Virginia
WEDDINGS

Virginia WEDDINGS

THREE ROMANCES PERSEVERE IN THE COMMONWEALTH

LAURALEE BLISS

BARBOUR
PUBLISHING

Published by Barbour Publishing, Inc., P.O. Box 719, Uhrichsville, Ohio 44683, www.barbourbooks.com

Our mission is to publish and distribute inspirational products offering exceptional value and biblical encouragement to the masses.

 Member of the
Evangelical Christian
Publishers Association

Printed in the United States of America.

Dear Reader,

What a beautiful area to kindle a romance—in sight of Virginia's mysterious yet awesome Blue Ridge Mountains. In *Virginia Weddings*, you are about to undertake a journey of the heart, soul, and spirit as couples, both young and old, solve mysteries while finding romance.

Just as I experienced love here on a mountain summit in Virginia some nineteen years ago, I welcome you to join these heroines and heroes who overcome their difficulties to discover enduring love within the realm of breathtaking and rejuvenating scenery. I hope their stories of faith will touch your life and fill you with the knowledge of God's unending love and concern for you.

I welcome you to visit my Web site at www.lauraleebliss.com to discover other books that will uplift your spirit while providing page-turning entertainment.

May God bless you.
Lauralee

Ageless Love

Dedication

To my mom, Lucille Braun,
and her wonderful enthusiasm for gardening
which I now enjoy so much.

Chapter 1

Daphne Elliot cringed at the melodious sound erupting from the store-house. Rodney was at it again, serenading his work with song. He burst into a merry tune the moment he arrived for work in the morning. It unnerved her to see him floating on a cloud with a song of love on his lips—and from a young man to boot. "Tweet, tweet," she mumbled. "Love's sweet song, blah. A pain in the pinfeathers, I call it."

"I heard that, Miss Elliot," said Rodney James, who came in carrying several bags of lawn seed on his shoulder. He plopped the bags on the floor of the garden center with a grunt. "Sounds familiar."

"It's from the wise old owl in *Bambi*. I don't wear these glasses of mine just for seeing, you know. There's great wisdom in age."

Rodney leaned over the counter with a boyish grin plastered on his face. Shocks of wavy dark hair framed his thin face that boasted luminous brown eyes. To Daphne, these young people seemed to be getting younger all the time.

"The problem with you, Miss Elliot, is that you aren't in love."

"You're quite mistaken, young man. I am very much in love." She picked up a feather duster and aimed it at the store shelves brimming with planting supplies, seed packets, fertilizers, insect control, and decorative planters. "With this, and this, and finally"—she pointed to a box of plant food—"this."

Rodney erupted into laughter, bringing a smile to Daphne's lips, which were colored a deep wine with swipes of her favorite lipstick. Despite the songs of love that permeated his work, Daphne enjoyed having the young man around. Rodney was prompt and helpful and did more around the nursery than anyone else she had ever hired. And he did it all without complaining.

She sighed, staring at the Garden Center Nursery that had been a part of her life since she was a young girl. It seemed unbelievable that she was still able to run this place. Her father opened the center back in the early 1950s. Normally a son would have inherited the family business, but her older brother, Charles, would have nothing to do with it. He lived out on the West Coast, far away from her home in Virginia. In fact, Daphne rarely heard from him other than the annual Christmas card that included a picture of him, surrounded by his children and grandchildren. When Daphne looked at the picture of Charles and his flock, she often wondered why life had passed her by. Then she would come back to the shop, work in the greenhouse, and find herself renewed. The feel of the cool dirt between her fingers and the flowers that bloomed from her efforts gave her a peace that this was where she was meant to be. Marriage and children were never a part of God's big plan for her life. This business was the plan, and the good Lord had prospered it far beyond her imagination.

Over the years, Daphne had many helpers come and go in the business. For a long time, she had a co-owner named Phyllis, an old friend from her high school days. She later became ill and had to leave. Daphne never once entertained the idea of a man becoming a co-owner. The men she preferred working at the shop had to be less than thirty years of age so they would do what she expected. They would be like sons receiving instructions from their matriarch, or so she liked to think.

By far Rodney had been the best of her previous employees. A lady at church recommended him. He had worked for Daphne in her garden shop just a short time before announcing his engagement to a young lady named Melanie. Six months later, they were married. A year had passed since then, and Rodney still carried a song of love on his lips. While Daphne disliked the connotation, she couldn't help but marvel at his beautiful singing voice. She informed him that he should try out for the summer theater program. Rodney only laughed and went off whistling another love song.

"There must be somebody I can fix you up with," Rodney said now, adjusting the sign advertising the lawn seed for sale.

With the spring planting season underway, Daphne made certain the store had a good supply of lawn seed. Many customers came in, complaining that the winter weather had killed their grass, the dreaded crabgrass had taken over like an invading army, or the heat of the past summer had steamed their lawns to a drab brown.

"How about in your church?" Rodney continued.

"Really, the only thing that needs fixing up around here is the sign for my store, which you promised to do yesterday."

"I'll go get the ladder. The hammer and nails are—"

"In the back on the workbench." Daphne returned to tidying up the counter after a long day of sales. Spring was the busiest time of the year, with everyone seeking to turn their property into bountiful gardens of flowers or fresh produce. Daphne had to bite her tongue when one customer came in asking for tomato plants. She patiently explained that it was too early to plant them now and she must wait for the last frost to be over. The bewildered customer chose packets of tomato seeds then and said she would grow her own. Daphne kept any further comments to herself. She was far too outspoken anyway.

At home she had no one to debate her daily struggles in life with but her dog, Chubs. Most evenings, the dog lay at her feet with his mouth hanging open, waiting for her to scratch his belly or throw him dog biscuits. Daphne never thought she would live her life as a spinster, but that must be the way God wanted it. Perhaps He knew no one could live with her tongue. Yet she refused to believe the good things in life had passed her by, even when gazing at her brother's many children and grandchildren. *There's more to life than marriage and children,* she told herself. *It all depends on how you look at it. And I'm going to be content right where I am.*

The bell to the door tinkled at that moment. Daphne looked at the clock and frowned. She had forgotten to turn the sign on the door, signaling that the shop was closed for the day. In the door walked a typical farmer of the region, dressed in dirty overalls with grass sticking to his knees, wearing a straw hat. A strange scar lay near the corner of his right eye, encompassing the right side of his cheek and extending to his neck. She wondered what could have caused such a scar. He did not look her way but scanned the aisles as if trying to decide what he wanted. Daphne stood watching his uncertainty for a moment before asking if she could help.

"I want to plant a flower garden," he said, "but I don't know how."

Oh dear. This is going to make me close up late. What will I do about Chubs who must be let out on time or he'll have an accident?

At that moment Rodney came in, lugging a small stepladder. He struggled with it, nearly losing his grip and bumping the ladder into the farmer's legs. He managed a smile and headed out the door. Daphne wanted to inform the man that she was about to close up shop and ask if he'd come back tomorrow. Instead, she came out from behind the counter. "Follow me." She proceeded to point out the various materials he would need to prepare a flower bed—humus, peat moss, fertilizer.

"I need all that just for flowers?" he asked, scratching a mound of gray hair beneath the straw hat he wore.

"It's important if you want your investment to survive. If you want to dig a few holes in this awful soil we have and throw in a few plants, you'll have a garden for about a week."

He raised an eyebrow. "You've got a lot of spunk there."

Daphne felt the heat rise in her cheeks. *And you have a lot of nerve coming in here when I'm about to close.* She clamped her mouth shut to keep the words from escaping. "It's been a long day, and I'm closing."

"I'm sorry. You looked as if you were open, and the sign there says—"

"Yes, I know. I forgot to turn it." Daphne pushed back a wisp of gray hair. "If you would like any of the materials I was telling you about, Rodney here will gladly help load them into your car." She glanced over to see a rustic truck parked in the lot, with mud up to the middle of the wheels. Wherever he lived, the place was hip-deep in mud, not uncommon with the spring rains. "Spring is actually an excellent time to put in a garden, with the soil nice and moist. I usually begin my flower seeds in February, replant them in small pots, then put them out in the greenhouse to harden them off. I have some excellent varieties here at the nursery that should do well, depending on where you wish to plant them."

The farmer crossed his arms and leaned against the side of the shop. "Well, I want to plant flowers in my front yard, you see."

"I'm certain your wife will enjoy looking at them out the window."

"I'm sure she would if she were alive. She died five years ago."

Daphne looked away. Rodney again peered at her, this time wearing a slight smile on his face. She could almost hear his thoughts. *Aha! An eligible widower and in your age range.* How she would love to shake that young man for grinning like a cat who nipped the canary, or more like Cupid ready to shoot the arrow. "I'm sorry to hear that."

"Thank you. I miss her, but I'm finding out the hard way that I can get along in life on my own."

She felt an internal sigh of relief creep up within her. At least he had not come here with some ulterior motive. She'd had a few customers in her day who sought more than just planting material or a healthy evergreen tree. They were also on the prowl. She would not soon forget Larson McCall a year ago. He had been congenial, offering her advice about her nursery, even taking her to the Hardware Store Restaurant for dinner. Only when Rodney found out the man intended to steal her business did she realize how close she had come to disaster, and all because of a yearning within her to enjoy the company of a man. Between the loss she'd suffered when she was young and the duping by Larson when she was older, she wanted to stay far away from any hint of a relationship. "Well, we have many varieties that will look wonderful in a garden spot. Of course, you also need to decide if you want annuals that only live a season or perennials that will bloom year after year."

"What would you say?"

"I like both. I plant different annuals each year. Perennials will come up in the same place I plant them. Since annuals live only a season, you can change the varieties." Daphne began showing him the different plants for sale. When she glanced up, she found his gaze centered not on plants but on her. Daphne felt her face grow warm and a strange flutter begin in her chest. Her heart was acting up again. Soon she would have to sit down and put her feet up, as the doctor had ordered on her last exam. "Excuse me, Mr.—"

"Jack McNary."

"Mr. McNary, I'm afraid I'll have to stop now. I'm getting a little tired. If you want anything, Rodney will be glad to help you."

A look of concern flashed across his rugged face, decorated with sparse wrinkles. His bushy gray eyebrows lowered over a set of ice blue eyes. "Are you all right?"

"It's been a long day."

"I'm mighty sorry. I'll come back tomorrow. When do you open?"

"Nine a.m."

He tipped his large straw hat at her. "Nine a.m.," he said, as if setting up some kind of date, then strode off toward the truck.

Rodney came down from the ladder and whistled while twirling the hammer. "Miss Elliot, now that was a D.E. if ever I saw one."

Daphne knew what he meant. *Divine Encounter.* In her eyes, she saw nothing divine about it—just a customer wanting a few posies to spruce up an otherwise dreary life. In fact, he was no different from her, though she hated to admit it. "Help me close up, Rodney. I'm feeling those chest pains again."

"I'll close up. You go on home and rest."

She smiled her thanks. That was another good quality of Rodney. She could trust him with closing the store tighter than a drum and making sure the money was locked in the safe. She was thankful she had already finished the books for the day. Rodney offered to do the bookkeeping on his computer at home, but Daphne preferred the old-fashioned way, in a long memo book. In the back of the store, she kept her father's books, etched in his stately handwriting. Occasionally he had allowed her to do the books as a young woman. Daphne marveled at how her writing had changed little with the passage of time, even if her heart acted up on her. At times she astonished young Rodney with her sharp memory when it came to ordering supplies for the store. Rodney told her she was a walking computer and could probably give the customers their change without using a cash register.

Daphne inserted the key into the door of her home, situated a mile from the nursery. Inside she heard Chubs barking his customary greeting, which also indicated his eagerness to go out. "Yes, I hear you," she told him, taking the red leash off a hook near the door. The dog, a medium-sized mutt of mixed breeds with a stomach that sagged near the ground, wagged his tail furiously as she hooked the leash to his collar.

Outside, a cool spring breeze blew. From her porch Daphne could look out across the busy street to the wide expanse of the Blue Ridge Mountains stretched out lazily before her. She enjoyed these spring evenings when the mountains shone crystal clear, displaying all their glory. When summer came, the haze would often mar the view she had come to love since she was a child.

The property Daphne owned once belonged to the Elliot family, but now she was the sole proprietor with brother Charles off in another state raising his family. Both her parents were long gone, as were numerous aunts and uncles. Daphne realized that with the passage of time came the pain of losing friends and family members once close to her. It gave her a deeper understanding of how fragile life could be and left her considering her own time remaining on earth. What would she do about the house and the business if she were to pass on suddenly? If she left it to Charles, he would sell it all in a heartbeat.

She then thought of ambitious, love-struck Rodney. He would make a fine businessman, if he could keep his head on earth and out of the clouds. If he took over the business, then he and his wife, Melanie, could live here instead of that crowded apartment. Daphne coaxed Chubs back into the small home. She would ask the young man about it. If he agreed, she would call her lawyer and make the arrangements.

Daphne went into the kitchen and looked in the cupboards, ready for her old standby—a can of soup—for dinner. It made no sense for her to cook elaborate meals when she was the only one to eat it. Sometimes she invited the ladies from church over for a meal and even once had Rodney and Melanie to dinner, but she found little interest in cooking for one person. *It's too much of a bother,* she would argue, and usually the argumentative side won out. Daphne reached for her favorite flavor, chicken and rice, and began heating it over the circle of blue flame on the gas stove.

The ruffle of fur at her legs sent her glancing downward at Chubs. He was wagging his tail politely. "No soup for you," Daphne told him. She opened a can of dog food and spooned it into a plastic bowl, which Chubs downed in several healthy bites.

When the soup was warm, she carried it over to the table, pulled out the evening paper, and began reading. This was the typical nightly fare—a dinner of soup or some other quick dish, and the evening paper to go along with it. Then she would sit in the family room to work on a bit of embroidery while watching a game show, or she would catch up on a favorite mystery novel. Afterward she would read her Bible, then climb into bed promptly at nine. Nothing swayed her schedule unless it was a matter of life and death. Daphne had to be on a schedule, or those pains in her chest would rise up to remind her.

After glancing through the newspaper, Daphne washed out her bowl, then moseyed over to the sitting room and turned on a lamp. She looked at her embroidery and her mystery novel, but neither of them interested her. Instead, her gaze fell on several old photo albums collecting dust on the bookshelf. Her hand shook slightly as she reached out and withdrew one. Dust bunnies flew. Daphne settled herself in a worn chair and opened the pages with a slight creaking sound. The white background where the photos rested was now yellowed with age. She had put these pictures in the albums close to fifteen years ago. They had been a jumbled mess in her bedroom drawer until she'd finally decided one day to take them out and arrange them in the albums.

Now she began opening each page, tracing the people in the pictures with her finger. The Great Smoky Mountains of Tennessee. A yellow framed house. A harvest festival. She paused at a page and stared. Piles of lumber occupied the background. And there he was—young, handsome Henry Morgan, similar to Rodney with his enthusiasm for life and for love. He had bushy black hair, a trimmed beard, and blue eyes. And he loved working with the trees. Working as a lumberjack was his trade. He and the trees were similar—strong, able to withstand harsh storms, giving shade and protection when the fierce summer sun came forth. He was her shelter and her love until he was cruelly taken away one dreadful day.

Even after all these years, the tears still gathered in her eyes. How could he have died, leaving her alone to face life? She shut the book when a wave of pain filtered through her chest. Her hand fumbled on the stand for the bottle of medicine that the doctor had prescribed for these symptoms. She placed one under her tongue. *I can't keep doing this. It's been forty years, and nothing has changed. Henry is dead. . . even though I was never able to wear my wedding dress or hold his arm while walking up the aisle of the church. Our children died with him. I can't do anything but forget.* If only she could.

Chapter 2

Daphne drove up to the nursery the next morning only to find the mud-drenched truck parked in the lot. Jack McNary sat behind the wheel, reading the morning newspaper. She glanced at her watch. There he was, right on time. She was a little late this morning, having slept in after suffering a restless night's sleep. She knew better than to stare at old photographs before going to bed. The memories were carried into her dreams, even though they should be locked in a closet and the key thrown away.

Daphne walked into the shop and found Rodney inside counting out the cash to place in the register. "Miss Elliot, he refused to come in."

"What?" she asked, a bit flustered.

"Your buddy out there. He was here when I came, but he wouldn't enter the store until—" Rodney didn't finish his sentence but instead waved his hand. "Good morning."

"Morning," said Jack McNary. He stepped inside holding a brown paper bag.

"I need to go check on some products in the storehouse," Rodney said, side-stepping away, but not before giving Daphne that grin she always detested.

She went behind the counter, trying hard not to look at the farmer's face.

"I brought you breakfast," he announced, holding up the bag.

Daphne jerked her head up, and at once her glasses slipped down her nose. She pushed them up with her finger. He wore a grin that sent wrinkles running through the huge blanket of scar tissue across his right cheek. "You what?"

"I brought breakfast. An egg biscuit from the convenience store down the road. And coffee. I don't know if you like any of those fancy coffees. Me, well, I like it strong and black, with none of those fancy flavors like hazelnut."

"Thank you, but I don't drink coffee. It gives me heartburn. And I don't eat eggs either. Too much cholesterol. Besides, I had my oatmeal." She turned and reached for the apron she liked to wear over her clothing.

"Sorry about that. I should have known."

"You had no way of knowing. There's no sense in apologizing for it."

"After I heard you complaining yesterday about feeling worn-out and all, I thought maybe you might have some kind of heart condition. We aren't spring chickens anymore. The old ticker can sometimes wreak havoc when you least expect it."

Daphne tried to conceal her flushed face. She couldn't believe how close the man had come to discovering her ailment, as if he could look right through her. Heart conditions ran in Daphne's family. Her father died young from a heart ailment. And Daphne had recently been diagnosed with high blood pressure—not that any of these situations cropping up in her life were helping in that area. "Mr. McNary, can we help you get your items for the garden? I would love to chat, but I have a lot of work to do."

Jack folded the top of the bag. "Good. Glad to hear you want to chat. Maybe I can come back after you close up shop, and we can sit a spell."

Again she felt a pain rippling in her chest. It was too much to bear. Surely the man had devious intentions, like that Larson character. "Pardon me." She went outside to the storage shed where Rodney's singing filtered out the door. "Rodney, please take care of Mr. McNary."

"Miss Elliot!"

"I mean it. Tell him I had to do something. My heart can't take it."

"What did he do?"

"I—well, I don't know. Just take care of his needs. I'm having chest pains again."

Rodney nodded and took her hand in his, giving a gentle squeeze. "Miss Elliot, you just need to open up that heart of yours a little. Maybe if you did, it wouldn't hurt so much." He winked and strode back to the store, whistling another love song.

Daphne trembled at the truth of his words. She peeked out the window of the storehouse to see Rodney and the farmer going through the stacks of planting material. She then saw him give Rodney the paper bag containing the egg biscuit. If only she hadn't been so curt. He was just being polite, but right now the thought of another man wishing to spend time with her was enough to send her to bed for a week. She had the stress of the business, after all. She couldn't take the stress of a relationship on top of it, especially when she barely knew him.

Before he left the store, Jack came lumbering over to her, his hands planted inside his dirty overalls—the same pair he wore yesterday, no doubt. "I just wanted to apologize for making you so uncomfortable. Really, all I wanted to do was chat about plants. The biscuit I brought was only a peace offering after making you stay open late on account of me. Nothing more."

Daphne blinked. Perhaps she had been hasty in her judgment and the man wanted only to learn from a plant specialist. Maybe it was Rodney who had inflated the whole encounter, enough to where she nearly had to take more of her medicine. "I appreciate your saying that. If you would like to come back and discuss gardening, I'd gladly arrange it."

With the smile that erupted on his face, Daphne thought she had invited him to a fried-chicken dinner complete with apple pie.

"I'd like that, thank you. I haven't yet bought the plants, so I would like your opinion on them. When would be a good time?"

"Come by around five o'clock."

Jack lifted his straw hat, said a pleasant thank-you, and strode out to his muddy truck. Daphne looked out the window as the truck pulled away.

"There—you see?" Rodney said with a saucy grin on his face. "That wasn't so hard."

"You read too much into things, young man," she said, returning to the counter. "We are only going to discuss gardening. Nothing more."

Rodney leaned over the counter. "And I know that the best way for a man to meet a woman is to share some common interest. That's how I met Melanie. She liked to hang out in craft stores, looking for posies to make those silk flower arrangements."

"She does a wonderful job. You're blessed to have her." While Daphne enjoyed live flowers more, the pretty silk flower arrangement Melanie had made for her last Christmas brightened up her home during the dreary winter months. Other times of the year, Daphne cut real flowers from her own garden to add color to the house.

"So I pretended I was interested in painting," he continued. "The art supplies were in the next aisle over from the fake flowers. She was standing there one day, trying to decide what flowers she wanted, and we happened to bump into each other. It was love at first sight. It can happen to anyone, at any time, and at any age."

"I don't know about you. It seems to me you always have something up your sleeve. You're definitely one who likes to plan mysteries."

"I only like to solve mysteries in people's lives, Miss Elliot."

She chuckled. "You'll never solve mine, young man."

The look in his eye made her nervous. "Is that a challenge?"

"Yes. I'm challenging you to do your work. We have a business to run."

He gave a wink before striding off to the back room to finish unpacking the goods that had arrived by truck. The words were disconcerting to Daphne. *As if I don't have enough to think about in life without wondering what that young man is up to.* Somehow she had to convince Rodney she didn't need or want a man, nor did she want to be involved in some mysterious plot he contrived. She wanted to be left alone with her shop, her flowers, and her memories.

ॐ

Despite the rocky start, the day had turned out pleasant but busy, with many customers coming by for their spring planting necessities. With the way she and Rodney scurried around the place, trying to fill customers' needs, Daphne wondered if she might need to hire extra help to ease the burden. She was thankful most of the customers knew what they wanted, which made life easier. A few had questions about specific gardening material or plants suitable for certain locations. The cash register rang endlessly. Now Daphne sat at the counter, hunched over the long memo book, adding up the day's totals. Rodney had already said good-bye, announcing he was taking Melanie out to her favorite Chinese restaurant. Daphne waved him off, but not before thanking him for his help.

She had just put down a long series of numbers, ready to tally them up, when a knock came on the door. After Rodney left for the day, Daphne always closed the shop up tight, along with turning the sign and locking the dead bolt. She peered between some shelving to see Jack McNary standing there, waiting expectantly. Daphne sighed. She'd forgotten she had told him to return at five o'clock after the shop had closed. She wondered if she should let him in without Rodney there. Daphne decided to ignore him and went back to doing the figures. The knocking persisted until suddenly she saw his face peer into a window near the counter. The image nearly made her faint.

She leaped to her feet and came to the door. "You scared me half to death!"

"I thought maybe you'd forgotten about our chat."

"I'm right in the middle of doing my books."

"I'm good at math," he said.

"So am I." She watched the look on his face change from one of expectation to obvious disappointment. Immediately her cold nature began to melt. If there was one thing she couldn't stand, it was seeing a sad face, especially one generated by some foolish statement that had escaped out of her mouth. "You can stay for a few minutes." She opened the door.

Jack took off his straw hat and stepped inside. Shiny gray hair stood up wildly on end. He smelled like the fields. He followed Daphne over to the counter where she had begun adding up the figures on paper. "Don't you have a calculator?"

"No, I don't."

"Be right back." Jack placed the hat on his head and headed out to his truck, returning with a calculator. "Okay, you read the numbers off, and I'll punch them in. We'll get this done in no time."

"Actually I prefer doing it myself." If the truth were known, she didn't want him discovering the amount of money they had made that day. He might be here to rob her blind, just like Larson McCall. He had been a sweet talker, too, but under it all lay a cold, crooked heart. For all she knew, Jack's offer of the calculator was only a guise for something evil lurking within, only to leap out when she least expected it.

A shiver raced through her. She looked around for the telephone in case she needed to dial 911. Rodney had told her many times she should get a cell phone, especially if she was here working late or at least while driving around in the car.

Daphne turned up her nose at the suggestion. Young people were forever throwing electronic gadgets in her face. Computers, cell phones, everything.

"Sorry. I was only trying to help." He pocketed the calculator and looked around. "I hope you still have time to tell me more about gardening. I'm sure you know everything."

"I do know quite a bit, and it would take much longer than the time I have to explain it. I think I told you yesterday what you would need for your garden. There isn't much else to discuss."

"If you could point out the plants that would be good, I'll pick them up. That is, unless your assistant is around to help me."

Daphne opened her mouth, ready to tell him he was long gone, then thought better of it. Instead, she led Jack around the nursery. When they came to the plants, Daphne began to relax. These living things were like her children, and who wouldn't want to boast about one's children? She picked up a pack of petunias, gently stroking the velvety petals. "Petunias are one of my favorites. They come in such wonderful colors and never fail to brighten my day. I also like rosebushes, but they're bug babies."

"Why is that?"

"Every bug and disease seem to love them. They must be treated right. They require proper fertilizing and pruning, and then they require different chemicals to treat them." She showed him the chemicals to manage the diseases of black spot and powdery mildew. "And then in June, we get those dreadful Japanese beetles. They chew everything."

"I heard about them. Chewed a good many of my apple trees one year and also my climbing rose. I hung those beetle traps, but it didn't work."

"The traps only make more come, usually from your neighbor's yard."

Jack crossed his arms before him. "Is that a fact?"

"They are actually quite easy to pick off, if you don't mind the feel of them, that is."

"I can't imagine a lady like you handling bugs."

Daphne gritted her teeth at the insinuation that she couldn't handle things. "I take care of all kinds of bugs, large and small."

Jack only smiled.

"I even killed a black widow spider on my property," she added, lifting her head higher. She would show him he was not talking to a limp weed, even if her heart did act up on occasion. She was as tough as an oak tree, all things considered.

"Is that a fact? You shouldn't fool around with those. They're highly poisonous, you know."

"Everything can kill nowadays. You could step into that truck and meet your end right there on Highway 29."

"I can't argue with that. I'm sure glad I know where I'm going. I'd hate to be someone who didn't know where he was going if I were to up and die like that. You think of people who die in accidents and such, and who knows if they've gotten right with the Lord. Makes my hair stand up just thinking about it. Like when that crazy lunatic was shooting up all those folks awhile back. They were shopping and pumping gas and all; then a bullet cuts them down. You never know when it's going to be your time." He relaxed his arms. "But I'm sure you know where you're going, right, Miss Elliot?"

"If you don't mind, right now I really need to go home. I have a dog to let out. He has accidents if I'm not there."

"I won't take up any more of your time. You just tell me how much this is going to cost." Along with several boxes of petunias, he added some decorative pots, rose chemicals, and several bags of fertilizer.

Daphne walked into the store and to the cash register. When the final total rang up to $40.14, she decided the extra effort was worth it. "I'll carry out a box of plants," she offered, observing Jack lift up the rest of the material he had bought. She marveled at his strength. No doubt hard work had put muscle on the man's body. Henry had the best muscles around from his work as a lumberjack. She used to love running her fingers over his hefty biceps, and he loved displaying them, too.

The thought made her flush. How could she think of such things, and especially with Jack McNary standing there? The box of plants began to tremble in her hands.

He opened the hatch to the bed of the truck, and she carefully placed the plants inside. "I sure would love to have you show me where to plant the flowers," he said, more to himself than to her.

Daphne's mouth fell open. "I hope you're not suggesting I go to your home and plant these? I'm not a landscaper, you know, though I can give you the name of a good one in town. I have enough to do trying to manage this business."

"I was only making a suggestion. I thought you would take it as a compliment." He loaded in the last of the bags beside the plants. Without another word, he entered the driver's seat.

Daphne walked back to the store, but not before casting a glance over her shoulder. She could plainly see his irritation. Again her mouth had taken over the situation as it always did. She doubted she would ever see him again. Did it really matter? Inwardly she should be thankful. God might have spared her further calamity in her life. Yet some interesting characteristics about Jack McNary drew her. He was polite and caring, for one thing. How many men did she know who would come bearing a breakfast sandwich as a peace offering? He had nice manners. Daphne always judged people on their manners. He had apologized more to her in the past two days than she had in her lifetime.

Daphne shook her head. She couldn't possibly find herself wrapped up with another man. She would not be left on a stoop wearing her bridal gown smudged with dirt, the tears causing wrinkles on the bodice of the gown, while men died or left town with all her money. She had been down that road. Time did not heal the wounds. Neither did her work in the nursery with the plants she lovingly tended. What then could heal them?

Chapter 3

I think it would do you good to go. Miss Elliot, are you listening to me?"

Daphne wished she had a set of earplugs to tune out that young man while she tried to keep occupied in the greenhouse, repotting the summer vegetables. She had ordered Rodney to work at the counter in the hope of keeping his convicting words out of earshot. He continued to insist that she come Sunday afternoon for a picnic at his church. Daphne disliked eating lunch with perfect strangers, even if they were good Christians. She sat with a few ladies she knew at her church on Sunday but rarely did much socializing.

Rodney often talked about his church, the same place where she had witnessed him and Melanie exchange their marital vows. The pastor had been amiable enough. The church was clean and neat, and the people friendly. But visiting foreign churches made her nervous. She only went to the wedding out of respect for Rodney. In fact, to Daphne's embarrassment, Melanie had a picture of Daphne, Rodney, and her blown up and framed. It now sat in a prominent position in the young couple's living room.

"You're like a mother to Rodney," Melanie said with a smile. "It means a lot to both of us."

Daphne wasn't certain whether to take this as a compliment or not. Now it appeared she was expected to attend other events at Rodney's church, including this Spring Fling—or whatever he called it.

"You'll get some nice fresh air," Rodney continued, "and eat a wonderful lunch in the great outdoors."

"With the ants and flies," she added curtly.

None of her arguments dissuaded the young man. When Daphne returned to the greenhouse, Rodney followed, helping her open a large bag of premium potting soil. Daphne's fingers were already at work in the soft soil, ready to place the delicate plants inside their new potted homes. "I'll have Melanie make a great dessert if you come," he said. "Maybe some fruited gelatin."

"I'm the one who makes a good fruited salad, if you remember," Daphne reminded him.

"Great! I'll tell everyone you'll be bringing a fruited salad to the picnic. The kids will love you."

Daphne spun around, her fingers caked with soil. "Young man—," she began, only to see him disappear into the store with the echo of a song trailing him. *Oh, he irritates me to no end. If he weren't such a good helper, I would get someone else. But that would be foolish. There's no one else like him. Without him, this place would wither away and me along with it.* Daphne inhaled a few breaths to calm herself, knowing that if she didn't, the heart pains would greet her once again.

The tinkle of the store bell alerted her to a customer. Daphne continued repotting tiny squash plants, barely able to make out the conversation in the shop. This was what she enjoyed doing the most, immersing herself in the work of repotting plants. She scooped out more soil onto the worktable; then out of the corner of her eye, she saw a dark figure hover over her. Her trowel went airborne. The dirt landed squarely in Jack McNary's face and straw hat. He stared, bewildered, like a child with chocolate on his face. Particles of dirt rolled off the brim of his hat.

"Oh no," Daphne moaned and gave him some paper towels. "You shouldn't sneak up on me like that."

"I didn't mean to startle you. I was here to get more dirt, and I guess I did." He cracked a grin. "What are you doing?" He pointed at the array of plants and their bare roots, laid out on newspaper. "Won't they die like that?"

"They would if they stay in the same pots where I planted them as seeds. The seedlings are now becoming root-bound. I'm repotting them into bigger containers."

"I've never seen plants like that, all naked and everything." He turned red. "What I mean is, you know, out of the ground like that, just lying there. I thought they couldn't survive."

"You must work quickly and give them plenty of water after they are repotted." Daphne picked up a small plant to show him the new roots. "See what pure white roots they have? Baby roots, just like a newborn. Fragile and in need of care. I just put my thumb into the soil like this and then slip the plant inside."

Jack stared, watching her every move. "You have a way with plants, Miss Elliot. I told you that you should have planted mine. I killed pretty near all of them. That's another reason I'm here—to buy more plants."

Daphne whirled to face him. The news stunned her. How could he have killed the plants—and so soon? "Oh no. What did you do?"

"I thought I had some time before they went into the ground, you see. It takes time to get the soil ready, as you told me. I had to dig it all up. Then I had to wait to rent a rototiller. I don't have one of my own. The fellow at the store said there would be one, but it didn't show up for three days. By the time I got the ground ready, pretty near all the plants were dead."

Daphne shook her head. She placed her hands on her hips, unaware of the dirty markings she was making on her apron. "Mr. McNary, did you by chance water them?"

"Huh? You mean water them in their little pots?"

"Of course! In the small pots we use, the plants easily dry out in this spring sun. You have to water them every other day. More if it gets warm out."

"You didn't tell me that," he began, then quickly added, "but I should've figured it out."

Daphne lowered her arms, only to find her hips now blackened with the dirt. She felt a familiar heat rise in her face. They looked like a pair from a comedy routine—Jack with his dirty face and her with dirty hips. "I can't believe you would let the poor things dry out like that."

"I can tell you I take better care of people than plants," he said swiftly. "In fact, I make an awfully good barbecue. People from all around have commented on it. Stick-to-the-ribs kind, too."

"I suppose that's nice if you have a good heart and low blood pressure, which I don't have." Daphne returned to her duty. "I'm sorry, but I must get back to this before the plants dry out."

He stood there for several moments, watching her work. His observing gaze made her nervous. She wasn't used to being on display like this, especially in front of a man who didn't know enough to water plants. How could he have done that? If only she had accepted his offer to go to his home and take care of the gardening. The sweet plants would be alive and well, ready to face the morning sunshine and even a terrific summer storm. He would've had a garden people could be proud of.

Jack made a few more comments about his barbecue that had won a prize at a cook-off. When she didn't respond, he planted his hands inside the pockets of his overalls and meandered back into the store. Rodney and he conversed for awhile longer. Daphne cast a glance inside the store, and Rodney looked at her and smiled. She quickly turned away. *I can't stand this. He truly thinks that Jack might be someone I should get to know. Dear Lord, please help me.*

At last Daphne heard the bells tinkle and the door close. On the worktable lay the paper towels he'd used to wipe the grime off his face. Daphne gathered them up, ready to toss them away. She stared at the paper towels and for some reason thought of Henry. Dear Henry, who accidentally upset her mother's dish of fine blackberry jam all over his lap. Daphne had rushed to find him some cloths to clean up the spill. Dark jam was everywhere.

"Now you have to kiss me," he told her. "You'll never find anyone sweeter than at this moment." And his kisses were sweet, better than clover honey, better than any dessert she could have tasted. She didn't care that he had spilt the jam. She only wanted him forever.

Daphne shook her head at the thought before discarding the paper towels in the wastebasket. She would do better to toss the memories away, too, rather than clinging to them. She should bury them deep, even burn them, anything to free her mind and her heart.

Daphne didn't know why she scooped up packages of gelatin from the shelf inside her favorite grocery store. Nor did she understand why she reached for several large cans of fruit cocktail and placed them in her cart. She had told Rodney a firm "no" to this Spring Fling at his church and even reiterated the point that very afternoon while closing up shop. Yet somehow, she felt moved to go to the store and buy the fixings for her famous recipe, just in case. After selecting a few more items, including dog food for Chubs, she rolled the cart to the checkout counter.

"Glad to see you again, Miss Elliot," said a young girl with black hair. Daphne couldn't remember her name, but she did recall that the girl had commented on a pair of old earrings she'd worn one day to the store. Daphne thought she needed glasses. The gold plating had long since chipped away, revealing the metal beneath. But they were earrings Henry had given her, and she'd worn them faithfully every Tuesday for the last forty years.

"Looks like you're going to make a fruited gelatin. My grandma used to make the best. She would put it out with the main meal, and we would always go for it rather than the rest of the dinner. There's nothing better."

Daphne fumbled for her wallet inside her purse. "Well, I've been invited to a Spring Fling, whatever, at my employee's church. I don't know if I'm going or not, but I thought I would get the ingredients together for it in case I changed my mind."

"It's supposed to be beautiful weather for a picnic," the girl said with a wink.

Daphne nearly believed Rodney had told this girl what to say in an effort to convince her to come. Or maybe it was God with another D.E. in her life. When she left the store, following the clerk who placed the bag in the trunk of her car, she considered the idea of a picnic in the great outdoors. While she loved plants, she was not much of an outdoor, picnic-type person. Still, Rodney might be right. Maybe she did need to get out of the stuffy places she had neatly constructed for herself and experience life anew. After all, the years were slipping away. With the way her health was these days, she might not even be able to enjoy the outdoors much longer. She would likely regret it if she didn't go, like other things she regretted in life.

Daphne arrived home and began at once to boil water for the gelatin. She retrieved from the cupboard her biggest mold with leaves carved into it. She had put on many a dinner party in her younger days, serving a fruited salad on a bed of crisp lettuce to the delight of visitors and family. Now she couldn't recall the last time she'd used the mold. Like most of the objects in her house, it had not been used in years. Daphne stirred up the gelatin and, when it began to thicken, added the drained fruit cocktail and chopped walnuts. For the last ingredient, she folded in a container of whipped cream and scooped it all into the mold to chill overnight.

Daphne wandered back to her closet to look for an appropriate picnic outfit. The closet was jammed with clothes from every year since she was a teenager. She hadn't thrown anything out, though she had been tempted several times to give garments away to the Salvation Army. She had clothing from every style of the twentieth century and even found clothes that had come back in fashion, like bell-bottoms and miniskirts. *It just shows how long I've been alive on this earth, when styles are already being recirculated in the twenty-first century.* She sorted through the clothes until she came to an evening dress, hidden away in a dark recess of the closet. Her hands began to tremble. Ever so slowly, she drew out the midnight blue, floor-length dress. She had worn this dress to a very special party, along with the pearl necklace and earrings Henry had given her at a Christmas party. That night she and Henry danced under the stars. It was a perfect evening, one for the storybooks.

Daphne stepped over to the mirror and held the dress up in front of her. In her reflection, she saw her face hovering above the elegant dress. Tiny wrinkles had begun to appear where she'd once had velvety-smooth skin. Henry loved to caress her cheek with his hand. Tears welled up in her eyes and dripped down her cheeks.

"I love the pearls you gave me," Daphne had told Henry that night. Her fingers touched each one, feeling their soft roundness. To her they were pearls of great price, though certainly not the greatest price.

"They are beautiful around your neck," he'd said, fingering the necklace before tracing a line across her cheek. The sensation sent chills running down her spine. He picked up her hand, and they waltzed to the music. Most young people then were embracing rock-and-roll tunes. Not Henry. He was like Daphne, preferring the waltz with an orchestra supplying the music. A walk in the moonlight topped off the evening. They stopped on a wooden bridge over a glistening river, with the shadowy line of Tennessee mountains framing the gray horizon. She'd told him that tomorrow she would have to return to Virginia. The nursery and the plants were calling her. He pulled her close and told her that one day he would return to Virginia and marry her.

That time never came. It died as he did—burned to ashes in the flames of a terrible fire that stole away his life and her happiness.

Daphne returned the gown to its rightful place in the back of her closet, among the other possessions she had gathered over the years. Now she concentrated on her newer fashions and pulled out a lavender pantsuit. The sleeves would need fixing, which she planned to do right now while she thought of it. Trotting over to the chair, she sat down and took out the sewing kit she kept inside an old cookie tin. It was so like her to take clothes out of the closet, even ones she had worn in the past, and alter them somehow. Move a button there; change the length of a hem here. She didn't like the sleeves hanging over her wrists so she couldn't see the face on her watch. She first tried on the garment and measured the length, then set to work hemming up the sleeves.

The clock struck nine. Though she was tired, for some reason, she didn't want to go to bed. There were nights when Daphne feared crawling into bed and drifting off to sleep, wondering if she would wake up. With her heart acting up the way it did, she had no idea whether the Lord would keep her going to see another sunrise. Not that she had much to look forward to. Tomorrow was another day, but one in which she would meet strange people at a church picnic and eat her lunch with ants crawling along the tablecloth.

Daphne crossed the room and hung up the pantsuit. Chubs followed at her heels to his place in the corner of her bedroom and a large pillow Daphne had bought him for Christmas. The dog performed his usual routine—turning himself around three times before settling on the pillow for the night. And Daphne did her usual routine, as well—washing her face, brushing her teeth, and slipping on a nightgown before heading to bed. Tonight her mind was consumed with worry over the picnic tomorrow. Why did she ever listen to that foolish young man? Perhaps she could still get out of going. After all, she had not promised Rodney she would be there. But what would she do with that huge fruit salad she had made? Daphne shook her head and turned out the light. No doubt God must be chuckling at the myriad of questions that brought about more needless anxiety. She needed to trust Him with the small things as well as the big.

ŝŷ

Daphne grimaced at the bright sunshine peeking through her window early the next morning. She had hoped it might rain and thus give her an excuse to stay home from the picnic. Instead she dressed, walked Chubs, and made a bowl of hot oatmeal for breakfast. She decided to forgo her own church service that morning, thinking it would be too difficult to go to her church first and then some strange church for lunch. Rather, she would watch a church program on television and attend the picnic at noon.

When the clock struck eleven, Daphne changed into the lavender pantsuit. In an afterthought, she put on the pearl necklace and earrings. She hadn't worn the necklace in years but felt sentimental today. After saying good-bye to Chubs, she took up the plate of fruited salad resting on a bed of lettuce leaves and gingerly went to her car.

The day was spectacular, with the Blue Ridge Mountains of Virginia clearly visible in the distance. It was days like this that Daphne wanted to be in the garden, feeling the cool soil between her fingers while planting rows of vegetable seeds. God's green earth beckoned to her with a persistence she usually could not ignore. But for now, only the picnic occupied her mind. She was determined to make it through these few hours, come what may.

Driving to the church on the busy highway, Daphne glanced in her rearview mirror to find cars whizzing by as if she were standing still. She looked at her speedometer. She was going fifty, a perfectly rational speed for such a treacherous four-lane highway, even if the posted speed limit was fifty-five. A truck roared by, nearly forcing her car off the road. Daphne bit her lip and tried to still the rapid beating of her heart. If anything happened to her or the car, she would blame Rodney for this. His incessant plea that she attend this event had worn her down to the breaking point.

Another horn beeped at her from behind. *Hurry, hurry. These people never seem to show any respect for older people,* she thought. Daphne gripped the steering wheel with both hands, ignoring the stares she received from other drivers.

Finally she made it to Rodney's church to see people gathering in the large yard for the Spring Fling. Tables and lawn chairs had been set up. Another banquet table, draped in a tablecloth that fluttered in the breeze, held an assortment of delectable homemade goodies. Daphne stepped out of her car to find Rodney greeting her with a huge smile on his face.

"I just knew you'd come," he said, taking the salad from her hands.

"This is the last time I do anything for you," she whispered but with a smile. It went without saying that Rodney was like a son to her. She looked upon this act as a small way of repaying him for his kindness and his excellent work at the nursery.

Rodney only laughed. "Miss Elliot, your heart is too big to think of something like that. Come on. I saved you a nice comfortable lawn chair."

She followed him to where members of the church had gathered. Rodney introduced her to everyone, along with comments about her wonderful nursery with the best assortment of plants this side of Charlottesville. Daphne felt slightly embarrassed by the way Rodney was gushing over her, but perhaps something could be gained from her willingness to eat with strangers out in the fresh air. If it brought more customers to the store, that was a good thing. She settled herself in a chair and watched young children zoom to and fro, playing with a ball. A woman came up and mentioned the beautiful rosebush she had purchased from the nursery last year and how she was looking forward to the gorgeous red blossoms. Daphne immediately perked up at this and offered her best smile.

"I'll be putting my roses on sale soon," she said. "You can save 20 percent."

"Well, then, I'll have to check it out. Thank you." The woman moved off to greet other church patrons. Daphne observed people roaming about, meeting each other, and conversing. She sighed, wishing she knew someone to talk to. Maybe it would have been better to invite a companion from her own church to tag along. At least she wouldn't feel so out of place.

She turned then in time to see a brown truck enter the parking lot. When she saw a familiar figure emerge from the driver's seat, dressed in a light blue shirt and jeans, her heart began to flutter.

Oh no! He couldn't have. But he did. Rodney had gone and invited Jack Mc-Nary to the affair. Of all the diabolical tricks. No wonder Rodney had been adamant that she come. Why he thought the two of them should get together anyway went beyond her sense of reasoning.

There was one way out of this, and that way was her car. She hurried off to the parking lot, only to find that another car had pulled in behind hers. She was blocked in with no place to go.

Chapter 4

"Miss Elliot, I'd like you to meet Jack McNary," Rodney said with a chuckle, taking her by the arm to lead her over to where the man was standing.

She wrestled her arm out of his grasp. "If I had a broom, I wouldn't hesitate to use it," she whispered.

"Look—you said strangers made you nervous. So I decided to invite a few people you did know."

That man isn't one of them. He killed all the plants he bought from the nursery. Daphne bit her tongue and glanced back to the white-frame church with the steeple that reached toward heaven, framed by the Blue Ridge Mountains. She would try to control her thoughts and her anxiety here on holy ground.

Jack McNary carried a foil-covered dish, which he placed on the table along with the other food. All at once, the pastor announced the blessing. Daphne bowed her head but kept it tipped to one side, watching Jack McNary out of the corner of her eye. He had removed his straw hat, bowed his head, and closed his eyes in a most reverent fashion. She wondered where he went to church.

With the blessing said, everyone hastened to form a line before the food. To Daphne's delight, the children shouted over the fruited gelatin salad, which was dished up by large spoonfuls. Jack came up to her, his plate already bursting with food, including a large helping of her salad. Daphne ignored him as she grabbed a paper plate and headed down the line.

"So how are you doing today, Miss Elliot?" Jack said.

Daphne realized it would be rude to ignore the man, even if he did destroy the plants from her nursery. What harm was there in being friendly, after all, especially at a church function? Daphne turned and nodded politely at him. "Just fine. A lovely day for a picnic." Her hand trembled as she tried to spoon up some baked beans.

"Can I help you with that?"

"No, thank you. I'm not quite ready for a nursing home."

The young girl behind her burst out laughing. "You sound like my grandma. She's nearly ninety and still lives alone."

"Well, I hope I don't look that old," Daphne remarked. "I'm only sixty-five, but the doctor says my heart is eighty. I have to be careful."

"Then you'd better not eat any of the ham," Jack said, nodding at the ham arranged on a platter, surrounded by slices of juicy pineapple and maraschino cherries. "Too much salt."

Daphne felt her ire rise. She had been contemplating sneaking a piece of ham onto her plate. She bit back a retort with the girl still behind her and instead reached for a chicken leg. With her plate about half full, Daphne headed back for the lawn chair when she saw Rodney frantically waving his hand from a distant table.

"Right here, Miss Elliot. Melanie and I saved you a place."

Daphne managed a smile at everyone, reminding herself that each face was a potential customer for her nursery. She had just set down her plate when Jack came and occupied the seat directly opposite her. If things were not difficult enough, he had to sit right in front of her. And likely she would need an antacid after this meal with the way he was staring at her.

Inhaling a breath, Daphne decided to get the conversation off on the right foot. "Nice to see you again," she said to Melanie. "I've been keeping your husband out of trouble."

"I wish you would. Trouble is his specialty." A small smile quivered on the corner of her lips at the quip, but her eyes seemed to tell a different story. Daphne could tell much about people by the way their eyes radiated either happiness or sorrow. Looking back at Jack, she saw his eyes conveying an internal message, as well—like appreciation. Or was it something else?

Jack lifted a forkful of the fruited salad. "I hear you made this, Miss Elliot." He swallowed, then exclaimed, "Delicious!"

"Thank you." She picked up a chicken leg and began nibbling at it, her appetite all but gone with this uncomfortable scene unfolding at the table.

"And I hear you made this, Jack," Rodney added, pointing to the heap of barbecue on his plate.

Jack nodded. "I was telling Miss Elliot the other day that I make a mean barbecue. But I left out the hot pepper sauce, in case you wanted to try some, Miss Elliot."

She dared not refuse with everyone at the table staring at her expectantly. "All right, I will."

Rodney immediately jumped to his feet to bring her a plate of barbecue while Jack grinned from ear to ear. Inwardly she hoped he would not latch onto this as a cue that she was seeking a relationship. *I'm only doing it because the pastor and his wife have just sat down at the table and everyone is staring.*

Rodney returned with the plate, and she smiled at him until he gave her a thumbs-up signal. How she wanted to scold that young man for his wild ideas. He might mean well, but little did he know he was contributing to her heart condition. She had told him countless times that she loved her life as it was right now. She and Chubs were getting along just fine, even if she did feel a bit lonely at times. Why did he seem to think she needed a man to balance it all out?

Jack waited in anticipation for Daphne to take her first bite of his barbecue. She did so, only to discover it was quite good, despite herself. When he wasn't looking, she took several more bites until his gaze returned to her. The people around the table made small talk about a summer Bible study coming up and other activities of the church.

"So where do you go to church, Jack?" Rodney asked.

"I think I'm sold on this place, to be honest. I've been looking around for a good church family, and I think I've found it here."

"Great! Glad to have you. And what about you, Miss Elliot?" Rodney asked with a gleam in his eye. "Are you ready to make the switch?"

"You know perfectly well I'm quite happy where I am." Then she added hastily for the pastor's benefit, "Though this is a lovely church with wonderful people." She began feeling lightheaded. "Excuse me, but I think I'm going to have to call it a day."

"Not already," Rodney moaned. "You just got here."

"Really, I think I need to go home and rest. It's been a pretty exciting day."

"No more exciting than a full day in the nursery, I expect," Jack added.

Daphne gritted her teeth. He could see right through her, as if her very soul were transparent. Why was this happening to her now? "Thank you very much for inviting me."

"Aw, Miss Elliot. We were just going to start a croquet game. You need a little exercise to settle the stomach." Rodney pulled Melanie up by her hand.

"Please come and play, Miss Elliot," Melanie implored. "Then I won't feel lonely."

Daphne gazed into the face of the young woman before her. Melanie was a sweet thing with a heart of gold. She had made a beautiful bride a year ago. Rodney loved her very much, she could tell. The love they shared shone through Rodney's work at the nursery and perhaps even propelled him to try his hand at matchmaking, much to Daphne's chagrin. "I might play for a little bit."

Rodney whooped and cheered as if a football team had just scored a touchdown. His enthusiasm made Daphne all the more determined to see this picnic through to the end, even if Jack's company left her feeling uncomfortable. She refused to display emotion when Jack trailed behind and selected his own mallet, ready to join in the game. He picked red. Red had been Henry's favorite color whenever he played. Daphne's brother, Charles, introduced Henry to the game when he came visiting one summer. They all laughed and cheered as the ball rolled through the steel wickets. Even when Henry had the opportunity of sending

Daphne's ball away after his ball hit hers, he never did. "If I sent you away, love, I would die," he said before throwing her a kiss that Daphne pretended to catch. It became a game, throwing kisses and catching them in the air. She often did it on the eve of his return to Tennessee, hoping he would not forget her, despite the distance.

Daphne shook her head, positioned herself at the starting pole, and hit her ball. It rolled cleanly through the two wickets.

"Good shot." Jack rested his mallet on one shoulder. "I can tell you've played this game before."

"Many times," Daphne said. She dearly wanted to expound on her croquet abilities and how she'd beat family members nearly every time. Instead, she swallowed her pride and whacked the ball, putting it in front of the next wicket. If only croquet had been introduced in the Summer Olympics, she often quipped. It was the only athletic-type event she excelled at, except perhaps for a marathon of repotting plants, of which the record stood at 110 in one day. Daphne smiled at her imagination as a ball went sailing past her feet toward the wicket. She jumped back with a slight yelp, only to see Jack racing toward her with a look of concern on his face.

"Did I hurt you, Daphne? Are you all right?"

She blinked, caught off guard by the tenderness of his words and the way he said her name. It was a sound she heard often in her dreams before they turned to nightmares. "I'm fine. The ball just startled me."

"You don't want to get hit by one of them."

"I should say not. I have been hit, and it nearly cost me my big toe." She blinked at his concern. It had been so long since any man of her age had shown concern for her well-being. If only she could be certain the concern was genuine and not born from some ulterior motive.

Just behind them, Melanie and Rodney were struggling with their mallets and balls, trying to overtake Jack and Daphne. Melanie hit her ball with a frustrated whack, sending it down a small incline away from the intended wicket. She tried to wear a smile, but Daphne could clearly see her aggravation. "It's just a game. Don't worry about it."

"I'll try not to," she said, then turned to see Rodney hit his ball with force, knocking it past the wicket and directly into Melanie's ball. "Aha!" he said with glee. "Revenge at last." He came and positioned the balls beside his foot.

"What are you going to do?" Melanie asked.

"If you hit a player's ball, you have the choice of taking two hits or sending the opponent's ball away and using one hit."

"Why don't you take the two hits?" Jack suggested. "It would put you in the lead."

An impish spark lit his face. "This is more fun."

Rodney raised the mallet and let it go with a smash, sending Melanie's ball careening past the field of play and over to where some of the picnickers were sitting at a table eating dessert.

"Thanks a lot," Melanie mumbled. "I should be the one sending you away after you didn't pay the electric bill."

Rodney's face reddened. "You don't have to tell the world about that, Melanie."

"Why not? You were the one who left me in the dark and without hot water for my shower." She turned to Jack and Daphne. "Here I was, in the middle of my shower, when the electricity goes off! I thought someone had hit a pole. I called the electric company. Come to find out, Rod hadn't paid the electric bill."

"It was an oversight," he declared, twirling the mallet around, his cheerful disposition slowly changing like a freshly peeled apple turning brown. "And I said you didn't need to go tell the world about our business."

"Let's not worry about it," Jack said. "I know I've made plenty of mistakes, too." He gave a sideways glance toward Daphne. She wondered if he was still trying to apologize for destroying the precious plants she'd sold him.

From that moment on, the game took a turn for the worse. Melanie and Rodney hardly spoke to each other while the balls trickled through the wickets and onward toward home base. Daphne found the joy in the game wane under the blanket of competitiveness. It reminded her of her brother, Charles, when she used to play games with him. He had to win over her in every game, as if to show off his dominion as the older brother. If she dared win, he would sulk for a week.

When Daphne continued to play well, cruising in to win the croquet game, she half expected Jack to throw a fit. Instead he smiled and congratulated her on her win. "I'm going to have to brush up on my skills if I ever hope to beat you," he commented.

"I don't see why. When do we ever plan to play again?"

"You have a nice lawn by your home. We could set up a course over there sometime and play."

Daphne stared at him in horror. "How do you know where I live?"

Jack paled and looked away.

"You've been snooping around, haven't you? Well, I won't have it. Please just leave me alone." She began striding toward her car.

"Daphne, I mean, Miss Elliot, wait now. I wasn't snooping. I did notice the other day after work when you drove home. It's not like your house is hidden. It's only a mile from the nursery."

"It doesn't matter. You shouldn't be prying into other people's affairs—" She stopped when she heard arguing near her car. She looked about, only to find

Rodney and Melanie shouting at each other. Melanie was holding a tissue and dabbing her eyes.

"I don't care if it was embarrassing to you. You embarrass me, living as we do, wondering how we're going to survive. And I want a baby. How can we have a baby with no money? You said I wouldn't have to go back to that awful office, and now it looks as if I'll have to."

"Melanie, it isn't that bad."

"It is bad! When we can't even pay the electric bill, that's bad. And how are we going to pay the other debts?"

Rodney looked up and saw Daphne standing there. No doubt she must've had a strange expression on her face, for he shook his head and strode back to the picnic. Daphne wanted to say something but didn't know what. Instead, Melanie took off in the opposite direction, to a bank of trees away from everyone else. *It's so hard to see young ones quarrel,* she thought.

All at once she saw herself and Henry standing by a bank of trees, with a raging river flowing before them. Henry was holding his favorite fishing pole.

"But you said we could take a walk!"

"We will, to my favorite fishing hole. Really, Daphne, the weather is wonderful, perfect for fishing."

"You mean perfect for doing what you want to do. What about me? I came here to visit you, and you'd rather go fishing."

"Daphne, it makes no difference whether it's a walk or casting a line into the river, as long as we're together."

"It makes a lot of difference."

She could picture the two of them bantering back and forth until a deep voice said, "They sound just like us."

The voice sent shivers racing through her, until she found Jack glancing down at her. He pointed at the young couple who had meandered off to separate locations.

"I don't know what you mean."

"You know, what happened between us just now and even back at the nursery when I told you about my plants. In fact, at the nursery you acted as if I had killed your relatives."

"The plants are my relatives. I have no one else on this earth. I'm all alone."

"Daphne, you aren't alone any longer. You may think you're alone, but there is someone who. . ."

Daphne searched through her pockets for the keys. Obviously the man thought he was the perfect person to ease her loneliness. Maybe he was, but at that moment, she couldn't accept it. "Excuse me, but I need to go home. Chubs needs a walk, and I need to rest."

"Daphne, if I said anything to—"

"Never mind. I just want to tell you that, yes, I am alone in this world. There is no one else. And it's all right. I'm content to be that way." She headed for the car without looking back to see his reaction. She was thankful the vehicle that had blocked her in was gone. Once in the driver's seat, she saw Jack walk up to several people and offer his hand. He was easy around strangers, giving them a smile and words of encouragement. Why did she have to be so short with him?

"Because I can't take any more pain in my life," she said aloud. She didn't want to admit that Jack had stirred something within her. It seemed to ease the bitterness that had held her heart captive for so long. If only she would let go completely and embrace the future. Perhaps Rodney was right. Perhaps the reason her heart ached so much was because she never did cast the disappointment into the Lord's capable hands.

Daphne shook her head. The whole picnic had been a fiasco, as she'd known it would be. Why had she ever agreed to go? And, to top it all, Rodney and Melanie were fighting. They were a picture of love, a symbol of what she and Henry might have been. The idea of their lashing out at each other sent waves of consternation flowing through Daphne. She prayed they would reconcile, and soon.

Chapter 5

Daphne considered playing the love song from *Bambi* over a small stereo she kept in the back room if she thought it would help Rodney's mood. Since the day of the picnic, the young man had brooded. He never smiled, nor did his beautiful tenor voice bellow out a favorite song. Daphne was amazed at how much his singing had become a part of her establishment. The silence brought emptiness to the place. If only she knew what to say or do. Daphne had to admit that personal relationships were not her strong point. Her brother had often said that a rabid dog would get along better with her than anyone. That's what made her relationship with Henry so special. They were meant to be together. He helped soften her rough edges, like a chisel to a piece of stone. He coaxed her along and showed her mercy, softening her hard heart.

Daphne stood outside the nursery as a large truck pulled in, transporting the plants and shrubs she had ordered for the early summer season. Two men jumped out and greeted her enthusiastically.

"Got any cookies today, Miss Elliot?" one of them asked.

"Sorry, fellows. I bake cookies only once a year," she said, referring to the large platter of oatmeal raisin cookies she had baked in February. When the men had arrived back then with her spring plants, they'd gobbled down the cookies faster than a pack of wild dogs.

"Too bad. Guess we need to work harder for the goodies." The men huffed, unloading box after box of plants, which Daphne directed them to place on several long wooden tables.

As they worked, she searched the road for Rodney. It was unusual for him to be late. She had counted on his being there to direct the men with the plants. She was thankful the men were easygoing and took to calling her their mom. The cheerful flowers waving in the brisk breeze sent warmth flowing through her. She looked over the flats and nodded. They included impatiens of different colors, begonias, and vinca, not to mention the vegetable flats of peppers, tomatoes, squashes, and herbs. They were all her babies in need of a good home.

Next came a new supply of rosebushes that looked like thorny twigs sticking out of their pots. With a little water, sunshine, and tender loving care, the roses would put forth leaves and then shoots of flowery heads with a fragrance that filled the air.

"So where's Rodney?" asked one of the men.

"I don't know. He's been having some problems. I hope that has nothing to do with his being late."

"Too bad. Hope it's nothing serious. That man seems so happy about everything."

Daphne agreed, realizing how Rodney's joyful outlook on life lifted her spirits. Seeing him like this, caught in the midst of some marital conflict, burdened her to no end.

"I'm sure you can help him, Miss Elliot. He thinks real highly of you. He told us so."

The comment pleased her, but she shook her head. "That young man has a mind of his own, unfortunately." She took the shipping slip the man gave her and wished him a pleasant day. Gazing about the area, she noticed the large bags of mulch and fertilizer that still needed to be stacked. Where could Rodney be?

The roar of an engine sent her whirling about, only to see a familiar dirt brown truck pull into the parking lot. The lone occupant wore a straw hat. She nearly groaned out loud but instead looked at the bags and how they made her nursery appear unkempt.

"You look like something's on your mind, Miss Elliot," Jack McNary observed, striding toward her.

"I don't know what to do. My employee isn't here this morning. He didn't call to tell me he wouldn't be in. I have all those bags that need stacking."

Jack lifted his straw hat and scratched his head. "I'll be glad to stack them for you."

"I can't pay you," she said quickly. "I have this huge shipping bill to pay and—"

"I didn't say you had to pay me. A smile would be enough." He strode over to the bags. "Where do you want them?"

Daphne gaped at him before pointing to the area. Jack hefted the bags one by one and set them in their proper place. His strength amazed her. Even Rodney grunted and groaned under the weight of the bags he was forced to bear. This man slung the sacks around as if they were filled with downy feathers.

"I guess you're used to carrying heavy loads," Daphne observed.

"Sure am. Worked on a farm for a few years. I got used to lugging feed bags and hay bales. This is nothing, really."

Daphne nearly cried with his willingness to help her out of her predicament, despite her rudeness the day of the picnic. At times she felt the Lord working on her heart, giving her the gift of repentance, but the flesh kept her silent. At last she turned and told him how delicious his barbecue was at the picnic and how she was sorry things didn't turn out better between them. He gazed back at her, somewhat amazed by her response. The look made her blink twice. It was a familiar look to her, a look of tenderness she couldn't quite place. Maybe it was just a longing within her to have a man gaze at her in such a fashion, even if her mind was telling her not to get involved.

Embarrassed by it all, Daphne hastily retreated to the store to take inventory of the summer stock. Every so often she glanced over to make sure Jack was stacking the bags correctly. She decided she must give him something for his labor. She would offer him several bags of mulch in exchange for his help. A meal would be more in keeping, as her father used to pay men for their labor by having Mother feed them a home-cooked dinner, like meat loaf and potatoes. But the idea of Jack eating at her home made her stomach lurch.

"All set," he said with a grin. "Now what did I come here for? I can't remember."

"Mulch," she said. "That is, you can take several bags of mulch."

"Mulch? What do I need mulch for?"

"I'm paying you with mulch. You need mulch with the kind of summers we get here in Virginia. It will keep the plants from drying out. Take several bags."

"Then I guess I'd better have some, since I already know what dry plants mean." Jack lifted up several bags of mulch and placed them in the bed of his truck. "Thank you very much, Miss Elliot."

"I should be thanking you. I needed the help. Now I'm going to call that young man and find out what happened to him."

"If you need any more help, let me know. In fact, I'll give you my phone number, in case."

Daphne's face colored at the thought. "That's all right. I don't need—"

He ignored her and fetched a crumbled piece of paper from the front pocket of his overalls, along with the stub of a pencil. He scrawled out the phone number and the name, along with his address. "Here you go. For a rainy day."

Daphne took the piece of paper and immediately stuffed it into the pocket of her apron. She said a quick good-bye to him as he trudged off to his truck. God had brought Jack McNary here when she needed him. She couldn't deny it. After the truck left, she reached inside her apron pocket and withdrew the slip of paper. The letters were short and choppy. She noted that he lived on Spring Mountain Road. She knew where that was, right beside the mountains. Rodney always said he wanted a place one day by the mountains. The thought reminded her of her employee's unexplained tardiness.

She entered the store, left the note on the back counter, and went at once to call Rodney. The phone rang incessantly until an answering machine picked up. After leaving a brief message, she hung up with a sigh. *Rodney, please don't do this to me. Dear God, what am I going to do?*

"Where were you yesterday?"

Rodney looked at her in surprise. He came that morning on time, to Daphne's relief, yet with a strange air about him.

"Didn't Melanie call?"

"No."

"Figures. I knew she wouldn't." He banged the counter with his fist, an uncharacteristic gesture for him, before striding to the back where he deposited his lunch and a magazine. "I told her to call you and let you know I wouldn't be in."

"I never got a call. Yesterday was the summer delivery, too. I'm glad Jack, I mean, Mr. McNary, showed up when he did. He helped stack the mulch and the fertilizer."

"It wasn't my fault, Miss Elliot. I left instructions for her to call, but she does what she pleases these days. And now I'm in hot water with you. Just my luck."

Daphne didn't know what to think. Never had she seen Rodney so irate. It made her wish for the old days and his songs of love infiltrating the place, even if the singing rubbed her nerves the wrong way. "Now don't fret. Things will get better with Melanie."

"Fat chance," he mumbled. "We haven't had a decent conversation since the day of the picnic. I'm sorry I asked you to go. I had no business trying to set you up with anyone. Believe me, you're better off not being married, Miss Elliot. No wonder God says it's better for a man to live on a roof than to be in the same house with a contentious woman."

Daphne began sorting out seed packets, finding some outdated packets still on the store shelves that Rodney was supposed to purge last fall. "Have you found out why Melanie is so upset?"

"It's this job."

Daphne whirled to face him. Any mention of her business, whether good or bad, piqued her interest. Not that she wanted to hear anything bad about the way she ran things. Oh, there was the occasional customer who said that a plant she'd sold them was diseased, or the customer who found a hole in a bag of potting mix. She did everything she could to fix the problem. "What did she say?"

"It doesn't matter." He disappeared into the storeroom.

Daphne could hardly contain her curiosity. Of course discussions should remain private between couples, but if the argument had anything do with her business, she must know what was going on. Did Melanie think she was treating Rodney unfairly? She only kept him beyond closing time one day a week at most. He didn't seem to mind. The spring was extra busy, after all. Or perhaps she expected Daphne to pay him more? But Daphne did pay him far more than other employees she had had under her care. And what about her idea of giving

Rodney the business? How could she do that if Melanie disapproved of his job?

Tossing the outdated seed packets into the garbage, Daphne went to the greenhouse where she found Rodney with his feet buried in dirt. He had upset a bag of soil kept on the shelf, the potting mixture Daphne used for transplanting her most prized plants. "Now I know something is wrong," she observed.

Rodney tried to scoop it up with his sneaker.

"A broom and a dustpan are probably better." She picked up a broom and began sweeping.

Rodney took the implement out of her hands. "I'll do it. This is my life right now. One big pile of dirt."

"It can't be that bad. Surely Melanie isn't still upset about your sending her croquet ball away on Sunday."

Rodney chuckled. "If only it were that." He leaned against the handle of the broom. "Miss Elliot, I'm afraid I'm going to have to move on to other pastures."

"What?"

"Melanie says we don't have any money. I told her when we got married she could stop with her office work and concentrate on her silk flower business. She wants to do those craft shows, you know. She couldn't stand the office. It was like a cage, and the boss was a dictator."

"I remember, I think."

"Well, she's mad the electric bill didn't get paid last month, and she's been complaining about the money ever since. She said I lied about my income and that I didn't make enough here to feed a flea. And what are we supposed to do if a baby comes along? Et cetera."

Daphne could feel the heat rise in her cheeks. "You make much more than any other employee I've had."

"She's not happy. So I'm going to have to look for another job."

He maneuvered the broom, sweeping the dirt into a pile. Daphne picked up the dustpan and gingerly knelt while Rodney swept. In the dustpan, she saw all her dreams ready to be thrown into the garbage. *Dear God, this can't be happening.*

"I know this must make you real upset, Miss Elliot," he said with a chuckle. "It means you won't have to hear any more of my singing or witness my numerous schemes in life."

I would take all of that and more. He simply can't leave! What will I do? She felt her chest tighten and her heart begin to race. She turned from him and made her way to the counter where she sat down in a chair.

"Are you all right?" Rodney asked.

"You can't do this to me. Please."

"Miss Elliot, I don't have a choice."

"There are always choices. I will go over the books tonight. I'll see if I can give you a raise."

Rodney rested the broom against the wall and came to her. His rugged face softened into the tender look of a son for his mother, so much so that Daphne nearly cried. "I won't let you do that. You'll be eating dog food for dinner if you give me any more money."

"If I lose you, I'll have to sell."

"No, you won't. You'll find another helper. I'll ask around church. I know some guys who would jump at the chance for a good job like this."

Daphne shook her head. She couldn't stand the thought of a major change in her life, especially training a new person. Everything right now was at a status quo, organized, in a daily routine. One change and she might slide down some slippery slope toward disaster. She had been through too many changes already in her life. She couldn't lose the young man who had helped her so much. Rodney gave her place of business character. He was helpful to the customers. And, yes, she treasured his songs of love, even if she was slow to acknowledge it.

"Miss Elliot, I must tell you the truth. If it comes down to my marriage or this job, you know what I have to do."

Daphne twisted her hands in dismay. She knew very well what he was saying. It was his character, after all. Rodney loved Melanie, and he loved being married, even if they were having difficulties right now. She couldn't expect him to be married to a job. That's what wrecked relationships and sent marriages tumbling into a dark abyss. "I know," she said quietly, though the words felt forced.

The rest of the day was somber, matching the dark gray clouds that began drifting across the spring sky. When Daphne closed the doors of the nursery that evening, she wondered how long the business would stay afloat now that Rodney had all but resigned. She hurried to the car, thankful she lived only a mile away as raindrops began falling from above.

She negotiated the short drive home, and pulling in, she heard Chubs barking. Lightning flashed. A violent spring storm was brewing. Virginia was known to have storms like this with flooding rain and even hail. Daphne hurried into the home as lightning struck again, followed by a boom of thunder that rattled the windows in their frames.

Chubs began to howl and scurried upstairs to hide under the bed, even though he desperately needed to go outdoors. Daphne managed to coax him out with a dog biscuit, hooked the leash on his collar, and allowed him to step outside the back door to do his business. The rain came down in a torrent. Chubs was soaked almost immediately, forcing Daphne to keep him in the kitchen lest he shake water all over the carpet in the living room. Muddy paw prints added a new decoration to the flowery print of the linoleum floor. Daphne watched the lightning dance across the sky. A bolt zipped between her home and the nursery. The indoor lights flickered. Despite his wet fur, Daphne hugged Chubs, thankful for the dog's companionship on this stormy evening. What a terrible day it had been, with Rodney's surprise announcement and now a storm that left her feeling weak and lonely.

She went to the living room and plopped down in her favorite chair. The rain outside continued in earnest, no doubt washing away the new soil she had put in her home garden not too long ago. She wondered if Jack had put down the mulch before the storm hit. She slid back in the chair, listening to the sound of the rain splattering against the windows. If only someone were here to share her innermost thoughts and, yes, her fears, too.

All at once she saw herself and Henry ducking between raindrops during a walk in the woods. She had thought to bring an umbrella, and together they snuggled under it while sitting on a small log just big enough for the two of them. The fragrance of the woods was even more pronounced. She shivered a bit before feeling the warmth of his arm cradled about her.

"Cold?"

"A little." Her voice quivered.

He removed his coat and placed it around her shoulders. Soon they were sharing a kiss beneath the umbrella. It didn't matter that the rain had begun to drip off the umbrella and fall into her lap. She only basked in Henry's warm presence and his lips that made her forget all her worries in life. Love could do that to you. Anxieties melted away under its fire. Problems were dissolved. Trials were but dust specks in the wind.

Daphne straightened in her seat. Melanie and Rodney had love, and that's what would see them through this difficulty. They needed to be like her and Henry, full of love for each other, even if they were caught in a storm with rain drenching them.

Daphne grabbed the telephone to call them.·

"Are you all right, Miss Elliot?" Rodney asked when he answered.

"Yes, but I know you two are not. So I'd like to invite myself over to your place for dinner. Ask your lovely wife if I can come."

"Of course you can come. But I'm warning you, if you think it will change anything—"

"I'm just lonely here, especially with this storm. I want to eat with someone tomorrow night." She heard conversation in the background and Melanie quickly agreeing to a guest for dinner.

"Of course you're welcome to come over."

"Will I see you tomorrow for work?"

"I'm not leaving yet."

"Good. See you tomorrow." Daphne replaced the receiver with a decisive click. She refused to let this relationship go to ruin, and likewise her business. She would coax them along on that sailboat of love and make certain it brought them into a safe harbor. If not, she had no idea where the storm might end up sending her and the garden center.

Chapter 6

Daphne tried to maintain an air of business at the nursery the following day, but she couldn't help her anxiety over the dinner that night. Rodney stayed busy outside, assisting customers with bags of fertilizer, mulch, and soil while she worked the cash register. Business had picked up with the spring planting season in full swing. The mere idea that Rodney might walk out on her during the busiest time of the year made her insides ache. By the time she trained another person to take his place, she would lose much of the season. And if a season went bad, she would have no choice but to close.

On her lunch break, she considered her options while trying to eat a dry turkey sandwich. Like other upsetting days, she found her appetite greatly diminished. Not that she couldn't stand to shed a few pounds, but anxiety was not the way to lose weight. As her doctor once told her, a diet low in salt and cholesterol, along with a brief walk, would help.

For now, Daphne put all that aside to concentrate on her dilemma. For some reason, she thought of Jack and his willingness to help her stack the soil and mulch after the delivery. Just as quickly, she shook her head. She couldn't possibly have that man fill Rodney's shoes. He was too old, for one thing. What if he died of a heart attack, trying to lift all those bags? And she couldn't boss him around the way she could Rodney. No, it would have to be someone young and with an openness to tolerate her way of doing things, like Rodney.

Daphne bit her lip and put down her half-eaten sandwich. Life was getting far too complicated. She had endured years of pain and uncertainty. At this point in her life she was growing weary of it all. Perhaps it would be better if her heart did give out so she could be at home with the Lord. But she wasn't a quitter. She was an Elliot and carried her namesake with pride. Her father had begun this business, and she would do whatever she could to keep it alive.

Before going to the dinner, Daphne outfitted herself in a pantsuit and the pearl earrings. She liked to wear them when times were rough. It made her remember all that she had been through with God's help. Daphne paused, her hand frozen with the lipstick ready to trace color on her dry lips. *God's help.* The very words convicted her. Had she truly been relying on God's help through all this? Or had she been trying to do it in her own strength, fueled only by pride? She applied the color, then used a tissue to wipe away the tiny streaks that missed her lips. She didn't want to miss God in all this. He had been there for her in the past and would guide her future if she allowed Him.

Daphne went to the chair in the living room and sat down. She closed her eyes and offered a prayer for help that God would guide her. Above all, she prayed that He would lead her to make the right decision with regard to her business. When she snapped open her eyes, the light of the lamp seemed to shine a little brighter. Her heart beat stronger. She smiled and picked up her purse. God was still there.

Daphne admired the many silk flower arrangements Melanie had created. The spare bedroom was filled with all kinds of arrangement paraphernalia—dried flowers, baskets, ribbon, picks. The strange aromas made her sneeze.

"These are wonderful," she said, picking up a small basket. "How much do you want for it?"

Melanie gazed at her in surprise. "If you want it, go ahead and take it."

"Nonsense. A worker is worthy of wages." Daphne opened her purse. "Is twenty enough?"

Melanie smiled and accepted the bill. She began wrapping plastic around the arrangement while Daphne examined the other arrangements sitting on a card table. "Have you done any craft shows?"

"A few. I've been trying to get that craft store in town to sell some of them on consignment. Of course I'm in competition with everyone else." She sighed. "But the way things are going right now, I may have to get rid of the business anyway and look for a job."

Daphne inhaled a breath. The door had opened already. She prayed she had the strength to handle whatever walked through. "So things are a little tight?"

Melanie chuckled. "*Tight* is hardly the word I would use. *Impossible* is more like it. I know you're very generous with your salary to Rod, Miss Elliot, but right now we're having trouble paying the bills. Not that it helps when he forgets to make payments on time and then we end up having to pay late fees. The bank had to pay on two checks because we didn't have enough funds to cover them. That's sixty dollars in service charges. It's a waste."

"Now we all make mistakes—" Daphne stopped when she saw the lines of consternation creep across the young woman's face. "I mean, I miss bills." She fingered a silk flower arrangement in a basket shaped like an old-fashioned baby buggy.

"I know I'll have to go back to that terrible office again. Rod promised me I wouldn't. He said I could do my flower business. Now I don't think he cares."

Daphne saw the shadow of Rodney on the back patio, using a small grill to barbecue chicken. At times the hazy smoke obscured him from view. She felt more and more like a concerned parent, trying to dole out advice to these two young people.

"He used to care. But I really think he does want me to go back to work. He says that most home businesses fail after a year anyway. Since I haven't had any major contracts for this work, he thinks it's a failure."

"A businesswoman can succeed," Daphne said with a smile, sparking one on Melanie's face. "I'm living proof. It isn't easy, but with God, all things are possible."

"Yes, but there's so much pressure for women to make it big in the corporate world. I feel as if I'm a failure because I want to run a home business and stay at home with any kids we might have."

"There's nothing wrong with a home business. And don't you listen to any of that chatter you hear on television. You have a very important role here, too. I do think you need to advertise your work more. It's really beautiful."

"Advertising costs money."

Just then the phone rang. Melanie picked it up, then marched away to give the receiver to Rodney. While she was gone, Daphne took stock of Melanie's inventory. She wondered if perhaps some of the customers at her nursery would want a few artificial arrangements for their homes. The thought made her cringe. If they bought them, they would never come and buy real plants and planting material for gardens. She shook her head, unwilling to make that kind of commitment yet.

Melanie returned. "Dinner's almost ready, Miss Elliot."

Daphne followed the young woman to the small kitchen nook. She saw the old flowered furniture in the tiny living room, given to Melanie when her grandmother passed on. The room was fairly bursting with furniture of various shapes and sizes. She could see right there that they needed a bigger place.

Daphne looked up to see Rodney emerge from the patio, carrying a platter of chicken and wearing a grin on his face. "I've cured all our ills," he announced, placing the platter on the table.

Melanie stared at him quizzically while Daphne exclaimed how delicious the food looked.

"We'll pray. Then I'll tell you my news," Rodney said with a grin.

The three bowed their heads while he offered up a prayer for the meal.

Daphne accepted a bowl of seasoned rice. "So what's the news?"

"You probably won't like it much, Miss Elliot, but I have great news. I'm set for an interview tomorrow with the company I e-mailed a resume to just yesterday. Isn't that terrific?"

Daphne stared. Before she knew what was happening, her hand trembled, spilling rice on the tablecloth. "Oh no."

"No harm done," Melanie said, grabbing a sponge to clean up the mess.

"If I get it, the job will pay big-time."

Daphne looked down at her food and found her appetite gone. Here she had come, hoping to solve this couple's problems, only to find more looming. What was she doing here then? Occupying a chair? She picked up her water glass and took a sip. "What does it pay?"

"Quite a bit. It starts at thirty-five with opportunities for more."

Daphne choked on the rice she had started eating. She picked up a napkin and coughed loudly. Rodney was only making twenty-eight in her little establishment. Her heart began to sink. She glanced over, expecting Melanie to smile at this announcement. Instead, she took only tiny bites of her food.

"It will work this time," Rodney told her.

"Right. I've heard it before, Rod. You go to these interviews, and then they make you sit by the phone for months. What happens to us in the meantime?"

Rodney glanced over at Daphne. No doubt he was hoping she would keep him on until he secured another job. Daphne bristled at the thought. If he was so eager to find a job paying thirty-five thousand dollars, why should she help? He would only leave anyway. She shook her head at such hardheartedness. Rodney was the best thing that had ever happened to her business. She could never let him go.

"In the meantime, I'll keep working."

"And in the meantime, we get more and more in debt," Melanie said with a groan. "We don't even have enough to make the car payment. I took out an ad today."

Rodney put down his fork. "What?"

"We can't afford the car, so I took out an ad to sell it."

Rodney rose to his feet, his face reddening. "Are you kidding? You're selling our car right out from underneath us?"

"We can't afford two cars. It's either that or we starve."

"Melanie, get real."

"No, you get real. And you haven't gotten real in the last six months. I got another notice about an overdue bill, too. The next thing we know, the electricity will be turned off again."

Daphne put down her fork. She felt dizzy and nauseated. The bickering weighed her down nearly to the breaking point. It seemed like a rerun from long ago. Finally she lifted her head and said, "That's enough. You two are hissing and barking like a cat and a dog. Next thing, you'll be scratching each other's eyes out."

Rodney sat down, and both he and Melanie bowed their heads, as if ashamed by their lack of self-control.

"I know what it's like not to have money. When my father died, there was a huge debt owed on the business. My brother, Charles, and I got into a terrible fight about it. He wanted to sell the business to pay off the debt. I wanted to keep it going and asked him to help. It was awful. We didn't speak. He left and went to live in California. I haven't seen him since. Is that what you want? Letting your marriage break up over this and living on opposite sides of the country?"

"It's not that bad," Rodney began, though his voice betrayed his doubt.

"Young man, I've seen many fine marriages break up over money. Yes, we need it to live, but money can end up breaking us and destroying everything we hold dear. That's when I made a decision long ago not to let money rule my life. I decided to live simply. I didn't buy fancy clothes. My furniture belonged to my parents. I bought a used car. And if I'm to have anything new, I'll leave it to God to bless me. And He has, I must say."

"I don't see anything wrong with wanting to buy a few new things," Melanie said in defense.

"Or having a car," Rodney added with a sideways glance at Melanie.

"Of course not. But, like everything in our lives, there's a right time for those things. Do you have a Bible?"

Rodney sat up, a bit startled. "Of course." He went to retrieve a Bible from the living room.

Daphne flipped it open. "Here it is. This is the verse God gave me when I was in debt. 'And my God will meet all your needs according to his glorious riches in Christ Jesus.'"

"So what you're saying is, we need to trust God in this," Rodney said, glancing toward Melanie.

"Yes. He knows what's best, and He knows our needs." Daphne realized she also needed to trust God more. Even as she spoke, the words convicted her own spirit. "Without faith, we can't please God. He wants us to trust Him, especially with our needs. He cares for the sparrow, and He makes the plants beautiful. Surely He will help us."

Melanie played with her napkin, folding and unfolding it. Daphne could see that the words were hard to accept. How she wanted to give these two young people a hug and tell them God would help, as He once helped her. He had answered her heartfelt cries when debts nearly forced her to declare bankruptcy and she had barely enough stock on the shelves to keep the nursery afloat. But somehow He had brought her through it. Now the business had a promising future—that is, if Rodney would stay on.

"I want my business to continue," she declared suddenly. "I don't want it to die when I do." She opened her purse and fished out a paper, one she had written the previous night by the light of a small oil lamp while the storm raged outside. She gave it to Rodney.

He took it and read it slowly, then flung the paper down. "Miss Elliot!"

"What is it?" Melanie asked.

Rodney gave her the paper. Daphne saw Melanie's cheeks pink and her lips tremble. "I don't believe it. You're giving the nursery business to Rod when you retire?"

"Yes, if he wants it. I had made the decision awhile ago, but I wasn't sure when would be the appropriate time to bring it up. Now seems a better time than any. If you agree, I'll have my lawyer make out an official document."

"I don't know what to say," Rodney began.

"You can say plenty. First of all, you can tell your pretty wife here that you love her. Same with you, Melanie."

Rodney and Melanie stared at each other. Suddenly they broke out into laugher that played like a soothing melody after the disharmony witnessed earlier that night. "I do love you, Melanie," he said. "And with God's help, we're going to make it."

"I love you, too, Rod. And if I need to work for a time, it's okay. We'll do what we need to do."

He glanced back at the paper. "I really appreciate this, Miss Elliot, but are you sure you want to do this? Do you know who you're getting?"

"Yes, I know. I know for a fact that you remind me of Henry. He worked hard and did what he could with the job he had. And he loved to help others. I think of this as a memorial to his name."

Melanie took Daphne's hand and squeezed it. "You still miss him after all these years?"

Daphne couldn't help the tear that slipped out of her eye as she nodded. She hadn't anticipated such a reaction, but Melanie had touched a sensitive area.

"You never did tell me what happened," Rodney said.

"What? I'm sure I did." When he shook his head, Daphne obliged. She wanted to relate the story, even if it was painful. She told about the day of his death and the mysterious fire at the mill that killed him.

"They were never able to tell you how it happened?"

"No. I went there myself and asked questions. No one would say. They just said it was a terrible accident. They said there was nothing left. . .only ashes." The tears gathered in her eyes. "I'm sorry." She blew her nose into the tissue Melanie had handed her. "I had a funeral for him, in my own way. I gave him to God. But that lumber mill stole him away."

"I wish I had known all this," Rodney said softly. "I know you mentioned Henry a few times and that he was your boyfriend when you were young, but I had no idea he died so tragically."

Melanie again gripped her hand. "Miss Elliot, I'm sure God doesn't want you to be alone like this. He will bring another man into your life. It's not too late to experience love."

The mere mention of another man instantly dried her tears and raised her defense mechanism like a solid wall. "No. My time is long gone, I'm afraid. The Lord is my husband. Scripture even says so."

Melanie released her hand and rose to clear the table. Rodney jumped up, as well, and before long had brewed Daphne a cup of tea. At first she regretted confessing her hurt over Henry's passing. Now, with her heart open and exposed, she realized the lingering sorrow that had crippled her. She had hoped to bring healing to this young couple but realized she needed some, as well.

Chapter 7

Daphne went to work feeling better than she had in months. Since giving the document to Rodney and Melanie and informing them of her desire to bequeath them the store once she retired, a heavy burden had been lifted from her shoulders. No longer would she lie awake nights, wondering what would become of her father's business if the Lord took her in her sleep. She could rest knowing that Rodney and Melanie would do a good job and keep the business thriving. Not only that, but she felt a renewal in her spiritual life, as well. For so long, she had shut out God. Sharing with the young couple from the Bible renewed her own interest in studying the Word and making it a greater part of her life. She read the Bible at breakfast over a bowl of bran cereal that morning and played a cassette tape of favorite hymns while she did a few chores.

Daphne worked with Rodney, arranging the roses for the new sale they had just begun. He returned to singing his love songs, which was cheerful music to her ears. He talked incessantly of what he would like to do with the business, including incorporating Melanie's talent for flower arranging. "I hope you don't mind my talking about this," he said suddenly. "I mean, it's not as if I want you to retire anytime soon. I guess I'm just excited about being a business owner."

"Don't worry about me. I have a feeling that retirement may be just around the corner. It's good to hear a motivated young man toying with new ideas. Now let's put all the red roses together, right by the entrance to the nursery."

"Red is the color of love, Miss Elliot," Rodney said with a mischievous lilt to his voice.

"Yes, and if my mother were alive, she would surely appreciate a lovely red rose on Mother's Day, which is coming soon."

Rodney frowned. "You know what I mean. Don't try to change my words. And speaking of love. . ."

A familiar truck rolled slowly into the gravel parking lot of the nursery. Daphne stood fast in place, her head high, and even wore a smile on her lips. She would not let anything or anyone steal her joy this day, despite Rodney's connotations.

"Hello, Jack," Rodney said with a cheerful wave. "Have we got a wonderful rose for you!"

Daphne felt her face color like the red roses blooming in the pots. "Rodney, please take these shipping papers to my office."

"Sure, Miss Elliot. I can take a hint."

The heat in her face crept into her ears and down her neck. And she was wearing a light-colored top, too. No doubt she looked like a tomato dressed in white. *The nerve of him,* she thought, even as Rodney strode off whistling. Daphne stooped down, trying to rearrange the potted plants into straight rows. She murmured a greeting to Jack's pleasant "Good morning." So much for her plan to be friendly. Rodney had again succeeded in putting her in a less-than-pleasant mood.

"You've got some nice roses there," he observed. "I used to have a climbing rose by the front porch until it pretty near died on me." He paused and stepped back. "I shouldn't be telling you about dead plants. It isn't as if I killed it, though. It broke clean away after an ice storm during the winter. And then the beetles came and ate it."

"Roses are like children. They need tender, loving care."

"And I'm sure you know just what they need."

Daphne glanced up at him. No doubt he must be referring to her vast knowledge of plants. She couldn't see his expression through the shadow made by the straw hat, but she could imagine what he looked like—with blue eyes staring down and a funny smirk on his face. "I know a few things. I've been in this business long enough."

"I see that young fellow decided to come back. I thought maybe you might have lost him. That's why I came to find out if you needed any help."

"No. As you can see, he's back and quite happy about it."

"Also, I wanted to let you know that the new plants are doing just fine."

"Glad to hear it."

"So there's hope for me as a gardener?"

Daphne refused to go that far but managed to bite her tongue before telling him so.

"Anyway, I was wondering if you might still need an extra hand?"

Daphne stared back, ready to issue a firm retort.

"I work cheap," he added.

"But I have Rodney."

He exhaled a sigh as if disappointed over the fact. "As I said, I wasn't sure if he would be coming back. I mean, it isn't as if I need the money or anything. It's just—"

Daphne didn't want to hear what he was about to say. The mere thought that he might want to spend time with her made her anxious. Soon he would be asking her to go with him to a lecture at the senior center or invite her to the famous Hardware Store Restaurant downtown. Her knees began to quake at the thought of sitting in a restaurant with a flickering candle on the table, staring at another man. The last time she had sat at a table like that was with that sweet-talking Larson McCall, and she almost lost her business because of it.

She picked up a rosebush and began walking toward the store, thinking a bush by the entrance might entice customers to buy.

"I get bored at the house," he said, following her. "I like what goes on here with the plants, starting new life, watching new plants take over and grow after others have died."

Daphne turned to face him. "Mr. McNary, did you need to buy something?"

He swiped off his hat. "Why are you angry?"

"I'm not angry. I just don't enjoy having a man follow me around, obviously looking for a woman to fill some unmet need. I can assure you I don't intend to be that person, no matter what you think."

"Daphne, is that why you think I'm here?"

"Aren't you?" The rosebush began to shake violently.

Jack's gaze focused on the large bush and how it wavered. He reached out, trying to grab the pot. The pot fell, breaking the rose in two. Sharp thorns pierced Daphne's hand.

"Oh no!" She began to cry.

"Daphne, I'm so sorry. Let me help." Without reservation, he took her in his arms. He grabbed a handkerchief out of his pocket and began dabbing at the bleeding wounds on her hand. "I have a first aid kit in the truck." He went off to fetch it. In no time, he had his arm cradled around her again. His other hand gently swabbed at the wounds with an antiseptic wipe.

Daphne remained in his presence, sobbing at the broken rose before her and the bleeding wounds on her hand. The tears were more out of frustration than anything else. How this scene illustrated her life right now—bleeding and broken, with thorns piercing her soul.

Rodney rushed out when he heard the commotion, only to stop short and stare. Daphne glanced up to see his look of surprise and suddenly realized she was in Jack's embrace with her head resting against his shoulder. She wrenched away. "Please leave me alone," she told Jack. "I mean it." She marched into the store and slammed the door shut.

≈≈

Daphne remained inside the store the rest of the morning, hidden in the back room, unable to venture out after the escapade with Jack and the rose. She hadn't realized it, but when she came in, muttering to herself about the encounter, several customers had been perusing products in the aisles. When they heard the commotion, they came out and stared. Some hurried away without buying anything. Daphne had never been so embarrassed in her life. How she could have made such a scene, and right where the customers could witness her tirade, was too much to bear. At once she placed the blame on Jack. He had put his arms around her, setting her off. That's all he wanted to do in the first place, take advantage of an opportunity to make a move on her. And now she had lost precious customers and money because of it.

Daphne tried hard to look at a memo book, but the tears clouding her eyes made the words waver like rippling water. How could she ever face the public again? Maybe she should retire right now and let Rodney take over. It would be easier. But Daphne was never one to quit, no matter what humiliation came her way.

Her throat became scratchy from her anguish. She peeked out, hoping to make a cup of herbal tea in the small microwave. A cup of tea was just the thing to bathe her parched throat and calm her frayed nerves. She sneaked out of the back room and toward the microwave, only to find Rodney there, removing a container of food he had heated for lunch.

"Are you all right?" he asked. "I wanted to go back and check on you, but you had locked the door."

"My hand hurts," she admitted. "Thorns can be very painful."

"That was sure nice of Jack to help you like that. He seemed very concerned."

Daphne said nothing but fumbled for a mug and a tea bag.

"He was pretty upset when he left. In fact, he gave me a note to give you." Rodney produced a small note, written on a scrap of paper from a seed company. At first Daphne didn't want it. Glancing up to see Rodney's questioning gaze, she took it and retreated to the storeroom.

Dear Miss Elliot,

I'm sorry about what happened today. I never want to hurt you. I hope you will forgive me. I didn't mean any harm when I came to see you about a job, but I see that I still manage to upset you, no matter what I do. I want you to know that I won't bother you anymore.

Sincerely,
Jack McNary

Daphne read the note twice. She should feel relieved after what she read, but instead, it made her sad. She remembered how gentle he was after the spill she had taken and how he tried to doctor the wounds on her hand. No doubt he had suffered wounds, as well, with that strange scarring on his face. A man with that kind of disfigurement must have gone through plenty in his life. What he didn't possess in facial characteristics, he most certainly did in his heart. He had been only a gentleman to her. He deserved much more than what she was giving.

Don't go that route, Daphne scolded herself. *Don't think about another man.* She was used to living alone and too old to experience love. It had passed her by as had the years that trickled away one by one, leaving her alone without children or a future. How could she even think of allowing such things to enter her life now?

She turned to find Rodney had come up behind her. From the look on his face, it was almost as if he could read her internal struggle.

"So is everything all right?" he asked.

"He apologized," she said carelessly, hoping her attitude would dissuade him from her real thoughts. "I think he had ulterior motives the moment he set foot on my property."

"Tell me, Miss Elliot—is it so wrong to consider that maybe God might have a special surprise in store for you?"

"If it's a man, I don't want it. You know what happened with that Larson character." Yet inwardly she knew it wasn't true. The scene on the stairs of her nursery told her she did need someone, desperately.

"Larson was a fraud, I admit. But Jack isn't. I've never met anyone more sincere. God must think you need a good man in your life. He's obviously tired of you running the show. Maybe it's about time you thought of someone else for a change."

Daphne gaped at him in astonishment. Rodney had never talked to her this way before.

"And most likely you now regret your decision to pass the nursery on to me," he continued. "But the truth is the truth. And the truth is, you've had so much anger in you that you've never even begun to live. You're like a plant stuck in the same pot of soil. You haven't grown an inch. And if you don't let God try to up-root and plant you somewhere else, you'll shrivel away to nothing." He marched out without his customary song.

Daphne never felt so ashamed. Not only had she caused a scene in front of her customers, but in front of Rodney, as well. Especially after sitting in their home, quoting Bible verses and appearing holier-than-thou, how could she turn around and do this?

Daphne dragged herself home that evening, her mind a whirlwind of mixed emotions. She took Chubs out for his customary evening walk, then returned to the empty home. No longer did the house seem comfortable to her. It was drafty and very lonely.

Daphne went to her room to see a picture of Henry sitting on her bureau. She had displayed the picture of him ever since the day he died in the fire at the lumber mill. He smiled cheerfully at her as he had these past forty years. Daphne exhaled a slow breath. All she had in life was the companionship of some black-and-white photo taken ages ago. A photo couldn't give love or companionship. It couldn't share heartaches and triumphs. And it would never bring her comfort. A photo was simply a memory that faded away with the passage of time.

Daphne kissed her fingers and touched Henry's face in the portrait. She was still bound to the past, as Rodney had said. She needed to start living again and with people who were alive, not dead. She put the picture in a drawer and walked out to the living room. The first thing she would do was call Jack and apologize for her rude behavior. After that, she might invite a few of her lady friends from church for dinner one evening. And she would have Rodney and Melanie over more often. She would open up her home and her heart to others. Maybe these steps would begin freeing her from her root-bound status, as Rodney had put it.

She began by hunting for the scrap of paper with Jack's phone number written on it. When she dialed, an answering machine came on. Daphne hated speaking into machines and usually hung up before leaving a message. This time she forced herself to speak.

"Hello, Mr. McNary. This is Daphne Elliot. I just wanted to say—"

The line clicked, and a male voice came over the receiver. "Hello? Hello, Daphne? Are you all right?"

Daphne straightened in her seat. For a moment she thought she heard a voice of long ago beckoning to her. Goose bumps erupted on her skin. *Ridiculous. Calm down.* "What? I'm fine. Just a few scratches."

"I'm so glad you called. I wanted to let you know that I mailed you some money today to cover the cost of the rose."

"What? But you didn't drop it. I did."

"I had no business asking you about a job. I only wanted to see if you still needed me." He paused. "I just wanted to make sure you had enough help and you weren't overdoing it, especially with that heart of yours. Not that I'm young myself, but I do have a strong heart. At least the doctor told me that ten years ago."

"You should see the doctor every year. You could be suffering high blood pressure and not even know it. That's what my doctor told me. He said many people don't bother to go to the doctor until it's too late and they've suffered a stroke. I can't begin to tell you how many I know have dropped dead from doing the simplest things in life. Though I'm sure you've been to the doctor a few times in your life."

She heard him cough over the phone. "What makes you say that?"

"Oh, well, uh—" She hesitated. Surely he must have been to a doctor with that strange patch of scar tissue on his face, though she didn't want to bring it up and cause him embarrassment. "I mean, everyone has gone at one time or another."

"I've been to doctors, yes, but it's been awhile. Maybe I should go again. Thanks for your suggestion."

Daphne began feeling warm and picked up a small magazine to use as a fan. "Anyway, I didn't want you to think I was ordering you off my property. As it is,

I chased other customers away during my outburst. Then I went and blamed you when you had nothing to do with it. You were only trying to help."

He said nothing. All she heard was the soft buzz of the open phone line.

"I guess I'm much too independent and stubborn," she mused.

"And it's my fault."

"Pardon me?"

"That is, I should have realized a woman like you knows what she's doing, especially with running a business. I had no right to interfere. It's amazing to see what you've done."

"Thank you. It did take a lot of hard work." She began to wave the magazine more urgently before her flushed face. "I need to go. Thank you again for your assistance today."

"Anytime you need me, I'll be there. I promise. Just call me."

His words chased her the rest of the evening. She desperately needed help in her loneliness. She needed comfort and security. She wanted peace. Perhaps she really was seeking the love of a good man.

Chapter 8

Rodney seemed pleased when Daphne told him about the phone call she had made to Jack. She then promptly invited him and Melanie to join her for lunch the next weekend. He agreed, telling her how much they'd enjoyed the last evening they'd spent together. He then broke into song with "What Now, My Love?" while going about his daily duties.

Daphne continued with an inventory of her existing supplies and readying another order of late-summer stock, including early fall mums and young trees. This time of year, both Rodney and she worked long hours to keep the nursery functioning. The customers liked to come later with the extended daylight to peruse the many varieties of plants and make their selections. Daphne tried to keep her sanity in the midst of the chaos. She dealt with this every year. With the majority of her money coming in during the spring and summer, she threw her entire being into her work. If the truth were known, she didn't have time to be neighborly, like having people over for dinner. The long hours tired her. But since the escapade with Jack and the lecture by Rodney, her conscience bothered her enough to continue with the plans, despite the hectic work schedule.

"I'm really looking forward to lunch," Rodney said a few days later while Daphne's hands were deep in soil, repotting the last of the summer annuals that would go on sale. "Any idea what we're having?"

Daphne hadn't even thought about it. "I don't know. What would you like?"

"Anything you cook will be first-class, I'm sure. By the way, I hope you don't mind, but I'd like to provide the entertainment for the afternoon."

Daphne peered up at him and that ridiculous smile he always wore. He made her feel as if he knew everything that was going on while she stayed in the dark. "I'm sure you're going to sing."

"If you want me to. What would you like to hear? 'Love in Any Language?' 'Lost Without Your Love?' 'Love Me Tender?'"

Daphne took up a small ball of dirt and threw it at him. He ducked, grinning from ear to ear. The soil sailed into the wall with a splat.

"Really, Miss Elliot. That's getting personal."

"What you're doing is getting personal, young man," she added with a smile of her own. "All I've been hearing the last few weeks out of you is love this, love that. And for your information, I think it's beginning to rub off just a tad. I'm trying to show more interest in others. I realize I've been too preoccupied with my own affairs and that something needed to change."

"Hurray! You have so much to offer, Miss Elliot. I remember a saying on a plaque that Melanie once got from a friend. It says, 'Count Your Age by Friends, Not Years.' It's the friends you make in life that count, not how old you are. Which leads me to my after-lunch entertainment."

For a moment, Daphne felt a wave of anxiety creep up within her. If he was planning another scheme like inviting Jack to the luncheon, she feared she might end up in the hospital.

"I'm bringing my laptop."

Daphne paused in her work with her fingers immersed in dirt. She reached for some paper towels. "Whatever for?"

"I need your help."

"My help? I know nothing about those machines. Whatever happened to good old-fashioned handwriting and ciphering? Everyone wants things easy nowadays. They have machines that do all the work for them."

"I need your opinion on something I've been working on. I've been trying to find the identity of a friend, and I've come across practically nothing on the person. It's as if this person never existed."

"Really."

"So I want to share with you what I've found and see what you think. You like mysteries, don't you? I know you read those mystery novels. Maybe you can help me solve this one."

Daphne nearly chuckled, recalling the stack of mystery novels lining the shelf in her bedroom. Yes, she loved a good mystery. Trying to solve a whodunit brightened up an otherwise dull life. But reading mysteries had its drawbacks, too, like drumming up a longing to discover more things about Henry's death in the lumber mill fire. After it happened, the businessmen at the mill remained tight-lipped about the incident for fear of lawsuits. She would never forget the face of one man without a hair on his scalp, looking at her over a pair of glasses. He announced quite matter-of-factly that Henry was in the wrong place at the wrong time. When she asked to see the spot where he died, the man refused, claiming it was under investigation. Daphne followed up with calls to the investigators but was supplied with little information. Everyone said it was an unfortunate accident and that she needed to go on with life. Daphne shook her head. Look where life had led her—a lonely spinster without happiness, entangled in a web of memories.

Perhaps helping Rodney with his little project would be good for her. She could act the role of sleuth, even if this did little to solve her own past. He wanted to play a game, and she would follow along. Maybe he even meant to play the game of Clue, which she enjoyed very much. "Everyone has a past, even if it might be shady at times. Bring your laptop, and we'll see what we can find out."

Rodney nearly leaped in the air before controlling his exuberance to help some customers who had ventured in. Daphne couldn't help but smile. Yes, Rodney was like a son to her, and yes, she was very glad she had signed the business over to his care. If only he would stop with his little matchmaking ventures and let her live in peace.

⊷

Rodney and Melanie arrived a half hour early for the luncheon, catching Daphne off guard. She hurried to finish setting the table with dishes in the pattern of ripe apples. Melanie immediately pitched in to help while Rodney set up shop in a corner of the living room and in Daphne's comfortable chair.

"Miss Elliot, I need a phone jack!" he called out.

"This is ridiculous," Daphne muttered to herself. "Why do you need a phone jack?"

"I have to plug in the modem on my laptop so I can access the Internet. I still have old-fashioned dial-up on this thing."

"I have no idea what you're talking about, but the phone jack is under the table. You'll have to unplug my phone. I don't like being without my phone, though."

"Are you expecting a call from someone?"

Daphne folded her arms. "No, but what if there's an emergency? I'll need to be able to dial 911."

Rodney took out a cell phone from his pocket. "Here. If you need to call 911, you can do it from my cell."

Daphne knew he was mocking her concern but took the phone anyway. She returned to the kitchen, a bit miffed over the encounter, even as Melanie stood by waiting to help.

"It will be another twenty minutes until the casserole is ready," Daphne said.

"May I see your gardens then? When we drove up here, I kept telling Rod how much I wanted to see them."

"You might as well. This will be your home one day."

Melanie looked at her, startled. "What do you mean by that?"

"I mean that when Rodney takes over the business, the house comes with it. You might as well see what I have growing in the garden so you'll know how to care for it. Unless you want to redo it all, which I'd understand. You don't have to keep the varieties I planted."

"But, Miss Elliot," Melanie countered, following her outside, "where will you live if you move out of here?"

"I'm sure a nursing home will take me in." She smiled slightly. "Just kidding."

"That's ridiculous. You will stay here as long as you need to. Rod and I can always look for another place."

"You need to be close to the nursery." Daphne strolled beside the gardens she had spent years planting and tending with a careful hand. Many of the perennials, such as bleeding hearts and painted daisies, were already in full bloom. Daphne explained the different varieties and which plants preferred sunlight or shade. Melanie then admired her selection of roses. Daphne had about a dozen of them, and they kept her occupied during the summer months when she wasn't at the nursery. Already the bushes had tiny buds ready for a showy display.

"These are going to be lovely," Melanie observed. "I suppose you have all different colors?"

"Red, pink, yellow, and blue."

"A blue rose! Oh, I'll have to get myself a blue rose someday. That sounds beautiful."

"The blue is very attractive. You must come over when they are in bloom."

Just then Rodney opened the window to the house and shouted through the screen. "It's ready, Miss Elliot!"

"I guess the timer went off for the casserole." Daphne scurried by Melanie and then Chubs who was asleep on the porch. She was walking past Rodney when something on the computer screen caught her eye. "What are you doing? Snooping as usual?"

"Miss Elliot, you have to come and see," he said as she went on into the kitchen and took out the casserole. "It's about Jack McNary."

Daphne nearly dropped the heavy casserole dish. She should have known Rodney would be up to something. If there was only some way to tell him to leave things alone. She would have to come up with some good scriptures about allowing the Lord to work and not make something happen out of nothing. But she also realized that love and concern were at play here. Rodney had obviously gone to great lengths to try to be helpful, even if she did consider him a bit nosy. The least she could do was play along while the casserole cooled a bit. And she was curious.

"All right, what is it?"

He pointed to a chair. "Sit down and take a look. I decided to do a little checking on Jack McNary. After that Larson character tried to dupe you once, I thought it would be helpful to know where he's from and everything. And guess what? I found out some interesting things."

Daphne sat with her arms folded.

"For one thing, the man has no past."

"You mean you can't find any record of his past?"

"No, I mean the man has no past. Before I came here, I called around to various record offices. There is no record of the man. In fact, the house he lives in isn't even his."

At this, Daphne straightened in her seat. "What do you mean?"

"It belongs to someone named Stuart Martin."

"They're probably cousins. Or friends. Or maybe he's renting the place."

"Maybe. It would be good to know if Jack and Stuart knew each other. If they do, I think you may have the answers to some of your questions about Henry."

Daphne felt her heart flutter. Warmth crept into her cheeks. "I—I don't understand."

"Rod, can't this wait?" Melanie asked. "You're upsetting her. I told you this should wait."

"No, no," Daphne said, rising to her feet. "What do you mean that Jack might know something about Henry? How could he possibly know?"

Rodney turned back to his computer, his finger sliding across a small black box at the bottom of the keyboard. Daphne watched incredulously as screen after screen lit up. At last he came to Stuart Martin and his personal data. Most of the rectangular boxes she saw remained empty but for a few facts. Stuart had been married to a Melissa Haverston of Tennessee. Rodney then highlighted the man's past work. Employment at the Harrison Lumber Mill near Cleveland, Tennessee. "I did some research on this Stuart. He does have a past, what little I could find. He was once married, and he worked at this lumber mill."

Daphne couldn't believe what she saw. There it was on the screen—the name of the lumber mill where Henry had worked and the same place where he'd died forty years ago.

"I even took the liberty of checking to make sure this was the same Stuart who worked at the mill. I called the Haverston family. They weren't too eager to give out any information, but it seems Stuart once stayed at the boardinghouse run by Mrs. Evelyn Haverston. While he was there, he married the daughter, Melissa. The house where Jack lives was passed on to Stuart by the Haverston family when his mother-in-law died."

"Then why does Jack live in Stuart's house?"

"I don't know. My guess is that they were good friends. Perhaps they worked together at the mill when they were young. Jack may be renting the place from him. If that's so, Miss Elliot, then you need to talk to him and find out what he knows about Stuart and the lumber mill. Maybe he heard something about the accident back in the sixties. I realize it was a long time ago, but this could be an open door to all those questions you've had."

All this came crashing down on her in one terrific storm. Daphne fell onto the couch, too overcome to know what to say or think. Who would have thought the man who frequented her nursery and tended the wounds on her hand with such caring fashion might have a connection to the past?

"Are you all right, Miss Elliot?" Melanie sat beside her on the sofa. "Should

I get you something to drink?"

"I—I don't know." She glanced over at Rodney. "Maybe you can talk to Jack for me and find out who this Stuart is."

"I already did. He didn't say much, only that the house is his, fair and square. He seemed a bit miffed that I was prying into his personal affairs. He didn't say it, but I could tell he didn't want me doing any more searching."

"I don't blame him," Melanie said. "This is too much, Rod. You get so involved with everyone else's lives that it really does amount to prying. You need to leave things alone before someone gets hurt. In fact, you may have already overstepped the boundaries."

Rodney gazed at the screen on his laptop. He stared into space for a moment before switching off the computer. "Melanie's right," he said, closing the laptop with resolve and restoring Daphne's phone. "I had no business snooping around. I should've never brought this up. I was only trying to help, but as usual, it comes right back in my face."

The three of them remained still and quiet in the living room, with only the ticking of a clock to serenade the moment. Daphne had not moved since she heard the news that Jack might know something about Henry and the lumber mill. While the past always haunted her, now it seemed to be pointing a finger directly at her. It dared her to make a move and discover the answers to the questions that had bothered her for so long.

Finally she remembered the casserole and went to the kitchen to serve it up. But the joy of the meeting had evaporated, replaced by uncertainty and confusion. During lunch, no one spoke. A rift seemed to have appeared between them all, but Daphne took little notice of it. All she could think about was the lumber mill and the possibility that Jack might have worked there. What she wouldn't give for just a glimpse of the past, if she had the strength to face it.

When Rodney and Melanie were ready to leave that afternoon, he again apologized. "Some entertainment," he said glumly. "I only wanted to do this for you, Miss Elliot, because you've done so much for me." He stuffed his hands into his pockets. "You helped us both and then are giving us the business and all. Believe me, I wasn't trying to hurt anyone."

Daphne patted his arm. "I know. It was sweet of you. You gave me a few things to think about, and it's good to get this brain of mine thinking before it turns to oatmeal."

"Are you sure? I thought I had blown everything."

"No. I must say you did drop a bomb. But I can tell you care. Both of you." She managed a smile, which was cautiously returned. "I'll see you tomorrow." She closed the door carefully behind them, turned to the living room, and suddenly broke down in tears.

Oh, God, after all these years You still remember the pain, don't You? Nothing is hidden from You, is it? You understand and You remember, even when my own memory fades. I try to keep it all alive with the stories I have of Henry, but I know they are disintegrating with time. Perhaps You truly want me to let go of the past, and Jack McNary is the one who can help me do it.

Chapter 9

Daphne didn't sleep a wink that night after learning the news concerning Jack McNary. It was all she could do to keep herself from picking up the phone and asking him outright about Stuart and the lumber mill. For several days, she tried to concentrate on her work at the nursery but kept looking for the familiar truck to roll into the parking lot, bearing the grizzly farmer dressed in dirty overalls. Surely he must have some gardening questions with this being the height of the planting season. Daphne sighed. Although she had apologized for the scene with the rose, she couldn't help but think her attitude might be keeping him away. If so, she could bury any hope of ever knowing what had happened to Henry. She thought back to the conversation with Jack and the final words he offered on the phone. *Anytime you need me, I'll be there.* Little did he know, but she needed him desperately. She needed to put the past to rest, cover it over with dirt, and place a tombstone on top. She needed the finality perhaps only he could offer.

At that moment, a loud rumbling sound sent her scurrying to the shop window. There came the old truck, the engine noise louder than usual, bearing Jack in his customary straw hat. Even in the warm weather, he still wore overalls and a long-sleeved plaid shirt. Daphne inhaled a quick breath. She felt like a schoolgirl waiting for her beau to arrive. She could have been a young lady of long ago, waiting for Henry to visit her from Tennessee. The comparison nearly made her faint.

Jack greeted Rodney who stared at him for a curious moment before casting a glance at Daphne. Jack then went inside the greenhouse and began looking at the assortment of vegetable seedlings. His thick fingers, stained with dirt, picked up a small, fragile tomato plant. With hands like that, he could easily break the stem in two. But his burly features did not match the heart that lay within. He had only been gentle and kind.

Inhaling a deep breath, Daphne came over and offered a quick hello. He whirled toward her and dropped the plant. Just as she had imagined, the plant snapped in two.

"Another plant destroyed!" He groaned, picking up the pieces and looking at the stem as if considering the possibility of gluing it back together.

"We must be related."

He flashed a look in her direction. He opened his mouth as if to say something, then shook his head. "I'll pay for it."

"No, it was my fault." Daphne took the plant and promptly tossed it in the trash. By this time, Rodney had come to the doorway of the greenhouse, still staring. Daphne wished she could close the door on him. Instead, she turned away and asked Jack how things were going.

"Pretty good. The climbing rose is doing better. The stump I had left in the ground put out new branches. It's looking as good as new. And those plants I bought a few weeks ago are still in the land of the living. So I thought I would try my hand at raising some fresh tomatoes."

"Be sure you have a bed ready for them. Tomatoes like lime and not too much fertilizer."

"I don't know of any plants that don't like fertilizer."

"If you fertilize them too much, they grow only leaves and no fruit. We want fruit, not bushy tomato plants."

Jack leaned against one of the long tables. "You're full of information."

"It's from years of working in the nursery since I was a little girl." Daphne pushed a tendril of gray hair behind one ear, feeling more and more like a shy schoolgirl. Yet in the back of her mind were the lumber mill, Henry, and this man who might hold the key to it all. If only she could ask him about it, but this was hardly the place. She couldn't invite him to dinner. A man alone in her house would be unthinkable. Maybe she could invite him for coffee at a nearby café? Would that be too presumptuous?

"I would like to know more about raising vegetables," he said, "but you must be pretty busy."

"Yes, it would be better to talk at another time."

"Well. . . ," he began, his grayish eyebrows furrowing as if contemplating it all. "I could come back after closing time."

"We close at eight o'clock now."

"Hmm. That means you must eat all your meals here."

"No, actually Rodney mans the place in the evening. I leave at five o'clock."

"Is that a fact? Well, then, maybe we can grab a bite to eat after work. What about that interesting restaurant in Charlottesville—the Hardware Store Restaurant? They've got those good specials on weekdays."

"All right. That would be fine."

Jack McNary gaped at her as if stunned that she had so readily acquiesced. Warmth invaded her face. Perhaps she shouldn't have appeared so eager, but the knowledge he had was too important to her right now. Surely he would understand it all once the purpose of the meeting came to light.

She hurried away to find him a box in which he could put some tomatoes and other seedlings. Inside the store, Rodney was sorting out insecticides when she came to the cash register.

"So are you two going to meet?" he inquired, gazing out from around the aisle.

"Yes," she answered. "And it will be your fault if things go bad."

"I'll take full responsibility. I already said I was sorry about the intrusion. In fact, you don't need to pursue this if you don't want to."

"Oh, you're a fine one to be telling me this now, after that so-called entertainment at my house! What am I supposed to do? Just forget everything you said?"

Jack suddenly appeared inside the store, carrying the box of plants.

Daphne ceased conversing with Rodney and began adding up the plant purchases, hoping Jack would not notice her trembling fingers. "Twelve dollars and eighty cents."

Jack shook his head. "That can't be right. I bought fourteen plants. Let me count them." He did so and nodded. "Yep, fourteen, and the sign back there said a dollar twenty-nine a pack."

"Well, don't worry about it. It was my mistake." Daphne held out her hand for the money.

He laid two tens in her hand. "Keep the change."

Daphne stared in astonishment. When he winked at her, her fretfulness disappeared, replaced by a strange sensation. Many men had winked in the past, but his gesture was different—as if he appreciated what he saw. Her gaze followed him as he went to his truck and placed the box carefully in the front seat. He then stood and stared back at the nursery, almost as if he were studying her, as she was him. He then climbed into the truck and sped off.

"So what do you think?" Rodney whispered in her ear. "Nice guy, eh? Perfect, as a matter of fact."

"I'm not thinking about that right now. I only want to find out what he knows about the lumber mill. In fact, we're going out to dinner." She clamped a hand over her mouth. "Oh no! We didn't agree on the day! I don't know if it's this evening or not. What am I going to do?"

"Wait a bit till he gets home, then call."

"I–I'm certain he meant tonight." But she wasn't sure about anything anymore. Her hand went to her heart as it began to flutter like a butterfly in her chest. *Oh, Lord, I have to resolve all this. My heart can't take much more. Help me.*

෴

The phone rang at the nursery later that afternoon. Daphne was grateful it was Jack, asking her what time he should pick her up for their dinner that night. She told him five-thirty, as she would need to change and take care of Chubs. He seemed enthusiastic about the meeting, saying he was looking forward to learning more about vegetable gardening. Little did he know, but she was looking forward to learning more about Stuart and the lumber mill.

As she dressed, she thought about how she might broach the subject. It would seem a bit out of the ordinary to mention the past suddenly. She had learned from Rodney how irate Jack could be if she went fishing for information. There must be a way to handle this tactfully. Daphne looked at her image in the mirror. How the years had crept up on her, along with the developing wrinkles around her eyes. She had tried some of those wrinkle-reducing agents but found nothing that worked. For a time, she dyed her hair also, but the chemicals became too irritating and the bill at the beauty parlor too expensive. Her hair was gray with strands of pure white scattered throughout. Was she even attractive to a man anymore?

Daphne picked up a bottle of foundation and applied a light coat. She remembered how her mother always made herself pretty for her father, even if she was working side by side with him in the nursery. She wore a thick, pasty type of makeup and bright red lipstick. And her father seemed to enjoy having Mother look her finest, even when working in the dirt. Daphne didn't relish the idea of looking made up for a man, especially to impress Jack. But if it lent some confidence to the night and helped her discover the past, then she would be the most made-up woman on the planet.

The doorbell rang. Daphne's heart skipped a beat. She checked her appearance once more in the mirror. At the last moment, she took out the pearl necklace and fastened it around her neck. Nodding her head, she scooped up her purse and headed for the door. The first scent she caught was not the scent of roses or honeysuckle, but the aroma of a powerful aftershave. She hadn't smelled aftershave like that in years. Before her stood a different man from the one she'd observed roaming about the nursery. Gone were the overalls and straw hat. Instead, Jack wore a pair of tan slacks, a red polo shirt, and shoes that shone in the final rays of the fading sun.

"I have to lock the door," Daphne said in a trembling voice, turning to fumble with the key.

He offered her his arm to guide her to the car, but she held fast to her purse strap and ambled along on her own. To her surprise, an old Lincoln Continental replaced the dirt brown truck in the driveway.

"Are you really Jack McNary?"

He cast her a quick glance. "Why would you say that?"

"I just want to make sure you don't have a twin brother. I was expecting to have my first ride in a truck."

He chuckled and opened the door for her. "No. I rarely take this car out. Only on special occasions."

For a moment, she wondered if Stuart might have left the car behind for him to drive. She peeked around the vehicle for anything that might have Stuart's name on it, even as Jack gave her a strange look. When he asked her to get his sunglasses from the glove compartment as the last glimmer of sunlight pierced through the windshield, Daphne opened it and began shuffling items around. She hoped for a car registration or something with Stuart's name.

"Can't find them?"

She sheepishly handed him the glasses case. "I like to see what people store in their glove compartments. Why they call it that is beyond me. There's barely enough space to put a pair of gloves inside." She quickly closed the small door and sat back in her seat, staring out the window. She tried to think of the questions she wanted to ask tonight, but already it seemed as if Jack had grown suspicious of her activity. For a long time she stayed silent as they drove to town. Finally she decided to forge ahead. "So have you lived in this area long?"

"About five years."

"Where did you come from before that?"

He drove into the parking garage. "I hope they can find us a nice, quiet place. Do you prefer a booth or a table?"

"A table," she said as they entered the restaurant. "The seats in a booth are always too far away from the table. At a regular table, you can at least pull your chair up close enough without having food spill on your lap."

Jack asked the waitress for a quiet table. They were led to a table for two in the rear of the restaurant. Daphne began feeling more uncomfortable when she saw the lit candle and even a rose in a crystal vase.

"I wanted to say you look very nice tonight. The pearls are beautiful."

"Oh yes," she said, fingering the strand. "A friend gave them to me."

"Oh, really?" He hid his face behind the menu the waitress had given him.

Daphne smiled at the waitress and asked her for a glass of water. She opened the menu book, but the words seemed to float about on the plastic-coated paper. She prayed she wasn't having some kind of spell. Likely it was the atmosphere and the eyes of a man staring at her from across the table. "Yes. He died a long time ago."

He put the menu on the table. "I lost my wife about five years ago, as I told you. I moved here to start over. But she loved eating out. I think she would have liked a place like this. Homey. Low prices. And not a buffet."

Daphne couldn't help but laugh. "Most of the food places in town are now buffets. I once counted over twenty Chinese restaurants in the phone book one day, of which more than half were a buffet. It's a waste for people like us. One plate and I'm full."

The waitress arrived to take their orders. Jack gave hers first, then his. "So you don't like Chinese?" he continued.

"I don't like the MSG. Bad for the heart. But what I really don't like are the fixed prices for buffets when I can barely eat a plateful. Rodney took me to a buffet once. I told him it was a waste of money. He only smiled. Have you seen the way he smiles? Just like a cat who swallowed the canary. Sometimes he bothers me to no end."

Jack laughed as if he took great delight in her grumbling. How she wished she could sound happier. Even as she spoke, she could hear her words—complaining, critical, bordering on bitterness. Is this the way she had been all her life? No wonder she was a spinster.

Daphne grew silent while the waitress placed the food on the table. Jack bowed his head and offered the blessing for the meal. After he finished, he delved into his salad. "I must say, I don't have a problem with food. I like most places. Steak houses, barbecue pits, even pizza."

"I get heartburn just thinking about it," Daphne added before realizing she was doing it again. "That is, I used to like pizza very much until it kept bothering me. The doctor finally gave me a prescription for it. I take a pill every night." She stole a glance at his face, and the scar that seemed more pronounced with the overhead light shining on it. She wondered how he received such a disfigurement. It wasn't from some kind of machine. It looked more like a patch, as if the skin's surface had been stripped away at one time and then replaced.

"Is something wrong?"

"Oh no, I was—I was just thinking about where you might have lived before you came here. You said you moved here five years ago."

"A neighboring state. Tennessee."

Daphne nearly choked on the lettuce in her salad. She quickly took a sip of water. "Then it makes sense."

"What makes sense?"

"What Rodney told me."

At this, Jack slid back in his seat and crossed his arms. "Now look, Daphne. I'm not sure what's come over that young man of yours. If you ask me, he's got a nose too big for his own good. He called me the other day, asking me all kinds of questions, like he was trying to investigate me or something. Do you know why he's doing this?"

"He's curious, I guess," Daphne said, playing with the lettuce leaves and tomato wedges on her salad plate. Finally she decided to come out with it. "Actually we were both wondering if you knew a Stuart Martin while you were in Tennessee?"

Jack had been sipping water. He jostled the glass, sending water running down the front of his polo shirt. He grabbed a napkin and wiped his shirt.

"You're treading in private waters."

"Rodney discovered you don't own the house you live in and that it belongs to someone named Stuart Martin."

He said nothing as he continued to wipe away the water, then asked the waitress for another glass and more napkins.

"So he called Stuart's wife's family."

Jack jerked his head upright. His face turned the shade of ripe strawberries. "What? What did they say?"

"Not much. Only that Stuart used to work at a lumber mill." Daphne could not hold herself back. "I need to know if this Stuart worked at the same mill back in the sixties. It's very important. Someone I knew died in a fire there and—"

"Daphne, we came here to have a nice dinner and talk about vegetables, not about lumber mills, Tennessee, Stuart, Evelyn—"

Something within Daphne snapped to life. She had not mentioned Evelyn's name. Jack did know something. She opened her mouth, ready to inquire, when she saw an angry look form on his face. Things were beginning to deteriorate. If she wasn't careful, she might lose everything she'd hoped to gain. For now she forced down her questions about the past and offered a brief apology. Yet Jack seemed to disappear inside himself. He said little during the main course. Daphne tried to talk about planting vegetables as he wanted, but the conversation felt forced. They finished their dinners, having talked about little else.

Jack drove Daphne home in silence, except for a few brief comments about the lack of rain. When he dropped her off at the door, Daphne felt worse than ever. She could barely unlock her door before collapsing onto the sofa. Chubs was at her side, yipping to be let out. Daphne didn't have the energy. She could only think about the night. She knew she had made a mistake by being so headstrong in her quest for knowledge. Instead of drawing out the answers, the questions had driven back whatever lay within Jack McNary. Now everything was lost.

Chapter 10

Daphne arrived for work the next day, worn-out after last night's escapade. She nearly called Rodney to ask him to keep tabs on the place while she spent the day in bed. She decided against it, realizing she would only lie there recounting the conversation between her and Jack. As it was, she didn't sleep a wink from thinking about it. She sat out in the living room, looking at old photographs while Chubs slept peacefully at her feet. One picture depicted Henry at the mill, standing beside several coworkers. She scanned the other men carefully with a large magnifying glass, wondering if any of them might be Stuart or even Jack. Oh, what she wouldn't give to know the truth. At times she wondered why she couldn't let this rest and go on with life. But God must have resurrected the past for some reason.

Daphne dragged herself into the nursery that morning, sipping on a cup of coffee which she knew was a no-no. But if she didn't drink it, she might fall asleep. Rodney was his usual perky self as he strode into the store, smiling from ear to ear.

"So how did it go?" he asked. "I'll have to admit, I was up practically the whole night wondering what happened. You don't know how much I had to restrain myself not to pick up the phone and call you for all the sugary details."

"We ate dinner, and he brought me home," she said, putting bills and change into the cash register.

Rodney groaned with a sound that startled her. In an instant, her heart began to flutter. She found herself gasping for breath and immediately sat on a stool. "Really, young man, must you do that?"

"I'm sorry, but you're giving me a heart attack. Please tell me what happened."

"You think you're having the heart attack? With the kind of stress I've been under lately, it's a wonder I'm not in the cardiac ward of the hospital." She opened her purse and took out a vial of nitroglycerin.

"Please—what happened?"

Daphne put a pill under her tongue, hoping it would relieve that terrible sensation in her chest as though butterflies were fighting to fly against a harsh wind. "I already told you. We went to the Hardware Store Restaurant. We had dinner. Then he took me home."

"Did you talk about Stuart?"

"I mentioned it, but he wasn't interested in talking about it. So I let it go." Out of the corner of her eye, she could see the expression of dismay on Rodney's face, as if she had allowed a huge opportunity to pass her by. "But he did mention Evelyn," she added hastily. "That is, he mentioned her name, and I hadn't even said anything about her."

"Really! Very interesting. Evelyn ran the boardinghouse where Stuart stayed, you know. Eventually Stuart married Evelyn's daughter."

"Oh, and I found out Jack is from Tennessee."

Daphne thought Rodney was going to leap over the counter with the way he began jumping. "Aha! I knew it. That proves it then."

"Proves what?" Daphne placed her hand on her chest, feeling her heart race beneath her fingertips. At least there was no pain, but the continual fluttering made her nervous.

"My original train of thought—that Jack knows Stuart and Stuart worked at the lumber mill in Tennessee. Now all we need is for Jack to tell us about their friendship and if Stuart worked at the mill during the time of Henry's death."

"He won't do it," Daphne stated. "It bothers him for some reason. In fact, he wasn't very happy when he dropped me off last night. I think he's tired of people poking their noses into his personal affairs. And I must say, I can understand it. If someone were prying into my business, I would be upset, too. I might even notify the authorities."

"Don't you want to know what happened?"

Daphne wondered right now if she did. The idea had seemed intriguing at first. But perhaps it wasn't the best thing to have all the knowledge in the world. After all, God forbade Adam and Eve to eat of the tree of the knowledge of good and evil. Sometimes He didn't want His children knowing everything about a situation. Maybe He felt it wiser to keep it from her. If the truth about Henry's death were known, it might create such an emotional strain that she could have a heart attack. For whatever reason, the knowledge of the past had been kept secret. "It's best to let it go," she said with a weary smile as several customers began trickling in to start off another busy day at the nursery. "There's a reason for it. So let's do what we do best."

Rodney said no more, though at times Daphne caught him looking at her in a strange way as if disappointed by her decision. She felt it the wisest thing to do under the circumstances. Life's challenges were hard enough without her trying to take on more than she could handle. And this was definitely a burden she couldn't begin to carry on her own.

The day went fairly smoothly with a steady flow of customers, but Daphne felt that she might need to close up shop early. Her heart continued to act up. She suffered a strange numbness in her left fingers and occasional twinges of pain. If there weren't a letup in these symptoms, she would call the doctor. Dr. Franklin was very particular about her condition. She liked him very much, especially the way his mustache twitched when he said "Miss Elliot." He was also very thorough with his examinations. No doubt he would see her after hours if her heart did not settle down and behave itself.

Melanie arrived before closing time, dressed up for her date with her husband. Since the argument that had brewed a few weeks before, Rodney made it a point to take Melanie out on special dates, even if it was for a walk. Daphne observed the couple from afar when Rodney came toward Melanie with his arms outstretched. He scooped her up, hugging her close, his lips searching hungrily for hers. Daphne shook her head. Tears invaded her eyes. There was nothing sweeter than young love, like the birds that fluttered around the old owl's head in *Bambi*. Daphne often commented that she couldn't take Rodney's love songs, but deep down inside, a part of her yearned for a similar kind of affection. The only man who had held her since Henry was Jack, after the rose thorns pierced her hand. His was a gentle but strong touch, much like the memory she once had long ago.

Rodney and Melanie drew apart and smiled sheepishly. "I was telling Melanie about the dinner you had with Jack," he said, bringing Melanie's hand to his lips for a kiss.

She giggled and stole her hand away. "I'm glad you both got together, Miss Elliot."

Daphne smiled. "It was nice, I suppose. So where are you off to tonight?"

"Pizza and maybe a movie. You want to come along?"

Daphne laughed. "Three is definitely a crowd. This is your special night. Have fun."

"We will." Rodney gave a wink before slipping his arm around Melanie and serenading her out the door to the tune of "Love Me Tender."

Daphne had to chuckle before a yawn nearly split her head in two. At least her heart calmed down enough for her to finish her work. She only needed to complete the bookkeeping for the day; then she would go home, take a nice hot bath, and go straight to bed. The figuring was slow to come when Daphne realized how exhausted her mind had become. Finally she gave up on it, promising to finish it when her head was clearer. Night shadows had already begun to fall across the landscape when she fished for her keys.

All at once, she heard the thump of footsteps on the porch of the shop. A familiar voice called her name. Her heart began its frantic fluttering once again.

"Daphne? Daphne, are you in there?"

She drew forward to find Jack standing there with a Thermos in his hand. What on earth was he doing here? After last night, she had not expected to lay eyes on him for a long time. But there he was, dressed like the evening before in a polo shirt and slacks. She hoped he wasn't here for another outing. She was too tired to think straight. "Do you need something? I'm closing up shop."

"I know it's getting kind of late." He stepped through the door and looked around at the dark interiors but for a small lightbulb dangling over the cashier counter. "I was hoping we could talk."

"I didn't think you were in the mood to talk," Daphne said in more of a huffy tone than she would have liked.

"I'm sorry for the way I acted at the restaurant. I guess your questions hit a nerve."

Daphne returned to the books, suddenly energized enough to rework the figures. All it took was Jack McNary to spur her to life. Usually it was something on the side of irritation, but now it was curiosity. Her hand patted the flutter in her chest that began again in earnest.

"I know things haven't been right since I first came to your store." He pulled up a stool. "So I took it all to the Lord last night and asked Him what to do."

Daphne listened with interest.

"He said I needed to come clean, to stop with the charades, and to tell it like it is."

Daphne continued to bend over the book, wondering what he was talking about.

"So you really don't want to hear what I have to say?"

Daphne put down her pencil. "Jack, I did want to learn more about you; yet when I tried to ask, it was as if I had committed a crime."

"So what do you want to know?" He sat back, crossed his arms, and waited.

For once, Daphne was speechless. She had spent the last few days planning out all the questions she wanted to ask him. After the fiasco of last night, she had pretty much dismissed them all, until now when the door had suddenly been thrust open.

"You wanted to know if I knew a Stuart Martin in Tennessee," he began.

Daphne felt herself growing nervous. "Yes."

"All right, then. Stuart is me."

Daphne blinked in astonishment. "What? You mean you're Stuart?"

"Yes, and the house where I live, the one your employee, Rodney, was trying to figure out about, does in fact belong to me. I decided to make some changes in my life when I moved here."

"I guess so, if you were once Stuart and now you're Jack. I don't know what to say."

"The reason I changed my name is because of what happened to me at the Harrison Lumber Mill."

At this, Daphne stood up. "You did work at the lumber mill! The same mill!"

"Sit down and let me explain." He brought out two cups and poured some tea from the bottle. "I knew you liked to drink tea, so I made up some fresh."

Daphne smiled shyly before picking up the cup, only to find her hand trembling. There was something in Jack's eyes she wasn't sure about. He stood on the verge of confessing everything he knew; yet she wondered if she had the strength to face it. He was there, at the Harrison Lumber Mill, the same place where Henry died. She wanted to know everything, even if it meant going through the fiery past herself, with smoke that burned her eyes and heat that singed her flesh.

"I did work at the mill on the day of the fire. At first it seemed like an ordinary day, but somehow I knew it wouldn't be. Maybe it was the Lord getting me ready. The fire broke out in the area where we were cutting up the logs. It was suspicious from the start. My face was burned pretty badly. I went for help and came across a boardinghouse owned by Evelyn Haverston, a few miles down the road. She took me in, got me a doctor and everything. It took quite a bit of doctoring to manage the burns. I didn't think I made out too bad, considering."

Daphne stared at the scar prominently displayed on his face before resting her gaze on his eyes. There was something in those eyes that seemed to plead with her. She shook her head. She was so intent on finding out what was going on that she was letting her emotions get the better of her.

"After awhile, I got to know Evelyn's daughter, Melissa, and eventually came to love her. We were married and lived in the area for quite a few years. Occasionally the family would come back here to Virginia, since they owned a summer home. Five years ago, I lost Melissa to cancer. It was very hard. Not long after that, Melissa's mother, Evelyn, died, too."

"I'm sorry," Daphne managed to say. "I know what it's like to lose a loved one."

Jack glanced down at his lap, examining the cup he held in his hands. He tried to speak but found himself choking. He took a sip of tea. "Anyway, Evelyn left me the summer home in Virginia in her will. And that's where I've been living."

"It is hard to lose the people you love. They all say you get over it, but you never do. So did you know Henry Morgan at the mill where you worked? Can you tell me what happened?"

"I—well—," he began, suddenly flustered. "I had my own problems that day, believe me."

Daphne leaned forward. "Did they tell you how the fire started? Did you hear if anyone had died?"

"I left after it all happened and never looked back. I haven't put my foot on the place since. I'm sorry."

She tried hard to contain the tears that welled up within her. The most promising lead into what happened to Henry had suddenly vanished. How she wanted to break down and grieve for him once more, especially after this disappointment. She sniffed and fumbled for a crumpled tissue inside her purse. "I can't blame you for not knowing what happened to Henry, but I had such high hopes you did." She looked up to see the scar on his face turning a bright shade of pink. "It must have been awful to be in a fire like that and suffer such a terrible burn."

"The disfigurement was the worst part. In one minute, I had lost all of my characteristics. I thought I would never be good enough for another living soul. What woman would want to be with a man like that?"

"Oh, it's not that bad. If we all dwelled on the tiny flaws in each other, we would never see the good on the inside." She shook her head. "And that's all I've done my whole life, finding flaws and not looking at a person's heart. Maybe it's better that I am an old spinster. I don't think Henry knew what he was getting."

"I'm quite sure he knew."

Daphne choked out a chuckle. She took out her wallet and from it a crumpled photo of Henry at the mill. "Here he is, doing the work he loved best. I will never forget the last day we had together. I wish now I had said certain things to him. You can think of a million things to share after a loved one has passed away. But what good is it?"

Jack put down his cup. "Daphne—"

"It's all right. I shouldn't be burdening you with this anyway. That's all I've been doing, burdening you and everyone else with my problems. I want Henry here—sometimes I even believe he's here, but of course he's not. I'm sure you understand, having lost your wife."

"Daphne—," he began again.

"It's like this ache that never goes away. Maybe that's why I have a heart condition. It's an ache I can't seem to get rid of. I was hoping you had the answer. I was praying that—" She stopped. Her throat tightened. She put her hand over her mouth to silence it. "Excuse me. This isn't right. It's wrong to place this all on you."

"Daphne, it's all right. It's more right than you can think. I—" He paused. Slowly he took out his own wallet.

She dried her eyes on the tissue. "Oh yes, do you have a picture of Melissa? We can share in the memories, can't we, if nothing else in life."

He took out a crumpled card from the wallet and handed it to her.

Daphne took it and blinked once, then twice. "I don't understand. This is Henry's driver's license. How did you get it?"

"Daphne. . .my name isn't Stuart or Jack. It's none of those. I–I'm Henry Morgan."

Daphne dropped the card.

"Daphne, please, let me explain what happened—"

"No, no, no." A terrible pain gripped her. She came to her feet, wavering. "You left me—you're dead. I know you're dead! You've been dead forty years! How can this be happening?" A sudden weakness overcame her, the weakness of a burden she had carried for too long. Her knees began to buckle.

Jack tried to reach her, even as she fell to the floor. "Daphne!" he cried, kneeling beside her, cradling her. "Daphne!" He shook her gently.

"No, no, no." She moaned until Jack's face disappeared in a cloud of white.

Chapter 11

Dear God, help me! The words repeated over and over in singsong fashion, but in another time and place. Daphne moaned and shifted about, struggling with both the reality of Henry's existence and the terrible game that had been played on her emotions. She could see Henry as if it were only yesterday—young, handsome Henry, his bearded face all smiles as he took her hand in his. How strong and warm his hand felt, though calloused by the heavy labor at the mill. Yet she wasn't afraid to have that hand hold hers and his lips press ever so gently on her own.

Daphne moaned again. Suddenly she remembered the news of the dreadful fire, the men who were injured and, yes, the death of her beloved Henry. She flicked open her eyes to see a pure white ceiling above her. Maybe she had died, too, and was now in the presence of the Lord. She struggled to sit up, only to find herself hampered by plastic tubing coming out of her arm. Strange metallic wires ran beneath her simple gown and were hooked to a monitor by her bedside. Heaven could not be like this. It seemed more like a horror movie instead.

A woman wearing a flowered-print smock and blue starched pants stepped beside her, holding a strange contraption. A probe was forced into her ear. Daphne nearly screamed at the obtrusive thing but let the machine do its work. The woman then attached some kind of monitoring device on her forefinger.

"I'm just taking your blood pressure and temperature, Miss Elliot," the woman reassured her.

No, she was definitely not in heaven, unless the Lord had a ward of nurses at His beck and call. The Bible said she would have a new body one day and not this worn-out model that had endured so much heartache and pain. Suddenly she shook at the scene that came to mind—of Jack taking out that old crumpled card, yellow with age, to display the name still inscribed on it: HENRY T. MORGAN.

"You need to relax," the nurse told her. "Your blood pressure is rising."

Daphne wanted to say that hers would skyrocket, too, if she had just been informed that her sweetheart from forty years ago had suddenly been resurrected from the dead. But she felt too tired and dazed to say anything. Even a whisper would take every ounce of energy within her, though her mind was a bundle of questions. Maybe she had dreamed up the whole scene with Jack. Maybe inwardly she had hoped he would be Henry. She didn't want to admit it, but she had feelings for the man. He was irritating yet comforting. He was craggy yet kind. Then she thought about it. The eyes. The voice. They had been teasing her the weeks she knew him, but of course it never dawned on her that he was actually Henry. Henry had a beard, black hair, a trim figure. Henry was dead. Now he had come back to life.

"Oh, God, help me," she managed to sputter. Her fingers groped for the leads on her chest that monitored the beating of her frazzled heart. How much more of this could she take? The Lord would help, but at this moment, she felt herself teetering on the brink of despair or maybe even death. If something didn't happen soon, she would be lost. She knew it.

At that moment, a parade of doctors assembled in her room. The scene caused her to shake once again.

"Miss Elliot, I'm Dr. French," said the lead doctor. "Your case was referred to me by your physician, Dr. Franklin. I have a few medical students with me today on rounds. I hope you don't mind them observing while I discuss your diagnosis and treatment."

Daphne did not have the energy to speak. She simply nodded her head. What did it matter anyway if these young people studied her like a mouse in a cage? She was in a cage after all, a cage of emotion with no way out. Her hand went to her heart as it began to flutter. The students pointed at the monitor and murmured to themselves. At least she was giving them a good show.

"Miss Elliot, your heart is undergoing severe strain at the moment," explained Dr. French. "You've been throwing what we call PVCs. That means your heart is not beating correctly. We have an electrical system within the heart that helps each chamber beat at the correct time. Sometimes when part of the system fails, the heartbeat becomes irregular and the heart can't perform its job. What we want to do is take you for a heart catheterization to see if anything might be causing the irregular heartbeat. If we find that the electrical system within the heart is malfunctioning, we can put in what's called a pacemaker."

"I've heard of that," Daphne croaked.

"Good. Then you know it's a simple procedure with excellent results. The nurse will provide you with instructions concerning the catheterization procedure. Of course, as with any procedure, there are risks involved." He took out his clipboard. "The condition could worsen; there might be extraneous infection, bleeding, heart and/or vessel damage, or death, though of course that's unlikely. Do you wish us to proceed?"

Daphne could only nod. Slowly she placed her signature on the document, allowing the procedure. The doctor nodded and paraded away with his flock of students, discussing the necessity of the procedure and what was involved. Daphne turned to the window to see a few clouds drifting by in the blue sky. She blinked back the tears that filled her eyes. Why was all this happening to her? Obviously God had a plan. Maybe He was trying to soften her hard heart by making it malfunction. Or maybe He had a better plan for her, and for now she must endure this. If only she didn't feel so alone.

A tear slipped down her cheek. If she died on the table during the procedure, who would care, really? Rodney and Melanie might be sad for a time, but then they would inherit the business. Perhaps Rodney would come and lay a wilted rose on her grave. But soon she would be a forgotten memory. All her hopes and dreams, everything about her, would be buried away forever. There were no children to carry on. It would be as if she'd never existed.

A nurse came in with an instruction sheet for the heart catheterization, along with a scrub brush soaked in an antiseptic solution to ready her for the procedure. The nurse looked at her for a moment and asked if she was in pain.

Daphne wanted to tell her that life hurt and maybe death would be better than living.

"Many people have gone through this procedure, Miss Elliot," the nurse explained. "It will help the doctors determine what the trouble is."

If only you knew, Daphne thought. *I have so much trouble in my life. I have a business in the height of the selling season that I can't manage. And Henry is both alive and dead. Oh, my dear woman, you don't know the trouble I have.*

"When I feel as if things aren't working out, I like to take time and pray things through," the nurse said.

At these words, Daphne felt a sudden burst of energy strengthen her.

"It makes me feel better if I can release it all," she continued.

"Yes," Daphne managed to croak out. "I—I'm a Christian."

The nurse smiled. "I thought so. I don't know how, but I had a feeling you might be. You remind me of my mother. She had heart trouble. But she always smiled and trusted in God. Eventually when it was time for her heart to be at peace, she went to heaven praising God. I know she is praising Him still. It helps me to think about her and realize that in tough times God gives the strength we need to get us through."

Again the tears began to fill Daphne's eyes. *Dear God, You sent an angel to my bedside.* Nurses were often called angels of mercy, but Daphne truly believed God had sent this young woman to encourage her. Even if she were all alone and no one else was there, God was. God knew everything that was happening. He knew her fears, her questions, her confusion, and her pain. He was ready and willing to bear it all in His strong arms.

When the nurse finished prepping her for the procedure, Daphne felt peace descend on her. She decided to let go of Jack and his wild tales and concentrate on getting well. It was the only thing she had the strength to do.

The nurse squeezed her hand. "I'll pray for you," she whispered.

"Th–thank you," Daphne managed to say, even as the orderly came to wheel her away. She was still frightened, but she felt peace. She was weak, but her spirit was strong. Even when she was wheeled into a large room with personnel hurrying about, arranging instruments, she felt the prayer of the nurse God had sent.

Daphne arrived back from the procedure, dizzy and sore but grateful to be alive. On her hip, she felt the pressure of a sandbag a nurse had applied to prevent bleeding from the site where the catheter was inserted. Nurses came by often to check her blood pressure and the machines clicking by her bedside. She looked around for the nurse who had prayed with her but discovered she had gone off duty while Daphne was in the catheterization lab. Now all she could do was wait and find out the test results.

A young nursing assistant walked in, carrying two flower arrangements. Daphne sucked in her breath when she saw them. Part of her hoped one of the arrangements might be from Jack, while the other part wished it wasn't. The first was from her church family, the other from Rodney and Melanie. The aide also gave her a note. Daphne took the letter and slowly opened it.

Dear Miss Elliot,

    I know you wanted to give me the business, but I'm not ready yet. So you have to get well soon!

Daphne couldn't help but chuckle at Rodney's opening statement, even if the motion caused pain in her hip. She continued reading.

    Don't worry about a thing. Melanie is my acting assistant, and she's doing a great job. I only had to scold her once when she didn't arrange the seed packets the way you like them. But really, she is doing a great job. There's something about having the love of your life working by your side that makes things run smoothly.

Daphne began to heave when she read the words "love of your life." Her hand fell on the bed, though her fingers still held tightly to the letter. Who was her love now? Jack? Henry from the past? Both Jack and Henry? Neither? When she felt her heart begin to act up, Daphne drew in a deep breath to calm herself. She refused to entertain such thoughts.

    I was sorry to hear what happened to you but glad Jack was there to help. He called me at home and told me what happened. I would have come to the hospital last night, but they said you were too ill for visitors. I will come this evening if you feel better and sing you some songs. And, I promise, no major bombshells. I only hope I didn't cause all this.

Daphne shook her head. "Of course you didn't," she murmured.

So just relax and get better. Everything is going great here. But I miss you.

Love,
Rodney and Melanie, my assistant

Daphne slowly folded the letter. No doubt Rodney would do well on his promise to entertain her when he arrived. It wouldn't surprise her if he came with a full-fledged orchestra, ready to accompany his singing. How like a son he had been in so many ways. She was glad, very glad she'd made the decision to give him the business. And it might come sooner than any of them expected, especially if her heart couldn't take the strain.

Just then the parade of student doctors dressed in white lab coats returned, headed by young Dr. French. Daphne tried to remain relaxed when she saw the contingent, but it was difficult. There was no telling what the diagnosis might be. For all she knew, he might be coming to tell her it was hopeless, that she would never recover, that the wounds of the past had caught up with her and she would soon die from it all. If only she had found Chubs another home before she passed on. Who would care for him?

"Just as I suspected, Miss Elliot," the doctor said nonchalantly. "We found it necessary to put in a pacemaker to regulate your heart. The bandage on your chest will be there a few days. We put in dissolvable stitches."

Daphne didn't realize there was a bandage on her chest until her hand felt something soft and bulky beneath the hospital gown.

"We will monitor you for a few days, then send you home. You did very well."

"So I'm not going to die?"

"You have many good years left, Miss Elliot, if you take care of yourself. I can tell you are a strong woman. And I know for a fact you run an excellent business."

A surge of excitement raced through her. "You do?"

"Of course. My wife has bought all our summer roses from your nursery. And I must say, they are beautiful. Now of course you will need to take it easy for a few weeks. I hope that assistant of yours can mind things for a time until you've recovered. After that, I must insist you cut back on your work schedule, if not consider retiring altogether."

"So you really think I can't go on."

"You'll go on, Miss Elliot. You just can't keep doing everything as you used to. At one time or another, we have to let the younger ones take over. And I think your heart has been saying that the past few years. Okay?"

She couldn't help but smile at him, especially after the wonderful news that he and his wife were loyal customers at the nursery. Watching the group depart, she rested against the pillows, mulling over what he had said. Things would be different now. Just how different, she wasn't sure. At least she thanked her intuitiveness in settling her business affairs before all this came up. The stress of having to find a successor to the business might have forced her back into this place. She wondered if Rodney was ready to accept the reins of owning a business so soon. He would surely appreciate the extra income, as would Melanie.

Daphne continued to think about the plans she must make in light of this new information, when a nursing assistant came into the room bearing another vase of flowers. This time they were roses with a bluish tint, to Daphne's amazement. How often she recalled telling others she preferred blue roses to red, despite their oddity. At that moment, she thought of Henry. He knew how much she loved the single blue rose he once brought her long ago.

A strange sensation came over her. When the aide gave her the card that accompanied the bouquet, she immediately tensed. The wound on her heart began to ache. The tape on the bandage pulled with the straining of muscle. She heard the beeping of the heart monitor take off like a galloping horse. *I can't read this. I'm not ready.* She nearly called the nurses to have them take the bouquet away, until curiosity got the better of her. For all she knew, Rodney might have surprised her again with a pretty arrangement. Maybe she had told him she loved blue roses. She couldn't remember, with all the talk of plants they'd had over the year.

Her fingers shook as she tore open the envelope.

> *I'm so sorry, Daphne.*
>
> *Jack*

It was not signed Henry but Jack. She looked at the dozen blue roses surrounded by baby's breath. She put the note on the nearby nightstand, even as tears began to collect in her eyes. He knew exactly what to send her—because he knew her from long ago.

Chapter 12

"Time to get up and get going!" came a cheerful voice.

Daphne had just begun to drift off to sleep when a deep voice awakened her. She was glad for the wake-up call, as her dream had begun to center around Henry and the first time he brought her a bluish-colored rose. Initially she had been upset the rose was not red. All young women in love were given red roses, or so she thought. But there was something intriguing about that rose. It was different. The color reminded her of the soft mist that occasionally shrouded the mountains. He had searched high and low until he found someone who had grown them experimentally, as such roses did not exist in those days. It was a rare find and extremely costly. It showed love beyond measure.

She blinked open her eyes to see past the blue roses arranged in the cut-glass vase to Rodney's smiling face. Behind him stood Melanie.

"Oh, Miss Elliot, are you all right?" Melanie asked, drawing up a chair to her bedside. The feel of the young woman's hand on hers was like a soothing balm. It nearly made her cry.

"I—I'm a machine now," she whispered.

Melanie glanced at Rodney. "I don't understand."

"They put a pacemaker in my chest to control my heartbeat."

Rodney waved his hand as he drew up a chair next to Melanie. "Oh, that's nothing, Miss Elliot. They do that kind of procedure all the time. Even governmental officials have pacemakers. 'It takes a licking and keeps on ticking.'"

"Now I won't take any more of your jokes, young man," Daphne managed to say but with a small smile. Before her sat her children, even if they weren't flesh and blood. No mother could be prouder. "So how is the nursery?"

"Doing well. We're making good sales. People have come by asking about you."

"Which reminds me," Melanie added. She opened her purse and withdrew a stack of envelopes. "People have also been dropping off cards. Some asked about sending you flowers, but since you run a nursery, they decided it might not be the best thing. So I'm collecting the cash and will get you a gift certificate at the mall or something."

"What? I don't understand."

"Guess you don't realize how much you're loved until the going gets tough, eh?" Rodney winked before turning to the roses. "And what a smashing bouquet!

87

Who's the secret admirer? Let me guess."

Daphne turned away. "Please don't say it." Out of the corner of her eye, she saw Rodney sit back in his seat as if he had been slapped. "I'm sorry. I wish I could tell you things, but I can't."

"You don't have to say a word, Miss Elliot," Melanie said, patting her hand while shooting a glare toward Rodney. "You've been through so much. You need to rest and take it easy. How long will you be in here?"

"A few more days. They want to make sure the pacemaker is functioning properly."

"Hospitals still smell the same," Rodney piped up, recovering after Daphne's remark. "I'll never forget the time my parents brought me in kicking and screaming after I fell off my bike. I needed thirty stitches in my head. I broke my arm, too."

"You never told me you broke your arm," Melanie said.

"Sure did. Right at the elbow." He rolled up his shirtsleeve to display the jagged scar.

"I thought you had only cut yourself."

"Surprise."

Daphne tried to concentrate on their conversation, but all she could think about was the scar on Jack's face. The fire had caused it, or so he said. But if he really was Henry and he had been burned—why didn't he tell her? Why did he run away, leading her and everyone else to believe he was dead? Why did he change his name? And then he married another woman to boot! All of it began a slow, steady simmer of anger that increased as time went by. Nothing of what he'd told her gave the real reason for his actions.

"Can you do me a favor?" she asked Melanie.

"Of course. Anything."

"I would really prefer it if you took those roses home with you. They are—well, I'm getting a headache and think I may be allergic to them."

"Allergic to roses?" Rodney declared. "You work around them all the time, Miss Elliot."

Daphne gritted her teeth at the young man who could see through her like someone peering in a shiny plate-glass window.

"It must be something new." Rodney shook his head as Melanie agreed to take them, exclaiming how beautiful they were. When Rodney asked who sent them, Daphne refused to say. He let it go and began discussing the business, including how to handle the new shipment of plants scheduled to arrive in the morning. Daphne tried to relate the business details as much as she could but soon grew weary from the visit.

"She needs her rest," Melanie told Rodney. "Before we go, we did bring you a present. Maybe it will make the time go faster."

Daphne took the gift, unwrapping it to reveal a mystery novel. "Thank you."

Melanie leaned over and planted a small kiss on her cheek. "You take care of yourself. And don't worry about the nursery. We have everything under control."

"I'll try not to. Just keep your eye on Rodney."

"Hey!" Rodney said indignantly. "I know exactly what I'm doing. After all, if I'm to be the heir to the throne one day, I'd better know what I'm doing. Take care, Miss Elliot. We'll try to stop by tomorrow."

"Don't forget to take the vase of roses."

Melanie picked them up, again exclaiming over their loveliness, before telling Daphne good-bye.

She watched the bouquet disappear behind the closed door, hoping and praying that everything else would likewise disappear. She looked at the mystery novel in her hands. Life itself had become a mystery. Maybe someone someday should write a book about her. She certainly had a tale to tell. Daphne pressed her eyes shut, wondering how everything would be resolved in the end.

❦

Daphne slept little that night after the visit by Rodney and Melanie, too overcome by anxious thoughts to relax. The next day, she was encouraged to get out of bed and walk around a bit. The doctor monitored her heart rhythm and blood work carefully, announcing that she was recovering nicely. She could go home in a day or two if everything continued to check out. This news brought about a new set of worries. How would she care for herself and Chubs once she arrived home? For now, Rodney had been letting Chubs out and feeding him. Perhaps she would have her strength back in a few days. But a simple shuffle to the door of her room and back had all but worn her out. If her energy level didn't return soon, she might have to hire someone to help. The mere thought went against her independent nature. God was certainly doing a work in her, both in the natural and the supernatural. All the ideals, beliefs, and traits she had worked up within herself were being beaten down. She wanted to throw up her white flag of surrender, if not for the thin wall of pride keeping humility at bay.

Daphne heard the nursing assistant come in, bearing a tray of food. She was a sweet girl, not more than twenty years old. She had told Daphne how she was in this job to help pay her way through college. Daphne admired her spirit. It was good to see a young person labor to achieve her dream. Daphne had worked hard also, but had her dreams been achieved? Glancing out the window, she couldn't help but disagree. Her hopes had been dashed so many times she couldn't keep count. The only reason she took over the nursery in the first place was because she couldn't bear the thought of her brother selling it. If any dreams were left to be had, even in her older years, she prayed God would soon bring them to fruition before it was too late.

Daphne slowly pushed the button, bringing the bed to an upright position to stare at the food. All the rumors of hospital food had come true as she tried to eat the unrecognizable mass of beef stew. Finally she gave up and had only the gelatin and decaffeinated coffee.

The door to her room opened. A visitor. At first she couldn't see who it was, until an image slowly came into focus. A man stood there holding a huge arrangement of flowers.

"Hello, Daphne," the voice said slowly, setting the arrangement carefully on a table.

No! Not him! She couldn't take it. Her mind grew foggy. Her head began to spin. "P–please leave."

"Daphne."

"I mean it. I'm trying to be nice, but I feel terrible."

"I do, too. I'll never forgive myself for what happened."

"I—I don't like what happened either, but right now I feel terrible. I didn't sleep very well, and the food here is awful." She fumbled for the call button, only to find a pillow had slipped between the mattress and the controls on the side rail. She tried to jerk it out.

"Here—let me get that for you."

She allowed Jack McNary this one act of kindness. He took out the pillow, laid it on the bed, then stepped back. He stood there, staring intently for several moments with his hands planted in the pockets of his trousers. Again he had dressed nicely for the occasion. She stared, trying to imagine the scar replaced by a beard he'd worn in his youth. If she didn't feel so horrible at that moment, she would ask him to smile and see if he really was Henry. But the thought made her sick. She knew perfectly well who it was and that he had abandoned her for another. He had left her alone, by herself, lost in memories for forty years.

Jack looked around the room. "The nurse at the desk said some roses had come for you."

"I gave them away."

He inhaled a sharp breath. "Why?"

His simple question caught her off guard. "Because—because—I didn't want them."

"Daphne, did you see what color they were?"

She wanted to tell him they were pink or white or any other color but blue. She knew what he was hinting at. He meant for her to accept what he told her that afternoon in the nursery, that he was her long-lost love. "Please—I need some rest."

"Daphne, if only you could hear the rest of the story."

"I know what happened. You pretend to be dead, make up stories, then end up marrying someone else. You—you leave me alone, miserable, a spinster until I'm old and gray and my heart is broken. And you think time heals. Well, it doesn't." Just then she felt a stabbing pain in her heart. Her finger pushed the call button.

Immediately two nurses appeared in the room to assess her pain while a dumbfounded Jack stood nearby. Daphne could see the tears welling up in his eyes. She didn't care. She had cried more tears than he could ever hope to cry, even if he did it every day for the rest of his life.

"You need to relax, Miss Elliot," the nurses told her.

"Please ask him to leave," she said, pointing to Jack. "He's upsetting me."

One of the nurses acknowledged him. "Sir, I think it would be a good idea."

Jack looked as if he were about to faint. He turned as white as the sheets on the hospital bed. He staggered backward. "Daphne—," he groaned, then turned and walked out the door.

"Please don't let him visit me anymore," she told the two nurses.

Yet the voice that uttered her name echoed in her mind the rest of the evening.

Chapter 13

Daphne slept poorly the next few nights in the hospital, distressed over the encounter with Jack and the way everything was turning out. He tried once more to visit her when the head nurse of the unit stopped him and made him surrender the teddy bear he had brought. Daphne asked the nurse to keep it at the station to accompany the bouquet that decorated the counter. She wanted no more reminders of the past. Maybe after this he would understand she needed time and to leave her alone. He had to realize he couldn't make up for forty years while he was married to someone else. Daphne ground her teeth at the thought. She knew she must try to avoid stress, but Jack McNary had succeeded in foiling any plans for peace and tranquility. On top of it all, she had other stresses to deal with—the nursery business, keeping her home, and caring for Chubs.

Daphne gingerly drew on a button-down blouse over the small bandages covering the wounds from the surgery. She still felt weak and run-down, but the doctor had decided to discharge her. He gave her strict orders not to return to work for several weeks. Maybe she could ask Rodney to continue walking Chubs before and after work, but he had already done so much. For a fleeting moment, she considered Jack. He would do anything she asked, but it was better for both of them if he stayed away. Even as she put on her slacks, she thought of all those photo albums of Henry in her home. Now she would have to get rid of everything. There would be no more memories to tease her now that the truth had been exposed. Still, she was left with the unending question, *Why?*

The young nurse who had shared the scriptures with her before she went for her heart catheterization now came to give her discharge instructions. As Daphne listened patiently to all the dos and don'ts, she wished the nurse also had instructions on how to deal with life.

"I'm sure you're glad to be leaving us," she said with a smile.

"Yes and no," Daphne admitted. The nurse's eyebrows arched in surprise. "What I mean is, I have a lot to think about once I get home."

"Just remember that you need to take it easy and avoid stress. That's why I gave you the brochure on stress."

"My dear, if you only knew what my life is like right now, you would see that's impossible."

"Miss Elliot, what is impossible with man is possible with God. And He is very good at carrying our burdens."

Daphne almost kissed the nurse on the cheek but nodded and smiled instead. She waited patiently until the orderly came to wheel her downstairs. Melanie would be picking her up and bringing her home. She was rolled along in the wheelchair and saw the huge bouquet and a teddy bear decked out in a red bow sitting on a counter at the nurses' station. It cheered the place up immensely, she had to admit. No doubt Jack was trying to do the same in her life. She stared at the bear for a moment. He was sweet, with his head tipped to one side as if asking what troubled her. But no flower arrangement or cuddly bear could diminish the storms that tossed her to and fro. If Jack thought flowers were a recipe for sunshine, he was wrong.

Melanie was waiting for her as promised, with a smile on her face that eased Daphne's misgivings. God had been good to give her these two young people who were like a son and daughter. She hoped she wasn't being a burden.

"How is the business?" she asked as Melanie helped her into the car.

"Don't worry about it, Miss Elliot," Melanie said. "Rodney is a very good businessman. I think it's in his blood."

"He does show quite a bit of promise, I must admit, even if he does wander about in a love-struck fog at times."

Melanie couldn't help but chuckle. The drive home took about thirty minutes. Daphne marveled at the changes to the scenery during the week she had been in the hospital. Summer had descended on the hills and dales. The trees were full and leafy. Early summer blooms brightened up the yards. Wildflowers planted in the median of the four-lane highway cheered her. When Daphne arrived home, she found her gardens vibrant with a showy display of flowers. She sighed in contentment. Everything looked better than she had anticipated. The barking of Chubs from inside the house was like music to her ears. Using Melanie's arm for support, she got out of the car and began walking slowly to the house.

"I'm as weak as a newborn kitten," she professed in dismay. "What am I going to do?"

"Don't worry about a thing," Melanie told her.

Upon entering the house, Daphne was astonished to find a bed already made up for her on the sleeper sofa. A stack of mystery novels, checked out of the library, rested on a stand. From inside the kitchen, she detected the aroma of soup on the stove. And decorating the fireplace mantel was an assortment of flowers in vases.

"I—I don't understand—," she began.

"Welcome home," Melanie said, squeezing her hand. "I decided to make up your bed here in the living room where you can read or watch television. That way you won't have to climb those stairs to your room."

"Isn't that sweet."

"I also bought a better mattress for your sofa bed. It should be more comfortable for you."

"What?" Daphne asked in bewilderment, eyeing the bed before her. "I'll pay you back. Let me know how much it is."

"It's a gift," she said.

"Melanie, you know you can't afford it."

"No, I mean it. Your church got together and took up a collection for it. So it really is a gift. They also brought over all kinds of food. Your freezer is full."

"Isn't that sweet," Daphne said again. Tears formed in her eyes. It never dawned on her that members of the church would care that much. It blessed her to see the outpouring of generosity at a time like this.

"Just make yourself at home. I'll go check on the soup."

Melanie went off to the kitchen, humming to herself. Daphne watched from the living room as the young woman slipped on one of Daphne's frilled aprons and took up a spoon to stir the soup. God had indeed been merciful and kind, even when she didn't deserve it.

Slowly she went and lay down on the sofa bed. My, how good a firm mattress felt to her weary body. The pillows were covered with the cases of embroidered blue roses she had buried away in her linen closet. She rested there, thanking the Lord for bringing her home alive, even if her spirit was troubled by all that had happened.

Her gaze fell on the familiar features of the living room before coming to rest on the fireplace mantel. She had pictures of her family displayed there, including one of Henry. Vases of flowers now stood among the pictures. At the end rested a faded photo of Henry, standing stiff and proud, with barely a smile teasing his youthful face. Next to it was a small vase with a single blue rose.

The sight of it angered her. With all the energy she could muster, she went over and took the vase off the mantel. "Melanie!" she cried.

Melanie hurried out of the kitchen. "What's the matter? Are you all right?"

Daphne nearly shook the vase in front of her face. "What is this doing here?"

"I thought you would like it. The roses were so beautiful that I thought it would be nice to have one on the mantel."

"Yes, but why is it sitting next to the picture of Henry?" She began to shake. Melanie rescued the vase before she dropped it and gently helped her back to the sofa. "I'm so sorry," Daphne mumbled. "I don't know what's the matter with me."

"I think you've just been through a major illness, Miss Elliot, and your body is telling you to rest."

"I—I think so. And please call me Daphne. I can't stand the thought of being a Miss. I wish—" She paused. The emotion caught in her throat, choking off her words. How could she tell Melanie that deep down inside she wanted to be a Mrs.? She wanted a man to care for her and love her. She wanted to fix him meals and raise a garden together. She didn't want to be alone the rest of her days. Inwardly she wanted Jack, but she was too stubborn to admit it.

"You'd better lie down," Melanie said, coaxing her to the sofa. Daphne did as she was told. To her dismay, Melanie returned the rose to the mantel beside the fading portrait of Henry. Then she left the room to dish up some soup.

Daphne glanced over at the cabinet where she kept her photo albums. Slowly she reached for an album that held her treasured memories. Settling back on the sofa, she opened up the first page to a close-up of Henry. She studied it for some time. Jack, she knew, was plumper and his hair gray, along with that unsightly scar on his face. He had no beard as Henry used to wear. But now she could clearly see a familiarity in the shape of the eyes and the broad shoulders. The comparison sent goose bumps riding along her arms. She flipped through a few more pictures, mostly taken from a distance with Henry doing his favorite things. One picture showed him with a croquet mallet over one shoulder. Daphne paused, thinking about the croquet game she and Jack had played at the church picnic. Jack had been a gentleman through and through. And if what he said was true, Henry himself had sat across from her at the table, commenting on her fruited gelatin salad. The very idea made her shudder. She shut the book with resolve, scolding herself for doing this when she knew better.

Melanie returned, carrying a tray with a bowl of soup and some crackers. She glanced at Daphne with a strange look on her face. No doubt Daphne could imagine what she looked like. "Are you all right?"

"Yes, just doing something I wasn't supposed to."

"Now, Miss Elliot, I mean, Daphne, that's why I'm here. I arranged things so I could spend a few days with you. I'll take care of everything. I don't want you overexerting yourself and ending up back in the hospital."

"I'll try to be good," Daphne said with a smile, looking at the chicken and rice soup that Melanie had prepared. "This doesn't look like canned soup."

"Oh no. I followed my mom's recipe."

"How wonderful." Daphne took a taste. "This is delicious, but I don't want you slaving over me and going to all this trouble. You have a life to live rather than taking care of a fussy woman."

"Daphne, you've been like a mom to both of us," she said, settling into a chair. "I know Rod appreciates everything you've done. And since his own mom died a few years back, you've meant a great deal to him."

Daphne chuckled. "I thought I was only a bee in his bonnet."

"It's okay. He could use a jolt once in a while. But, honestly, you've been so helpful to us. I know how much you cared about our marriage, especially when you came to visit us that one night. It meant a lot to us. I realized then that God did bring Rod and me together for a special reason. I had no right to tear us apart just because things weren't working out the way I'd planned."

Daphne rested the spoon inside the bowl. The words jabbed at her like the tines of a fork. Isn't that exactly what she was doing with Jack? Perhaps God had brought them together for a special purpose; yet she was batting it away. Daphne shook her head and tried to eat another spoonful. Melanie watched her as if trying to analyze her thoughts. At least the young couple didn't know anything of what went on between her and Jack. Rodney would have a field day with it if he knew.

At that moment, a knock sounded on the door. "That's probably Rodney," Melanie said with a smile, rising to her feet. Chubs began to bark, drowning out the greeting that was taking place in the foyer. Daphne continued to eat until she felt a presence enter the room. The strength was so tangible that she could nearly touch it. She glanced up, and there he was. She dropped the spoon inside the bowl. Though her flesh wanted her to look away, her spirit remained mesmerized, especially after the pictures she had just seen in the photo album.

"I wanted to make sure you got home safely," he said slowly.

"Yes, thank you." Her face reddened when his gaze traveled to the mantel. No doubt he saw the blue rose resting beside the picture of Henry. *Did he think I did that? I hope not.* "If you don't mind, I'm feeling very tired."

"Please stay and have a bowl of soup," Melanie offered to Jack, running to fetch him some.

Daphne watched in a daze as he took a seat opposite her, in the chair where she often sat and gazed at photo albums, reminiscing about days gone by. If only she had the strength to run away from this embarrassing scene. She would take Chubs for a walk, go upstairs to her room and lock the door, anything rather than see this.

Melanie returned with the soup. Jack gulped it down in several swallows, to Daphne's amazement. He acted as if he hadn't eaten in a week.

"I really do need to get some rest," Daphne said in as controlled a voice as possible.

"I understand. I just wanted to say I was sorry for what happened in the hospital."

Oh no, not in front of Melanie! I don't want her to know he's Henry. Daphne's heart began to race. "I'm feeling very tired," she said once more. "I—I think I'm getting heart pains again. I don't want another spell."

Jack rose to his feet. "Daphne, if I could only tell you about—"

"Please, not here, not now. I have to safeguard my health. Please go." She turned away and closed her eyes.

Jack said no more. He bade a quick good-bye to Melanie and left.

Melanie stared wide-eyed, first at the closed door and then at Daphne. This was just the scenario Daphne wanted to avoid. Jack had brought up all kinds of questions in Melanie's mind, which she would take to Rodney. And Rodney would not give her a moment's peace until he knew everything.

Without a word, Melanie took her tray and retired to the kitchen. She said nothing about the encounter. But Daphne thought about it the rest of the evening, wondering why God was doing this to her and at a time when she felt so weak.

To Daphne's relief, Melanie never mentioned Jack's visit. Instead, she was busy caring for Chubs, cooking up the meals offered by the church members, and taking care of business. Rodney came by in the evenings to advise Daphne about the nursery and to cheer her up with his usual playful antics. One evening he sang while Melanie accompanied him on the guitar. Daphne had never heard a more beautiful duet. After the performance she told them they should make a CD with a Christian recording company, to which they both shared loving glances. When Daphne saw them kiss good night in the foyer of her home, she thought of Jack. There had been no word from him since the day he'd left the house. Daphne figured the end had finally come for them. He had been chased away from more places than a mouse. But her life's book still had blank pages left to be written on. She had no idea what the future held. Even though the blue rose had long since faded away, she had the distinct impression that something else lay ahead of her. Only God held the answer.

Melanie called Daphne for dinner inside the kitchen. After a few days on the sofa, Daphne insisted on eating her meals at the table. She didn't want to be an invalid for the rest of her days. Melanie had warmed up the last of the beef stew brought over by a member of her church. Daphne sat down at the table, bowed her head, and began to eat. "Aren't you having any?"

"I hope you don't mind, but Rod is picking me up. We're going out to dinner."

"How nice. Where to?"

"Believe it or not, to the Hardware Store Restaurant." She nearly laughed out loud. "It seems strange, but we really like that place."

Daphne stopped eating. The Hardware Store Restaurant was one of Jack's favorite places. She wished her a pleasant evening. "And after tonight, you can go home," Daphne told her. "I can take care of myself now."

"Are you sure?" Melanie asked. "At least I'll come over for an hour or two and make sure Chubs is all right."

"That would be wonderful, thank you." Daphne stared out the back window, lost in thought. She hated the idea of being alone in the house. She enjoyed having Melanie around. It made her feel young again to sit and chat about womanly things over cups of tea. She was grateful Melanie never mentioned the scene with Jack. Instead she talked about her flower business and how she hoped one day to make it thrive. It was during that particular conversation with Melanie that Daphne suggested she sell some flower arrangements at the nursery. Melanie hugged her afterward.

"It's the least I can do after everything you've done for me."

"Daphne, you know I don't want you paying me back. We're supposed to be there for each other."

But Daphne couldn't help paying her back in some small way. Without Melanie and Rodney, who knew what might have happened to her?

Just then a car sounded in the driveway. Rodney came to the door, all smiles as if eager to spend the evening with his love. The aroma of aftershave filled the house. Daphne watched the two of them kiss. How she would love enjoying a relationship like that, if only it were meant to be.

"So did you tell her?" Rodney asked in a low voice, loud enough for Daphne to hear. She had a keen sense of hearing and could distinguish even the slightest sound.

"Tell me what?"

Both Rodney and Melanie turned to face her. "We've been talking—," Melanie began.

"Actually we've been talking to Jack," Rodney corrected.

Daphne felt her face grow warm and her heart begin to thump. No doubt the pacemaker would have to kick in with what was about to come out of Rodney's mouth.

"I think you need to talk to him."

"I will take it under consideration," Daphne said icily.

"There's more here than meets the eye. If you only knew—"

"I know plenty, and what I found out landed me in the hospital."

"You can't blame Jack for your sickness," Rodney exclaimed.

Daphne bristled. He was right, of course. And she owed Jack an opportunity to explain, as he'd tried to do many times.

"We care about you, Daphne," Melanie said. "And so does Jack."

"And we also know he's the one you thought was dead long ago," Rodney continued. "It's amazing. A miracle, really. I think you owe him a chance to explain why he did what he did."

"I don't owe him anything. In fact, he owes me forty years. Forty years of grieving for a man who wasn't even dead! Forty years of thinking he had been burned alive when he was married to another woman."

Rodney sighed. "You know I can't tell you what to do. But you were very good when you came to us during a hard time in our relationship. Maybe now you can use a bit of your own wisdom—how we need to trust God even when things don't look right. Melanie and I, we were only looking at things through our eyes. All I want you to do is think about Jack through God's eyes. And use a bit of that faith you were telling us about. See if maybe there are things you hadn't considered—like healing those scars you both have right now."

Daphne stared, dumbfounded, as the couple headed out the door. She returned to the sitting room, exhausted by the verbal battle with Rodney. Yet his words rang true. She had not looked at any of this through God's eyes. She had imagined all kinds of scenarios with regard to Jack and not once considered there might be other possibilities. He wanted to tell her the facts, but she refused to listen. She thought about the scar on Jack's face and how it changed colors with his moods. She wondered about the pain he must have gone through, suffering such a wound. And maybe like her, he had scars within that also needed attention.

She pondered it all until her eyelids grew heavy and sleep won her over. Soon she was dreaming of Henry during their final meeting before the fire. She appealed to him to consider moving to Virginia, even working at the nursery.

"It isn't time yet, Daphne."

"Of course it is! Who knows what the future holds? And we love each other."

"Daphne, when that time comes, I'll know. I'll come back for good. And when I do, I will gather you in my arms, and we will get married. I promise."

Daphne flicked open her eyes in a start. The lamp on the table shone full in her face. Had the time come? Had Henry returned at last, ready to fulfill his promise?

Chapter 14

Rodney was surprised to see Daphne at work the next morning, shaky but determined to help him with the summer rush. When he asked about her health, she brushed the question aside and put on her best smile for the customers who came to select flowers and other plants. She knew what he was thinking, that she had ignored both his advice and her health to satisfy an obstinate heart. He said little, only inquired about a new shipment of late-summer plants that included the fall selection of brightly colored mums.

"Also, I hate to mention this, Miss Elliot, but I cut myself a check while you were in the hospital. It was close to payday, and since I knew you couldn't do it, I went ahead and paid myself. You know how Melanie gets if I don't pay the bills on time." He showed her the ledger and the amount he had deducted.

"You don't have to justify your actions. In fact, I plan to give you more for the management you did while I was sick."

"You don't have to do that."

"A worker is worthy of wages," Daphne said with a smile. She pulled out the check ledger and began writing him a check when the door to the shop burst open.

"Rodney, can you give me a hand?" the voice called out. The man stopped short and stared. When their gazes met, Daphne felt a rush of warmth flow through her. He quickly turned and left. Rodney threw her a look before leaving his post and walking after him. Daphne came to the window, just in time to hear Jack mention how he didn't know she had returned to work.

"Don't let that stop you. You need to interact."

"And I told you I won't come unless she asks me. I made myself a promise. I won't chase her anymore. I was wrong to do it in the first place."

"It isn't wrong to show her you love her. And, believe me, she needs all the TLC she can get, even if she won't admit it."

Daphne hung her head low at these words. She desperately craved love, even if she was stubborn and hardhearted. She once thought love meant her place of business, her dog, or her life as an independent spinster. But now other things were at work, other emotions she never would have dreamed could bubble up after so many years.

She peeked out the window to see the sunlight shining full on Jack's face

100

and the scar he said he suffered from the fire. Is that why he left, because of the scar? Is that why he found comfort and purpose with another woman, believing she wouldn't want him anymore? If so, he was foolish to think it. A man was not a machine that could be thrown away over some insignificant defect. She would have received him with open arms, even if he had two heads and twelve fingers. She had been madly in love. . .once. If only he hadn't run away as he did.

"I do appreciate everything you young people have done," Jack said. "I believe the Lord used you in this situation, even if it isn't turning out the way I'd hoped."

"Hang in there, Jack. Things will change. Just be patient. I've learned by working in this place that patience is definitely a virtue."

He chuckled. "I've been learning it also. I've waited a good long while for the Lord to work on my own heart. I think about how patient He's been with me. I can hardly say a word against Daphne and her response in the situation. As she's said, it's been forty years. But I know coming forward as I did was the right thing to do. You see, Rodney, when God resurrects something in one's heart, it's meant to happen. And I know the love is there. I believe we're meant to be together, somehow, some way."

His words melted Daphne's heart. She walked to the rear of the shop and took a seat, pouring tea she had made into a cup. Tea. The truth had come out in the conversation she and Jack shared over cups of tea. What would become of it all now?

Daphne returned to writing out the check to Rodney when he came back inside. She sensed his thoughtful perusal, but he made no mention of the encounter with Jack. Instead, he showed her a list of bills that needed to be paid and the profit secured within the last month. Daphne was pleased to see how her business had been blessed, even with the topsy-turvy spins and twists in her life. It also confirmed to her that Rodney was indeed an excellent choice to take over the nursery when she retired. Both he and Melanie had done a wonderful job. She owed them a great deal. If only she could be sure what her own future held.

op

He paced back and forth, wondering what to do. His hand sifted through his gray hair. Yes, Henry was very much alive. He had kept the man hidden away for forty years, but the truth was begging to be released. She had to know the truth. And she had to know he'd done it to protect her. If only she would let him tell her what happened, to let the confessions come forth, to make her realize that even if he had loved and married Melissa, it didn't mean he cared for her less now than he had so long ago. He didn't want to be an old widowed farmer the rest of his days. He wanted to be her love and her husband.

How I long for you, even after all these years. I know I was only a memory, a picture

101

you would gaze at in the darkest of nights. But I've come back. I'm alive. I've been alive for forty years, even if I spent much of my life with a woman whose companionship I cherished. After Melissa died and the years began falling away one by one, I knew God was resurrecting you in my heart. I remember our walks in the rain, the ball where we danced, the tender touch of your soft lips. Yes, the years have passed. We are no longer the same people. It may even be too late. But I truly believe love can be renewed, Daphne, with God's grace and mercy.

He flicked away a tear, as he laid aside his thoughts and rose to his feet. He would try one more time to reach Daphne's heart, even if it was concealed behind a stone wall. He would try once more to see if love might be there or if it had disappeared with the passage of time.

The meeting she overheard between Jack and Rodney affected Daphne more than she realized. The words shared had been tender and sincere. Even now she reflected on it and the meaning behind it.

But I know coming forward as I did was the right thing to do. You see, Rodney, when God resurrects something in one's heart, it's meant to happen. And I know love is there. I believe we are meant to be together, somehow, some way.

Did he truly mean what he said? Did he think their love would last a lifetime? Or was he hoping not to be alone for the rest of his life after losing the woman he married? All these things spun around in Daphne's mind in an endless circle. She could hardly eat that night or even read one of the mystery books stacked by the sofa bed. She could do nothing but sit and think about Henry the young man, Jack the mature man, and herself caught in between.

When the doorbell rang, she almost didn't hear it. Only Chubs's incessant barking made her rise to her feet and shuffle to the door. She peeked out between the blinds to see him standing there, as big as life itself. Her breathing nearly ceased. What was he doing here? She hesitated, watching him. He stood still, waiting patiently. He obviously knew she was there. She also knew if she didn't answer that door he would be gone forever.

Almost in a daze, Daphne opened the door.

Startled, Jack took a giant step backward and nearly fell off the porch. "Hello, Daphne. I—I probably should have called and told you I was coming." He faltered. "I know you don't want to see me, but if I don't get these things out in the open, you will never know the truth."

"I—I don't like strange men in my home," she said, "especially in the evening."

"I was going to ask Rodney to come along. If you want, I'll call him and ask him to come be a chaperone of sorts."

"No, never mind." What she didn't need right now were two men giving their opinions on how she should think and feel. She opened the door wider and allowed him inside. Glancing around the living room, she noticed she still had the portrait of Henry sitting on the mantel. She tried to ignore it and took a seat on the sofa. Jack appeared melancholic as he sat down stiffly in her favorite chair. His eyes were dull. There was no cheer in his facial features and certainly not in the scar where the light of the lamp illuminated the ragged edges. He looked down at his fingers intertwined on his lap.

"There are some things I must tell you, Daphne. But before I do, I hope you will believe me when I say that I am Henry Morgan."

Daphne looked away to focus her gaze at the framed portrait of a smiling Henry. A lump formed in her throat. "It's hard for me to believe that. For all I know, you could be a clever imposter out to dupe me. It's happened before."

He shook at the statement. "Daphne, please don't say that." Pain laced his words. "I will tell you then how much I loved the waltz more than any of those other fancy moves. I gave pearls to a beautiful woman one Christmas and walked along a bridge overlooking a quiet river. I blew kisses so she might catch every one." He inhaled a deep breath. "And I told her that when I returned to Virginia I would marry her."

Daphne's knees began to shake. This couldn't be happening. Too much had changed. They were not the same people. Even if the memories were his as well as hers, she didn't know if she loved him. She was in love with a young and vibrant man, one who cared for her and would do anything for her, except the night of the fire. "Why did you fake your death at the lumber mill?"

"I didn't fake it. The authorities believed I was dead. There was no trace of me found, except for a few personal belongings. I ran off and found refuge at Evelyn's boardinghouse. I was hurt. My face was a mess."

Daphne crossed her arms. She had heard all this before.

"Daphne, they wanted me dead anyway. It was better for everyone to believe I was dead."

At this, Daphne looked at him in confusion.

He leaned forward in his chair, intently focused on her without wavering. "You see, I was about to tell on the corporate bosses. They were involved in extortion and embezzlement. I found out the scoop through some careful detective work I'd done at the mill. Fellows at the mill were upset there had been no pay raises in several years, even though the company profits were skyrocketing. Someone somewhere was pocketing the extra cash and not giving it to the workers. I found out who it was. I was about to become the greatest whistle-blower the company had ever seen."

Daphne managed to draw a breath and remained riveted on his story.

"The bosses heard about it. They threatened me, trying to keep me silent. But, worst of all, they threatened you. They were going to use you to keep my mouth shut. I didn't know what to do. I wanted to warn you, to tell you to stay away, that there were men who wouldn't shirk at hiring assassins if they could to keep their money and their lifestyles. So I waited. I prayed. I asked God what to do. So many times I wanted to call you and tell you what was happening. I felt so alone."

Daphne had to admit she would have been scared if he'd told her strange men were threatening her life. Silently she thanked the Lord he hadn't told her. Just the idea sent her shivering once more on the sofa.

"Are you all right? I'll stop if you want me to."

"No, I'm fine." She took the afghan off the back of the sofa and wrapped it around her legs. "Go on."

He hesitated.

"I want you to go on," she added.

He relaxed a bit. "Anyway, I considered letting you know what was happening when the explosion occurred. It wasn't an accident. Something sparked inside the chain saw when I turned it on. The thing blew up in my face. I was thrown nearly forty feet, and I hit my head against a tree. I think I was knocked out for a while. When I woke up, a fire had spread into the woods. My face was so raw and painful that I didn't know what to do. When I realized what had happened, I took off into the woods. If they were trying to kill me, I didn't want them to think I was alive."

"So you pretended to be dead?"

"I didn't tell anyone one way or the other. I just ceased to exist. It was the safest thing to do. I walked for miles that night and reached Evelyn's boardinghouse at daybreak. I wasn't even sure how far I went. When I got there, I told the family my name was Stuart and that I had burned myself working on some machinery. I never told them about the fire at the mill. From that moment on, Henry Morgan was no more. Evelyn was able to find medical care for my face. They heard there was a fire at the mill. They had some questions. But I refused to tell them I was involved and stuck to my story. I didn't want them in on what had happened. Evelyn's daughter, Melissa, helped me a great deal. A lot of nursing was involved, and Melissa did it all. She was a trained nurse. In time we did get married, and for the next thirty-five years, I was Stuart."

Daphne felt her teeth grind. How could he run to Evelyn and Melissa who were strangers, seeking out their protection and love, but couldn't run to the one who loved him with all her heart?

He paused and stared once more at his hands. "Daphne, if I'd told you I was alive, then those people might have come back for both of us. I had no choice but to leave the life I once had with you. I knew also that for me to return to you, a young and beautiful woman, as someone scarred like this—I knew it wouldn't be right."

"What? Do you think I can't take a man who's scarred?"

"Daphne, you wouldn't have been able to take any of my scars. It wasn't just my face. It was my life. And that wasn't a life I wanted you to live."

"So you created another scar instead. Pretending you were dead and allowing me to grieve all these years. Reliving all those memories. Never being able to put away the pictures." She began to heave in distress.

"I'm sorry, Daphne. I wish there were a way I could help you. I only hope you can believe I did it all to protect you. I believe you're alive because of it. We both are alive."

"This is living?" she cried, standing shakily to her feet. The blanket fell on the floor. "You don't know how many times I wanted to die! When I heard what happened, I thought my life was over. And for years, I felt as if I were walking around dead. If only you had told me what happened. We could have gone away together. I would have left everything to be with you, even my father's business."

"Daphne, that nursery was your life. It still is."

"But it wasn't at first. You were." The tears began to roll down her cheeks. "You were everything to me. You were my sun and moon. Maybe I loved you too much. Maybe it was getting in the way of other things. But I know I would have been there for you, if you hadn't kept this from me."

Jack also rose to his feet. "I didn't know that for certain, Daphne. I honestly didn't know if you would be there. I believed after what happened to me, with the burn and everything, it would have been too much of a shock."

"So you're saying that Melissa was better than I was? That she could live with a changed appearance while I couldn't?"

Jack ran a hand through his hair, making it stand on end. "It was different. Melissa cared about someone named Stuart."

"And now you're someone named Jack. Don't you see? No matter what you say, Henry is still dead. As much as you want to, you can't bring him back to life."

Jack stood there quietly, his eyes shifting back and forth as if considering her words. "Then I want to do something new. Even if I'm not the same person, and you aren't either, is there still hope that God might want us together?"

How could he ask her that? She had no idea what God wanted. Right now her life was turned upside down. She didn't even know how to breathe, let alone think and act. Why did life have to be so complicated? Why couldn't there be a manual on what to do when life came crashing down in the most unexpected ways?

"What can we do?" he asked once more. "I love you. Is there any chance we can create something together? Or is it just wishful thinking?"

"There are still wounds to heal," Daphne said, slowly picking up the blanket.

"It can't happen overnight. You can't expect to come back and begin where we left off, not after all this time. It's impossible. And I think that's exactly what you hoped to do."

"I had hoped the sparks would be there," he admitted. "That's why I kept myself back for as long as I did after I came here to Virginia. I wanted to see if anything was left. I wanted to see if you remembered Henry, if you were seeing anyone else, or if you had other things in your life. But you and I are so much alike. Trying to get along but seeing the years catch up. Trying to keep going but knowing how fragile life can be. Wondering if love can still happen."

His words shook her to the core. Fresh tears welled up in her eyes. She didn't resist as Jack came and took her in his arms. She knew she was still a fragile plant, unable to thrive where she was. She was as Rodney once described—a plant suffocating in its tiny pot unless she was transplanted soon. And Jack was desperately trying to transplant her.

When she felt his hand gently lift her chin and his eyes stare into hers, a sudden fear swept over her. It had been so long since she had been in another man's arms. He gazed at her with the same intensity she remembered long ago.

Daphne twisted out of his embrace and wiped the tears from her face. "It's getting late."

He nodded, picked up his set of keys from the stand, and said a swift goodbye. Daphne never looked back but kept her head bent, staring at the carpet. *God, please tell me what to do!*

❧

Jack came home that night, torn in his heart and his spirit. *The answer was close, so very close, but I rushed. Look what I've caused all these years, and even now, when she suffered that heart attack. Oh, God, I know I've been selfish. I should have let her go. I should never have returned to Virginia after Melissa died. But it all seemed so perfect, with Evelyn leaving me the vacation home here and so close to where Daphne's nursery was located. And to find out she had never wed, as if she had been waiting all these years for me to return. I thought when she found out who I was she would leap into my arms. But I was shortsighted. She's right. I have been trying to resurrect Henry. Even though I am Henry, I will never be Henry. Henry is gone. He died in the fire. I'm Jack now, Jack McNary, and one whose heart is linked to another. That is the person Daphne must come to love somehow, some way. But I won't push her anymore. I will leave it in Your hands, God.*

Chapter 15

Daphne spent the next week searching for answers. She went to church whenever they had services, hoping the pastor would say something that would tell her God's will concerning Jack McNary. She had several of the ladies over for tea one afternoon in the hope of finding answers. Instead, they chatted about their grandchildren and what their families were planning to do for the upcoming summer vacations. All the talk made her feel even more miserable.

On Tuesday, Daphne decided to take a day off from the nursery. She was feeling lonely again and maybe even a bit selfish. One look at the calendar told her the reason why. Today was her birthday. She informed no one about it; she didn't want to make a big deal of it. But to Daphne, it was a big deal. Another year older, and another year of trials and tribulations. She dressed in a comfortable outfit, then paused when she saw the earrings Henry had once given her long ago, the pair she always wore on Tuesdays. She slipped them on, then went to listen to Bible messages on cassette, hoping for words to soothe her soul.

That evening the doorbell rang. Daphne tiptoed to the window and looked down below to see Rodney's car parked out front. What was he doing here? Had he somehow remembered her birthday? She glanced in the mirror, ran a comb through the row of gray bangs on her forehead, and came down the stairs. At least she was grateful for her strength that had returned after the surgery. A visit to the doctor last week confirmed that the pacemaker was doing very well.

Rodney and Melanie stood at the door. "Happy Birthday!" Rodney said with a big grin. He came forward and planted a kiss on her cheek before presenting her with a wrapped gift.

"You didn't need to come here," she said, opening the door wider to allow them in.

"Of course I did. I had to see my mother on her birthday."

Daphne shook her head. "You could use some discipline, too," she said jokingly.

Rodney grinned. "What—are you gonna make me sit on the stairs for coming to see you? That's what my mother used to do to punish me when I was little. These days I guess they call it time-out." He went over and plopped down on the sofa. Melanie headed into the kitchen. She returned a few minutes later, a big

107

grin on her face, singing "Happy Birthday." In her hands, she carried a layer cake decorated with blue roses.

Daphne tried not to cry, but it was difficult, especially when Melanie placed the cake before her on the coffee table. In blue icing were written the words, HAPPY BIRTHDAY, MOM!

"And many more!" Rodney sang, giving her a hug. "Now open your gift."

Daphne took the package from him and sat down. She carefully undid the tape that held the flowered wrapping and opened it. Inside was a digital camera package.

"Time for some new pictures in those albums of yours," Rodney said, folding his arms.

Daphne stared at it. How would she ever operate something like this? She managed a small thank-you before putting the box on the table.

"Don't you like it?"

"I don't know much about cameras."

"This is the same one I have," he said, taking the camera out of the box. "I'll show you how it works. Then you go to the store and use the picture machine to select your prints. Or I can upload them on my laptop and do it from there."

"What? I don't understand a thing you're saying."

"It's simple. We'll go though it step-by-step. I figured you'd need to start filling your albums with new memories."

Daphne shuddered at his words. He must be hinting at her and Jack. Well, there was no future. It was as lifeless as the plants Jack forgot to water.

"In a little under nine months, to be exact," Melanie added.

"Nine months," Daphne repeated. She straightened in her seat as smiles spread across the faces of both Melanie and Rodney.

"That's right—you're gonna be a grandma!" Rodney announced with a laugh.

"Oh, stop it. I'm not your mother."

"Of course you are," Melanie said. "You mean just as much to us as our own mothers did. And we want you to share this special time with us."

"That's wonderful! I'm very happy for you, I must say."

"We just found out the other day," Melanie continued. "I wasn't feeling too good so I took a pregnancy test. I'll tell you, Daphne, there's nothing more exciting than seeing that magic *x* appear in the little window. Rod leaped so high he bumped his head on the doorway. He got a nasty bruise."

"Really now, young man," Daphne said with a chuckle. "You always did do things in excess." Her heart overflowed with joy at the couple's news.

"So it's time for new things," Rodney repeated. "Just like the flowers that are all in bloom, and everything is coming up roses. And, speaking of roses—"

"Rodney found the most gorgeous blue rosebush, Daphne. It came in on one of the shipments while you were in the hospital."

"I'm glad," she told them honestly. "Red and pink are lovely, but there is something about a blue rose that is so unique." She fell silent then. If only she had her own good news to share with the excited couple sitting before her. Instead, she felt like a hollowed-out shell, without hope. Or could it be that God had sent this sweet couple to give her hope? That newness of life is still possible? Just this morning she had read the verse about trusting in the Lord and not leaning on one's understanding. In her own eyes, nothing made sense. Through God's eyes, everything was perfectly planned and would be completed in order, just like a new baby.

After they left, Daphne went over to the drawer of a small table. Inside lay a folded piece of paper with the address and phone number Jack had given her. With shaky fingers, she took it out. In his own hand, he had written where he lived. Spring Mountain Road. She knew where the road was located. She had been in the area a few times over the course of her life. It was a pretty road, too, at the foot of the Blue Ridge Mountains. Maybe a drive would be in order.

After work the next day, Daphne took care of Chubs, then drove off on a special errand, heading straight for the range of mountains looming before her. She rarely went for a drive unless it was to town for groceries or to church, but something stronger was beckoning to her. She decided to obey the feeling that grew inside.

She enjoyed the sight of the Blue Ridge Mountains in all their glory. This area had been her home for as long as she could remember. Even if Henry at one time wanted her to leave Virginia and live in the mountains of Tennessee where he worked, she couldn't bring herself to leave this place. It was part of her. Nothing would take it away. And now God had seen fit to bring Henry back, even if he was a different person. He had returned despite all the obstacles, just to find her. The thought made her smile.

Soon she was winding her way around the curvy road of Route 810. Spring Mountain Road came up on the right. She had no idea what his house looked like but continued on. The road grew steeper, climbing the shoulder of a foothill that guarded the grand Blue Ridge. Suddenly she saw it—the dirt brown truck he always drove, parked before a modest ranch home overlooking the valley. She slammed on the brakes with a terrific shriek, sending the car into a small ditch.

Jack burst out of the house and ran across the lawn. "Are you all right?" came his anxious voice, only to stop short. "Daphne! What are you doing here?"

"I—uh—I was on a drive," she said quickly, too embarrassed to tell him the real reason for the trip. "Now I have to get out of this mess."

"Allow me." He waited for her to exit the driver's seat. She watched as he backed up the vehicle with skill, into his driveway behind his old pickup truck.

For an instant, she wondered what she was doing here, early in the evening, and at Jack's house, of all places. He looked like an old farmer, dressed in his usual overalls he had worn the first day he came to her nursery. "Actually I came here to find out what you've been doing with all those plants you bought from me," she said.

He cracked a grin and waved his hand. She followed him to the backyard and gasped. The gardens were expertly formed rectangles and looked free of weeds. Tiny plants in picture-perfect rows stood surrounded by mulch. "I don't believe it."

"Did I do something wrong?"

"Of course not. This is simply beautiful." She gazed up into his face to see it shaded by the brim of the straw hat. "I thought you didn't know a thing about plants."

"So they really look all right, then?"

"I should say so. They look extremely healthy."

In the vegetable garden, Jack had already placed cages for the tomatoes. The broccoli heads were full. "I was about ready to cut a head of broccoli. I also cooked up some of my barbecue. Have you eaten dinner?"

Daphne stared at the home behind her, uncertain about what to do.

"There's a small table and chairs on the patio," he added.

She breathed easier and said that, yes, she was hungry. A big smile broke out on Jack's face. He hurried into the house and came out with a knife and, under Daphne's direction, cut off a huge head of broccoli as the vegetable for the meal. While she roamed the property, looking at the thriving apple trees and even the rosebushes that appeared healthier than her own, Jack was in the kitchen finishing dinner. When he called, she returned to find a small table set for two, along with a lit candle. He had also changed clothes.

"I hope you don't mind the candle," he said, "but if it gets dark, we can still see. Unless you don't want to see what you're eating."

"Of course I do." Daphne promptly sat down in the chair he pulled out. She lowered her head while Jack said the blessing, then began eating. Neither of them said anything for a time while they ate, listening to the last call of the birds for the day. The steady hum of insects soon took over as the sun dipped behind the mountains.

"You do have a nice place here," Daphne finally said, wiping her lips on the napkin. "I haven't been back to this area since I was young. Remember Jane Neely? I think she lived down the road not far from here."

"Yes. You said she had a crush on me."

"She did. She never used to say anything to me in high school. For some reason, the word got out that I was seeing some muscular lumberjack from Tennessee.

Then she was around the nursery all the time, asking questions." Daphne gazed out over the landscape, watching the daylight melt with the approach of evening. "So this was Evelyn's home?"

"Her vacation home."

"Did you ever come here with Melissa?"

Jack bent over his plate in silence for a moment. When he answered yes, Daphne nodded. "I figured you must have come here for vacations, with this home being in Melissa's family and all."

"It was hard moving here at first after Melissa died," he admitted. "There were many memories. But working in the garden helped. It was good to see life come again after experiencing death—first Melissa's, then Evelyn's. I think I know why you like the nursery so much. Life grows there. And I understand better now why you reacted the way you did when I told you how I killed the first batch of plants."

"I was totally unreasonable that day," she said. "Getting upset over silly little plants." Daphne was thankful the dim light masked her flushed cheeks.

"Daphne, they aren't silly. They are part of God's creation, and His creation is perfect." The look in his eyes softened. "And just the same, you're also part of His creation. As much as I want to be with you, I've decided I'm going to let God determine my future. I know what I would like to have happen. But if it isn't His will, then I'll just be hitting my head against a wall. And I think that's what I've been doing these past few weeks. I've been pretty selfish."

Daphne stared. How could he sit there and say such things when it was she who had thrust up walls and been basking in her own hurt and jealousy?

"I'm glad you came," he added. "I won't deny it. But I won't let it speak for anything either. We can call this a nice visit between friends."

"Is that what you want?" Daphne heard herself say, shocked by her own words. Yet she couldn't help how she felt. If only he would take her in his arms and tell her everything would be fine. If only she would not die alone but leave this world experiencing the love of another.

His head popped up. "What?"

"Do you want to be just friends?"

"Daphne, I want only what's best for us. And if that means a friendship, that would be fine with me."

"But is that really what you want?" she pressed.

Jack lifted his glass of lemonade and took a long swallow. The glass clinked on the table with resolve. "No. No, it isn't. I don't want to be just friends. I love you. It's a season for new things, just like the gardens I planted. I'm hoping it's also the right time for us, too."

Daphne's heart nearly leaped at these words, the same words she had been sensing in her own heart. Could this be a confirmation from God?

"Look—the moon is beginning to rise." Jack pointed at the faint rays of golden moonlight rising in the east. Daphne turned to look. When she did, she heard a chair scrape. She felt his presence come up behind her and then the feel of his strong hands on her shoulders, gentle, soothing, slowly gliding down her arms. A tingle shot through her like the tingles she had when she was young and in love. She began to shake.

"It's all right," his voice said in a light whisper. "I'm here, and I won't leave you." He came around the chair and knelt before her. He gazed longingly into her eyes.

"Henry—," she said with a sob. She buried her face in his shoulder. The strength of his arms around her was powerful, filling in the empty hole, soothing the ache, healing the wounds. When he kissed her, everything came to life. The planting of long ago had finally sprouted. Peace flowed like the warmth of love in her being. God had answered her prayer.

♒

" 'Love in any language. . .straight from the heart. . .pulls us all together, never apart! And once we learn to speak it, all the world will hear, love in any language, fluently spoken here!' "

Today Daphne felt no animosity toward that beautiful singing voice of her employee. It bounced across the walls of the shop and carried outside to the tables of plants that customers perused on a busy summer day. She even found her foot tapping in time to his song. She knew from the volume of his voice that Rodney was trying his best to irritate her. No more. The rough edges had been made smooth.

Her fingers gently slid the tiny little impatiens into a new pot. When she'd arrived at the nursery that day, she was amazed to find Rodney already there. He had done the morning count and had taken up a broom to sweep out the remnants of dirt and dust from last evening. The sight of it all confirmed her feeling that today was the day. She wasn't exactly sure how to break the news to him. Perhaps if she just came out and said it, the Lord would supply her with the words.

Wiping her hands on a towel, she ventured out of the greenhouse to find Rodney tending to several customers. Everyone turned and smiled in her direction. The warmth of their expressions soothed her heart and soul. When the customers left the store, carrying boxes of plants, Daphne came to the counter. "Everything going all right?"

"Looking good."

"And is Melanie feeling good?"

"I wouldn't exactly call throwing up in the bathroom every morning feeling good. But she knows it's because of the baby, so I guess that's to be expected."

Daphne ran her finger across the smooth counter. How she would miss this place. It had been her home for so long. "I guess it's a good thing then that you will be getting some extra income."

"Babies can be expensive. And Melanie keeps saying we need a bigger place." Rodney let out a sigh. "I'm not sure what to do."

"It's all right." She reached over and patted his hand. He stared back as if surprised by the contact. "Everything is going to be all right. Trust me."

"If you say so."

"I know so." She inhaled a sharp breath before gazing around the store. "I'm going to miss this place so much. But I know it's the best thing to do."

Rodney leaned over the counter, staring in confusion. "Miss Elliot, you're not making any sense."

"Rodney, I'm giving you the business. Today I'm announcing my retirement." His mouth fell open. "What?"

"I've decided it's time to move on. You were right, you know."

"I was right about what? I can't even begin to imagine."

"That I need a bigger pot in life. This place was causing me to get root-bound. I needed to be transplanted, but I was fighting it tooth and nail. God tried to send people in my path to let me know He wanted to change things. But I didn't want Him to do it. I thought I had it all figured out, but it only made me more miserable. Besides"—she continued to run her finger across the counter—"the doctor thinks it would be good for my heart to leave this place. The stress level hasn't made things better for me."

"But what will you do? I mean, you've been at this place since you were little."

"Ten years old, to be exact. I started as you did, counting seed packets and sweeping out dust with a broom. My, those were the days." She chuckled at the memory of her pigtails flying in the breeze as she helped her father. In the distance, her brother, Charles, would groan about lifting the heavy bags of mulch into their respective stacks. But for Daphne, there was nothing better than working among God's creations of plants and rich earth. It was her calling. Little did she realize, but this place she loved so well kept her until another life called to her.

"How can you just leave? Won't you miss it?"

"I'm sure there will be things I'll miss. That voice of yours, for instance. Meddling in other people's affairs. Trying to run lives." She chuckled, then added with much conviction, "Being a caring young man who loved a mean spinster as he would his mother."

"I hope you aren't doing this out of some need to pay me back. If anything, I should pay you back for all you've done for Melanie and me."

"No, sir, young man. On the contrary, as I said, life has a way of changing. It's time to go work in other gardens."

At that moment, the door to the shop creaked open. The footsteps were solid upon the wooden floor of the shop. Daphne smiled at the vision that walked in, as if the sun had just risen.

"Aha!" Rodney exclaimed in a loud voice. "Now it all makes sense. Have you an announcement to make?"

"Well, not quite," she said, feeling the heat in her cheeks. "Maybe soon."

"Sooner than you think," Jack added, grabbing Rodney's hand and shaking it heartily. "I had to thank you for everything."

"I didn't do anything."

"You did. . .more than you know."

He offered his arm to Daphne who slipped her hand through the crook in his elbow. They moved off toward the door that led to the greenhouse. This had been Daphne's place of joy, the place where she nursed plants until they could find a home with a customer who would care for them with loving hands. Yes, she would miss this place. Maybe she could come back once in a while if Rodney needed a hand, especially when Melanie had the baby. But for now, she was content to walk around, gazing at the workstation still cluttered with potting soil, peat pots, a pair of gardening gloves, and her trowel with the decorative pink handle.

"Are you sorry?" Jack asked.

"I would be sorry if I turned my back on what's ahead of me," she said. "Of course I loved this place very much. My father showed me right here how to transplant seedlings."

"I remember coming here when you had your elbows in dirt, both forty years ago and now." He gently turned her toward him. "And I remember how sad I was when I had to leave and go back to Tennessee to continue on at the lumber mill. But all things work together for good."

Daphne never forgot the day when he took off in his rickety old car, heading back for the woods of Tennessee. When his death was announced, life had taken a turn down some dark alley. Now it had emerged into the light and at the right time. "But you came back."

"When I came back here five years ago to live, there were so many times I wanted to see you and talk to you. I wanted you to know I was alive. I just didn't know how to say it."

"I'll admit I never knew you were Henry, though there were instances when you reminded me of him. Something in the eyes. During the croquet game. All that dirt on your face. Holding me after the thorns pricked my hands. When you showed me that license, everything made sense. Of course my mind wouldn't accept it at first, but my heart did."

"I almost killed that heart, too," he said mournfully, rubbing her hand.

"No, you gave it new life. If I hadn't fainted that day in the shop, it might have been too late. I could have been here, working with my plants, lonely and miserable, and suffered a heart attack. You never know."

His arms curled around her. "You aren't going to leave me, Daphne. I know one day we'll be called home to be with the Lord, but I want it to happen knowing you were by my side and with a ring on your finger."

"So is this a proposal?" she asked with a laugh.

He reached into his pocket and brought out a box. Daphne gasped. Her heart leaped, not with pain but with joy. She took the box and opened it. The ring was just as she used to dream about, a pretty diamond with her birthstone set on either side. She'd always told Henry she wanted a ring with her birthstone in the setting. *Because if I wasn't born, we wouldn't be engaged!* she used to joke. The sight of the ring brought tears to her eyes. Dear sweet Henry. "Y–you remembered."

He bent over her and kissed her gently. "Yes, I remembered. How could I forget? You were very clear about what you wanted when we talked about it. Could it be forty years ago?"

"Yes, all those years ago. During that time, we both lived different lives."

"We may have grown in different gardens, but we share the same Creator who knew when the time was right to bring us together again." He then became serious. "Daphne, it's forty years later, but will you marry me?"

She glanced at the plants aligned in a row on the workbench, some with flowers that waved from the breeze blowing through the open door. Nodding her head, Daphne took the ring and slipped it onto her left hand. "It's beautiful."

He grinned and offered her his arm. "How about some lunch to celebrate? The Hardware Store Restaurant is running some good specials."

Daphne laughed and hooked her hand through his arm. Like the plants she so lovingly tended, love, too, could bloom at any age.

Epilogue

U nder the authority vested in me, I now pronounce you man and wife. What God has joined together, let no man separate. You may now kiss the bride."

The kiss was marvelous, the lips tender as they found hers, just as she envisioned it would be. Then suddenly he kissed her again, prompting a round of laughter from the congregation that rose to the very rafters of the church. Daphne couldn't help but laugh herself. What a strange sound to hear—laughter from her lips that so often criticized or spoke words of sadness and depression. Today she felt sprightly, ready to face the world for another forty years, even as they turned to greet the enthusiastic congregation, ready to present themselves as Mr. and Mrs. Jack McNary. They stepped off the platform, arm in arm, to the cheers and smiles from those Daphne had come to know. Loyal customers of the nursery. Friends. Her doctor. And to her surprise, an older man with a craggy face and graying hair but familiar nonetheless. Her older brother, Charles.

Daphne inhaled a swift breath and went at once to embrace him. He seemed startled by the greeting. Despite their estranged past, Daphne felt nothing but happiness that he had come all this way from California to be here.

Suddenly she saw the tears in his tired eyes. "I'm sorry for everything, Daphne," he mumbled.

"You're sorry. . . ?" she began. "You don't have anything to be sorry for."

"Yes, I have. For many things. Most of all, for not being there when you needed me. I hold nothing but admiration for you. And I'm happy that everything turned out for you in the end." He reached over to shake Jack's hand. "I have to admit, your story has been a shock to me. Maybe I can talk with you more about it sometime."

"Please do," Daphne said, gripping his arm. "It really is a miracle of God. It taught me so much about how He cares for us, in the small and the large things. But I'm so glad you're here, Charles. You can't know."

His smile warmed Daphne's heart, even as she and Jack walked the remainder of the way down the aisle. When they reached the rear of the sanctuary, a high-pitched wail greeted them. Melanie was there, trying desperately to calm her two-month-old baby girl, Rose. Daphne couldn't help the tears that sprang to her eyes. "And how is my dear grandbaby?" she said, reaching over to give the infant a kiss.

Melanie smiled. "You may regret having invited her to your wedding, Daphne."

"Nonsense. Even if she isn't my blood relation, I still consider her mine." She handed Jack her bouquet of blue-tinted roses and took the little baby in her arms. All at once, the crying stopped and the tiny crook of a smile formed on her wee face.

"Daphne, you have a way about you that makes everyone smile," Jack said with a chuckle. "Even the littlest ones."

"It wasn't always that way, you know. I'm happy God doesn't give up on us. And He didn't give up, did He?"

Jack kissed her on the ear. "No, He didn't. And I am so glad you didn't give up on me either."

"I thought you might get a few comments on the dress you're wearing," Melanie said, taking little Rose back in her arms. "Most brides wear white. But you always had your own ideas, Daphne."

Daphne looked down at her midnight blue dress that once hung in the back closet for years upon years, only to be resurrected for this special occasion. "My dear girl, how could I not wear this dress? You remember it, Jack."

"Of course I remember it. You wore it to our first ball forty years ago. And the pearls to match."

"It needed fixing up, but with my sickness and all last year, I had no trouble fitting into it. I guess there is some good that can come out of being sick and getting a pacemaker. I never would have thought I could wear the dress again."

Melanie laughed, linking her arm through Daphne's as they proceeded toward the church hall and the reception. All at once, Rodney came out from behind the door and presented them with a huge Mylar balloon. "Happy Wedding Day to you!" he sang.

"What mischief are you up to now, young man?" On the balloon was the head of a smiling Bambi along with the word CONGRATULATIONS.

"Don't you remember? You were quoting Bambi to me one day in the nursery, calling love a pain in the pinfeathers. I just had to get it."

"You do beat all," Daphne said. "What would I do without you?"

"Admit it. Life would get boring. But you must be a little happy how the nursery business is going."

"You mean getting a front-page news story about it in the lifestyle section of the *Progress* this past Sunday? Yes, I am very happy. Everything has worked out, beyond my dreams." *Everything,* she thought, watching Jack as he went over to speak to the minister of his church and some church friends. At that moment, he looked over at her. She threw him a kiss. He smiled, raised his hand and caught it, just like those times long ago. The scar on his face disappeared. He was Henry again, with his twinkling eyes and youthful appearance. He was all hers, to have and to hold, from this day forward.

When Rodney turned on the music and a waltz from long ago filled the room, Jack came forward and swept her up in his arms. "You still remember how to dance, don't you?" he asked.

"Oh, dear. I'm not so sure. That was a very long time ago."

It came to her easily, as if she had been doing this all her life rather than forty years ago. Maybe the dress sparked the memory. Or the excitement of the wedding. Or simply the man whose arm cradled her while his free hand led her across the linoleum flooring of the reception room. Rodney saluted them with a glass of bubbly apple-flavored beverage.

"You're having no trouble remembering," Jack noted with appreciation. "It looks like you have been doing this for years."

"I have," she confessed, "in my memories. But now I can live it. We can have new memories with a love that never really went away."

"Ageless, just like you."

Daphne had to laugh. "No, I am older. But not too old at least to dance."

"Or for love."

Resting her head against his firm shoulder as the music enveloped them, Daphne couldn't help but agree.

Time Will Tell

Dedication

In memory of my beloved grandmothers:
Grandma Schreiber for her old cuckoo clock,
the princess glass shoe, and the candy dish.
And Grandma Braun for her delicious kuchen
and the fascinating laundry chute.

With thanks to:
Lorena Perez
Wanda Hume
The Clock Shop of Virginia
Charlottesville, Virginia

Chapter 1

*B*UZZ.

Not again. Connie jumped out of the shower at the sound, racing to switch off the alarm clock at her bedside. A pattern of water droplets decorated the carpet beneath her feet. She never remembered to turn off the alarm come Saturday morning. Her internal clock worked beautifully every weekend, awakening her to a picture-perfect day filled with the hope of finding treasures at the yard sales she planned to attend.

Friday nights were spent scanning the newspaper, circling the yard sale ads that interested her. On a map, she starred in pencil the streets holding the sales. This Saturday, to her delight, she found a moving sale right down the street from where she lived. Many times she'd had to drive long distances to find one that appealed to her. This sale in particular—held by her neighbor Mrs. Rowe—tickled her interest. In the ad, Mrs. Rowe cited several antique treasures and old books.

Connie rubbed the towel over her shoulder-length dark brown hair while scanning shelves of books purchased at previous yard sales. Half the books she owned were juvenile in nature. Connie often wondered why as a young, single woman she bothered buying children's books. Perhaps that maternal instinct was on the rise, or maybe it was the plain nostalgia of owning children's classics that had entertained her as a youngster.

Connie blow-dried her hair and quickly dressed. With the sale just down the street, she hoped to be one of the first arrivals in her quest for a bargain. All around her apartment were telltale signs of previous yard sale finds—old plates, a small wooden table, a lamp, a painting of the ocean. . . . Her wages from her job at the department store didn't quite cut it for her to be buying expensive possessions to fill her place. Instead, she resorted to yard sales to find decorating ideas. A few of her coworkers went with her on her journeys on Saturday mornings and were amazed at Connie's ability to sniff out obscure bargains. Soon they began giving Connie their lists and asking her to keep an eye out for items that would interest them. Connie was able to find an origami book for one worker's daughter, queen sheets in rose print, and even a crib for an expectant coworker. No doubt she could win Yard Sale Customer of the Year if such an award existed.

Connie quickly drank down a cup of coffee and ate a piece of toast spread with strawberry jam before heading out the door. No need for the car on this venture, with the first yard sale a mere five houses away. The clear blue sky slowly awakened with the first rays of morning sunlight. Birds chirped merrily from the trees as she hurried down the sidewalk. Neighbors' yards were all abloom in tulips and hyacinths. It was a perfect spring day.

Claudia Rowe was still dressed in her duster with a cloth turban wrapped around her head when Connie appeared in front of the house. Boxes were scattered on the lawn. The older woman stared at her in amazement before glancing at her watch.

"I don't open for another hour."

"I know," Connie said breathlessly. "I only live down the block. When I saw your ad, I knew this was the first place I wanted to look."

"You must be that young thing who lives in that apartment building down the street from me. I think I know everyone in this section of West Street. It will be hard for me to leave the neighborhood, but it's something I need to do."

Connie had never considered herself a "young thing," but she must seem young at twenty-five to someone over sixty. "I'm Connie Ortiz. My coworkers call me the Yard Sale Queen."

"Really now. And why is that?"

"Because from March until August, I'm at yard sales. I usually bring lists from others that tell me what to hunt for."

"Well, I suppose you can look around if you want. I'm going inside to get dressed. I'll be right back."

Connie smiled and began browsing. Most of the items for sale were typical of other yard sales she had been to—clothes, shoes, glassware, cookware, luggage pieces. . . . There were a few toys and a box of books. Connie knelt down to sift through the books. She picked up a heavy hardcover with slick pictures of the nation's parks and sighed. How she would love to tour those parks one day. It reminded her of trips her family used to take every summer when she was young, traveling around in their old pop-up camper. She glanced around, reminiscing about it all, when a particular item caught her eye. She put down the book and picked up a clock that was sticking halfway out of a dusty box. It was no ordinary clock either, but an old-fashioned cuckoo clock. Connie looked at the carving of wood and the tiny door above the clock face where the little bird would pop out and call, "Cuckoo." She was still examining it when Claudia Rowe appeared, carrying a cup of coffee.

"Isn't it a beautiful clock?" the older lady said with a sigh. "I've had it for many years."

"I suppose it works all right?"

"Of course. It cuckoos every half an hour. It requires winding every eight days by pulling the chains here. I've actually had it in storage a very long time. I felt with the move and all it was time to get rid of it. No sense keeping memories like that around anymore, especially when there's nothing left to hold on to."

Connie traced the polished wood with her fingers, noting the configuration of carved leaves and the profile of a bird etched into the top. A clock like this must be worth a fortune—far above her humble means. It was silly to even consider it.

"I really should have sold it in the paper," Claudia continued, "but I thought I would put it out and see if I had any takers. Besides, if you advertise something in the paper, you never know who will respond. I don't want strange people knowing my phone number and calling me up or coming inside my home."

"I don't blame you. You have to be careful nowadays." Connie continued to stare at it, thinking how much it reminded her of her grandmother's clock that once hung in the living room. After her grandmother passed away, Connie had tried desperately to find the old clock, only to discover, like many of Grandma's possessions, it had been sold at auction. Now it seemed as if God had resurrected the clock from long ago. "How much do you want for it?"

"Well, I'm not really sure. I haven't thought about it, to be honest. But you seem like a nice young lady who would take care of it. I suppose you can have it for a hundred."

Connie gulped. The most she had ever spent at a yard sale was thirty, and that was after she'd managed to dicker on the price for the small wooden table now sitting in the foyer of her apartment. She glanced at the woman, wondering if she was in the bargaining mood this early in the game. "Would you take fifty?"

She shook her head. "I'm sorry, but I think a hundred is very generous. I know the clock doesn't mean anything to me now, but I am in the process of moving, and I need the money."

Connie sighed. She turned away and opened her wallet to find twenty-five dollars. In another part of her wallet, she kept her gas money for the next two weeks. Pulling out the bills, she discovered she had seventy-five dollars but no more.

Claudia Rowe moved off to arrange some clothing on a table while Connie returned to the cuckoo clock. How much it reminded her of her grandmother's home and that time in her life. Tears filled her eyes just thinking about it. As a little girl, she could still see the rescue squad arriving to take her mother to the hospital after she fainted on the bathroom floor. When they said she'd suffered an aneurysm and might never wake up, Connie cried for hours. She refused all comfort, even from family members. The only comfort she found during those long days and nights spent in her grandmother's home was from the old-fashioned cuckoo clock hanging on the wall. The faithful bird popped out every half hour to greet her like a friend. Grandma would try to think of things to do while she and her younger brothers waited anxiously for word about their mother. But it was the cuckoo that Connie looked to time and time again until she was reunited with her mother.

Just then other customers began arriving for the sale—several women and then a man wearing a hat, bearing a distinct limp. Connie saw them edging toward the table where the precious cuckoo clock rested. Immediately she picked up the clock and approached the older neighbor. When Claudia hastily agreed to the seventy-five dollars, she handed over all the money in her wallet, including her gas money for the next two weeks. At that moment, she didn't care. In her eyes, the clock was tantamount to finding a precious gem. When life brought troubles her way, she would look at the clock and remember God's faithfulness in bringing her through times of turmoil to a joyful end. It was just like the day her mother walked into Grandma's home after awakening from her two-week-long coma. This clock was God's gift to her, a gift that symbolized a miracle and one she would treasure forever.

Arriving home, Connie immediately found a place on the wall of her living room to display the clock. She eagerly set and wound the clock. In no time, the half hour passed and the door opened to reveal the cuckoo bird, ready for its first greeting in its new home. Connie couldn't help smiling. The clock had been worth its price, even if now she must scrimp to meet her needs. Maybe she could find some extra hours at work, like doing inventory, to cover the cost. She decided to call her friend Donna, who'd worked the previous evening at the customer service desk. Maybe Donna knew if any extra hours were available on the monthly calendar.

"There must be a reason you're looking for work in inventory," Donna said with a chuckle. "What did you waste your money on this time?"

"You'll never guess."

"You're right—I won't. I never know what you'll come home with. Which reminds me, any luck at finding a nice-looking table lamp?"

"I only went to one yard sale today and ran out of money. So I came home."

"Wow. Must have been one terrific sale."

"It was." Connie inhaled a breath. "I got a clock."

"Did you say *a* clock? How much did you spend?"

"Seventy-five."

Connie could imagine Donna's "Are you kidding me?" expression as she asked, "Who would spend *all* her money on *one* clock?"

"It reminded me of being in my grandmother's house when I was little and the time my mom went to the hospital after a brain aneurysm burst. For days, the only thing that comforted me was my grandmother's faithful cuckoo clock. It's symbolic, I guess; this clock reminds me that God took care of her. Mom not only survived, but she is healthy to this day."

Donna seemed disinterested. "Still, seventy-five bucks is quite a bit for just a clock," she finally said.

"Yes, if it was any old clock. But I'll tell you, it could be the twin to my grandmother's cuckoo clock. For all I know, it might even *be* her clock. I mean, her things were sold off at auction. Maybe I should check with the lady down the street and see if that's where she got it. Wouldn't that be incredible?"

"Definitely not of this world," Donna agreed.

Connie was glad to hear this statement as she had been talking with her friend about the Lord. She didn't preach but rather shared with Donna the times in her life when she felt God was looking out for her interests. She hoped it might minister to her friend in some small way. Which reminded her, she needed to have Donna and some of her other women coworkers for lunch soon. Connie tried to have people over as often as she could. There was something about sharing meals together that brought people closer. Now if only there might be a love relationship in her life as well as good friendships. Not a day went by when she didn't dream about a man waltzing into her life and whisking her away to some island paradise. She sighed and gazed at the clock once more. God had His perfect timing as He did when He brought the beloved clock into her life. He would bring a man into it, too—at the right time and in the right place.

"Oh, and guess what the news is at work, Connie? We've got a new employee. And he is out of this world."

At the word *he*, Connie listened more intently. Not that a guy at work would interest her all that much. Most of the men who worked at the store were stock boys earning money to put toward their college degrees and were much younger than she. The head manager was married. And mainly women worked as cashiers or manned the customer service counter.

"His name is Lance Adams. He's training to become part of the management team."

"That's nice."

"C'mon, Connie. I've seen goldfish show more enthusiasm."

"I'm hardly going to be enthusiastic about some guy who's probably married if not already attached. Besides, if he hates yard sales, I'm fresh out of luck."

"You're too much. I'll try to discover his phone number and find out some other tidbits for you. Then maybe you'll feel more comfortable."

Warmth spread across Connie's face at the thought of Donna snooping into some stranger's life—and just for her benefit. She tried to tell Donna she wasn't interested, but something inside her held out a hope that perhaps this man was unattached and looking for someone like her.

Connie began considering her lifestyle and characteristics. Besides her love for the Lord and her interest in yard sales, there wasn't much else spectacular about her. She had shoulder-length dark brown hair parted down the middle, her mother's German nose, and her father's dark brown eyes and dark skin tone from his Hispanic ancestry. Many considered her job at the store on the low end of the employment scale. She had nothing of real value in her home but the sentimental value of the cuckoo clock she'd purchased today. Her clothes were ordinary jeans and tops, with a few pairs of slacks and blouses for the workday. She disliked buying clothes; consequently there was little hanging in her closet. She did love Christian music and would often listen to her favorite artists on her iPOD. Occasionally she might play a game on the Internet with her brother Louis. If Lance liked computer games, they might actually have something in common. Then she recalled her assumptions about the man—married or with a steady girlfriend who had a nice job, beautiful clothes, and a flashy smile. She might as well accept it. There was no hope.

"You haven't heard a word I've said, have you?"

Connie gulped, realizing she had no idea what Donna had been talking about.

"Don't worry," Donna continued good-naturedly. "I still plan to find out what I can about Lance. When can I come see your clock?"

"I'll have you over for lunch soon," Connie promised.

"Sounds good. See you Monday."

The phone clicked, precisely at the moment when the little bird popped out of the clock and began its merry serenade. Connie had to smile. At least she wouldn't be lonely tonight. God had provided her a feathered friend, even if it was made of wood. And maybe, just maybe, He might have others waiting in the wings, too.

Chapter 2

I hope you'll do the smart thing and sell that clock on the Internet."

Connie had just taken off her jacket and hung it in her locker when Donna bounced up behind her. It was Monday morning, a new start to the workweek, and already Donna was after her about her precious clock. "Of course not. I love it."

"Haven't you heard about these people who resell their stuff on the Internet and make tons of money? I know people who do it all the time."

Connie wished her friend would consider other things besides money. As it was, she would never dream of selling her sweet clock. She had just slipped her lunch bag into the small employee locker when Donna grabbed her arm.

"Look! Quick! Over there! Isn't he magnificent?"

Connie thought a movie star had suddenly graced the premises, ready to sign autographs with the way her coworker was reacting. Donna pointed to a tall man with dark hair who was chatting with several of the cashiers. All the young girls had dreamy looks, their fingers slowly pushing strands of hair behind their ears in shy displays.

"That's him. Lance Adams. Make your move."

"I'm not making any move," Connie told her tersely. Her hand shook as she shut the locker. "Whoever he is, he's obviously a womanizer. He has all the girls eating out of his hand."

"He's interacting with the employees, silly. And he's training for management. Lots of money—that is, after his training is complete. What a keeper."

Connie stole a glance at the new manager-in-training while his back was turned. He was tall in stature, with brown hair in a shade close to her own. He wore tailored slacks and a broadcloth shirt with a silk tie befitting his status. She shook her head. There was no possible way this man would give her the time of day, especially with the number of females working at the store. Ten to one was poor odds at best. And he was in management training, after all. Those in the upper echelon of the business world didn't associate with mere laborers. Connie adjusted the watchband on her wrist before tossing back her hair. There was only one thing she could do—concentrate on her work at customer service and forget about Lance Adams. As it was, she needed to check the schedule for some overtime so she could earn enough money to buy a tank of gas. *Either that or I'll have to drag out the old bicycle from storage.*

A young woman named Sally, with auburn hair and freckles, rushed up to her. "Oh, Connie, I just know you can get me out of my predicament. I need a rocking chair."

"A rocking chair!" Donna echoed with a laugh. "Aren't you a little young to be thinking about that?"

Connie cast her friend an irritated glance, wishing at times that Donna wasn't so blunt. She turned her attention to the young girl who smiled meekly. "You mean you want me to find you a rocking chair at a yard sale?"

"Everyone tells me how you can find the greatest deals at yard sales. All my mother does is reminisce about the rocker her grandmother once owned. I would like to get her one for her birthday."

This statement drew Connie's interest. "I'll have to tell you sometime about the wonderful cuckoo clock I just picked up on Saturday. My grandma had one almost exactly like it."

Sally grabbed her arm in excitement. "I just know you can find me a rocker, Connie. I'll pay you whatever it costs and even extra to cover your trouble."

"You don't need to do that."

"But I want to. The money's worth it. A rocker will absolutely make Mom's day—I just know it."

Connie smiled as Sally raced off to man her cash register, until she caught Lance Adams gazing in her direction. His dark eyes were large and luminous as they stared at her for a few seconds before turning to Mr. Drexer, the store manager. Connie wondered why he looked at her the way he did but pushed the thought aside to enter the customer service area. She sighed in dismay at the amount of garbage strewn across the desk—candy wrappers, coffee cups, papers with doodles on them. . . . No doubt Donna had tried to keep herself awake Sunday evening while working overtime and hadn't bothered to clean up, leaving the mess to sit until Monday morning. All Connie needed was the new manager-in-training to see this sloppy workstation and get the wrong impression of her.

Connie had brought over the wastebasket, ready to toss out the trash, when suddenly his face peered over the counter. She dropped the wastebasket on the ground, dumping out the trash that included a half-filled can of soda. A brown stream trickled across the shiny linoleum.

"Oh!" she cried, glancing around for something to clean up the mess.

"Not a good way to start a Monday morning," Lance Adams observed.

Connie looked beyond him, thankful Mr. Drexer wasn't there, or he would have surely reprimanded her even though she was innocent. "Please believe me—I didn't make this mess."

"I'm sure you didn't." He reached out his hand. "Just wanted to introduce myself. Lance Adams."

Connie offered her hand in return only to find she was still clutching a chocolate wrapper, one she'd retrieved from the litter-strewn desktop. She tucked away the offending hand and offered him the other one. "Connie Ortiz."

"Ortiz. Is your family from Mexico?"

"No, we're not from Mexico," she retorted, a bit miffed. People were forever asking her this question. "My father's relatives are from Guatemala. And my favorite food isn't enchiladas either. Actually, I prefer a good Mediterranean pizza, the kind with prosciutto, black olives, and artichokes. Luigi's makes the best."

Lance blinked in surprise before offering a smile. "Sounds terrific. We should go there sometime."

Connie gaped at him in astonishment. Her hands began to shake at the mere thought of the man offering the semblance of a date—and when she didn't even know him. He must be more of a womanizer than she'd thought. She turned back to see the river of soda creeping toward her shoe. "Excuse me, but I have a mess here to clean up."

Instead of moving away, Lance came behind the customer service desk to see the garbage on the desk and the soda adding a distinctive pattern to the floor tiles. He grabbed up the phone and paged the janitor. "You'll be cleaned up here in no time. So tell me, do you have any concerns you'd like to discuss with regards to customer service?"

"Yes, as a matter of fact. Half the time, the register here doesn't work. We've never had enough pens. And we could use another employee for the evening hours, except that I need the job."

His eyebrow rose. "You already have a job."

Connie was becoming more and more flustered by this conversation. If only the man hadn't suggested the idea of going out for pizza. The statement had totally wrecked her nerves. Maybe Donna had tickled his ear about her. Then again, maybe he was just a nice guy looking to have everyone in the store love him. Perhaps he offered pizza outings to all the girls on the staff. Maybe he should throw them all one big pizza party and be done with it. "What I mean is, if we did hire another clerk, I wouldn't be able to pick up overtime, which I could really use right now."

"Money's that tight?"

Connie said little else about the money angle, nor did she mention her prized find at the yard sale that led to her poor financial status for the coming week. Instead, she told him how an extra paycheck was always nice as she cleared the workstation of wrappers and stray paper.

"I'll see to your other requests—the extra pens and a technician to look at the cash register. Nice meeting you." He turned to greet other employees but not before offering her a wink.

Connie watched him interact with several women at the main cash registers, giving them each a friendly greeting and a handshake. The women reacted with smiles and wide eyes that scanned him in curiosity. With his winning personality, no wonder he was picked to be an assistant manager. She could see his lips move as he spoke, probably trying his pizza ploy on the others. Connie shoved a strand of hair behind one ear while mopping up the spilled soda since the janitor had failed to appear. There was no sense in being disappointed over the encounter. She knew all along this was too good to be true, though inwardly she wished Donna hadn't planted so many hopeful seeds.

Connie had just gotten her act together at the service counter when her first customer arrived, a young woman returning several articles of clothing. She went about her daily work and soon forgot the encounter with Lance. The day became busy, with the line for refunds and exchanges growing before her. She looked around for Donna in the hopes she could help out but realized she had likely been snagged to do inventory as it was nearing the end of the month. The people in line grew antsy. Some began to sigh loudly and stare at their watches.

Suddenly the cash register jammed. Connie's face grew hot as she tried to make the system work, only to find it had frozen.

"What's the holdup here?" snarled a man with a balding head, waving a wrinkled shirt. "I only wanted to return this measly shirt, and I've been waiting here thirty minutes."

"I'm sorry, but it seems the cash registers are down."

The man swore before turning to the other customers in line. He began ranting about the incompetence of the employees while they chattered on the phone to their boyfriends. He continued on with his plan to take his shopping needs elsewhere, even if this was the only major store in the area. "And I hope you go out of business," he redirected toward Connie.

Connie bit her lip while trying to maintain her composure enough to page maintenance. When she failed to receive an answer to her call, she tried once more. This time, her shaky voice echoed over the store's loudspeaker. "Stan Harrison, will you please come to customer service? Stan Harrison?"

Several of the customers began drifting away until only the bald-headed man and one other lady stood before the counter. Again the man used choice words that nearly curled Connie's hair. This is what she hated most about her job, dealing with irate customers who blamed her for things totally out of her control. If only she could get the cash register to open.

Just then Lance Adams appeared, along with Stan who jiggled a set of tools. She breathed a sigh of relief, but not before the bald-headed man called her a name that mocked her Hispanic heritage. He then told her to go back to Mexico where she belonged. Connie nearly fainted on the floor.

"Excuse me, but that wasn't necessary," Lance told the man directly. "If you need assistance, I'll gladly take care of it. But don't harass my employees."

"I've been waiting here over an hour to return this thing," he barked before tossing the article of clothing into Lance's hands. "You can keep it and your store. I'm never coming here again."

Connie stood there, stunned by the encounter. Never in her life had anyone said such things to her. Of course she had heard stories from her father and how he was ridiculed for his heritage, but never once did she think it would happen to her.

"It looks like you could use a break," Lance whispered to her. "I'll get Donna to cover."

Connie nodded, unable to speak after the incident. She managed to walk to the lounge, her mind in a fog. She wished now she hadn't ignored Papa when he spoke of the old days and what happened to him as a young immigrant to the United States. To her, they were just tales told for effect. She was an American, after all, even if she was born to a Hispanic father and a German mother. But little did she realize she carried within her a heritage that had suddenly been attacked when she least expected it.

"I'm sorry that happened," a soft voice directed her way. Connie glanced up to see that Lance had followed her into the lounge. He went and poured her a cup of coffee. "You take sugar?"

"One packet of the fake stuff. And a little milk." She threw herself onto the sofa. "I've never had that happen before. Papa told me how he was teased in school, especially over his accent. He kept bringing it up like it was the worst thing he had ever been through. I just ignored it. Now I wish I hadn't. It's like I ridiculed him, too, by refusing to listen."

Lance handed her the coffee. "Don't be so hard on yourself. That customer was completely out of line. And you did warn me about the cash register. I should have had someone look at it right away. I let you down, Miss Ortiz."

Connie blinked in surprise at this statement before taking a sip of her coffee. There were interesting features about this man named Lance Adams. He wasn't just a typical manager; he had a merciful heart for others. He sat down in another chair.

"Please call me Connie. Ortiz makes me sound like a brand of tortilla chips." Lance laughed even though Connie shook her head. "There I go again. Really, I do like my name and my heritage. I guess I just don't want to make a big deal out of it. But my eyes were sure opened today to some of the hate that's out there."

"It's hard when people become that way. Sometimes I don't understand why God would have us love people like that, but He does. And yes, He loves that man, too. Are you a churchgoer by any chance?"

Connie nodded and described the community church she attended, only to see Lance's dark eyes widen. A smile erupted on his face.

"Would you believe, that's where I go, too?"

Connie stared in astonishment. She tried to picture the man among the members of the congregation but couldn't place him. As it was, the church had grown quite a bit over the last few months. Connie wasn't very good at introducing herself to strangers. She had a group of women she liked to sit with and paid little attention to others.

"Then we do understand the same language when it comes to dealing with irate people."

"If you mean we should be dumping coals on their heads, I guess so. Though I don't think that customer's scalp could get much redder. He looked boiling mad," she said.

Again Lance chuckled with warmth that made her feel good inside. It was almost as if she had known him for years rather than having just met him this morning. There was a friendliness about him that put her completely at ease. He sympathized with her struggles, and he had already helped her out of several predicaments. Maybe God had divinely set all of this up—first with Donna and then through the actions of the irate customer. Perhaps He was working to bring them together for some special purpose. She would then have two delightful gifts to call her own, the adorable cuckoo clock and handsome Lance Adams.

"It's hard keeping your cool in these kinds of situations," Lance agreed. "I've already found myself dealing with interesting situations here at the store, and I only began a few days ago. But I did work at another giant store, so dealing with problems comes naturally."

"You seem at home here," Connie agreed. She wanted to add that she was glad he had switched jobs and decided to grace their humble store with his presence but kept such comments to herself. Instead, she answered his questions about church and some of the activities she was involved in. With that, Connie began sharing her yard sale experiences, deciding she might as well spill the beans about her interests. He said little about it and asked about some of the items she had purchased in the past. When she mentioned the precious cuckoo clock, Lance straightened and inquired where she bought it.

"My neighbor down the street. She's moving, so I guess she wanted to get rid of it. I did an Internet search and found that cuckoo clocks can cost several hundred to several thousand dollars. I really got a bargain."

"I guess so." Lance glanced at his watch. "Time to get back to work." He stood up and opened the door of the lounge for her.

"Thanks again for coming to my rescue," she said, then caught herself when she realized what had come out of her mouth.

"Don't mention it. If you have any other trouble, call me on my pager. That's the quickest way you can get ahold of me." He gave her his business card before striding away to greet several people. Connie glanced down at the card he gave her with his name inscribed on it. Lance Edward Adams. The name sent tingles shooting straight through her. Lance Edward Adams, her benefactor, her rescuer—the one who pledged to share her favorite pizza one day soon. She floated on a cloud of emotion to the customer service counter where Donna gave her a curious look.

"I see it's working out well," she said with a grin.

Connie squeezed the card Lance had given her. "You were right, old buddy, old pal. I'll treat you to an ice cream sundae after work. Oops, I don't have any money right now. I'll have to give you a rain check."

Donna laughed loudly, drawing the attention of several customers who again began to congregate in front of the counter, looking to bring back returns. "Connie, love will do wonders in your life."

With the warm, fuzzy feelings floating through her at that moment, Connie couldn't help agreeing.

Chapter 3

Connie found it difficult concentrating at work after the encounter with Lance, though she rarely spoke to him for the remainder of the week. The way he helped her early on, especially when confronting the irate customer, remained in the forefront of her thoughts. She'd never met a man quite like him. On occasion, her brothers would stick up for her when confronting the neighborhood bully. Louis even took a punch in the lip to ward off such an attack. But the idea of an almost perfect stranger coming to her aid gave her a feeling of worth and confidence. The incident with the customer no longer affected her when she considered how Lance supported her. And from the conversations with other employees, compassion seemed to be his trademark. Mr. Drexer must be thrilled to have someone like Lance on the management team.

At the business meetings, the head manager often encouraged the employees to act like a family and be neighborly to one another. Lance exemplified the role to a T. He was like a father, nurturing them, helping them out of difficulties that would creep up during the cycle of a normal workday. After the first week at his new job, Connie learned of at least ten different episodes where Lance was required to help a customer or an employee out of a jam. Surely he was a blessing in disguise.

Connie began a tally of the day's refunds before leaving the customer service counter to Freda, a young girl who worked the evening shift. Looking at the schedule, she was pleased to see that Freda was only working three days next week. Hopefully Connie could snag one or two of the days and make up for the money spent on the clock. She quickly jotted down her name and the hours she would work before forwarding the slip to personnel for approval. With a nod, Connie hastened to her locker to grab her purse.

"A great week so far, eh?" Donna asked with a wink.

"It started out a little strange, but yes, it's ending on a higher note."

"I was telling Lance all about you when I saw him earlier today," Donna said, taking out her own large black handbag from the locker. She rummaged for a tube of lipstick.

"You didn't."

"Of course I did. I told him how we were friends and how I knew all kinds of secrets about you." Donna traced some color on her lips before casting Connie a grin. "Just kidding. I did tell him, though, about your yard sale adventures. I must say he seemed very interested about that ridiculous clock you bought last Saturday."

"Maybe he likes antiques," Connie mused. *Wouldn't that be a catch—to find a guy who actually liked yard sales?* It seemed too good to be true. She could imagine getting together with Lance one fine Saturday morning. She would come equipped with the Saturday morning paper and the sales circled while Lance would provide the street map. Together they would drive around in his sports car searching for sales. He would follow her as she explained about the bargains to be had, even buying her a pretty vase in which to place a bouquet of red roses—

"Or maybe he likes the person who buys the antiques," Donna said, interrupting her thoughts. "He did ask why you like to buy other people's junk. I wasn't sure what to say, but he really answered his own question. He said, and this is what I loved, 'Connie must be someone who can take another person's junk and make it beautiful. It takes a special person to do that.' Isn't that just the sweetest thing you've ever heard? What a guy. If you let him go, honey, you might as well give up on life altogether."

Connie couldn't believe her ears after hearing this news. She said good-bye to Donna and headed for her car, all the while thinking about Lance's words. She wondered after Monday's mess at the customer desk, the scene with the customer, and then stories of her sales, whether Lance had already made up his mind about her. Could it be she had found her match in life and so soon? It seemed unreal. Yes, she had had a nice conversation with him, and he had said some sweet things, but they'd just met. She needed to take this one step at a time and not rush it, even if everything was looking good. Connie knew that many times what seemed right could turn out wrong. And she didn't want to be wrong about Lance Adams, even if he was turning her heart topsy-turvy at the moment.

Connie stopped at a small grocery store on her way home. With the ten-dollar bill she had found in a desk drawer last evening, she bought some apple juice on sale, corn tortillas, cheese, a bunch of bananas, a head of lettuce, and some ground beef. She hoped the meat would last all next week if she divided it up into sandwich bags to put in the freezer. At the cash register, the amount came to $10.23. Connie paled as she scrambled to search in the bottom of her purse for the coins, only coming up with a dime. Behind her, the customers were growing irate. *Doesn't anyone have an ounce of patience while waiting in line?* Finally she took off one banana from the bunch, had it reweighed, and found the amount totaled exactly ten dollars.

Red-hot with embarrassment over the incident, Connie quickly made her way to the car, setting the plastic bags on the backseat before flinging herself into the driver's seat. She resisted shedding a tear over the incident but scolded herself for buying the dumb clock. Donna was right. She had no business making a purchase she couldn't afford right now. Her parents would have a fit if they found out how she was scrimping on food this month. Papa loved the huge meals Mom always fixed. If they found out that she only had a small tortilla with cheese, meat, and lettuce for dinner each day, they would make her pack up and move home.

Connie bit her lip and started the engine. No, she must have faith in all this. God would provide. If He fed the sparrows, He would feed her. His Word promised not having to worry about food and clothing if she trusted Him. She lifted her head higher and headed home, feeling better after the incident that marred an otherwise upbeat day. Then she thought of Lance. What would he think if he found out she was as poor as a church mouse? Would he think she only liked him because of the money he made as an assistant manager? She shook her head. Lance appeared as genuine as could be, without giving a thought to another person's status—besides the fact he was a Christian with a servant's heart. She truly believed if God meant for her and Lance to be together then it would work out somehow, someway.

When she neared her home, Connie found a stranger pacing back and forth before the door of her apartment. Despite the warmth of the spring afternoon, he wore a pale brown trench coat that came past his knees, along with a dark hat. He might have been a twin of Sherlock Holmes, except he walked with a distinct limp. After a time of pacing, he slowly eased himself down to sit on her doorstep.

Connie drove past the apartment and down the street, taking a good look at the man as she did. She then paused in front of Claudia Rowe's house, the same place where she purchased the cuckoo clock, and sat behind the wheel. What should she do? Obviously the man was waiting for her. She couldn't imagine why. Maybe he was an undercover cop or detective of some sort. A chill raced through her. Could something have happened to a family member? The mere thought made her quiver with anxiety. She saw the news each night on her little portable television. Pictures of lost family members or those involved in some type of crime flashed in her brain. But the man appeared a bit too feeble to be a detective. He had a limp, after all, along with gray hair poking out the brim of the hat he wore. Then she considered that he might have been sent by the bald-headed man as retribution for the incident at the customer service counter earlier that week. Or maybe he was the man himself, wearing a disguise.

Get ahold of yourself. Remember you can do anything through Christ who strengthens you. Connie also realized that the ground beef she had bought would not last unless she got it into a refrigerator soon. Finally she turned around in the street and approached the apartment. To her relief, the man seemed to have disappeared. She thanked the Lord under her breath, parked the car, and began taking out the two plastic bags of groceries.

"Miss Ortiz."

The sound of a man's deep voice behind her made her jump. *Oh no, I'm being mugged! What should I do?* One of the bags slipped out of her hand, sending the head of lettuce rolling across the seat and onto the pavement.

"I'm sorry for startling you." His hand, clad in a black glove, slowly reached out to the road and picked up the head of lettuce.

Connie nearly cried out for help when she turned and found a craggy face peering into hers. He was only an older gentleman dressed in his trench coat. He gave her back the lettuce, torn and bruised by the encounter with the pavement.

"I'll buy you another head of lettuce," he said.

"No, no, that's all right." Her jittery hands managed to slip the lettuce back into the bag. No mugger would offer to buy her a head of lettuce. But he did know her name. Perhaps he was a detective after all. "Is there something you need?"

"Actually, yes."

Connie wondered what he could possibly want. Certainly she was no one of interest, only a humdrum store worker who had grabbed the attention of a handsome man for the first time in her life. Maybe the grocery store where she just bought the food had sent him to clarify the problem with money. But she'd cleared it up by taking away a banana, right?

"I—I don't understand what this is all about," Connie said. She walked gingerly to the door of her apartment and froze. It would be foolish to invite a stranger inside her apartment. What if he was someone of ill repute? But if she stood outside talking, the meat would go bad.

As if reading her mind, he said, "If you have groceries to put in the refrigerator, I'll wait outside. I do need to talk to you, though. It's very important."

Connie nodded meekly. Inside, she thought about the man in the trench coat waiting for her on the front doorstep and began imagining all sorts of possibilities. If this week hadn't been packed with excitement already, she was now ready to face her first inquisition by a genuine detective. She only prayed there wasn't a problem with her family. Not that her younger brothers could stay out of trouble—especially the youngest, Henry, or Enrique as Papa liked to call him. He'd already had a run-in with the law, having been caught selling marijuana.

When her parents found out about it, her mother cried and her father refused to speak to him. Papa ordered Henry out of the house. Connie tried to reach out to him with love as the Bible taught her to do. Henry refused to forgive their father for the way he had been treated. Now Connie feared perhaps Henry had delved into the drug scene again and that detectives, such as the one waiting for her outside the door, were on his trail.

She put away the groceries, went to get a glass of water, and then headed to the window to see the man still waiting for her on the doorstep. From the looks of him, he seemed ready to topple over. His fingers gripped the doorway. His legs wavered. She hastened outside where he had once more settled himself on the step. She wanted to invite him in but still felt uncertain about the whole encounter.

"I'm sure you're wondering why I'm here." The man slowly began to stand.

"Oh, please don't stand on my account. Yes," Connie said as she descended the step, then turned and faced him. "Has my brother done something wrong?"

"Your brother?" The man took off his hat, revealing sparse salt-and-pepper hair. Deep wrinkles decorated his face. The gray mustache he wore twitched back and forth.

"Yes, he was. . ." Connie could tell from the blank look on the man's face that this visit had nothing to do with her family. "Sorry. I thought you might be a detective. I'm not used to seeing a man standing in front of my apartment wearing a trench coat."

He chuckled and grasped the collar of his coat, straightening it in dignified fashion. He then took off his gloves and pocketed them. "I've been told by family that I should join the twenty-first century, but I refuse to part with my coat."

"I'm certain you've been called *Sherlock* more than once."

The man lifted his head and laughed loudly. Connie glanced around to make certain no one down the street was listening. Yet she couldn't help smiling at his hearty laughter, putting her at ease for a moment.

"The reason I came to see you is because I noticed you at the yard sale last Saturday."

Connie stared, surprised by his comment. "Oh, really."

"Yes. And you bought a cuckoo clock from Mrs. Rowe, did you not?"

Her heart began to beat rapidly. What else did he know about her? He must really be a detective or maybe a private investigator.

He went on. "I would very much like to buy the clock from you. I will pay you handsomely for it."

Buy my cuckoo clock? His statement stunned her. Connie didn't know what to say. At first she wanted to tell the man he must be mistaking her for someone else, even though she knew it was a lie. She recalled the sale and how numerous people had begun arriving just as she decided to purchase the clock. In fact, it was the onslaught of customers all headed in the direction of the priceless item that made Connie decide to buy it outright. She didn't know at the time that someone else was actually interested in it.

The man began withdrawing his checkbook. "I would very much like the clock. I collect antiques, you see. And this is a very special clock."

His insistence unnerved her. She desperately wanted to tell him to go elsewhere and find his clock, when the telltale sound of the cuckoo beckoned to her. It was the bird's chirp for the five o'clock hour. The cuckoo seemed to sing endlessly. The man paused with the checkbook in his hand, listening to the sound. Connie glanced back at her apartment and then at the man. Was that a tear she detected in the corner of his eye?

"As you can hear, I did buy the clock," Connie confirmed, "but it means a lot to me. My grandmother had one exactly like it."

"I'm sorry, but it means a great deal to me, too. That's why I'm prepared to offer you quite a bit for it." He took out a pen and clicked it open. "How does one thousand dollars sound?"

Connie stared in disbelief. One thousand dollars! Could this be real? In an instant, she saw her money problems disappear quicker than water down a drain. She could buy a whole new wardrobe and matching shoes. Her clothing had been screaming for a lift, especially with her job at the department store. Even Donna had offered to buy her a few new blouses. She claimed the red top was getting a bit old with Connie wearing it twice a week.

"I can see you're seriously thinking about it," he said. "Shall I go ahead and write you out the check now?"

His quiet persuasiveness was deafening. It proved difficult to say no. But she had already become endeared to the quaint object that cheered her during the night, when all she had was the clock to keep her company. She didn't think it would happen so soon, but she loved the old clock and what it represented. The mere thought of parting with it, especially after the great deal she had found at the yard sale, made her pause. Yes, with the money he was about to give her, she could purchase an even better clock and maybe the list of clothing Donna had once drawn up for her. If she took his offer, there would be no clock on her wall to cheer her when she stepped through the door after a busy workday.

"I'm sorry, Mr. . . ."

"Silas Westerfield." He extended his hand, which Connie shook.

"Mr. Westerfield, I'm sorry, but I've grown very partial to the clock. Like I said, it reminds me of the past—a miracle that happened, actually. I really can't part with it."

She watched the man's expectant expression fall. He put back the checkbook. "I see. So there's nothing I can do to change your mind? What if I upped the offer to twelve hundred?"

Connie shook her head, though her insides were screaming to say, *Yes!* "It means too much to me. I'm sorry."

"I see that we are very much alike, Miss Ortiz. If only you knew." He nodded his head and exhaled a long sigh. "I won't waste any more of your time." He bowed slightly and limped down the street to a taxi waiting for him on the corner. For an instant, Connie felt a wave of sadness followed by puzzlement at the man's final sentence to her. What did he mean that they were alike? Alike as in their desire to possess an old clock? Connie shook her head. If he was willing to spend twelve hundred dollars, he could certainly afford to buy another clock elsewhere. This was her possession, after all—the clock God had given to her. She was convinced of it.

Yet the man's sorrowful face was not soon forgotten, nor was the exorbitant amount of money he'd offered to buy a dusty old clock from a yard sale. She began to consider it. Could it be that she had stumbled upon a unique treasure? Or did the clock hold something else of value that only the older man knew?

Chapter 4

Y ou're crazy, girl! Absolutely crazy. Have you gone cuckoo like your clock?"
Connie was about to think she had, as she made herself a rolled corn tortilla for dinner that night. She decided to call Donna about Silas Westerfield's offer, only to have her friend literally scream at her for not taking the man's generous offer. When she first told Donna about her visitor, her friend immediately asked if she had taken the money. When Connie answered no, Donna ranted and raved.

"And for your information, the particular cuckoo I'm referring to is you," Donna added. "Is that clock connected to you so much that you can't part with it even for twelve hundred dollars?"

Connie wanted to say yes. She was connected to it far greater emotionally than any item she had ever owned, save for the little princess glass shoe from her grandmother's collection. Perhaps no one would ever understand her feelings—except for God, who was there when it all happened. One had to be in the midst of it to see how a simple thing such as a clock could bring forth a response that money couldn't buy.

In her heart, Connie felt a peace with her purchase and with keeping it out of the hands of some stranger. Silas Westerfield was a well-to-do gentleman who could afford to buy another clock. He just happened to see her buy the clock at the yard sale and wanted it for himself. No doubt if Mrs. Rowe knew how much he was willing to pay for it, she would have grabbed the clock out of Connie's hands and given it to him with a gold bow attached. Instead, Connie had snatched it up for seventy-five dollars, and now it was hers. She hoped the man would find another clock somewhere else, anywhere other than Connie's humble abode.

"I think you're making a big mistake," Donna admonished. "And I suppose you don't have any money now until payday."

"Don't worry—I'm not going to starve. God provides." *Sometimes through family,* she thought. In fact, she planned to ask her brother Louis for some money to tide her over until her paycheck arrived next week. A tortilla a day wouldn't be wise or healthy. Louis had always been protective of her when they were little, as they were the closest in age. He was making it big right now, repairing computers. But what would he say if she told him she needed the money because

141

she had spent everything in her wallet on a silly clock instead of food? He would understand, she decided. After all, Louis was there at Grandma's when it all happened.

"I don't know about that religion of yours, Connie. Seems foolish to me sometimes."

"It's actually helped me in more ways than I can say, Donna. Talk to you soon."

They said good-bye, and Connie took the final bite of her tortilla while gazing at the clock. Right now it was silent with the cuckoo bird tucked inside its little dwelling before the half hour struck and the door flipped open for the little cuckoo to announce the time. She went over to admire it. For its age, the clock was in remarkable shape. It appeared as if Mrs. Rowe hadn't used it much, if ever, and had merely kept it in the attic for the longest time, just waiting for the right time to sell it. Connie reached up to touch the smooth wood sides of the finely crafted instrument. God had divinely arranged this to be her clock of remembrance. God alone would have to bless Silas Westerfield with a clock, as He had blessed her. There was nothing else she could do.

Now she turned to her computer and e-mailed Louis, asking him if he would loan her fifty dollars. That should be enough to buy a few more groceries, pay the water bill, and leave her with money to fill the gas tank.

At that moment, the cuckoo bird appeared for its eight o'clock greeting. Connie listened, counting the eight cuckoos before the bird ducked inside. All at once, she was a mere eight years old, gazing up in wonder at her grandmother's stately cuckoo clock hanging in the living room. When Mom told her they would be visiting Grandma, she was delighted. Family relations had been strained after her mother married "a foreigner," as Grandma put it.

Connie didn't consider her father foreign, even if he was born in Guatemala and much of his family still lived there. For a long time, Grandma and Mom were not on speaking terms. Finally Mom had decided the children needed to see their grandmother. She let go of the hurt caused by the separation, and they began visiting on a regular basis. Connie was eight at the time. Louis was seven; Henry, six.

Upon arriving at Grandma's home for frequent visits, Connie immediately went to her favorite areas—like the back stairs where they liked to play hide-and-seek. Her favorite items were Grandma's princess shoe made of glass—which Connie often pretended to slip onto her tiny foot like Cinderella—a blue covered dish filled with fruited candies, and finally the cuckoo clock hanging on the living room wall. Connie used to stand under the clock and wait patiently for the bird to emerge. When it did, she would gaze at it intently until the bird went into hiding and the door snapped shut.

One summer, they decided on a lengthy visit when Papa was called away to take care of some business dealings with his family in Guatemala. They were to spend three weeks at Grandma's fascinating home. For a few days, she and her brothers roamed the large house, investigating the small rooms and the large walk-in pantry in the back, which was always cooler than the rest of the house. Inside the pantry was a long counter and enclosed shelves. Grandma always had bunches of bananas ripening on the counter and, next to the bananas, large German coffee cakes sprinkled with cinnamon sugar she had made. She called it *kuchen,* and it was delicious.

Upstairs was a huge bathroom with an old-fashioned tub supported by clawed feet. Along the wall was a little trapdoor. Connie used to open the door and peer down the dark, foreboding shaft. When she heard it was a laundry chute that sent clothes to the washing machine in the basement, she scrambled down the metal staircase and to the washer where the chute door opened to reveal clothes gathered in a heap on the cold floor.

One day, Henry dangled her dolly above the laundry chute and, with an evil grin, let it go.

"You killed my doll!" Connie screamed, looking into the chute to see her doll disappear into a deep, dark abyss. "Help! Help! Henry killed my doll."

Louis raced to find out what had happened, only to head to the basement and retrieve Connie's doll from the laundry piled up at the washing machine. After that incident, Connie made certain to hide her belongings from the mischievous Henry. He would not hesitate to drop other things down the chute if given the opportunity.

Besides the fascinating house, Grandma also liked to show off her garden. She had a green thumb, as some would put it. After Grandpa died, she continued planting and caring for the vegetable garden. Connie and her brothers went to investigate the vines of tomatoes and helped Grandma pull out a carrot or two. She admired how her grandma could do so many wonderful things, even though she lived all alone in her huge house with the awful laundry chute.

Then came the day Connie would never forget. It started normally, for the most part, except that Mom complained of a terrible headache that wouldn't go away. Suddenly Louis found her unconscious on the bathroom floor. Connie cried at the sight of her mother, unable to wake up even as she called out desperately to her. Grandma ran for the phone and dialed the rescue squad.

As they were lifting Mom's unconscious form onto a stretcher, the head EMT said she might have suffered a stroke. Connie didn't know what that was at the time, but she later learned that her mother had suffered a ruptured aneurysm in her brain. Most people died from such things.

God's hand had been upon her mother, even though Connie didn't realize it at the time. All she knew were the lonely days and nights while her mother was in the hospital in a deep sleep, as Grandma called it. A neighbor would come over and watch them while Grandma went to be with Mom. Connie never felt so alone in her life. Her pillow became wet with tears as she cried for her mother to come cuddle her. The only comfort she found during this difficult time was the cuckoo clock that she waited upon each hour. He was her friend, a cheerful interruption to the uncertainty happening around her.

Papa returned from Guatemala to be with Mom. He was the one who told them of the severity of Mom's condition. She stayed in a coma for two weeks. When she woke up without brain damage, everyone hailed it a miracle.

Connie walked over and touched the cuckoo clock she had purchased at the yard sale. She felt sorry for Silas Westerfield, that she had to decline his offer to buy the clock, but this instrument symbolized a miracle to her. Not only had her grandma's clock kept her company as a child during the most difficult time in her life, this clock reminded her of God's merciful hand in restoring her mother. She would never part with it, not for a million dollars. In her opinion, memories such as these were priceless.

She decided then to call her brother Louis. Even though she had already e-mailed him, she wanted to talk about the clock and the emotions that had surfaced this night. She managed to catch him with his mouth full of food. Thinking of him before a gigantic smorgasbord reminded her of her sparse meal and her need for a little cash to make ends meet.

"So what are you eating?" she asked.

He went into a long exhortation about the necessity of eating foods that were good for you. He had been shopping at the health food store down the road and had made himself a vegetarian meal. "Do you realize how many preservatives are in all the food we eat?" he said before taking another noisy bite.

"I had a tortilla for dinner," Connie announced.

Louis laughed. "You still eat those things? I tell you, if I even step into a Mexican restaurant, I get nauseated. That's all we ate growing up. Papa always had Mom make his favorite dishes, though at least she did manage to talk him out of having his main meal at noon like he was used to doing in Guatemala. And remember the time she forced him to eat her German food of sauerbraten and red cabbage? He turned as purple as the cabbage, if I recall."

Connie had to laugh, thankful Louis was also in the mood to take a stroll down memory lane. She glanced at her clock and told him about her purchase, along with the memories that resurfaced, such as Grandma's house and the time their mother took ill.

"I don't remember much about it," Louis confessed. "I was only seven. I remember the loud noise the rescue squad made when it came to the house.

I remember that Mom wouldn't wake up. In fact, she didn't wake up for the longest time, did she?"

"It seemed like a long time, but actually it was only two weeks. I know of others who have suffered brain injuries where it takes much longer. I just heard the other day of a man who woke up after nineteen years. Can you imagine? And his wife was still there at his bedside, waiting for him. When he had been in the car accident that put him in a coma, they were newly married."

Louis sighed over the phone. "Glad those days with Mom are long past. And I'm glad we didn't have to go through anything like nineteen years. So what do you need, Connie? I know this can't be a social call. Money?"

Connie gaped at his presumption. Was she that easy to read? She had asked Louis for money before, but the times were few and far between. "I did catch myself a little short this month after using my spending money to buy the clock. Could you spare fifty? I e-mailed you about it, but a phone call is a little more personal."

"Fifty, eh? Okay, I'll transfer some money to your account. And this time, you don't need to pay me back."

"What? Of course I do."

"No. Call it an early birthday gift."

"But my birthday isn't for three months."

"No problem. You're my sis. I'm sure I owe you for some kind of payback at one time or another in our lives."

"The only incident that comes to mind is the time you decided to float my play dishes down the creek. Remember that? I screamed at you and told you to go get them. You just stood there on the bank, watching them bob up and down, saying what cool boats they made. For all you know, I could have permanent psychological damage for not having play dishes growing up. Maybe that's why I can't make myself decent meals. I've been deprived."

Louis laughed at her joke. "Okay, then this is payback time for losing your play dishes. You can buy a new set."

Connie giggled, thinking of a set she wouldn't mind owning—the tiny china dishes decorated in rose print, enclosed in a wee picnic basket. She had seen it in a country store once. After hanging up the phone a few moments later, she felt better. Louis never failed to cheer her with his positive outlook on life. He had been successful at whatever he put his mind to, including school, college, and now his computer business. Mom and Papa were proud of him.

Now if only she had a better relationship with her other brother, Henry. He tended to be a loner. He and Louis didn't get along at all, especially after his run-ins with the law. Connie did what she could to reach out to him, but Henry was his own person and did what he pleased in life. At least she was grateful to have the open communication with Louis. She wasn't too proud to ask him for a loan now and then. And he always obliged.

Connie then thought about Silas Westerfield's offer of twelve hundred dollars that would have taken her out of this monetary slump and then some. The mere notion he wanted to give her such an exorbitant sum for a clock from a yard sale left her puzzled. Why did he want it so much? Did he know something intriguing about the clock that she didn't? He must if he was a collector of antiques. Perhaps she had stumbled upon something huge when she bought the clock and didn't even realize it.

Connie ventured over to study the timepiece. There was nothing unusual about it from what she could tell. It was in perfect working order. She didn't think it could be as valuable as he said, but it must be. She had heard stories of people who stumbled upon great treasures in attics, basements, and at yard sales. She used to watch that program on television where people would take their most treasured items and have them appraised for their value. Maybe she should take this clock to such a place and find out its true worth.

Connie shook her head. It didn't matter. Silas Westerfield seemed compliant with her request to keep the clock, and she had a treasured memory that cost but seventy-five dollars. She would be content with that, at least for now.

Connie arrived for work the next morning, tired from the nightmare that besieged her during the night. In it, Silas Westerfield showed up at her doorstep at 2:00 a.m., ordering her to give him back the clock. She could still see his gnarled face and gray eyes blazing as he waved the checkbook at her. *If you don't give me that clock, I'll make your life miserable, like sending you a dozen angry customers to mob your service desk!* From beneath the folds of his huge trench coat came a parade of angry customers, all waving merchandise and demanding that Mr. Drexer fire her and toss her into the street to become a helpless beggar.

"Hello out there!" hailed a friendly voice.

Connie whirled and caught her elbow on the corner of the desk. Pain shot through her arm. "Ouch!"

"Are you okay?" The calm face and dark brown eyes of Lance Adams stared into hers.

"Y–yeah. Just not quite awake." She nearly told him about the escapade at the grocery store, the corn tortilla for dinner, and the man with the trench coat who wanted her precious clock. Likely after all the stories, he would recommend commitment to some insane asylum. Instead, she fumbled in the drawer for slips of paper and pens to start the day.

"You look like something's bothering you."

"I didn't sleep very well last night." Besides the dream, her stomach kept her up with cries for nourishment. The corn tortilla for dinner hadn't lasted long. Finally, in the middle of the night, Connie made herself a lettuce salad to tide her over until breakfast. She planned to make another trip to the grocery store after work for more substantial food purchases. Before she left that morning, she checked her banking account on-line and found that Louis had transferred the fifty dollars. She thanked God for the generosity of her brother. Now she could buy good stuff, like some delectable apple crumb muffins.

"So did you decide to sell him the clock?" Donna asked, bopping up behind the desk.

Connie cringed, wishing Donna hadn't brought up the subject of the clock in front of Lance. "No. I told you I wouldn't sell it for a million dollars." Connie tried to look busy in the hopes this would blow over.

"Mr. Adams, did you hear what happened?" Donna now inquired of Lance. When he shook his head, Donna launched right into the tale without giving a thought as to how Connie might feel. "And this elderly man comes to her door, asking to buy the clock for twelve hundred dollars. Can you imagine? Twelve hundred for a clock that only cost—how much did you pay for it at the yard sale, Connie?"

Connie pretended not to hear her until Donna stepped up and nearly shouted the question in her ear.

"Seventy-five," she said in a low voice.

Lance raised his eyebrow. "Really. He must want it very badly."

"I'll say. And knowing how poor Connie is, I would have jumped at the chance. I mean, she complains she doesn't have money to fill her gas tank; then this man pops up at her front doorstep offering her cold, hard cash. I don't understand why she wouldn't take it."

Connie felt her face begin to heat up. Now Lance knew her financial situation along with the clock episode. If only she could put a cork in Donna's mouth. But when would that ever stop her? She rattled on about it for another five minutes and even turned to several of the cashiers who had come up, telling them the tale of the man in the trench coat who wanted Connie's clock for "twelve hundred smackeroos."

"This must be some clock," Sally said, staring at Connie with a look that made her all the more uncomfortable. "Can I come see it after work, Connie?"

"It's just a cuckoo clock."

"Does it really work?"

"Of course."

A crowd of employees now gathered around the customer service counter, giving their opinions as to whether they would have accepted a twelve-hundred-dollar check for a clock that cost seventy-five. The majority agreed they would have jumped at the chance. Only a few believed that a high-priced antique was worth holding on to. The battle intrigued Connie. At first she wanted to sweep the encounter under the rug, but the employees' enthusiasm proved infectious. "I guess it must be a unique clock," she agreed. "Maybe I should give tours." *That would be one way to get myself out of a financial pinch. Charge a five-dollar admission fee for a glimpse of the mysterious cuckoo clock.*

"Great!" Sally exclaimed. "When can we have a tour?"

"Yes, yes!" others clamored. "When will you let us come see it?"

Connie observed the assortment of eager faces, each one wishing to see her famous clock. Maybe she shouldn't let the opportunity slip her by. How often she thought about reaching out to coworkers with the saving message of the gospel but could never quite find a way to do it. Now she had the opportunity of showing them the clock God had provided and sharing the miracle of her mother's recovery from an aneurysm. Perhaps God might use the clock to bring people closer to Him.

"Let's have a luncheon on Saturday," she decided. "I'm off that day. And those of you who aren't off, maybe you can stop by on your break and join us."

Everyone pounced on the idea of a get-together. They all talked at once about having lunch and seeing the infamous clock. Connie tore off a sheet of yellow paper from a legal pad and had people sign up to bring a dish to share. She bubbled over with excitement at the thought of this luncheon turning into an outreach of sorts. When the others had left to perform their duties, Lance stepped up.

"Guess you do know how to gather a crowd," he observed. "And it just so happens, I have Saturday off."

Connie glanced at him while trying to contain the glee welling up within her. Not only was there the opportunity of an outreach to the other employees, but Lance Adams planned on gracing the event, as well. "Great! How about signing up to bring something?"

"I don't cook, so how does a bottle of soda sound?"

Connie giggled and scribbled down his name along with the item he volunteered to bring. "Maybe you can make it two bottles. Or a bottle of soda and a gallon of spring water." She tapped a pen on the counter in thought. "I'll need paper plates and cups. Disposable forks. Napkins."

"If you need me to bring anything else, just let me know. I know you're short on cash."

The joy of the event quickly soured at his knowledge of her tight finances. "I'm fine," she said swiftly. "God provides."

"I agree He does, and sometimes He provides through the giving of others. So if you need anything, please call. And if you don't, I'll get mighty upset."

Lance wandered off toward the management offices, leaving Connie with her yellow sheet of paper and warmth that invaded her heart. *Dear God, I'm so glad You brought the cuckoo clock into my life! Look at the blessing it's bringing. Now everyone is coming over for a lunch—including the star of the show, Lance Adams.* If this was any indication of what might lie ahead, Connie decided the clock was the best investment she'd ever made.

Chapter 5

Connie bustled around her apartment, readying everything for the luncheon at noon that would bring several friends from work along with her special guest, Lance Adams. She smoothed the rumpled fabric of the old sofa that once stood in Grandma's living room, straightened out the magazine rack, and took up a feather duster to give Mr. Cuckoo a shine. So far the bird had been doing his thing all morning and right on schedule, much to her delight. The piece appeared proud and majestic, hanging on the wall of the living room, ready for the array of curious onlookers.

She wondered what Lance would think of her home. As an executive, he must live in a fine place with new furniture and high-tech equipment. Actually, she knew very little about him, even if he did know everything about her—courtesy of Donna. The idea made her feel miffed. At times she wished Donna would stay out of her life but knew that attitude wouldn't be in keeping with her Christianity. Somehow Connie envisioned the opportunity of reaching Donna with the gospel message. Instead, she found her friend's ways grating on her nerves. Maybe God was using Donna to do a little refining in her own heart—to have patience and seek peace no matter what circumstances might come her way.

Connie set to work making up one of her grandmother's recipes on her father's side, a dish of stuffed tortillas with black beans for lunch. She only recalled meeting her foreign relatives twice in her life. Both times, they came to the house for Christmas when Connie was young. Her *abuelita*, as her paternal grandmother was known, couldn't speak a word of English. Connie found herself unable to communicate at all except for a few words of Spanish she picked up from her father. Papa's two brothers who also came spoke broken English, and her *abuelito*, or grandfather, said nothing but merely stared into space. Somehow Connie never felt much of a connection to her father's side of the family. Perhaps she ought to consider changing that somehow, maybe even by joining one of those mission trips to Guatemala. That would be a good way to see her relatives.

Now Connie considered the luncheon and what she would say about the clock. She didn't want to preach, but she did want them to know the miracles God had worked in her family. She hoped her hospitality skills would help make Lance feel welcome. Thankfully, with Louis's money, she was able to purchase items for the luncheon like matching paper plates, cups, and napkins.

Perhaps it was in her blood to throw a nice gathering for others. Papa loved to throw gatherings for people from his workplace. Often he had associates come to their home where he cooked up food native to Guatemala. The house would be filled with the scent of corn, cilantro, and onions. The guests would all laugh and share stories, to the wide eyes of her and her brothers who only stared at the assortment of people gathered around the table. Sometimes the guests would give them presents. Connie still had the small furry monkey a guest had given to her during one of Papa's dinners. She wondered if Lance might bring her a present. *You're crazy, girl. Just crazy.* Lance appeared the dignified type, not the fuzzy kind that would give a lady stuffed animals and boxes of chocolates.

The doorbell rang. Connie looked up at the clock to find there were still fifteen minutes to go before the guests were scheduled to arrive. Who could be here so early? She checked between the blinds to find Lance standing there. She might have guessed it would be him. It seemed his character, though most men were usually late, as her brothers often were. Many times her mother yelled at Louis and Henry to hurry up. She opened the door to find Lance holding a gift bag.

"I figured I would come a little early and see if you needed help setting up."

What a gentleman, she thought in admiration. He then presented her with the bag. "Just a little something."

Connie turned to one side, trying to conceal her flushing face from his gaze. She took the bag and opened it to find a small stuffed bird.

"The tag says it's a cuckoo bird. He's called Clarence."

"Clarence the cuckoo," she said with a laugh. So Lance was indeed the stuffed-animal, chocolate-bonbon type, after all. "Thank you very much." She proudly displayed Clarence on the antique table in the foyer.

"Looks like you have everything ready." He nodded, staring at the matching cups, plates, and napkins, along with a small centerpiece of flowers. "Is there anything I need to do?"

Connie shook her head. "Just make yourself at home."

"Oops, forgot the drinks in the car. Be right back." He made a mad dash to his vehicle parked out front. Connie peeked out the window to see that he drove a navy blue compact car that sparkled in the rays of sunlight. She could tell from the looks of the car that he liked things to be clean and neat. She was grateful she had spent extra time earlier that morning dusting and straightening her humble abode. She didn't want him thinking she was messy, especially after what happened at the customer service counter the first day they met. The vision of the candy wrappers and spilled soda on the floor still made her cringe.

Lance returned with a bottle of soda and a container of spring water. He followed her into the kitchen where she placed the drinks inside the fridge to chill. "You eat sparse," he noted, scanning the empty shelves.

Connie had forgotten about her meager food supply. The shelves were bare but for the few items she had purchased the other day. He looked at her as if remembering Donna's discussion of her financial situation. *He probably thinks I go to the neighborhood soup kitchen for my meals.* "I don't eat very much."

"Maybe we should think about a cost of living raise at the store," he said as though thinking out loud. "I'll have to check into it."

If only Donna hadn't said anything about my money troubles. But a raise would be nice, she had to admit. Keeping up with the rent, plus utilities, car bill, and food did take every penny out of her check. She refused to say anything one way or the other but allowed him to mull over the idea.

Just then the doorbell rang. The other employees from the store had arrived, carrying delectable luncheon entrees while chattering away. It didn't take long for the small apartment to feel crowded, yet Connie was glad for the companionship. How often she had envisioned coordinating a get-together for the employees but never quite knew how to go about it. Now, thanks to a fortunate purchase at a yard sale, everything had come together. She directed them to the kitchen where they set down their food items on the counter.

All at once, Mr. Cuckoo came forth for his noontime serenade. Her coworkers rushed to the living room to watch the bird perform. The noise continued for some time until the bird suddenly disappeared behind the tiny trapdoor.

"How sweet!" Sally exclaimed in glee. "I absolutely love it! I can see now why you want to hold on to it, Connie. What a wonderful find."

"Yes, but you can get that model of clock anywhere," Donna interjected. "I looked it up on the Internet myself. In fact, it only sells for a few hundred dollars at most, depending on what it does and how often you need to wind it. It's not as elaborate as some of them, which can cost over a thousand. So I say if someone wants this clock that badly and for twelve hundred dollars, let him have it. For two hundred bucks, you can get a clock almost exactly like it and pocket the rest of the cash."

Anger began stirring within Connie, and the guests had only been there ten minutes. She ushered them to the small dining area, hoping to avoid a major confrontation between her and Donna. She didn't want to debate money or anything else. She knew if she said anything, the emotion it raised might squelch whatever God wanted to do among her guests. She showed them the food and encouraged them to help themselves. Everyone obliged, taking paper plates and dishing up the food. Several mentioned how delicious Connie's tortillas were, including Lance.

"This is great," he told her, "but I thought you didn't like Mexican food."

"This is a special recipe from Guatemala, not Mexico. And I do eat Spanish food. The same as I'm sure you eat roast beef, even though you've probably had it every Sunday while you were growing up."

Lance looked at her in surprise. "How did you know that?"

"You seem like a person raised on meat and potatoes."

"Yep, an all-American guy," he added with a wink.

To Connie's disappointment, he took a seat at the other end of the table and began engaging Sally in conversation. She had hoped he might want to sit with her after the encouraging meetings the past few days. Instead, Donna sat beside her and again voiced her opinion about the clock and the way Connie had mismanaged the wealthy gentleman who came calling. Her teeth began to grind in agitation. Tension filled her muscles. If only there was some polite way to tell Donna to lay off the whole scene with Silas Westerfield. Finally Connie managed to change the subject by sharing with others why she kept the clock. The table grew silent as they heard of Connie's mother and how a cuckoo clock had kept her company at her grandmother's home while her mother lay in a coma at the hospital.

"That's awful," Sally said in sympathy. "I can see now why money can't replace something like that."

"But it isn't the same clock as your grandma's," Donna pointed out. "You could get any other cuckoo clock, and it would still serve the same purpose."

"Perhaps, but this clock looks very similar to my grandmother's," Connie answered in defense. "And I know all about those clocks you're mentioning. They're half the size of this one and with all kinds of newfangled modifications. This is an older version, and one I will treasure. So can we just let it go?"

Donna sat back in her seat with a stunned expression on her face. Connie began clearing the plates and brought out the dessert. Looking around the table at the assortment of thoughtful faces, she hoped the exchange between her and Donna hadn't chilled the meeting.

Suddenly she noticed Lance missing from the group. She peeked around the corner and found him in the living room, staring at the clock in obvious fascination. When she called him to come have dessert, he whirled and returned to the table without saying a word. The rest of her guests began discussing sports, movies they had seen, and other items of interest in their lives. After some time passed, several of them bid Connie farewell as they needed to return to work. Donna and Sally hung out awhile longer, talking about the yard sales they had been to and some of the bargains they had discovered. When they were ready to leave for the spring sales at the mall, Donna looked back at Connie as if ready to give her another opinion. She then tossed her head, thanked her for arranging the lunch, and took off with Sally. Connie tried hard not to take offense by what had happened, but sometimes she wondered if it was wise having Donna as a friend.

Connie returned to the living room and again found Lance staring at her clock. He stood in a thoughtful pose with his hands tucked into the pockets of his trousers, gazing up at it as she often had. He seemed mesmerized by the piece. Maybe like her, he had seen a similar clock in his youth. Or perhaps the memories she shared about her mother had affected him in some way. She wanted to ask him about it, when suddenly he reached up and began taking the instrument off the wall hanger.

At once, Connie came forward. "Is something wrong?"

He jerked around, his hands trembling, nearly losing his grip on the piece. Connie gasped, praying he wouldn't drop it. "No, no. I was just looking is all." He slowly returned the clock to its proper resting place. "Where did you say you got it?"

"A neighbor down the street from me. Claudia Rowe."

"Claudia Rowe," he repeated, still gazing at the clock. "And she sold it to you for seventy-five dollars?"

"Yes."

"It's in excellent condition. Where did she keep it?"

"A box in the attic, or so she told me. I don't think she ever had it out—or at least not for very long. I saw no scratches on it, wear and tear, or anything. Except for the dust, it looked practically brand-new."

"Sad she never had it displayed."

Connie looked at him, puzzled. "Why? That means I got a great deal on a clock in mint condition. She wanted to get rid of it anyway. She's moving. I guess she had too much clutter."

"So that's why she had the sale?"

Connie nodded. "She already sold the house. More than likely, she will leave by the time summer rolls around. I hope she has another yard sale, though. I would love to see if she has anything else stored up there in the attic."

Lance said nothing but only continued to stare at the clock. "So you wouldn't consider parting with it, would you?"

"Huh? Don't tell me you want it, too?"

"Not for me, but I was thinking if that man wanted it—"

"As I said earlier, the clock means a lot to me."

"Yes, but maybe it means a lot to others, as well. And certainly you could use the money, right?"

Connie gaped before turning away. It seemed Donna had hoodwinked Lance into trying to make her give up the clock for a fat check. This was becoming more aggravating by the minute. "I really think this is my problem. I know you may be the manager-in-training, but that doesn't mean I can't make my own decisions."

"I just want you to consider all the angles here. I can tell the clock means a great deal to you because of the past. But like Donna said, there are other clocks in this world."

"Yes, and there are other clocks for antique hunters, as well. And despite what Donna said, I don't need the money that badly. The memory of how God saved my mother is more important to me than whether I have filet mignon for dinner." She turned away and marched back to the kitchen. Why was everyone fighting with her over this clock? Didn't any of her words at the table matter to them? Here she had tried to use the clock as a means of sharing God's blessing, and now everyone wanted to talk her out of keeping it. Could they be so callous as to think that money means more than memories?

Her aggravation soon turned into anger. She shook her head when Lance offered to help with the cleanup. He was in the same category as Donna as far as she was concerned. Maybe it would be better for him to make a move on Donna instead. They both operated on the same wavelength when it came to getting ahead in the world.

Lance remained in the kitchen, even after she'd refused his help. "Connie, I don't want you angry over this. I only think you need to consider other points of view besides your own. That's why the Bible says there's wisdom in a multitude of counselors."

Connie snorted at the thought of either Donna or him as counselors. Right now they were both bothersome gnats flying around in her face. "There are millions of clocks in the world. Let Mr. Westerfield and others find some at yard sales."

"That's what I'm trying to say, Connie. There are millions of clocks for you to choose from, also. Maybe you should let the man have it, and you find something else when the time and money is right."

She must've had a horrible look on her face, for he quickly backpedaled, offered a hasty good-bye, and headed for the door.

Connie inhaled a deep breath to calm herself. Why was this happening to her? After cleaning up, she plopped down on the sofa to stare at the clock. Why, out of all the clocks in this world, did this one have to mean so much to Silas Westerfield? And now even strangers were going to bat for him. She tried to consider this from the older man's viewpoint but couldn't. The man was obviously a dealer who found something at a yard sale that caught his eye, and she had snatched it away. Wasn't there a saying for such things? Finders keepers, losers weepers?

She sat mulling over it all—Silas Westerfield, Donna, and finally Lance. She was certain Lance entered his opinion out of a concern for her financial status. He had seen the empty fridge. He thought it would do her wallet good to sell the clock and look for another. He wanted what was best for her. Perhaps the conversation showed that Lance truly cared about her.

Connie gazed at her purchase. Little did he realize, but what was best for her right now was this clock. It brought her companionship and a wealth of fond memories from days gone by. If only she didn't feel so troubled. Instead of joy, she now wrestled with confusion. *God,* she prayed, *help me sort this all out, somehow, someway.*

Chapter 6

Over the next few weeks, little was said at work about the clock. It was as if the cuckoo had been a passing fancy and now everyone's attention returned to their daily lives. Connie was glad things had quieted down. The clock still remained the focal point in Connie's apartment, especially on her days off when Mr. Cuckoo faithfully announced the time every half hour. The rhythmic ticking assisted her when mopping the floor or even cleaning out a corner cupboard where she had put away old cards received over the years. Searching through them one day, she found a couple from her grandmother, etched out in her stately writing. These cards were worth their weight in gold.

To her surprise, tucked away inside one card, she found the recipe for kuchen, the famous German coffee cake that Grandma always made when they came visiting. She gasped when she saw it, having forgotten that Grandma sent her the recipe in the hope that the tradition would be carried on within the family. Scanning it, Connie decided to splurge a bit with the paycheck she had recently received and buy the ingredients to make a few cakes. No doubt the employees would love the baked treats when they came into work the next morning. She could just imagine the exclamations as they cut healthy wedges of the coffee cake to accompany the morning coffee, brewed strong the way Donna always made it.

Connie began assembling the ingredients after a quick trip to the grocery store. While waiting for the milk to scald in the saucepan, she reflected on the luncheon at her home and Lance as he walked about examining everything, especially the cuckoo clock. For days afterward, she analyzed the comments he had made. At church last Sunday, he appeared rather aloof, offering her a pleasant good morning but otherwise ignoring her. At work, she hoped for a few clues as to why he was so emphatic that she accept the older man's offer. He said nothing about it. It didn't matter anyway. By now, Mr. Westerfield likely had located a different antique clock to satisfy his need. Still, she wished she knew the motivation behind Lance's insistence. If he did care about her, as she hoped, then she prayed he would understand her need to keep the clock.

Bubbles began appearing on the milk's surface when Connie removed the pan to a trivet to let it cool. What a pleasant way to spend the day—in the kitchen with her hands immersed in fragrant dough, working to make her grandmother's beloved recipe, with the cuckoo chiming in the background. There was nothing better except perhaps an outing with Lance, if he ever offered one. At one time, he did suggest they go out for gourmet pizza. Connie figured he'd forgotten about the invitation. Either that, or he'd found someone better to dine with than a woman who loved memories more than money. She began adding ingredients to the warm milk in the bowl until a soft dough formed. The pleasant aroma of yeast was more soothing than a cup of hot tea.

Before long, the dough had risen beautifully, with the help of a trick she learned from a cooking show—placing the mixture in a warm oven with a small pan of water on a separate rack. Parceling out the dough into four pans and drizzling each with butter, cinnamon, and sugar, she placed the pans back into the warm oven to rise one last time.

Grandma would be proud of her if she were alive. She would laugh and talk about her days as a young girl when she lived on the farm. Connie wished she were still alive. How she would love to share about what was happening in her life right now—and especially after buying the clock. *At least there's a little of you here, Grandma, even if you aren't alive to see it.* When Connie removed the crusty brown treats some time later, she stared at her creations in approval before snapping pictures on the camera. *Just wait until I tell my brother Louis that I made kuchen,* she thought proudly.

At work the next day, Connie juggled the bread, along with her purse, while struggling to open the door that led to the employee lounge. Suddenly a familiar face peered into hers as his hand reached out to open the door.

"What's that?" he inquired.

Connie looked up into the face of Lance Adams who helped her with the breads she had brought, carrying two of them to the table.

"It's something I made," Connie said breathlessly, placing the baked goods near the coffee and cups. Several employees gathered around to stare at the treats like puppies with their tongues hanging out.

"Coffee cake!" Sally exclaimed.

"No, it's kuchen," Connie corrected. "I made it."

"Wow." Everyone looked at her in appreciation. Connie brought out a knife from inside her purse and cut the bread into wedges, then served them on paper napkins.

"This is fantastic," Sally said. "Can you get me the recipe?"

"It takes a long time to make," Connie confessed. "It's like a yeast bread."

"So you can't make it in a bread machine?"

"Oh no. You have to make this the old-fashioned way, like my grandma used to do. It's a German coffee cake."

Lance had already eaten one piece and was cutting himself a second. "This is really great, Connie," he said in appreciation. "You're a woman of many talents."

"Well, not really."

"Of course you are." He acknowledged the swarm of employees who descended on the lounge when word spread of home-baked treats waiting for them. "You know how to bring everyone together. You have a gift for hospitality, which is really needed nowadays. Everyone seems so busy all the time. They tend to forget the number two rule of loving your neighbor. But you certainly haven't."

Connie was glad to see Lance talking to her again. She figured he was still upset over the way she'd spoken to him at the luncheon. Instead, he made a few more encouraging remarks, including how great the bread tasted and if he could also have the recipe to send to his mother back home. "She likes to make fancy breads," he added.

"Sure. I'd be glad to write it out." *Guess you scored big-time with Lance, Connie ol' girl, even if the conversation at the luncheon didn't go so well.* She enjoyed the warm fuzzy feeling floating around inside her. With the clock but a distant memory, perhaps everything would get back on track in their newfound relationship. The outlook improved all the more when Lance asked her to go over some ideas with him before the store opened for business that morning.

She followed him to his office, thinking how nice he looked for his job. He was impeccably dressed in fancy pressed trousers and a navy blue shirt. The navy blue solid-colored tie he wore matched the shirt to a tee. Connie loved seeing a man dressed in solid colors and often bought Louis shirts with matching ties for Christmas.

"Come on in."

Connie entered the small office to find a rubber plant decorating a corner and a desk filled with mementos. Several pictures graced the windowsill including, to Connie's dismay, several portraits of women.

"Have a seat," he offered. "I just wanted to tell you first off that I appreciate the many ways you've been bringing the employees together."

Connie sat back in her seat, surprised by this statement.

"I wasn't kidding when I said you have a gift for hospitality. As it is, I've been trying to think of ways to have the employees interact. I'd like to have us more like family, working together to run this store. And I'd like you to think about heading up a hospitality committee."

"A hospitality committee?"

"You know, come up with ways to bring the employees together. I know in other companies there are business softball leagues, company picnics, that sort of thing. Would you be interested in heading up such a committee?"

His dark brown eyes leveled directly on hers. Her heart skipped a beat. "I guess so, if I can find people to help me with it. I'm sure Donna would jump at it."

"That's a good idea. I don't expect you to do this all on your own. We need each other to make things work."

Connie began fiddling with her watch, sliding it around on her wrist. "Sure, okay."

Lance smiled. "Good. I knew I could rely on you, Connie. So—" He began pushing papers around on his desk. "How's that infamous clock of yours?"

Connie stared, unable to believe he had brought up the subject out of thin air. If he was going to ask her again to sell the clock to the elderly man, she might tell him to find someone else to run the hospitality committee. "It's working fine, if that's what you mean."

"You still don't plan to part with it?"

"No, I don't. I'm sure the man has already found another clock." Uneasiness swept over her. Yes, she would do just about anything else for Lance Adams, like helping with his committee, but she would not sell her clock. "By the way, I do have something I want to discuss."

He perked up as if he couldn't wait to hear it. When she launched into questions about the new policy of drawing up money orders at the customer service counter, he frowned. Surely he didn't mean to discuss the clock more? She tried hard not to read into his nonverbal reaction but couldn't help the confusion that began to build. How she wished she could make him understand where she was coming from. Like the kuchen recipe and the princess glass slipper, the clock was a part of her past and would remain in the present to bring joy to her and others. Maybe if she could convince him that it was her witnessing tool of sorts, a reminder of God's miracle in preserving her mother's life, maybe then he wouldn't worry about the elderly antique dealer or her monetary situation.

The meeting promptly ended without another mention of the clock, to Connie's relief. But she couldn't help noticing that Lance's gaze followed her out the door, and with it, an obvious disappointment over the decision she had made. Well, it was not his choice. It was hers and God's. And right now, she felt completely comfortable with it.

⁂

Connie left work that day with mixed feelings. While she liked Lance and thought him handsome, to boot, his preoccupation with her cuckoo clock irritated her to no end. *I guess he assumed I would take his advice since he's the assistant manager,* she thought, pulling into a gas station. The action of filling the tank and paying the cashier reminded her of everyone's solution to her financial situation—selling the clock. Thankfully, at this point, she was doing fine. After careful budgeting and the money from Louis, she was in the clear for the rest of the month and then some. She even had a bit left over, perhaps to do a bit more browsing at some yard sales this coming weekend. She still needed to locate that rocking chair for Sally, who'd mentioned it to her on lunch break earlier that day.

Connie continued on until she spied an older man limping along the sidewalk, trying to manage two sacks of heavy groceries. In an instant, she pulled over to the side. Normally she would never consider picking up a stray person off the street, but the man appeared harmless and in need. "Do you need a ride?"

"I was going to wait for the Connector there at the corner," he said, mentioning the transit service in town.

"Where do you live? Maybe I can take you there."

He paused as if to consider the offer, then said, "Blue Ridge Avenue."

"That's not far from where I live." Connie opened the trunk, came around, and loaded the two sacks. Seeing the multitude of heavy cans in one of the bags, she wondered how the man managed such a load this far from the store.

"You're very kind," he added, gingerly settling into the front seat. "I believe we've met before."

Connie blinked. She didn't think she had ever seen him before, until she recalled the man in the trench coat waiting for her at the door. He did appear familiar with his characteristic limp, though this man wore a cardigan sweater. "Have we?" She took off down the street.

"Yes, we have met," he concurred. "Several weeks ago. I offered you money for a cuckoo clock."

At this, Connie felt the red flush entering her cheeks. *Oh no! Why out of all the elderly men in the world did I have to pick up him?* "Oh, really?" she managed to say.

"Of course you must remember that. I was waiting by your front doorstep. I suppose it was a little bit presumptuous of me to be waiting there, expecting you to hand your clock over to some stranger."

Connie said nothing, though inwardly she agreed with him.

"Although I must say I'm particularly fond of antiques. And that clock has sentimental value. Worth the cost and more."

"I know."

He looked over at her, puzzled.

"It means a great deal to me, too. My grandmother owned a clock exactly like it."

"I see."

"And I stayed with her during a particularly hard time in my life. I was only a little girl, and to have your mother near death in the hospital, it brings about feelings that are very hard to describe. Feelings of loneliness, of emptiness, wondering if anyone will love you and take care of you."

"So you stayed with your grandmother while your mother was ill?"

Connie nodded, surprised by the tears that erupted in her eyes. She flicked them away to concentrate on the road before her. "Yes. The clock helped keep my mind off my mother. She did get better, which I was thankful for. I felt that God had given me the clock to remind me of the time He'd blessed my family."

"I see," the man said again. "So there's no possible way you would reconsider. Even if I offered you more than I offered before?"

Connie noticed the determined look he wore on his face. Even after sharing her innermost secret, the man was not swayed. Why was the clock worth that much in his eyes?

"I'm sorry, but I have no interest in selling. I hope you understand." She drove up Blue Ridge Avenue. "Which house is it?"

"The brick one, just up there." When the car stopped in front, the man thanked her and began removing his wallet.

"You don't need to pay me for the ride."

"Well then, thank you. You've been very kind."

Connie went to retrieve the groceries. "I'm sorry about the clock, but I had hoped you might find another one."

"I wish I could," he said sadly, taking the bags from her. "But there's only one like it in the world. Good day."

Connie watched the man walk gingerly to his home, pondering his words. What did he mean, there was only one like it in the world? Could the clock really be that valuable? Now she couldn't wait to go home and look at it. Maybe she had actually stumbled upon something of tremendous worth and didn't even know it. Only an antique dealer, with an eye for such things, would know the value of the clock. The mere idea it might be worth thousands intrigued her.

She came home in time to see the cuckoo bird emerge for the five o'clock round of chirping. She took the clock off the wall and examined it. What untold mysteries surrounded this timepiece? It wasn't like that clay box a curator once found that supposedly held the bones of Jesus' brother in it. But there must be something of intrinsic value to have the man pursue it, enough for him to claim there was only one like it in the world. To Connie's eyes, it was only an old cuckoo with a pleasing sound that rekindled childhood memories. But he spoke of it as an object of great worth.

Connie held the clock tight in her arms. "If that's true, Mr. Cuckoo, then I would be a fool to let you go."

Chapter 7

Connie awoke the next morning feeling worse than she had in weeks. A tension headache teased her, along with a sour feeling that stemmed from her circumstances. Ever since the meeting with Silas Westerfield, she sensed the peace of God leave her. She couldn't imagine why. Many times over the course of her life, she felt God's displeasure with her decisions, and last night was the latest example. She still believed her intentions were good as far as the clock was concerned, but the older man's unmistakable sadness, along with his strange comments, raised a three-pronged battle of wills within her. One side questioned the idea of selling a clock that meant everything to her, simply to fulfill the desire of some antique dealer. It parleyed with the side that felt she should be willing to let go of the clock if God desired it. Yet another wondered whether the clock did have more of an intrinsic value than she was led to believe. After all, Silas Westerfield did say there was only one like it in the world. The whole situation left her feeling anxious and upset. At work, she found herself snapping at the customers, especially at a lady who couldn't find her sales receipt.

"I'm sure I had it. I might have dropped it outside the door while trying to get my baby into the car seat."

Connie nearly growled. "I'm sorry, but we can only give refunds with a dated sales receipt." Her fingers felt for the pain throbbing at her temples.

"Can you make an exception just this once?"

No one makes exceptions for me, she thought. "I can give you a direct exchange if you don't have a receipt." The pain in her head mounted with each passing moment.

"But I can't use this toy. It's too small for her, and she could choke." On and on she went, claiming how she could use the money for other purchases that needed to be made. For all Connie knew, the woman had been given the item as a gift and was looking to make an easy buck. She continued to refuse the customer a refund until Lance suddenly appeared.

"Trouble, ma'am?" he inquired in his friendliest voice.

The customer explained the circumstances, all the while casting Connie a vicious look. Lance came around beside Connie, opened the cash register drawer, and gave the customer her refund. The humiliation of it all irked Connie to no

163

end, especially the smile Lance gave to the woman. Didn't he realize he may have just been duped?

"I was only adhering to company policy, Mr. Adams," Connie told him tersely, shoving the cash drawer closed with a resounding thud. "For all you know, that lady didn't even purchase the item here. She was just looking to make some easy money."

"Maybe so, but I want to keep customers, not drive them away. So what's the matter? You aren't yourself at all."

Connie nearly told him about her run-in with Silas Westerfield but kept it buried within. If she did, no doubt he would hound her once more about giving up the clock. Instead, she looked away and helped another customer with a return item. During her morning break, Connie plunked herself onto the couch inside the lounge, wondering why she felt the way she did. The headache was driving her crazy, too.

Just then Lance appeared in the lounge to pour himself a cup of coffee. Connie wondered why management didn't have its own coffee for the offices. He added cream and sugar, slowly stirring the concoction together before his gaze settled on her.

"So what's going on, Connie?"

"Nothing. Have you ever had a bad day?"

"Plenty. But I don't think you're having a bad day here, are you?"

"Not here. It's just that my life seems to be going badly right now."

His facial features softened. "How so?"

"You would think it's silly. You're a guy. You wouldn't understand things like this."

"On the contrary, I have sisters. I understand more than you think."

"Really? How many?"

"Four. They're all older and married. I have four nieces and five nephews with number ten on the way. They have to remind me when their birthdays are. Too many to keep track of. And of course all my sisters are wondering when they're going to help plan their kid brother's wedding. In other words, they think I ought to get a move on."

Connie couldn't help marveling at the idea of Lance surrounded by women. That explained the pictures she saw in his office and the soft touch he had with everyone. No doubt older sisters were beneficial in his understanding of the female mind. How Connie wished she had sisters to confide in about her difficulties. Brothers had little sympathy for such things. They were creatures of fact, not emotion. "That's funny, because I have two younger brothers."

Lance chuckled. "So then you must understand the male mind."

"You mean, do I understand the colors of black and white, straightforwardness, without the emotional mushy stuff that gets in the way of the real facts?

Yes, I suppose I do."

"At our house, it was one big emotional party. Either the crying party or the happy-go-lucky, stay-up-all-night-and-chitchat party. I would have to go to Dad for a little male input at times." He cracked a grin and took a sip of his coffee. "Anyway, since I do have a little experience in dealing with women's problems, perhaps you can clue me in on yours. Unless it's personal or something, then I'll have to leave it alone."

"No, it's not personal. More spiritual, I guess. Honestly, I don't even know what the trouble is." Her hand supported her chin as she paused in thought. "All I know is that I woke up with a weird feeling inside, like the peace of God just zoomed out of me overnight."

"Any particular reason?"

Connie refused to elaborate on the possible cause. She only said that things had been a little tight, and she found herself wishing that life could be easier to handle.

"We all go through that. The good old trials and tribulations. But God's Word is clear. 'Be of good cheer, I have overcome the world.'"

"I think it's more a matter of knowing His will," Connie said. "I have trials at times, but sometimes I think they come about because I don't know what He wants me to do."

"Have you asked Him?"

Connie straightened in her seat. The answer was so obvious she nearly gasped. "Asked Him? You mean pray?" When he nodded, she turned away before he could see her trademark flush creep into her cheeks. "I guess I haven't prayed about things like I should. I mean, I do pray, but not consistently and certainly not about this situation since it blew up."

"One thing I've learned is that God is interested in everything we do in our lives. He wants to be involved. He wants to carry our burdens. But He can't do it if you don't allow Him to. And the way you allow Him is to put your cares on the altar of prayer. After that, He can tell you what to do—whether by the Bible; His still, quiet voice; or by way of other believers."

Lance spoke so matter-of-factly it was as if he had revealed the most common truth in the world, yet the words themselves were powerful. Of course as a Christian, Connie knew the necessity of prayer. Sometimes the situation clouded over her responsibility to seek peace and pursue it. Even now she felt a peace over how to proceed, for which she thanked Lance.

He offered her a quick, "You're welcome," before disappearing to conduct his rounds of the store. Despite his heavy-handedness with regard to the cuckoo clock, Lance had only been helpful with her situations. She thanked God for bringing the man to the store and into her life.

That evening Connie went to prayer over the clock, along with poring over the scriptures, hoping to hear the mind of God. Even with her own arguments in favor of keeping the timepiece, she couldn't get the picture of Silas Westerfield's sad face out of her mind. It was then that she came across the Gospel of Matthew. *"Give to the one who asks you, and do not turn away from the one who wants to borrow from you."* Connie sucked in her breath as the words seemed to leap out at her from the pages. *Give to the one who asks you. . . .* Could this be the word she should abide by? After all, didn't Silas Westerfield ask for the clock?

Connie slowly closed the Bible and gazed at the treasured timepiece. It would be difficult parting with it. She had to admit she had grown fond of the cuckoo popping out to greet her, even if it was a mechanical object made by man. The clock had become a part of her life. Just as Mr. Westerfield said, there was nothing like it in the world. But she also knew the clock couldn't become an idol either. She should be free to give it to whoever wanted it and feel no regrets—besides the fact that there were plenty of other clocks available. She could still preserve the memory of long ago by purchasing a similar cuckoo clock while satisfying the desire of an elderly man at the same time. Connie nodded and closed the Bible. Tomorrow she would look up Mr. Westerfield's number and inform him of the good news.

♁

Connie was flipping through the phone book, looking for Silas Westerfield's number, when a knock came on her door. Peeking through the blinds, she found her neighbor Claudia Rowe standing on the step with a plate in her hand. Connie gasped in surprise. Claudia had never visited Connie, let alone spoken with her before the woman's recent yard sale, even though Connie had lived on West Street a few years. Like most people in the neighborhood, Claudia kept to herself. Occasionally Connie went out to greet the neighbors but found many of them indifferent or busy with their own lives, except perhaps for the McCalls who lived right next door to Claudia. She had often considered getting together a block party to meet more of the neighbors but never had the wherewithal to pull it off.

Connie opened the door with an enthusiastic greeting and invited her in.

Claudia smiled and stepped inside. In an instant, her gaze fell on the clock hanging on the wall. She inhaled a deep breath and ventured forward. "I made some cookies. I hope you like them."

"That's so thoughtful of you, Mrs. Rowe. How about I make up some tea?"

The older woman nodded and took a seat in the living room. Minutes later, with tea bags brewing in the cups, Connie ventured out to find her still looking at the clock. Were it not for the fact that Claudia once owned it, Connie would think she had the most unusual piece in the world with all the attention it wrought. She placed the cup on a coaster and settled in her seat. "How's the packing coming?"

"Oh, it's a lot of work," she confessed, dipping the tea bag in the hot water. "You find things tucked away in places you never knew existed. I'm amazed how much junk I've accumulated over the years."

Connie glanced around at her sparsely furnished apartment. That was one thing she never had to worry about—an overabundance of possessions. At least she was grateful for a roof over her head, even if the furnishings were old and a bit ratty looking.

"I really should have one more sale before I move," Claudia continued.

"Well, I simply love the clock I bought at your last sale," Connie purred. Then it dawned on her that she had made the decision to sell the clock to Mr. Westerfield. She bit her lip, refusing to tell Claudia her plans and the money she would make in the venture.

"Actually, that's why I'm here." Claudia sat back in her seat and placed the cup on the table. "I wanted to make sure you were holding on to the clock."

"Holding on to it?" she said, her voice quaking. "Well, uh. . ."

"I put it in the yard sale in the hopes that whoever bought it would take care of it. And that means not reselling it. You understand, right?"

"I'm not sure I do."

"My dear, I'll be frank. There are some people in this world who would love to get their hands on this clock. But you must promise me you'll never sell it to anyone."

Connie blinked in astonishment. The seriousness of Claudia's request was plain to hear. It was almost as if the woman had an inkling she was prepared to sell it to Silas Westerfield. But how could she know? "I'm not sure what to say, Mrs. Rowe. I've bought plenty of items at yard sales, and yes, I have resold a few of them. I've never had anyone come to my door asking me not to sell something that's mine, though."

"I know, but this situation is unusual." She began twisting her fingers in obvious agitation. "Unfortunately there is one man in particular I don't want to have it. I saw him at the sale, you see. I was so glad you were interested in it. Quite frankly, if you hadn't given me the seventy-five, I might've let you take it for a lot less. Anything rather than letting that man have it."

Connie stared in bewilderment. "You mean you saw Mr. Westerfield at the sale?"

"You know him?"

"I don't know him personally, but yes, I've met him. And I know he is very interested in the clock."

At that moment, Claudia jumped to her feet and began to pace. "This is what I was afraid of," she moaned. "I wish he would stop with this. What does it take to have my wishes followed?"

Connie could not believe it. Obviously at one time, Silas Westerfield had been after Claudia Rowe about the clock, as he had with her. There seemed no limit to where the man might go with his interest. Were all antique dealers this nosy and determined to get what they want? "I'm sorry about this, Mrs. Rowe." Connie hastened to the bathroom to fetch a box of tissues.

Claudia Rowe dabbed her eyes. "I'm sorry you're caught in the middle of all this. I really thought I was doing the right thing by selling it. Now it seems I have to endure more heartache. I don't know when it will end either."

"It will end here," Connie said, unable to take the tears. "I'll keep it safe." She inhaled a deep breath. "It's strange you came when you did. I was getting ready to sell the clock to him. He offered me twelve hundred dollars for it."

Claudia Rowe nearly dropped the tissue. "Twelve hundred dollars!"

"Yes. It wasn't the money I was after, believe me. I just thought the clock was starting to become an idol of sorts in my life. I really loved it, as it reminded me of my grandmother's house and a difficult time that God saw me through as young girl. But I'm a Christian, you see, and I didn't want even a clock that served good memories to be a barrier in my life. A friend of mine at work encouraged me to pray about it. I did and decided after reading the Bible that it might be better to sell it since he seemed to want it so much."

"I hope after this I've managed to convince you otherwise."

"Is there—I mean, is there something I need to know about this man? Is he a crook or something?"

"No, he's not a crook. He's—" She paused. "Let's just say he's been after my things before. He used to be poor, you know. I guess he thinks since I have such nice things he should be able to take them and resell them at his leisure."

"He doesn't seem poor," Connie observed. "Especially if he's able to offer that much money for a clock."

Claudia said little else. Connie could tell she was becoming more and more agitated by the meeting. In a way, it reminded her of her grandmother when her ideas were questioned. Grandma would bristle, much like a cat when confronted in a corner without a means of escape. Angry words would come forth. Then Grandma would leave the room, followed by a slam of the door as a signature of her disgruntlement.

Again the verse weighed heavily on Connie's heart. *"Give to the one who asks you."*

But two people have asked me for opposite things! What should I do?

"I didn't mean to upset you," Connie said. "Of course I will keep the clock. I only thought I was doing the right thing by getting rid of it. And he seemed to want it very much. He said there was nothing else like it in the world."

Claudia's face colored, but she said nothing. Instead, she grabbed her purse.

"Well, I must be going. Thank you for the tea."

"Thank you for the cookies and. . ." Connie never finished her statement as Claudia Rowe exited her home in a flourish.

Connie sat still on the sofa, looking at the plate of oatmeal cookies and then at the clock that seemed to bring more trouble with each passing day. Maybe this was God's way of telling her to forget the yard sale scene. Maybe she was learning a valuable lesson through all this, not to buy things that could bring division among people. But then who would have thought a simple cuckoo clock could do such a thing? She had been to countless yard sales, bought things for herself and others, and never once found herself in the middle of a storm like this one.

There had to be a reason for it. God certainly knew what the clock meant to her. It was no mistake that she ran into Silas Westerfield not once but twice. And now Claudia Rowe had graced her doorstep for the first time. What could be the meaning behind it all? Would she ever learn the real answer before she became, as Donna suggested, kookier than the clock?

Chapter 8

Connie had to admit the encounter with Claudia Rowe left her feeling more confused than ever. As she lay awake that night, she wished she had never bought the clock. It had ushered in situations she never would have dreamed possible. And what made it all the more confusing was the assortment of people gravitating to the instrument. First there was Silas Westerfield, dressed in his trench coat, standing outside her front door and asking her to sell him the clock for twelve hundred dollars. Next came Lance, who all but ordered her to give in to Silas's request to sell the clock. Then there was Claudia Rowe, who had hardly ever spoken to her, much less come to visit, arriving with a plate of cookies and begging her not to sell the clock to Silas under any circumstances.

Connie climbed out of bed and padded to the living room to gaze at the timepiece. How she wished the bird could speak to her, beyond those half-hour serenades alerting her of the time. She wished it could tell her why all these people were so interested in the clock while she remained in the dark. She thought she was doing the right thing by selling it so it wouldn't become an idol in her life. Just as she was prepared to do so, she was urged to keep it.

"God, I know Lance told me to come to You with my problems. I thought I had an answer to this mess, but I only seem to be growing more confused. Please show me what to do." She plopped down in the chair to ponder it all. She thought of asking the pastor of her church for advice, but wouldn't he think her troubles minor compared to the real problems of life? What if she went back and told Lance what Claudia had said? What kind of advice would he give? Connie wasn't sure she wanted his opinion. She had already found herself challenged by his suggestions in the past. She didn't think she could handle another round of rebuking, especially now.

A yawn nearly split her head in two. Connie wandered back to bed, knowing she had a full day of work tomorrow. Life was too short to worry about an old clock anyway. Unfortunately that was exactly what was happening.

Connie arrived the next morning to find Sally asking if she had gone in search of the rocking chair like she'd promised. Connie told her not yet but that she would go soon. Inwardly she had already made up her mind that cruising yard sales just wasn't what it was cracked up to be, especially after this scenario with the clock.

But she didn't want Sally to know this, as she had promised to search out a rocking chair for her mother's birthday. She moseyed on over to the customer service counter to find Donna already there, arranging the workstation for the day's influx of returns and other business. She was surprised to see Donna looking so organized. Ordinarily she was as messy as they come, especially when she had a sweet attack. Then the place would become saturated with candy wrappers and soda cans.

"Hey, long time no talk."

"Yeah," Connie said wearily. "It's been kind of hectic."

"Yeah? Like how?"

Connie wasn't certain whether to divulge her escapades concerning the clock and the people involved. After all, it was Donna who insisted she give in to the older man's offer in the first place. The clock meant little to her friend other than as an item worthy of cold hard cash.

"C'mon," she coaxed. "I know I was a little heavy-handed about the clock, but I'm ready to listen and not jump to conclusions."

The statement surprised Connie. She sensed a bit of softening within Donna. She wondered if by some chance Lance had anything to do with it. Maybe he had taken Donna aside and talked with her. Connie saw him as a guy who could easily witness to the employees about God if the need arose. It would be an answer to her heartfelt prayer. At times, Donna's opinions aggravated her to no end. Even though she knew Donna didn't have a relationship with Christ, Connie realized she needed to show Donna the same mercy God gave her whenever she made mistakes.

"Okay. I was all set to sell the clock like everyone was suggesting," Connie started. "I felt it was the best thing to do since I didn't want the thing ruining my life. Of course it still means a lot to me, especially with what it represents about my past and all. But if having the clock itself is causing things to go wrong in my life, then I thought it wise not to have it around. So I was all set to call Silas Westerfield when my neighbor stops in."

"Your neighbor?"

"Claudia Rowe. The lady I bought the clock from. She came knocking on my door, holding a plate of cookies and everything. I was pretty surprised to see her, considering we've hardly spoken to each other. I couldn't believe she was coming to my home for a visit. Of course, looking back on it, I should have invited her over a long time ago."

"So what did she want?"

"You won't believe this, but it seems like she found out that Silas Westerfield planned to buy the clock from me. She insisted that I not sell the clock to him or anyone else. She apparently believes she sold it to me on the condition that I would take care of it and not profit from it, so to speak."

"But it's your clock. You can do whatever you want with it."

Connie traced the smooth countertop with her finger. "I know. For some reason, this clock is acting like a magnet, drawing people right to my doorstep. First it was Silas Westerfield. Then all the people at work wanted to see it. Lance has some kind of strange fascination with it. Now my neighbor. It's like this clock holds a secret."

"I think you're making mountains out of molehills."

"Maybe, but I know that an older lady, who has mostly kept to herself since she moved into the neighborhood, is now moving away, and a person like that doesn't suddenly start making house calls without a good reason. Don't you think it's strange?"

Donna smiled at a customer holding an active toddler who had come to return a toy she said had missing parts. "There's only one way to find out, Connie. Take the clock to a clock shop. There's a good one in Charlottesville. Maybe you'll find out it's actually some kind of rare antique worth thousands."

"More likely I'll end up right back where I started from."

Donna gave the woman her money, then deposited the toy into the large plastic bin earmarked for toy returns. "If so, you're no worse off than you are right now. And if the clock isn't worth anything, then you can still sell it and make a little money."

"But I promised my neighbor I wouldn't."

Donna rolled her eyes. "Connie! Why did you promise her that?"

"She insisted that I keep it. I guess this man has been after her rare antiques in the past. She doesn't want him to get ahold of this clock. Believe me, she had the tears to go along with it. I can't stand seeing people cry, especially if I have anything to do with it."

Donna snickered. "Connie Ortiz—in the middle of a real mystery. Maybe you should go on one of those mystery shows."

"I just want my life back together," she said glumly.

"Cheer up. After work we'll check out that clock guy and see what's going on. And if there isn't anything to this, then you can rest a little easier. At least you'll know you don't own a clock that once made Henry VIII happy."

"I don't think they had those kinds of clocks back then. I think they only began making them in Germany around two hundred years ago."

Donna patted her elbow. "I was just kidding."

The day went by slowly. Connie kept glancing at her watch, waiting anxiously for the shift to end so she and Donna could head right for the shop. She had already called the proprietor, and he agreed to give the clock a quick examination right after work. She would need to stop by the apartment and pick up the clock, then drive to Charlottesville in hopes of finding the answers. There had to be a reason why everyone was showing up at her place with an interest in this simple timepiece.

Near the end of the shift, Lance came over to check on the returns. When he saw Connie and Donna bustling about, he asked why they were in such a hurry.

"We have a very important errand to run," Donna told him. "We need to see if Connie struck gold."

Lance raised his eyebrows and glanced in Connie's direction. "If so, I hope she'll divvy it up with all of us. But I didn't know the Blue Ridge Mountains had gold."

Donna snickered. "No, we actually think there may be hidden gold inside the clock."

Lance stepped forward, intrigued. "Really now. And what makes you think that?"

"Why else would an old guy pay over a thousand dollars for it?" Donna took Connie's arm. "C'mon, we gotta get going."

Connie could clearly see the confusion painted on Lance's face but thought little of it. She and Donna headed right for her apartment. She managed to find the box for the clock while Donna raided the fridge for something to drink, complaining about the lack of food on the shelves. Once the clock was tucked away safely inside the box, they headed out. During the drive, Connie watched the splendor of the Blue Ridge Mountains in all its beauty rise up before her. The sight eased the misgivings about this whole venture. Donna chatted away about Connie's fame and fortune if she discovered that a clock bought at a yard sale was actually worth a huge sum of money. Maybe she would even be picked to do a talk show on bargain shopping. Connie only wondered what she would do after finding out the result of this visit.

They arrived at the Clock Shop in the downtown area. Hanging on the walls were clocks of every shape and size. From behind the counter, a small elderly gentleman ventured out, wearing magnifying spectacles. Connie noted in interest that he had a hook for one of his arms. She applauded the efforts of the man to do such delicate work, despite his physical challenge. He appeared like the perfect image of Geppetto from *Pinocchio*, but instead of puppets, clocks surrounded him.

"So this is the clock," he said when Connie opened the box. "Yes, indeed. An original Black Forest cuckoo clock. I recognize the workmanship."

Connie and Donna exchanged glances as the shopkeeper lifted the instrument out and set it carefully on the counter. Donna went on to tell the tale of the clock's past, including the offer of twelve hundred dollars for it, while Connie stood by.

The man carefully lifted off the front piece, using a fine whisk brush to dust away the dirt. "It's in excellent condition from what I can tell." He then turned it over and, with his magnifying spectacles, scanned the panel. "I assume you knew there's an engraving here on the back panel."

"What?" Connie leaned over the counter. The man brought out a magnifying glass so she could take a look. Even though the etching had faded with time, she could make out the words on the wooden panel: GENE AND BETTE, 1960.

"I wonder who Gene and Bette are?" Donna mused.

Connie shrugged. "Maybe Mrs. Rowe purchased it from either Gene or Bette. Is there anything else special that you can see about the clock besides the engraving?"

He looked it over. "It's a well-kept instrument."

"It's very accurate," Connie added. "I wind it every eight days."

"I've seen many like it. While the age and condition of it would fetch a higher price, the engraving does lower the value. I don't believe it's worth much more than five hundred dollars." The man offered to keep the clock and give it a thorough cleaning, but Connie decided against it. Finances were tight enough as it was without having to pay a cleaning bill. She thanked him and returned the clock to its box before heading out the door with Donna.

"There, you feel better?"

"No. I feel worse. The only thing I know is that this is a nice clock with some kind of engraving on it from a previous owner. It doesn't explain why Silas Westerfield wanted to buy it for such a huge amount of money or explain his claim that there's only one like it in the world." Connie sighed. "Oh, Donna, maybe you're right. Maybe I am making mountains out of molehills. Maybe I should just hang the thing on my wall and forget about it." But she knew she couldn't. This was not something easily forgotten. For a moment she could understand Claudia's exasperation with the thing and perhaps the reason why she had tucked it away in some obscure corner of the attic. Maybe she had found others wanting it because it was a treasured piece and then hid it away so as not to be reminded of it. Maybe that's exactly what Connie needed to do to restore the peace in her life—put the clock away for a time. Once the storm blew over, she could again have the clock gracing her living room wall.

Connie dropped Donna off at her apartment, thanking her for tagging along to the clock shop, then proceeded home. Her fingernails tapped on the box cover, the timepiece tucked away inside. "You're definitely full of mystery, Mr. Cuckoo," she murmured. "If only I had answers and not all these questions."

She pulled up to the apartment building to find a shadowy figure waiting on her doorstep, reading the evening newspaper. All at once a familiar dread came over her. At least this person wasn't wearing a trench coat. In fact, he looked vaguely familiar. In the lamplight, she could see a crop of dark hair. He turned then and gave a friendly wave. Lance Adams.

Oh no. She glanced down at the box sitting on the passenger seat of the car. She decided to leave the clock inside the car and lock the car door. It made no sense to spark further discussion about the clock right now. Her head was already spinning.

"Hey there," Lance said, folding the newspaper in half. "How's it going?"

"Okay," she said tentatively, wondering what the motive could be behind this impromptu visit.

"I'll bet you're wondering why I'm here."

No joke, she thought but offered a pleasant smile. "Are you homeless or something?" She grimaced at the remark. What an absurd comment to make—and with the connotation that he would seek refuge at her place.

He ignored it. "I was curious to know what happened with the clock."

I can't believe you came over here to talk about that clock, she thought in exasperation. How she wished he might pay *her* a little more attention. Or was he only paying her attention *because* of the clock? "I just wanted to make sure there was nothing strange about it, so I took it to a repair shop in Charlottesville."

"What do you mean? What's strange about it? Doesn't it work right?" The concern in his voice puzzled her.

"It's working fine," she said, wondering why he cared so much.

"Donna told me that Mrs. Rowe had asked you not to sell it."

When did Donna tell him that? "Yes, my neighbor did say that to me on her visit." She wished she could tell Lance that this was a private issue and she would handle it. But for some reason, the clock fascinated him, and she really wanted to know why. Could it be that Lance Adams had some kind of connection to it?

Suddenly she blurted out, "So why are you so interested in my clock, Lance? I've been wondering that for a long time. It can't be some passing fascination on your part. Most guys couldn't care less what's hanging on the wall. At least that's the way my brothers felt."

He stepped backward, as if her words had clobbered him. "Well," he began. She tensed at his reaction.

"You could say that I'm also interested in the clock for personal reasons," he offered. "If you come with me to Luigi's, I'll tell you all about it."

The Italian restaurant that made her favorite pizza. He was making good on his promise to take her out for pizza, even if it did include conversation about the cuckoo clock. Connie smiled. No matter. She would enjoy a bite to eat and maybe in the process, find out a thing or two about Lance's connection to the clock. If only she were more of a gumshoe on par with Nancy Drew. Connie never felt she had the brains to solve a mystery, especially one involving herself.

But a few clues would certainly do no harm—and maybe help her achieve that long-sought-after peace. "Okay. I am a little hungry."

His face relaxed, as if relieved she had accepted. They strolled along the sidewalk to where his car was parked. Connie looked back at her own vehicle and the clock sitting quietly on the front seat. What a web of a mystery the timepiece had woven. She could hardly wait to discover the ending to it all, if she could make it there without going crazy.

Chapter 9

Connie wasn't certain what to think or believe as she sat in the passenger seat of Lance's immaculate car. The interior was as clean as a whistle and smelled of polish, as if he had just spiffed it up at a car wash. The mere thought that he might have washed the car just for her sent tingles shooting down to her toes. She said little as they drove to the restaurant, making only casual comments about work. Lance then began chatting away about his first job as a grocery boy who delivered parcels to customers.

"And one time—" He began to laugh. Connie couldn't help smiling in return. Lance had a friendly, easygoing laugh that never failed to put her at ease. "I had two gallons of ice cream to deliver. This lady, Miss Paula we called her, loved her ice cream. Her tooth was sweeter than anyone I had ever met. I had the ice cream on the backseat, and before I could deliver it to her, my car had a flat tire. At the time, I was driving this really old rust bucket I affectionately called Rusty. In all honesty, I was lucky to start it in the morning. So there I was, in the middle of nowhere, with two gallons of ice cream melting in the backseat. By the time I managed to get the tire changed, a glacial ice cream lake had formed on the seat and dripped to the floor. I called it Lake La Crème."

Connie laughed in glee. "Oh, Lance, you're hilarious."

He grinned. "So I had to run back to the store and tell Mr. Carson, the grocery clerk, what happened. Then I had to clean out my car. What a mess! And yes, you know what happens to milk when it sits awhile in a warm car."

"Ew!" she exclaimed, holding her nose.

"I never quite got the smell out after that. But Rusty was soon for the junkyard anyway."

"Lance, it's a good thing you're not telling me this story when we're about to eat or anything," she said with a wry grin.

Their lighthearted conversation instantly calmed her. Perhaps Lance realized her anxiousness when she first entered the vehicle. Like the good manager he was, he'd smoothed over the rough edges with a humorous tale about himself. She took it as a sign of a man who understood feelings, and like he claimed, one who grew up surrounded by the emotional complexities of women.

When they pulled into the restaurant lot, Connie was feeling much better and more confident—ready to face whatever Lance came here to discuss. She couldn't quite imagine what he might say. Right now the whole clock scenario was like a revolving door. Somewhere it had to stop. She prayed it would at the right entrance. When Lance held open the door for her and she gazed into his dark brown eyes, she wondered if perhaps the mysterious revolving door was meant to lead her to him. Maybe he was the one God had chosen to give her the answers.

Settling at their table, Connie immediately began giving the waitress an order for her favorite pizza with Italian prosciutto, black olives, artichokes, and Italian cheese. She then looked up into Lance's expectant face. "I'm sorry. I wasn't even thinking. I'm used to ordering the same pizza when I come here. Perhaps you want something else."

"Sounds good. I told you I wanted to try it sometime." He added to the order two glasses of iced tea, then sat back expectantly with his arms crossed. "So, how often have you eaten here?"

"A few times. Donna and I like it. She loves the atmosphere, the flowery curtains, the pictures of Italy on the walls." She pointed out the paintings. "She says that one day she would love to go over there and visit. Afterward, we head to the nearest video arcade."

"Really. She doesn't seem like the type who plays those kinds of games. I thought her pretty dignified, made-up—polished."

"Donna can be a little kid at heart when she wants to be. She likes to have fun, that is, when she's not bossing me around. I guess it's good, though, since I don't have a sister. And she's been a great friend—even if she can be rather opinionated."

"But she isn't a Christian, is she?"

The drinks arrived. Connie poked a straw into the tea and took a sip. "No. I've talked to her some about it. Even tried to invite her to church. Once I was able to get her to go on an outing with the church ladies to that big outlet mall in northern Virginia. She had a blast, but she did say she was a little perturbed how everyone talked about God so much. I tried to use it as an occasion to say something about having a personal relationship with Christ. She thought it was strange."

"You did the right thing by inviting her along," Lance said. "You planted the seeds. We need to do more friendship evangelism. And I can tell you have a heart for it, Connie. It's no coincidence that you come from a background where families and friends join together to share meals and good times. We need to do more of that nowadays. We tend to shy away from it when it comes to these things. We're afraid to invite others into our world, afraid what they might think or how they'll react. But people are craving attention in their lives. They want five-star treatment. They want to know that others care about them. I hope maybe we can both begin organizing some of the events for the employees like I discussed awhile back."

Connie listened patiently, wondering if this was all a precursor to the conversation about the clock. Maybe Lance wanted to do more with the clock, like have another luncheon with coworkers. She sighed. And here she had been hoping to learn more details about the timepiece and especially Lance's involvement. Maybe there wasn't anything else to share. She grimaced in disappointment. Now she was right back where she started.

Lance gazed at her quizzically. "I guess you don't like my ideas?"

"Sure, it sounds great. I just thought we were going to talk about—oh, here's the food." The waitress arrived with the pizza. The aroma sent the juices swirling in Connie's mouth. At least her appetite hadn't been affected. It showed how comfortable Lance could make her feel, even if the conversation wasn't going the way she planned.

They both ate for a time, commenting every so often on the different kinds of pizza they had tried in the past, from a Philly cheesesteak variety to Hawaiian, barbecue, and even seafood.

"So did the clockmaker where you took the cuckoo say anything interesting about it?" Lance suddenly inquired.

Her stomach lurched. Luckily Connie had only eaten one slice of pizza when Lance popped the big question. So he had not forgotten the main crux of this outing. "He said it was in great condition."

"Did he say if he saw anything unusual about it?"

Connie coughed into her napkin. "Unusual? Like what?"

He waited patiently, as if expecting her to come out with it. Finally he said, "Like an engraving."

Connie stared in disbelief. How could Lance know so much unless Donna told him about the engraving? But she couldn't have. Lance was waiting at the front doorstep when she arrived home. Did he already have some preconceived knowledge of the clock all along then, as Connie had begun to suspect? "Yes, he said there was an engraving," she admitted. "I still don't understand how you would know about it, though. Maybe you can clue me in like you promised."

Lance picked up a napkin and began to fold it into a paper airplane. "It's pretty simple, Connie. The man who was trying to buy the clock from you—he's my grandfather."

Connie opened her mouth so wide she was sure he could see her tonsils. She clamped her lips together. "You mean that man in the trench coat is—I don't believe it. Silas Westerfield is your grandfather?"

"Yes, that's my granddad."

She sat stunned by the revelation, staring at the pizza slices before her. Now that her appetite had swiftly taken flight, there would be plenty of leftovers to take home.

Lance continued to fashion the airplane before resting it on the table. "And the engraving on it says GENE AND BETTE, 1960, right?"

Speechless, she could only nod.

"Gene is my grandfather," Lance explained. "It's his middle name. Silas Eugene Westerfield. He actually hated the name Silas. Everyone calls him Gene."

"No wonder he wanted the clock. Then why does Claudia Rowe have it?" She paused. "Is she Bette?"

Lance winked. "You got it, lady. You're sharp. Yes, it was his nickname for her."

"And it must be that your grandfather gave her the clock. Now he's upset that she's parting with it, so much that he's willing to pay a lot for it."

"Right again. At first I tried to talk Granddad out of it. I said how you were my employee at work and had really taken a liking to the piece. Granddad agreed at one time to leave it alone, but I guess he changed his mind. I know he's asked a few times about it. He mentioned how you gave him a ride home the other day. That was really kind of you, Connie."

"Now everything he said to me makes sense, especially the comment that there's no other clock like it in the world. So he had the clock engraved for Bette?"

"It was an engagement gift of sorts. A gift of promise. They both loved antiques. I don't know if you've seen the inside of Mrs. Rowe's house, but she's quite a collector. That's how they first met, you know—at an antique store over in Fredericksburg. They were both living in this area at the time. Virginia is an antiquer's paradise, you might say.

"As a promise of a future life together, Granddad bought her the clock as a gift. Not long after, a few months maybe, they broke off their engagement and Bette moved away. Granddad never really told me why they parted. But he always wondered about her and what happened. I'm sure when she moved back into the area a few years ago he wanted to open up communication. By that time Grandma was dead. I think Bette had lost her husband, as well. But Granddad was never one for chasing women. He's a gentleman. He had hopes Bette might want to see him. She never did. And when he saw her selling the clock at the yard sale, he knew she meant to erase any memory of what they once had long ago."

"How tragic!" Connie moaned. "Your grandfather and Mrs. Rowe engaged in a lover's quarrel."

"I can't say that he loves her now. They probably did love each other at one time. Now he simply wants the clock back. He believes it's his after it was given out of a promise. When that promise was broken, he felt he should have had it returned. And I think he saw his opportunity when a nice young lady purchased the clock at the yard sale."

"Of course I'll return the clock to him." She paused. "Oh no. I promised Claudia I would keep it. Wow, now everything she said on her visit makes sense. She said this elderly man wanted the clock really bad—that he was after her priceless objects, or something to that effect. She made your grandfather sound like a crook. She sat in my apartment and shed tears about it all. After all that, Lance, I promised her I wouldn't sell it."

Lance blew out a sigh. "Then I guess Granddad will have to accept it. At least he can find comfort in knowing the clock is in good hands." Just then he leaned over and grasped Connie's hand. "And speaking of hands, I must confess that I've wanted to hold yours for quite a while. You have such long, lean fingers. I notice them while you're working at the customer service desk. But holding hands isn't quite what a manager and an employee should be doing."

A buzz like a bee filled her ears. Warmth flowed through her. Here they had been discussing a love that was lost, and now a new love was blossoming in its place.

He released her hand to take up the airplane he had made out of the napkin. "So I guess we're going to have to let this go, aren't we?" He held up the paper plane, preparing to fly it across the restaurant.

"Don't you dare let that go," she said with a giggle. "You'll cause a stir! Anyway, it doesn't necessarily mean we have to let your granddad and Claudia go their separate ways. If there's anything left from the past, maybe we can coax it along a little."

"And just how do you plan to do that?"

"At one time, Bette and your grandfather were in love. They had to be if they were engaged and your grandfather bought her a clock with their names engraved on it. It's just like lovers who engrave their names on a tree. After all that, I think we should see if there might be some sparks left from long ago. I'm sure there is."

"I'm not so sure, Connie. It sounds to me like whatever argument they had left scuff marks on their hearts."

"Then we need to buff up those hearts a little. We need them to shine once again. The Bible says to be reconciled. We need to see that this couple is given the opportunity to do just that. Who knows? Maybe other fruit will happen, too."

"You're incredible, you know that? Granddad was fortunate to have that clock fall into your hands. It was definitely no accident that you love yard sales and that clock caught your eye."

Connie smirked, realizing she had been thinking the same thing. For a time, she thought the clock might well be a curse that brought tribulation to her life. Now that she had learned the story, how the clock served as a link between two young people who were once in love, it took on a greater meaning. Perhaps it might bring the relationship back to life. "Only time will tell," she murmured.

"What?"

Connie confessed to him the play on words she had devised, to which he laughed.

"I don't think you're too far off. It would be nice to see them reconcile after all these years, and especially since they're both lonely people."

"Does your grandfather ever talk about Claudia—or Bette, I guess is her name?"

"A few times since Grandma died ten years ago. That's how I found out about the clock and the engraving. That's not to say Grandma's passing wasn't hard on Granddad. He loved her very much. They did everything together. When he broke his hip, she stayed by his side constantly."

"Is that why he walks with a limp?"

"Yes. He broke it eleven years ago. One leg is shorter than the other. All he needs to do is get a shoe built up, but he isn't fond of doctors or the way they do things. He believes the doctors messed up his leg to begin with. So he's gotten used to walking with a limp. Sometimes he uses a cane, but he hates it. Says it makes him look old. When I told him he *was* old, you should've seen the look I got!"

Connie snickered. "He talked about how the family made comments concerning his trench coat."

Lance nodded. "Another testy subject. I did talk to him a little about his taste in clothes. He's fairly set in his ways. That's why I don't see much coming from a reunion between Granddad and Mrs. Rowe. He knows it's been a long time, and they are different people. I'm sure they will be polite to each other, but that's about as far as it's likely going to go."

"We can at least try. It can't do any harm. After all, God has unique ways of bringing people together. I mean, look at how we're sitting here talking about a clock I bought at a yard sale. That little cuckoo bird is being used in more ways than one."

Lance got to his feet and left some bills on the table. "This has been fun, Connie. I'll have to admit, at first I dreaded this meeting. I know you weren't too happy about my involvement with your clock. When this all came up, I debated telling you right off that Mr. Westerfield was my grandfather. Somehow I didn't feel comfortable about it until I knew you better and could gauge your response."

Connie dropped her head, realizing how her attitude had affected the situation. If she hadn't been so vexed about his involvement, she would've had the answers to her troubles a lot sooner. She was thankful the clock's magnetism had drawn them together for a special purpose. "I'm really sorry how I came off at first. I was deep into my own personal feelings and still am, I guess. But I must admit I find this scenario between Claudia and your grandfather to be quite intriguing. I'd like to see this cuckoo clock bring them back together. It will make all the trouble worth it and more."

They strode out of the restaurant toward the car. Above them, a crescent moon shone overhead. It was a perfect spring evening, despite the slight chill in the air. Lance opened the passenger door for her, and soon they were on their way down the dark road. Connie sat huddled in her seat, reminiscing about the evening, wishing it didn't have to end so quickly. Though she needed to work tomorrow, Connie knew sleep would be slow in coming tonight. "Do you think it would be all right if I did a little probing?" she inquired. "Maybe ask Claudia Rowe a few questions and uncover some clues about their past relationship?"

"As long as it doesn't upset her. I'd proceed with caution. Maybe once you find out a few tidbits, we can figure out where to go from there."

Connie nodded, excited at the possibility, when Lance pulled up to her apartment. He waited for her to enter the dark apartment before driving off. She flicked on a light, only to find the clock missing from the wall. Panic assailed her until she remembered the clock was still inside her car on the dark street. The wall seemed empty without the merry piece to entertain her. If all this worked out and Bette or Gene decided they wanted their clock back, Connie knew she must be ready to part with it. The clock had once knit two young lovers together until some kind of misunderstanding forced them apart. She would like nothing better than to see them reunited, even if it did cost her the most prized object she had ever purchased.

Chapter 10

Connie didn't want to admit it, but she was nervous about the meeting with her neighbor. She spent much of the morning rehearsing what she might say so Claudia wouldn't become angry. It was a risky endeavor, she knew, but worth it if by some chance God might be knitting this long-lost couple back together. Mixed in with all of this were her strong feelings for Lance. She recalled with pleasure the warmth and strength of his hand on hers during dinner at the restaurant. At first the contact startled her. She had always found Lance a strong and attractive Christian man, but it didn't dawn on her that he might also be attracted to her. Now she considered their various interactions over the past few weeks. He met up with her almost daily in the store, accompanied by a friendly word or greeting. At first she assumed it was a part of normal managerial relations. Now she wondered if there were other reasons behind the communications. Of course they had a link with the clock. She owned the very piece that could unite his grandfather with the woman he would have married had they not broken their engagement. Yet there was also sincerity in Lance's gaze during dinner and the way he commented about her hands. It led her to believe his interest extended far beyond business and a simple wooden cuckoo clock to something much more personal.

For now, Connie put Lance's interest on the back burner to focus on the encounter with Claudia. She had walked by the home earlier that morning to find boxes strewed across the front porch. No doubt her neighbor was in the midst of packing. Perhaps Connie should make a visit on the guise of offering some assistance with the packing, along with returning the plate that once held the delicious oatmeal cookies. There was no better opportunity than using the ministry of a servant's heart to bring forth a topic of deep importance. Connie had done such things with others on numerous occasions, including Donna. While the person sometimes didn't always respond the way she had hoped, at least it provided an avenue in which to tackle difficult subjects.

Just then the phone rang. Connie hurried to answer it as the cuckoo on the wall interrupted with a cheery greeting.

"I can hear the clock," Lance said with a chuckle. "It must be a sign."

"It's been a sign ever since I bought it. Every half hour on the half hour."

"Connie, it was a sign long before you bought it. And I'm hoping it might bring happiness into two people's lives. That's why I'm calling, to wish you faith and grace on your visit with Mrs. Rowe. Have you thought about what you want to say?"

"A little. Actually, I decided just to make myself useful and hope the words will come out. She has a bunch of boxes on her front porch, so she's probably hip-deep into packing."

Lance blew a sigh over the phone. "I hope we aren't too late. Once she moves away, that's it. Granddad won't track her down. I know it. He won't interfere with her plans. We need to do something as soon as possible."

"I have to say, I'm a little anxious about the meeting. We could be setting ourselves up for a big fall if something goes wrong."

"It won't."

"Easier said than done. It seemed like a good idea, too. I guess I'm getting cold feet."

"Then warm them up a little. Confess some good scripture like, 'I can do all things through Christ who strengthens me.' I don't think it's an accident that you live a few doors down from the woman my grandfather once loved. When I saw Granddad the other day, I could tell he'd been thinking about the past. He had a note with Bette's old address on it lying on his desk. I asked him about it, but he only put it away and said nothing. If you could see the longing in his eyes, Connie, it would give you the strength to go forward with this, as uncomfortable as it might seem."

"I believe you. Just pray for me, and we'll see what happens. And maybe in the meantime, you can work a little more on your grandfather. Maybe encourage him to give Mrs. Rowe a call. Something to open up the doors of communication."

"Sounds good. Talk to you later."

Connie hung up the phone, breathing a sigh of relief. As was his nature, Lance had instilled in her a confidence she sorely lacked. She picked up her purse along with the plate that Claudia had used to bring over the cookies, took one last look in the mirror, and made for the door. She breathed a prayer for God's will to be done.

※

Claudia Rowe greeted Connie with a surprised look when she opened the door. Her hair was bound up in the turban she'd worn at the yard sale. Tiny beads of perspiration dotted her forehead. "Oh, my plate," she said when she saw the dish in Connie's hands. "Thank you for returning it. I nearly moved away without it."

"Looks like you're packing," Connie observed, acknowledging the open boxes and the dishes Claudia had just begun to wrap in tufts of paper.

"Yes, and it's hard work, I must admit."

"I'd be glad to give you a hand. I can wrap the dishes, and you can pack them."

"Well. . ." She seemed to consider the offer while scanning the many dishes on the counter. "All right, but please be careful. Many of these are antiques."

"No problem. When my grandmother had to move, I helped pack up her antiques. She had quite a few in a display case. And many Hummels, as well." Connie took up a sheet of paper and began wrapping a glass. "I loved this one Hummel she had of a little girl holding an umbrella. She had such a sweet expression on her face, as if wondering whether the umbrella would protect her from the storm."

"Is your grandmother the one who owned a cuckoo clock?"

Connie nodded, placing the glass carefully in a cardboard box half full of Styrofoam peanuts. "She had quite a few antiques. I was grateful to get one piece before it all went to auction—a little pink glass slipper with gold etching."

Claudia Rowe glanced at her in curiosity. "A glass slipper! It sounds like something from *Cinderella*."

"I always thought I would turn into a princess if I could get my foot into it," Connie reminisced with a laugh. "Unfortunately, it was the size of a toddler's shoe. And I was about five or six at the time. Still, I don't have very big feet, even as an adult."

"You're quite petite," the woman observed. "You look a lot like my youngest daughter, Karen. That's where I'm moving, near where my two daughters live. They both live in Virginia Beach. I'm not getting any younger, you know. I want to be close to them and their families. One of my grandsons is getting ready to graduate from high school. Can you believe it?"

"You don't look old enough to have grandchildren that age! I think it's a great idea, though. It would be wonderful living near the ocean, watching the waves roll in and seeing the sun rise in the morning." Connie wrapped up a few more pieces, all the while wondering how to broach the subject concerning Lance's grandfather. It appeared Claudia had her heart set on moving near her family. Obviously Silas Westerfield was nowhere in the picture. She continued on with small talk about her grandmother's house and some of her antiques. "You have quite a collection here."

"Yes, many years' worth. I really should just get rid of it all, but it's difficult. Some of the pieces are very old. A few I collected pretty near forty years ago."

"Really. I'll bet the clock I have was one of them, huh?"

Claudia paused. Her hand jerked as if Connie had touched a nerve. "Not really. The clock was given to me."

An open door! Connie decided to pounce on it before it slammed shut in her face. "It must be a secret admirer, then. Or else the clock did have some other kind of secret between two people."

"I'm not sure what you mean."

"I had it looked at by a clock repair shop in Charlottesville. The man there discovered an engraving on it." Connie turned to look at her. The color had drained away from the older woman's face, leaving it white like the petals of an Easter lily.

"Well, it doesn't mean anything," she declared.

"The shopkeeper told me it said GENE AND BETTE, 1960. I'm guessing someone else had it before you did?"

Just then a teacup slipped out of Claudia's hand and crashed to the linoleum in a million sharp shards. "Oh, look what happened!" she cried.

"I'm sorry. Where's the broom? I'll clean it up."

Claudia ignored her request and hunted down the broom and dustpan herself. With methodical strokes, she began sweeping it up. "I only have two of these left now," she moaned. "They were original cups from my wedding china. I don't know, but in the last few years, I've had wedding china breaking right and left. Now I only have a few pieces left."

Connie didn't know what to say. The pitiful look Claudia gave was enough to make her want to share in the tears that came trickling down the older woman's face. This visit may well have already turned into a dreadful mistake.

Claudia now took a seat on the sofa. "My Herbert died ten years ago from colon cancer. When the doctors found out about it, they didn't treat it until it was too late. He should have never died at such a young age."

"I'm so sorry for your loss."

"We had a wonderful marriage. He was a lovely man, just the man Daddy wanted me to marry. And I was glad I did, of course." She seemed lost in thought.

"Is he. . . I mean, did he give you the clock?"

"Oh no. That came from someone else. Someone before Herbert. Someone who is trying to come back, even though I want him to stay away. What we had was so long ago. We both took different paths in life. I wish he would accept it."

Connie stood still, her heart pattering away, hoping and praying she would continue.

"It wasn't that Gene was a bad man. Just the opposite. He was sweet and kind, but my family was suspicious of him. He was poor, and I was the daughter of a wealthy businessman. Daddy always wanted me to marry the vice president of his company. They thought Gene was a street urchin trying to wheedle his way into the family fortune. But he was wonderful to be around." She reached over to grab a tissue out of a box. "We had a lot in common, too. We both loved antiques. Gene was a whiz at finding antiques and getting the best deals. I told him he should become a dealer. We would browse through all kinds of shops. He could negotiate the most wonderful bargains. I really did love him." She paused. The lonely sound of the grandfather clock serenaded the moment.

"Then one day, Gene bought me the cuckoo clock. He had seen me looking at it in one of the shops. He brought it over to my parents' house when they weren't home. He said it was an engagement gift, a promise that we would always be together. 'As time endures, so will our love,' he told me." She blew her nose. "Isn't that romantic?"

"Yes, it is." Connie tried to imagine Silas Westerfield, outfitted in his trench coat, saying such things under the faint rays of moonlight. No doubt he was a dashing man with a romantic heart, and still was to have a grandson who followed suit.

"He showed me the engraving he had put on the clock. I was so touched. Oh, I did want to be with him, I must admit. But when Daddy found out that Gene was serious about marrying me, my parents did everything they could to keep us apart. Daddy went so far as to send a person to spy on him. He discovered that Gene's brother was a swindler and believed Gene was the same way. I knew Gene didn't have a lot of money. He had no nice clothes. He drove a lemon of a car that always seemed to break down—and at the most inopportune times. He rarely had money to take me out."

Connie winced when she heard how Silas Westerfield's financial status had cast a pall over their relationship. She certainly hoped such things would not hinder her relationship with Lance, even if her own finances weren't as stable as she would like.

"At first the money didn't matter. But Daddy was insistent. He said Gene was after our fortune. He wasn't a good man for me. Eventually I believed him. Why wouldn't a daughter believe that her father had her best interests at heart? So I told Gene we couldn't get married. Without my family's blessing, there was no hope for us anyway. There would always be contention and resentment somewhere, and I didn't want to live like that. Gene refused to accept it. He said we could elope. We were meant to be together. But I wouldn't. I was my father's girl, and I would honor his decision."

Claudia began to cough then and went out to the kitchen to pour some filtered water into two glasses. She returned, handing one to Connie. "I said to Gene it would be better if we stopped seeing each other. Not long after that, we went our separate ways. I took the clock with me, as I did like it very much. Gene tried to contact me on several occasions, but Daddy told him to leave us alone or face the consequences. Gene stayed away after that. We lost track of each other. Then I found Herbert, a coworker in the company. Daddy highly approved of him. He was a nice man and gave me everything I wanted. But I must admit, deep down in my heart, I never forgot Gene or the clock he gave me, even if I kept it hidden away in the attic all these years."

Connie could hear the wistful tone in her voice, of one who wished circumstances might have played out differently. Of course she was glad it hadn't, for

Lance wouldn't be here. Still, God had a way of orchestrating events in people's lives, even years later. "It's not too late for you and Gene," she told Claudia.

"I'm afraid it is. We both went in different directions. I found a husband. Gene found a wife. We raised families, and now we both have grandchildren."

"His grandson believes it isn't too late."

Claudia looked at her quizzically. "You act as if you know who Gene is."

"I do, Mrs. Rowe. I know that Gene is really Silas Westerfield, the one who wanted to buy the clock from me."

Claudia gasped. "Don't tell me he dragged you into this mess! How could he do such a thing?"

"He didn't say a word about this to me. His grandson, Lance, is the assistant manager at the store where I work. We've come to know each other pretty well. He recently told me how Mr. Westerfield bought you the clock as an engagement gift."

"Why he wants it returned to him after all these years, I have no idea. I can't believe he suddenly cares about it."

"He must care if he's willing to offer twelve hundred dollars for it. Or maybe he cares about the owner and feels the clock is the best way to reach her heart."

Claudia shook her head. She stood up and returned to wrapping up the dishes. "What we had died a long time ago. He shouldn't try to resurrect something that never was and never will be. And to think he tried to get it from you by offering such a huge amount of money."

"I think it's sweet."

Claudia cast her a look that sent a chill racing through her.

"I mean it's obvious he wants to communicate with you again. But he's a gentleman and doesn't want to seem as if he's interfering."

"He is interfering by wanting something that can never be. It's over. No clock will bring it back."

"Is it really over? You even said at one time you wanted to be with him. There must have been something there between you two. The years don't have to erase it."

Claudia stood still as if stunned by the words. Connie watched the lines of aggravation break out across her face. She said no more and helped finish packing up a box. Once it was filled, Claudia taped it up.

"I think we're done for today," she announced. "I can tell that you came over here to try to arrange something between Gene and me. I'm sure his grandson helped, too."

"I only thought that maybe after all these years there might be something left of a young couple who was once in love. And I know you both were in love. I could hear it in your voice and see it in your face."

Claudia winced and turned away. "Thank you for your help. I should be able to finish this myself."

Connie reluctantly picked up her purse and moved toward the door. She wanted to say more but bit her tongue. She had said too much already. At least she was thankful her neighbor had revealed a few facts to her. If only there weren't such barriers existing between Claudia and Lance's grandfather. If this was indeed a match that could transcend time, was it possible for Lance and her to bring it to pass? Both Gene and Bette had families, children, and grandchildren. And forty years was a long time. But there must be some spark left, even if Claudia's family had tried to smother it. Perhaps a breeze of opportunity might fan the flames. If only she knew what the next step should be—or if there was a next step, whether it should be hers.

Chapter 11

"Why didn't you answer your phone last night?" Lance inquired as soon as Connie dropped her purse inside the employee locker. "I nearly drove over to your house to ask what happened, but I managed to restrain myself."

Connie knew he had called. His number flashed on the caller ID. Yet she couldn't bring herself to answer the phone after the encounter with Claudia Rowe. She was grateful the woman had opened up about her life, but the avenue to Silas Westerfield appeared closed with the detour sign reading Virginia Beach. Her neighbor was determined to move. She had given the clock into Connie's care with the hope of sealing shut the past. Connie felt if she pursued it any further, she would be setting herself up for a big fall.

Lance peered at her intently before pouring a cup of coffee. "I guess it didn't go very well."

"I learned quite a bit, but I don't think this is worth pursuing. From Claudia Rowe's standpoint, she believes they took separate paths, then got married and had families. It's those families they should look to now, not some long-lost love of decades ago."

Lance's face twisted in obvious disappointment. He opened his mouth, ready to speak more, when Donna came bopping in. "Hey, you two!" she said with a shrill. "So how was the date the other night?"

"Date?" Connie asked blankly.

Lance excused himself and headed out the door. Donna looked at her quizzically. "Wow, must have been a bummer."

"If you mean the pizza, that part went fine. It was the conversation surrounding it."

Donna groaned. "Connie, you're going to have to quit with your opinions and lighten up a little. So did you sit there and tell Lance what to do with the store?"

"No. And don't try to guess either. You'll never even scratch the surface."

Donna stepped closer, the challenge igniting a fire in her eyes. "Just try me."

"Okay. You know that older man who wanted to buy the clock?"

"Of course."

"He's Lance's grandfather."

Donna's mouth fell open, exposing the gum she had been snapping. "No way." She pressed her lips together and began to chew.

"Yes, and that's not all. My neighbor who sold me the clock, Mrs. Rowe—it turns out she and Lance's grandfather were once engaged to be married. The clock happened to be a gift he bought for her."

"So the engraving that said 'Gene and Bette'?"

"*Gene* is Silas Westerfield's middle name. And *Bette* was his nickname for my neighbor."

"This is too wild to believe! Our manager is the grandson of Gene? Wowsie! No wonder the man was so interested in your clock. This couldn't get any stranger."

"So now Lance and I are trying to think of a way to get them back together after all these years."

"Wouldn't that be sweet! I guess they're both widowed?"

"Claudia Rowe lost her husband to cancer. I'm not sure how Lance's grandmother died. He never told me. But Claudia said at one time she cared a lot for Gene. There must be some kind of feelings left, even if she's denying it."

Donna took a seat at the table and cupped her face with her hands. "So what exactly do you plan to do? Give me all the juicy details."

"There's nothing much happening right now. She got angry when I told her that Gene must still care about her if he was trying to buy back the clock after all these years. She saw no connection but only pronounced the relationship dead in the water."

"You need to coax the two of them along a little. Look at the success I had with you and Lance!" Donna winked.

Connie stepped back. "You didn't have anything to do with us. I mean, Lance and I just started talking. It's true you first mentioned him to me. When you think about it, though, that clock also brought us together."

"So what's the next step?"

"Right now there isn't one."

"Honey, there's always a step to be made. You need to come up with a way for the two of them to meet face-to-face. Think of a common interest they share."

Connie paused to consider this. Donna seemed gung ho over the idea of uniting the older couple, despite what happened with Claudia. If only she could be certain about what to do. There were no manuals in this area but biblical guidance. And there it said to live peaceably with all men and, above all, to trust God. Maybe in His own mysterious way, having Donna enter the picture might create a path between Gene and Bette, if that were possible.

"They both like antiques," Connie suddenly declared. "That's the whole reason Gene gave her the clock in the first place. And she loved it from what she told me. When they went their separate ways, she kept the clock hidden until the yard sale where I bought it."

"Then maybe you can arrange to have them meet at an antique market. That seems the most logical place. It's worth a try." Donna hopped to her feet, gave a wave, and took off.

Connie puzzled over the suggestion in light of the visit she had just made with her neighbor. It seemed harmless enough, arranging for the couple to meet at an antique market. There was a nice one out on Route 29. She could ask Claudia to go with her one Saturday, perhaps on the notion of needing advice on old rockers for Sally's mother. Nodding her head at a possible game plan, Connie made for the customer service desk.

The workday passed by without any major shake-ups, for which Connie was grateful. To her surprise, there was no sighting of Lance all day. After the plans they had made, she was certain he would appear at various times to talk about what had happened. Even at lunch, he was nowhere to be found. Rumors soon spread of high-level business meetings within the store management. She could picture him sitting tense at the meetings, his personal data assistant in hand ready to take notes, a silk tie hanging loose around his neck, the sleeves of his white cotton shirt rolled to the elbows, his dark eyes alert. The mere thought of him made her tingle. She glanced down at her right hand, the one he held that night at the restaurant. There must be something brewing between them for her to feel the way she did, and for him to hold her hand on their first outing together.

Just then a deliveryman appeared at the customer service counter. "I'm looking for a Constance Ortish."

"Ortiz," she corrected, staring in surprise at the basket filled with a variety of spring flowers, from daisies to tulips to the heavenly scent of hyacinths that filled her head with a sweet fragrance.

The man left the basket on the desk. Donna immediately bounced over and took the card. "I bet I can guess who sent this."

Connie thought she could, too, even as her fingers shook while opening the envelope.

Thanking you for your kindness.
Silas Eugene Westerfield

Donna repeated the simple message. "Wow! It wasn't who I thought. Hey now, if that isn't a go-ahead to try to bring them together, I don't know what is! Reading between the lines, I'd say he's thanking you for helping him and Bette out."

"But I haven't done anything," she said. "And I refused to sell him the clock."

"Lance probably told him how you talked to Bette, and he's thanking you for it. That means he wants to get back together with her."

"I suppose it does. Maybe this is the sign I've been waiting for." She touched one of the soft tulip heads, then inhaled the fragrance of the hyacinth.

Just then Lance appeared. Seeing him, Donna shot Connie a quick smile before busying herself with sorting out returns.

"So they came," Lance observed. "Granddad said he was going to send you something. I told him it wasn't necessary, but he wanted to."

"They're lovely. Does this mean he's giving us permission to try to work things out between himself and my neighbor?"

"He won't do it himself, so I guess we should take up the torch. How about we grab some food for a picnic and meet at the park? We can talk over a game plan there."

"That would be nice."

"Good. See you after work." He waltzed away, whistling a tune as if happy about the plan.

Donna gave her a thumbs-up signal. "Looking good. Our manager is falling head over heels in love. Like grandfather, like grandson."

Connie wasn't certain she would categorize their relationship in that light, but at least she was spending more time getting to know Lance. She sailed through the last remaining hour of the workday, all the while anticipating the picnic that evening. After the work shift ended, she headed home to dress in something more comfortable and give a drink of water to the pretty arrangement of flowers. She wondered if Silas Westerfield really did send the flowers or if Lance did it in disguise. Whatever the reason, Connie enjoyed how the arrangement spruced up her apartment.

When Mr. Cuckoo emerged for his five o'clock serenade, she lifted up the basket of flowers. "All this is because of you," she informed the famous clock. "Not only do I get a basket of sweet-smelling posies but also an outing with a wonderful guy."

Just then she heard the sound of a car. Glancing out the window, she saw Lance approaching the door. "Sorry I didn't tell you specifically where and when to meet," he said, digging his hands into the pockets of his jeans. "We can make a stop at a deli and grab something to eat."

"I'll be ready in a minute." She ran around breathless, fetching her purse and some paper products left over from the luncheon. It had been a whirlwind of an invite, but she was looking forward to sharing about his grandfather, Claudia Rowe, and tidbits about themselves. When she returned, Lance held the door open for her. The sky was an azure blue, the birds active as they fluttered about, even with the sun dipping low on the horizon. It was a perfect evening to have dinner and talk beneath a canopy of trees.

The picnic was a great success. With Connie's disposable dishes and the food Lance had purchased at the deli—including a rotisserie chicken and potato salad—it couldn't have been better. They chatted for a time about the store. Lance mentioned how he might be away next month to help start a sister store in the valley over the mountain. Connie marveled at the responsibilities he had been given, wondering why he would want to associate with someone of her status. None of it seemed to matter to him, though, as he delved into the main topic of their get-together—Gene and Bette.

"When I talked to you earlier, you didn't seem too thrilled over the meeting you had with your neighbor."

Connie nodded. "She wasn't thrilled at all. In fact, she was pretty upset, so I didn't want to press the issue."

Lance considered this. "I tried talking with Granddad about her. He didn't say much. In fact, he never really told me why they broke off their engagement. Not that I'm upset about it—I wouldn't be here if they had married!" He cracked a grin.

"That's true. I guess we need to be thankful that it didn't work out. When Mrs. Rowe told me what happened, though, I'll have to say it was pretty sad."

Lance leaned forward, his eagerness for information spelled out in his eyes that reflected the coming twilight. "What happened?"

Connie proceeded to tell him of the falling out they had because of the differences in their social status. "It's sort of like us—hypothetically, I mean—you're a guy with a great and wonderful career, and I'm just a little old clerk behind a desk."

"Connie, we're people. . .not items to be compared with on a store shelf. Anyone who puts a price tag on a human being is crazy."

"I think that's what happened with Claudia and your grandfather. Claudia's father told her she couldn't marry him, and she abided by his wishes. They ended up moving away. She lost contact with your grandfather after that."

"Poor Granddad. At least he did find someone else in my grandmother. She died ten years ago."

"So did Claudia Rowe's husband. Of cancer."

"Same with my grandmother. Strange coincidence. And now we have two lonely people who were once engaged, trying to find their place in life."

"Claudia feels her place is with her daughters in Virginia Beach. I don't think your grandfather is anywhere in the equation. But I'm wondering if perhaps something can still be done. It's obvious your grandfather cares a great deal about her. I don't think he would have sent a basket of flowers to thank me if he felt I was doing something wrong."

"You're right about that."

Connie gazed up into the tree branches. It was a perfect place for a picnic, right beside the glistening waters of a gurgling brook. "We need to find a way for them to meet. Donna suggested we try to bring them together using some common interest. Since they both love antiques, maybe we can use that area. In fact, I was thinking of that nice antique center out on Route 29."

"Hmm. A possibility. Granddad likes going there. I wouldn't have any trouble coaxing him to come. But what about you? How do you plan to get Mrs. Rowe there? I'm sure she's plenty busy with moving and all."

Connie traced the back of the park bench with her finger. "I have an idea. Sally wants a rocking chair. I'm hoping Claudia can lend me a hand deciding which style chair might be suitable. Sally wants me to find one at a yard sale, but I can still look around at an antique place, too."

"You've got the brains to match your looks," Lance said.

Connie gazed at him in wonder. To her delight, she found him staring at her with a look she couldn't decipher. How she wished she could read his mind. Did he truly like what he saw? Her question was answered when he scooted over ever so slowly and curled his arms around her, ushering her toward him. The next moment, Connie was experiencing the warmth of his lips and the fragrance of his cologne washing over her. A bird landed on a limb just above them to serenade the moment with a song. Lance pulled back and chuckled.

"Maybe that was a song of approval," he said softly.

"I don't know, Lance. I'm not sure."

He straightened as if he had been reprimanded. "I'm sorry, Connie. I thought maybe you—I guess I read this wrong. Sorry."

"What do you mean? I was thinking about how to get Claudia to go antique shopping with me." She giggled at the confusion that distorted his features. "Anyway, I've been hoping you *were* reading this right."

He smiled. "Good. I'm glad to hear it. I wasn't sure how you would react at first. Normally I'm not that impulsive, but you look gorgeous sitting here by the river. And that look in your eyes when you talked about trying to get my granddad and your neighbor back together—the timing seemed perfect."

"As long as we're in this together."

"Through thick and thin," he promised, taking her hand in his.

She prayed so. She couldn't take any more upheaval in her life right now.

Chapter 12

Lance discovered that the antique center, the Country Shops of Culpeper, was holding a special open house the following weekend. When he called Connie with the news, they decided that this might prove their best opportunity to bring two people together in the hope of reconciliation. Connie sometimes wondered whether they were intruding after her encounter with Claudia Rowe. She only wanted peace in this situation. If there was one thing Connie desperately craved in her own life, it was peace. When she found out what life was like without it—that raw sense of anxiety mixed with an unsettled feeling like one lost in a dark forest—Connie did whatever was necessary to restore peace in her life. It was hard for her to understand how people like Claudia Rowe and Donna could live without the peace of God in their hearts. What did they do when the going got rough? Connie knew what Donna liked to do—shop or eat. Maybe Claudia was the same way with her antiques. Still, she was hopeful that through all of this, God might open a door, not only to reconciliation but a hope in Him, as well.

Connie eagerly prepared herself for the encounter with her neighbor. Before picking up the phone, she offered a prayer that the older woman would not shun her after what happened during their last visit. With the tears that were shed, along with the broken china, there seemed little reason to believe Claudia would agree to the excursion. She placed it all in God's hands.

Her confidence soared after making the call. Claudia was delighted to hear from her. Then came a surprise question—if Connie would come over and help her do some more packing.

"Since my daughters are so far away, there's no one here to help. And you did such a careful job the last time. I know we had that discussion about Gene, but that still doesn't mean you didn't do a wonderful job here. I'm grateful."

Connie smiled at this open invitation. She agreed to help, deciding to broach the subject about antique shopping after she arrived. There was little doubt that the best way to her neighbor's heart lay in offering a helping hand. Maybe if all went well, Connie would find her acquiescing to the excursion. Claudia would then run into Silas Westerfield, they would talk, and presto, love would be reborn like in the movies.

Connie arrived to find Claudia trying to pack heavy books into boxes. She scolded herself for not thinking of having Lance come help, especially with the heavier items. Two instead of one might have been helpful in this endeavor. Claudia greeted her with a pleasant smile, a glass of iced tea, and a request to help sort out some of the older books. They chatted about various topics until Connie mentioned Sally and the need to find her mother an antique rocking chair as a surprise birthday gift.

"Oh, rocking chairs," Claudia said with a sigh. "I have a book somewhere in this stack that shows many rocking chairs dating back several centuries. They were all made back then by superior craftsmen. It took precision work." She found a thick book on antiques and settled down on the sofa. "Yes, here it is. See how lovely they are?"

"Is it possible to find an antique like that in a store?"

"I'm not sure. Of course with the move and all, I haven't had a chance to look around at the antique stores here in town."

"Honestly, if I tried to look for one, I'd probably get something that was a fake. And I heard some good things about that antique center on Route 29. Any chance you might get some free time on Saturday to come with me and look at a few rocking chairs?"

A glint of anticipation danced in Claudia's eyes. "Oh, that would be lovely. I need to get out of this house. We can make an outing of it. We'll go antique shopping, and as my treat for all your help, I'll buy lunch."

Connie smiled smugly. This was going better than she had anticipated. And maybe after all was said and done, it would be Gene accompanying Bette to lunch. The mere thought sent tingles shooting straight down her spine. For all the concern over the outcome of this day, she could hardly wait to tell Lance how everything had fallen into place.

The afternoon flew by while they packed up the whole library. When she was ready to leave, Claudia thanked her profusely for her help. "I'm looking forward to antique browsing and lunch," Connie said. "Does ten thirty on Saturday sound good?"

"That's fine. See you Saturday."

Connie felt like she was floating on a cloud. She drifted down the sidewalk toward her apartment. Not only did she have the outing planned with Claudia Rowe, but the kisses of Lance Adams also lent energy to her steps. Nothing could be more perfect.

When she arrived home, she nearly embraced the cuckoo clock. The piece had been a trial at first, but doors were opening that had once been closed tight—like reconciliation, forgiveness, and, for Connie, love. She wondered then what it would be like to be married to the assistant manager of a store. There was no sense in pondering that quite yet. Yes, Lance had kissed her, but there was still plenty of time before they would run down the aisle. At one time, Connie vowed only to kiss the man she would marry. She had made that promise to herself long ago, even though she told no one about it—not even the few guys she had dated. When she opened herself up to accept Lance's kiss, she knew there was something special about him. And it wasn't just the kiss but his whole manner. They had been drawn together since day one and had only grown closer as time passed. Surely God would not have brought such a man into her life if he weren't meant to remain a permanent fixture in her heart.

Just then the phone rang. It was he, the man she thought of day and night.

"Hello, Connie."

He spoke her name in such a tender way that she nearly melted. The voice came from sweet lips that had touched hers just a few days ago. How she wanted to say, *Hello, Prince Charming. You have swept me off my feet,* but said simply, "Hi, Lance."

"So how did it go?"

"Marvelous! Absolutely marvelous. Claudia is definitely coming to the antique center this Saturday. And she plans to take me to lunch as a thank-you for helping her pack. I'm hoping it will turn into a luncheon date with you-know-who."

"Well, I hate to put a damper on all this, but there's a problem. Granddad refuses to go."

Her mouth fell open at this revelation. It never dawned on her that Silas Westerfield wouldn't go. She was certain he wanted to see Claudia again but was too shy or proud to arrange such a meeting himself. "What? Why?"

"He knows this is all a setup. Granddad is pretty smart. Sure, he might have been poor in money but definitely not in brains. He knows Bette will be there, and he knows what's going to happen—a tense scene he would rather not be a part of."

"How can he know what will happen? For all we know, it could be a wonderful time for the both of them."

"You and I might believe that, but he doesn't. The mere idea makes him very nervous. It's been over forty years. A lot has changed, and he isn't a spring chicken anymore. He would rather do something less drastic, like call her on the phone maybe. But since she's moving, he feels it's all a waste of time anyway."

"But this is a perfect situation—in a nonthreatening setting that they both love. This is the time, Lance. It's now or never."

"For someone who wasn't sure about this whole thing, you're sure excited now."

"Of course I am. Claudia is anxious to go. I mean, I did give her the alibi about checking out rocking chairs, but it fit perfectly with our plan."

"I'm not sure what do from this end. I can't make Granddad go."

"Give me his phone number. Maybe I can try talking to him."

"You?"

"Why not? He did send me the beautiful basket of flowers. He knows I've been talking with my neighbor. To me, that means there must be something there. If he was angry over my involvement, he would have sent a basket of poison ivy instead."

"Connie!"

"Well. . .the point is, maybe I have a little leverage. I did get the lowdown from Claudia about why they broke off their engagement. The least I can do is try."

Lance finally relented, giving her the phone number and telling her to call before 8:00 p.m. "But don't try to pull the wool over his eyes. He'll read right through it."

Connie promised. With the phone number in her hand, she thought about the words to say, as she had to do quite often these days. God again needed to guide the conversation. She did want to see things restored and prayed this message might be reflected in her words.

Later that evening, she dialed the number Lance had given her. When she introduced herself, she heard a cough.

"Miss Ortiz, this is a surprise."

Connie managed to clear the frog in her own throat. "Mr. Westerfield, I wanted to thank you for the lovely basket of flowers."

"You're quite welcome."

"I'm not sure I deserve it, but I wanted to thank you anyway."

"What? What do you mean you don't think you deserve it?"

"Oh, after the way I acted when you came calling. All I wanted to do was hold on to this cuckoo clock at all cost. I didn't even take into account your feelings."

She sensed his hesitancy. "But I know it was a priceless item that reminded you of your grandmother," he said.

"Yes, but you also mentioned how priceless it is to you, as well. Of course I had no idea what you meant, but I know now. Love really is priceless when you think about it. We can own all the things in the world, even be as rich as a king or sultan, but when it comes right down to it, love is the costliest possession of all."

Again, she felt his confusion on the phone. He coughed several times. "I'm not exactly sure why you're bringing this up."

"Well you see, I know your grandson quite well. And I've also been getting along with my neighbor Mrs. Rowe."

"Really. In what way?"

"The Bible talks about the rewards one gets for being a servant. That's what I've been trying to do, not to put myself on a pedestal or anything. I've been helping her pack and all. I found out that sometimes it's the little acts of kindness that can win hearts. It's so easy to get caught up in our own little world. Once we break out of it to reach out to others, we find things we didn't even know existed. Companionship, conversation, even reconciliation. And these are all worth much more than any clock, don't you think?"

Silence came over the phone. Connie began to pray, hoping she hadn't overstepped her boundary. Sometimes her passion for a subject overshadowed discretion.

"I guess I've been trying to run away from it," he said slowly. "I'm a Christian, too, you see. I thought all I wanted was the clock, but what I really want is to reach out to the one who owned it. I'm afraid I'm too late."

"It's never too late, especially if God is in control. The only sure way to find out is to come to the antique center on Saturday with your grandson. God might surprise you."

He chuckled. "My dear girl, I've been surprised quite a bit by God and certainly not in ways I had anticipated. I had a wonderful marriage with my wife, Margaret, God bless her. I was content to live alone the rest of my life. But when I saw the ad for the yard sale at Bette's house and then saw she was selling our beloved clock, something stirred to life; something I thought was gone forever. At first I wanted to contact her. Then I thought perhaps if I got the clock I could use it as a way to reach her."

"It's not too late, Mr. Westerfield. The best way to find out is to do a test this Saturday. I know that sometimes people abuse the Gideon-type test of hanging out fleeces, but it's okay to take a few steps forward and see where the path leads you. That's what I did, and that's how I found a clock and eventually your grandson."

"Lance has grown quite fond of you. He talks about you all the time. All right, I will consider it."

She sighed before hanging up the phone. It was all she could hope for, considering the circumstances. Now it was up to two wandering hearts and the Lord Himself to do the rest.

❦

Connie found her neighbor bubbling over with excitement as they drove through town to the antique center. Claudia shared about the town of Culpeper and how it had grown from when she was a little girl. She mentioned the store where Connie worked and how a large farm once stood there when she was a young girl. The owner happened to be a nice old man whose wife often baked cookies for church bake sales.

"I thought you only lived here a few years."

"I spent my childhood here. I moved away in my early twenties." She pointed to the rustic buildings that withstood the test of time. Those that used to stand were now replaced by modern shopping establishments and the solid brick buildings of downtown businesses. "I know towns change, but I wish some of the old places were still around. For instance, I remember the old soda shop. I was so sad when it closed two years ago. That's where my young man once bought me my first ice cream float. It was a wonderful time, too. Ice cream was cheap back then, certainly not like it is now. I once had to pay nearly three dollars for a simple hot fudge sundae with a cherry on top. I told the manager it was highway robbery. When I was growing up, such a treat would have cost thirty cents."

Connie nearly asked her if the young man she was referring to was Silas "Gene" Westerfield but decided against it. She drove out onto the main highway and soon arrived at the antique center. The parking lot was overflowing with customers. Outside looked like a carnival. Vendors were selling homemade goodies and even cotton candy. Inside the center were all kinds of stately antiques from a bygone era. Connie was surprised to find items for sale that were available in recent memory—like older Barbie dolls, metal dollhouses, even an original little baking oven that outdated the newer models now available.

Claudia delved into the antiques as if she were young again, exclaiming over each one. She was a wealth of information, talking about the age of the item and its market value. Connie tagged along, trying to listen to her explanations, all the while wondering if Lance had arrived yet with his grandfather. When Claudia stopped to examine wares inside a curio cabinet, Connie spotted them across the aisle. She exhaled a sigh of relief. Lance caught her eye and nodded. Connie wondered how to proceed when Lance beckoned to her while his grandfather was engaged in a solid cherry bedstead. Connie told her neighbor she wanted to check out a booth across the way, then slipped over to meet Lance at the end of the aisle.

"I'm so glad you're here," she whispered, giving him a hug of relief.

"I guess that talk you had with Granddad did the trick. I don't know what you said, but when I asked again if he would come, he said yes."

The two of them peered around a wooden pie safe to see Lance's grandfather making his way across the aisle. The man suddenly stopped short. Connie gasped, putting her hand on her chest to feel the rapid beating of her heart. This scene was almost too much to bear. Lance slipped his hand over hers and gave her a gentle squeeze of encouragement. They inched closer, hoping to hear bits and pieces of what was transpiring.

"I see you still like antiques," they heard Gene announce.

Bette whirled at the voice. She grabbed hold of the edge of the curio cabinet to steady her gait. "G–Gene!"

"Hello, Bette."

Bette bristled. A red flush filled her cheeks. "What are you doing here?"

"I suppose the same thing you're doing. Browsing."

Bette looked around hurriedly, as if scanning the establishment for Connie's whereabouts. Connie gripped Lance's hand as they ducked behind the pie safe. When they peered around it to observe the scene, Bette and Gene were staring at each other as if scrutinizing a memory from long ago.

"So how are you? I heard you're moving out of town."

"I'm fine," Bette said quickly, shoving the strap of her purse over her shoulder. "And yes, I am moving. The closing is a week from Monday. I'm moving to Virginia Beach to be with my daughters."

"That's nice." He gazed at the ground. "I knew you had moved back here quite awhile ago, but I decided it wouldn't be wise to come calling."

"No, it wouldn't. We really have nothing to say to each other." She straightened then and folded her arms. "But I am curious to know why you were trying to hoodwink a young lady into selling you the cuckoo clock. When she told me how much you were willing to pay for it, I nearly had a coronary."

"It's really my business, Bette."

"No, it's mine. After all, it was my clock."

"It was *our* clock," he corrected. "I gave it to you on the condition of a promise."

"That was your promise, not mine. I never promised to marry you. It was your choice to give me some kind of fancy clock that I must say never saw the light of day."

The harsh words Claudia spoke were difficult to hear. Connie was surprised that Lance's grandfather didn't march away right then and there. She looked over at Lance, wondering how he felt about it all. Yet he only stood by as did his grandfather—two strong towers in the midst of a battle. His lips moved in silent prayer. Lance always knew the right thing to do in a difficult situation.

"I'm sorry to hear you say that," Gene continued. "It meant a lot to me, just as you do. I was hoping you might feel the same way."

"I'm sorry to say I don't. I suppose that now you've fallen by a little money with your antique dealing you think I should fall all over you after forty years."

"Bette, you don't know me at all. I thought the love we once had would be able to see through the past. Yes, we did find love with others, and now have wonderful families because of it. But that doesn't mean we need to forget what we once had."

"Maybe you want to live in the past. I don't. It's gone. It's forgotten."

"Is it? The past has a way of influencing the future. I don't want the years I have left in this world clouded over by rumors that were never true. You must know it. Ask your heart, Bette. Maybe we can find somewhere to talk about it."

She shook her head and strode away. Connie bade Lance a hasty good-bye and headed toward a booth, just as Claudia approached. "I was just going to..." Connie began, then paused. "Mrs. Rowe, is something wrong?"

Claudia took a tissue out of her purse and began blowing her nose. "I can't believe this happened. Right out of the blue, forty years later, he shows up wanting to reconcile."

"What do you mean?"

"Gene! I can't believe it. After all these years." She shook her head. "I'm sorry, but you'll have to take me home. I'm getting a terrible headache. He nearly made me have a nervous breakdown."

"What happened?"

She tearfully explained her encounter with Silas Westerfield while they headed for the car. "He's still the same man Daddy warned me about so many years ago. Serving his own self-interests. Trying to take over my life."

"Maybe he just wanted to say hello."

"Well, I know for a fact he wants that cuckoo clock. Just remember, you promised not to give it to him. I don't want him to have it. He'll parade it around like some kind of trophy, hoping I'll come running to him."

"And what if he does parade it around? What does the clock mean to him other than a representation of the love he once had for you?"

Claudia stared at Connie, speechless.

She started the car and headed for the road. "If I had someone who loved me that much, I would be so glad. I would thank God every day for it. That kind of love is hard to come by these days."

"H–he never really loved me. You didn't know him back then. He loved money and antiques."

"Maybe he did, but what he loves right now is the engraving of two names on the back panel of the cuckoo clock that speaks of something long ago. Yes, you both have suffered losses, but why not see if there's something else left while there's still time?"

Her face reddened. "I wish you would leave this situation alone. I appreciate your concern, but I need to deal with it as I see fit." She turned away and stared out the window. Connie could think of a million things she wanted to say but decided not to press the issue. She drove her neighbor home in silence. With a quick thank-you, Claudia got out of the car and strode away. Connie never felt lower in her life. All the joy she nursed over a possible reunion had evaporated into thin air. Now there was nothing but emptiness.

Chapter 13

After the episode at the antique center, Connie allowed the phone to ring in her apartment, even though she knew it was Lance. She felt confused by everything. Though the seed planting might have been admirable, the fruit from it was diseased. Connie always looked to the consequences of her actions. While she wanted things to come out right, when they didn't, she decided she must have done something wrong. If this were right, wouldn't God have blessed the encounter? Maybe the idea of setting up the meeting bordered on a deception that the Lord had frowned upon. At any rate, she felt miserable. Everything was hopeless.

Before church began on Sunday, Lance left his circle of friends to come find her. She had taken a seat in the back and began leafing through the Bible, hoping to lose herself within its pages. "Are you okay?" he asked. "I tried calling you, but there was no answer. I nearly went over to your place to knock on the door."

"I just wanted to be alone for a while."

"Did something happen between you and Mrs. Rowe?"

Connie shrugged.

Lance took a seat next to her, despite the looks they received from members of the congregation. Connie winced. No doubt everyone was eager to know if something was materializing between them. Why would it, after all? Lance was well thought of within the congregation. He served on many committees and was involved in helping lead the youth group. And he was the assistant manager of a megastore. She was just ordinary little Connie, a simple desk clerk, barely making ends meet.

"Hello, hello, wherever you are," Lance whispered in her ear.

The sensation of his breath on her ear sent shivers racing up her spine. She nearly leaped to her feet. "Look, I just have a few things to think about." She stood then as the worship team came forward to lead the congregation in the opening song.

Lance left her to take his place with several men in a separate row. She sat alone in the row usually reserved for latecomers, trying hard to become a part of the worship. Yet self-pity clouded the time. She felt disillusioned about everything—Claudia Rowe, Silas Westerfield, her relationship with Lance, maybe even God.

When the service was over, Connie was quick to make a swift exit out of the church, but not as quickly as she'd hoped. Lance had left by a side entrance and was there at her car when she arrived.

"Well, aren't you Speedy Gonzales?" she murmured.

"I can see you're down in the dumps. Don't let yesterday bother you. I thought it was quite encouraging."

"Huh?" She stared at him in bewilderment.

"Sure. I mean, you didn't think after forty-some years they would take each other in their arms and confess their love, did you? At least they're starting to talk about the past."

Connie fumbled for her keys. "I guess, if you call that progress."

"C'mon, I'll take you out for brunch. I know a little hole-in-the-wall that would be perfect. It's been around for ages. A locals' hangout called Baby Jim's. Granddad loves it."

"Baby Jim's, huh? Sounds like my kind of place." Connie reluctantly went along to his car. He said little as they drove to the old restaurant connected to the basement of a regular house. He led the way into the restaurant, filled to capacity with the after-church crowd. Customers were served every kind of greasy food available. Connie couldn't imagine this place being a hangout of Lance's grandfather's. She stood in line with Lance until he placed their order for two breakfast platters. Connie wasn't sure what to say but stared at the interior of the restaurant that represented the old-fashioned lunch counters of long ago. "I've passed this place a few times, but I've never been here."

"Like I said, this is the local hangout. It's been around since the thirties. They only serve breakfast and lunch. Granddad took me here a few times. He and Bette used to come here, too. We'll sit where they used to, at one of the picnic tables."

"Oh." Connie winced when he mentioned the sore subject of Gene and Bette. Of course they would end up sharing a meal at the same place where the couple once ate.

"What's on your mind?" he asked.

"I'm just trying to imagine Claudia Rowe and your grandfather as young people madly in love. Maybe they once sat there, side by side, sharing in a tall frosty milk shake and a plate of fries."

"For all I know, they did just that. They loved coming here. They also enjoyed strolls through the meadow that's now part of the park where we had our picnic."

Lance grabbed the platters while Connie took the drinks and headed for a picnic table. The eggs and sausage looked very appetizing, but right now the lump in Connie's throat quelled her hunger. Lance, on the other hand, dug right in. She tentatively picked up the fork and took a few bites. It was good, despite the mood she was in. They said little else but enjoyed their brunch. Connie was glad for Lance's optimism, even after what they had witnessed at the antique center. She thought he might be deeper in the dumps than she was. She admired his faith in tough situations.

Finally Connie put down her fork. "Maybe we should've never gotten involved, Lance. None of this is our business anyway."

"I beg to differ. It became our business when you bought the clock."

"Then I'll get rid of it. Maybe I'll give it to Donna. She can keep tabs on this whole situation. In fact, knowing her, she would probably love to be in the thick of things. I'll tell Claudia I gave it to a friend. I can't take much more of this."

Lance leaned over. His hand gently reached out to take up hers. She trembled under his touch. "Okay, what's this all about, Connie? You were so confident. Now you act like this is the worst thing that could have happened."

"I was just surprised at the hurt I saw between the two of them. Maybe I was expecting more, like words of kindness instead of bitterness. I know I couldn't expect a hug and kiss, but I thought after being separated over forty years they would be a little more friendly. Especially on my neighbor's part."

"Granddad was surprised by the encounter, I must admit. He said that Bette still has a lot of bitterness about the past. I tried talking to him, to make him see that maybe she doesn't really mean it, that she was just startled to see him. He believes she's still hounded by all that nonsense her father once planted in her brain. He had hoped all these years would make her see the light. He feels someone in that kind of darkness isn't worth pursuing."

"So it's hopeless."

"Connie, you and I both know that with God nothing is hopeless. These two had a falling out forty-some years ago. It was never resolved. This is why God wants us to reconcile with each other as soon as possible. It's a perfect example of what happens when too much time is allowed to elapse without a resolution. The heart can turn to stone."

"And it looks to me like they have no intention of resolving their differences. So what are we doing in the middle of it?"

Lance took his coffee and dumped in a cream and two packets of sugar. Instead of answering her question, he posed another. "Do you think we should give up?"

"I don't know. I've been considering it all night and most of the morning. Claudia has already told me to leave her alone. I don't have an invitation to communicate with her anytime soon. And she is set to move in a little over a week. I say we drop the whole thing."

"I think before we throw in the towel we should find out what to do. And I know just the ticket."

Connie was about to ask for details when she saw the twinkle in his eye. She realized they had been down this road before, with his wisdom shining like a bright bulb in a dark and difficult situation. "I know exactly what you're going to say. Pray and ask God."

"Bingo. I said you were sharp, and I meant it. Even if things don't go as planned, Connie, we need to persevere until God chooses to close the door. While Claudia may think she has closed the door, I'll wait for God to do it Himself. In the meantime, let's you and I both take the rest of this Sunday to take the matter to Him. I think it will surprise us to find out that He wants these two people to reconcile more than we do."

"I hope so. I don't want to think that the encounter inside the antique center has shut the door for good."

"This is a lot like the clock. I'll bet when you took it to the clockmaker he probably did a little cleaning and all."

"He wanted to do more, but I didn't think it was necessary."

"Sometimes our hearts need a little fine-tuning and cleaning to make everything run in good order. I don't think anything here has been a mistake. God wants to use people, but they need a little sprucing up, even repairs to the damage in their lives. Once that's accomplished, I believe there's a destiny planned for Granddad and Mrs. Rowe, the same as I feel there's one for us."

The expectant look on his face told her that he might indeed be considering his own happiness as well as his grandfather's. It warmed her to think that he might think of her in that way. If only she felt as confident about the future.

He drove her back to church to pick up her car, rattling on about the days ahead and how God had everything planned out. After thanking him for brunch, she went home to ponder the encounter. Lance was indeed a rare gem. If only she didn't feel so doubtful about everything. Inside the apartment she barely heard the cuckoo singing until she glanced over at the tiny painted bird, making his appearance at the two o'clock hour. She came and took the clock off the wall. Putting it facedown on the table, she examined the engraving on the back. She thought of Lance's grandfather and his eagerness to buy the clock from her. If only there was some way to convince her neighbor that Silas Westerfield's intentions were genuine, that he still loved her even after all these years. But Claudia Rowe was a woman frozen to a belief that the man was only looking out for his own interests. It would be difficult to thaw out a heart like that and make her think otherwise.

Connie replaced the clock and decided to take a walk. It was a picture-perfect afternoon, with the sun gleaming and the temperature pleasant. She walked down the street until she came to Claudia Rowe's house. It sat still and quiet. Most of the boxes on the porch were gone. The storage shed was open, revealing the boxes stacked inside, ready for the moving van when it appeared. She swallowed hard. If Claudia moved away before reconciliation could take place, it would spell the end for the couple's chances. They would go their separate ways and never look back.

Connie continued on, dreaming of walking down the aisle into Lance's arms. Flowers surrounded the pebbled path. The breeze sent her fine veil billowing. She could see a perfect church set up in God's glory, beneath the trees at the park where she and Lance first shared in a kiss. A true covenant would commence in that special place. If only there was some way for another couple by the name of Gene and Bette to likewise make such a commitment.

Connie returned home, anxious to call Lance and tell him about her dream—just the part about Gene and Bette. He'd talked about them having a future, but she knew it would be presumptuous of her to tell him she'd been daydreaming about walking down the aisle into his arms.

When he answered, she said, "Hi, Lance. I've got another idea. Maybe we should set up a table for two in that special grove of trees by the river, the same place where we had our talk. We can tell your grandfather and my neighbor there will be a picnic, but instead, it will be a private get-together."

"Are you serious? Why the sudden change?"

"I was thinking about weddings and saw a beautiful one in God's creation, right there in the park. I think it would be nice if your grandfather and Claudia could meet one final time. In a place like that, anything can happen. Look at us."

"Weddings, huh?" Lance chuckled softly. "It's a nice idea, except I don't believe they would fall for another outing. What's the saying? 'Fool me once, shame on you; fool me twice, shame on me.'"

"I don't think Claudia suspects that I set her up at the antique center. Your grandfather knew about the encounter, but she didn't. So it wouldn't seem out of the ordinary to have a picnic in the park, at least from her point of view."

"I thought Mrs. Rowe asked you not to be involved anymore."

"She did. I'm thinking perhaps of trying to get one of her daughters or a friend to help out. Someone she knows who might be willing to invite her to a gathering."

"I'm not sure, Connie. If you ask and the daughter doesn't want her mother involved, it could boomerang. We know from Bette's past that having family caught up in everything isn't always the best solution."

"Good point. Then what would you suggest? I'm out of ideas."

There was such a long pause Connie thought the call had terminated. "Lance?"

"I'm still here. Just thinking about what you said and how we can get them both to the park for a picnic. I still don't think it would be wise to involve her family. Maybe if we pretend to have a gathering hosted by friends—like a going-away celebration since she's moving away. That might work."

"What about your grandfather? How would you get him to come to the park?"

"Oh, Granddad likes a stroll in the park anytime, so long as we take it easy. I'll pack us a lunch, and he'll think we're going there for our own picnic and to talk about business. He likes it when I ask him for advice. He's always giving me pointers from a business standpoint."

"Maybe I can find out about the friends Claudia has in the area. If she thinks it's a friendly get-together to see her off, she wouldn't be suspicious. Since she's moving, especially as far away as Virginia Beach, it would make sense that people would want to give her a send-off."

"Sounds like you have a plan, lady. Let me know if I can help in any way."

Connie immediately went to work creating an invitation on the computer. She paused to consider it all, realizing the whole thing could fall apart if Claudia refused to come. She dared not deliver the invitation herself after the fiasco at the antique center. She considered the neighbors in the area who might help and recalled the elderly couple living next door to Claudia. Perhaps they would be helpful in encouraging her to accept the invitation.

Connie spruced up her hair, grabbed her purse and the invitation, then made her way down the street. She carefully sneaked up to the neighbor's house, hoping Claudia wouldn't suddenly glance out her window and catch her moseying up the driveway.

At the door, a kindly woman answered. "Hello. I think I recognize you."

"I'm Connie Ortiz. I live down the street in the apartment building."

"Yes, that's right. I'm Hilda McCall. Would you like to come in?"

Connie was grateful for the open invitation. She went in and, to her astonishment, saw a cuckoo clock hanging on the wall. She nearly gasped out loud but managed to control her emotions. "I'm sorry for barging in like this," she began.

"It's no bother. I was just telling Stanley the other day that we really don't know many of our neighbors except for Claudia. And now she's moving away. The last I heard, some young couple bought her house."

"Do you know Mrs. Rowe very well?"

"Oh yes, ever since she moved in. She has so many beautiful antiques. We get together for coffee sometimes."

"I actually bought one of her antiques at the yard sale she had not too long ago. Would you believe it was a cuckoo clock?"

"Really?" Hilda's gaze settled on her own clock hanging on the wall. "Aren't they just precious?"

"Yes, and it just so happens that the clock was involved in a mystery of sorts." Connie delved into the history of the clock and how it symbolized the love between Claudia and Lance's grandfather named Gene. Hilda listened with interest.

"You know, I seem to recall Claudia mentioning a certain gentleman in her past. She said she nearly married him but they had a falling out."

"Well, believe it or not, Gene's grandson, Lance, and I are hoping there might be some sparks left. They both have been widowed for many years. I know that Gene really wants to talk to her. But Mrs. Rowe hasn't been too keen on the idea. So Lance and I came up with a plan, a picnic for two at the park. The problem is, I don't think Mrs. Rowe will go if she knows Gene will be there. So I was thinking of having someone invite her to a pretend farewell party given by her friends. I immediately thought of you, since you are her closest neighbor."

"Will this Gene be at the party?"

"That's the point. The party will not be a true party at all but a special picnic for the two of them. Lance and I want to see them come together if possible and try to work out their differences."

"So the party idea is a ruse for a special picnic. You're going to an awful lot of trouble, Connie. Why are you doing this, if I might ask?"

Connie paused. Why did she want to do this? "I've never really considered it up until now. I have no personal reasons for bringing them together, I guess. But Gene is Lance's grandfather. And they are very close. If his grandfather's happiness means Lance's happiness, then I'll do what I can to see it through."

Hilda laughed. "Aha, I see. But you must know if Claudia doesn't want to associate with the man then there's nothing you can do to make it happen. Even if your intentions are good."

"Oh, I understand. But I don't see any harm in trying one more time for a reunion between the two of them before she leaves this area for good. It might mend both their hearts instead of having them hurt for the rest of their lives. And I've talked with Mrs. Rowe about the past. Believe me, I can tell she's hurting. Sometimes talking things out is the best medicine in the world."

"I can't argue with that. Stanley and I have talked through many difficulties, even when it was uncomfortable."

Connie withdrew the envelope. "This is the invitation. I was wondering if you might take this over to Claudia and see if she will come. I thought since you knew her, she might agree to it."

Hilda stared first at the envelope, then at Connie. "I don't know what it is that makes you young people get involved in things like this. I hope it's worth the effort."

"It will be if two broken hearts are mended."

Hilda smiled as she took the envelope. "I'll take it over to Claudia and let you know what she says. And I do know a few friends of hers. I can have them call and encourage her to come."

"That would be wonderful. Thank you so much." Connie nearly danced her way down the sidewalk. At least she had put the wheels in motion. Now it was up to the Lord to make it everything work out to the final destination, wherever it ended up.

Chapter 14

So far the plan had worked, according to Hilda McCall who had phoned Connie with Claudia's reaction to the invitation.

"At first Claudia was startled to think anyone would care enough to throw her a going-away bash. She went on to say she hoped there wouldn't be too many people, as she didn't like crowds." Hilda chuckled. "You know, I actually enjoyed being a part of this secret," she confessed. "In a way, I wish I was throwing the surprise party."

"If all goes well, maybe you can throw an engagement party instead."

Connie could just picture Hilda on the other end, shaking her head in wonder. "Don't you beat all, young lady. I've never seen anyone so determined. I guess if it's meant to be it will happen. But if it's not, then you must be willing to let it go. You can't force two people to reconcile, no matter how much you may want it to happen. Ultimately it's between them and the Lord."

Connie agreed. How often she wanted to change the circumstances of life through her own devices. She prayed she wouldn't suffer disappointment if things didn't go the way she planned. One might sow the seed and another might water it, but only God could cause the growth.

During the rest of the week, Connie was on the phone with Lance, sometimes several times a night, to go over details concerning the picnic. He'd marveled at her ingenuity, especially at recruiting the neighbors to help with the whole scheme.

Near the end of the week, they met at her place to finalize the menu that would be served up on china plates. As they discussed it, Connie thought about the two of them. How like Bette and Gene they were, two young people in love, but one well-off and the other poor. What would she do if Lance's family suddenly decided to treat her as an outcast? What if they convinced Lance to abandon her as Bette did to Gene? How would she ever live through that kind of rejection?

"You've gotten quiet all of a sudden," Lance remarked, staring at her in confusion. "Is something the matter with these plans?"

Connie traced her finger across a pillow decorating the old sofa that once belonged to her grandmother. "Just thinking about something."

"Thinking can sometimes cause more harm than good, Connie. And just to make sure it comes out right in the end, I'll offer a twenty-dollar bill instead of a penny for your thoughts."

She wanted to giggle at his play on words that spoke of his affection, but somehow the offer of money made her feel worse. He could put down twenty dollars if he wanted. She was lucky if she could put down a dime. Her finances certainly hadn't worsened as they had when she purchased the clock, but they hadn't improved much either. There were still weeks of penny-pinching no matter how much she scrimped and saved.

Lance reached into his pocket, took out his wallet, and withdrew a twenty-dollar bill. "Here. Take it. I'm desperate to find out what's happening in that pretty head of yours."

"I don't want your money. I just want to make sure there aren't any bomb-shells coming our way."

"Like what?"

She hesitated. He would think her foolish if she came out with it. But the consequences could be far worse if she stayed silent. It would be better to settle things now before they went any deeper with their relationship. "I need to know something. Are your parents against you being with someone who isn't finan-cially secure?"

His eyebrows lowered in confusion. "What brought this up?"

"We're trying to bring together two people who split apart because of fi-nances. One of the families did everything in their power to break up the en-gagement. I don't want that happening to us. So if there's any chance at all, then maybe it would be better for us to go our separate ways now and not get hurt."

"Connie, you're not making any sense. You know my job is secure."

"Not yours," she said in exasperation. "Mine. I'm the one as poor as a mouse. I was hardly able to buy groceries last month. I don't want your parents unhappy because you're hooked up with someone so poor."

To her dismay, Lance bit his lip as if to stifle a chuckle. "Do you honestly think that will happen?"

"I don't know. Can it?"

"Connie, if you must know, I'm the first one in my family to get a managerial position. Everyone has to save to make ends meet, except perhaps for my sister Alice. She's making a heap of money right now, but she worked hard like all of us to get where she's at. I've learned valuable lessons, too—that one's walk with God and their loved ones are far more important than how many bucks a person makes. Granddad learned that, also. And I'm hoping Bette will see the light and realize that what her father did to their relationship long ago was foolish. Sure we need money to exist, but there are other things more important."

"So I won't get looked down on by someone better off, like your sister?" Connie cringed at the thought of this Alice calling her up, asking her how much money she made before pronouncing her a leech to the entire Adams clan. In turn, they might shun her as Bette's family did to Lance's grandfather. She would be left with nothing but the memory of a love gone sour and the monotony of a job behind a customer service counter.

"In case you didn't know it, you already have a fan club. Granddad has been telling everyone what a wonderful lady you are. All my sisters want to meet you. They think you'd be perfect for someone like me." He chuckled. "They all want to help plan a huge wedding."

Connie grinned at the thought. It would be nice to have sisters to talk to. And her brother Louis would enjoy getting to know Lance. Maybe Lance could even influence Henry's life, too. Only God's divine hand could bring it to pass.

"So have I put your worries to rest?" he asked.

"I guess so."

"I will admit, though, that your questions have confirmed some things that God has been speaking to me about."

"Like what?"

"I'll let you know as time goes by. But for now, let's put the finishing touches on this picnic for two."

Connie went over the menu once more, yet now she was clearly distracted by his comment. What could God have been whispering to him in that still, small voice? Just when she had one question answered, another came to take its place. There was little time to ponder it while planning out the final details for the reunion between Bette and Gene.

At work the next day, Connie took out a notepad and began jotting down what they would need for the outing. *Small table* went on the list. *Pure white table-cloth and candlesticks in pewter holders.* The menu of chicken cordon bleu sounded elegant to Connie, accompanied by a bottle of sparkling cider served up in crystal goblets. She was furiously writing when a face peered over her shoulder, examining the paper.

"Wow, is all that for our manager?" Donna inquired with a smirk.

Connie covered the paper with her hand. "It's a secret."

"Oh, Connie, don't keep secrets from me. Are you planning a special dinner?"

"Yes, but it's not who you think. It's for Lance's grandfather and the lady he once loved."

"Oh, how sweet." Donna gently pushed Connie's hand away from the paper. "Sounds nice. Where do you plan on having it?"

"At the park. We found a really nice place. And I managed to get Bette's neighbor in on it. She's invited Bette to the park under the guise that some friends are throwing her a farewell party. Actually it will be an intimate dinner with Gene, though Bette doesn't know it yet."

Donna's eyes sparkled at the romantic ploy about to unfold. "I never knew you had it in you, Connie. I mean, you do know how to plan get-togethers, but it's amazing to see what you're doing for these people in particular. They've become your special project."

"I had a good trainer." When Donna raised an eyebrow, Connie pointed the pen at her. "Who was the one who first pointed out Lance to me? Who kept insisting I sell the clock, which eventually led to Claudia making a surprise visit at my apartment? And who discovered the mystery of the clock by going with me to the clock shop and finding that engraving on the back panel?"

Donna giggled and sat down beside to Connie. "I thought at first you considered me a bit too opinionated for my own good. I never told you this, but my parents always put me down for everything I did. I had an older sister who went into modeling, and they thought she was the greatest. I felt like I always had to compete with her. They would ask me why I couldn't do something with my life. When I left the house, I decided I would make something of myself. Of course I didn't think that this store would be a stopover along the way. I hope one day to go back to school and maybe work on a business degree. I wouldn't mind doing what Lance is doing—being a manager and all. I like working with people."

"I'll tell him."

Donna grabbed her arm. "Oh, don't tell him that! I don't have a degree anyway."

"But maybe he has some ideas on how you can further your career so you can become what you want to be. I really believe we have God-given goals for our lives. Like you, I'm wondering how this job will fit into my future plans. But I know if I didn't work here, I wouldn't have met you or Lance or had my adventure with a famous cuckoo clock." She chuckled at the wonder of it all. "Yet here I am. God worked it out for Lance to become a part of my life. And I think real soon he may even ask me to marry him."

"Wow. So it's heading in that direction already?"

Connie couldn't help blushing. "It seems that way. His family wants to plan the wedding. As nurses sometimes fall in love with their patients, it seems a manager may have fallen in love with his employee."

"How sweet." Donna fumbled with several register receipts she held in her hand. "So you really think God is running your life, don't you?"

"I know He is. I wouldn't have made it this far if He wasn't. It's much better having someone else at the helm. I'd probably mess it all up—maybe even end up like my brother Henry, who's still searching for his identity. But I'm glad I found my identity in God. I'd much rather have His plans for my life than any other."

Donna didn't reply but went over to the register where a line of customers had begun forming. Connie didn't realize the store had opened for business. She was so intent on sharing her love for the Lord that the time had flown by. But she sensed a joy in her heart concerning Donna. Even if she wasn't the one to bring her friend to the Lord, at least she could throw down a seed now and then.

ज़

The day of the picnic arrived. Connie was more nervous than she had ever been in her life. She wondered what led her to do strange things like this. It must be that special Someone who had given her the grace to go forth. Most people would let life run its course and not get involved. But she was heavily involved now. Her neighbor was once the love of Lance's grandfather. All of them had been united by her cuckoo clock. She felt obligated to at least try to make something wonderful happen.

She gingerly placed a box containing dinnerware in the backseat of the car. Lance arranged for a waiter from a nearby catering business to arrive at the appointed time and serve the couple dinner. Lance had taken care of the music—supplied by his portable CD player—and the small table and chairs. The night before, while they finalized plans on the phone, Connie could hear the excitement radiating in his voice. She sensed his hope regarding his grandfather and her neighbor. If the Lord meant it to be, everything would work out.

Connie asked if Hilda and her husband could bring Claudia to the event in the park. At first Hilda balked at the idea, but after seeing the energy and enthusiasm put into the meeting, she agreed it was the best thing to ensure that Claudia arrived as planned.

Connie drove over to the park and headed for the grove of trees to find Lance setting up the table and chairs. He had also brought along a few other chairs, as well.

"What are those for?" she inquired.

"I don't want your neighbor thinking this is a setup. Some extra chairs around will convince her at first that this is an actual party. He then put up a small stepladder and, with Connie's help, looped streamers through the tree branches.

"I didn't know you had a decorator's touch, Mr. Adams," she teased.

"I didn't know I had a knack for devious undertakings either." He glanced at his watch. "I'll need to pick up Granddad soon. I promised him that innocent walk, you know." He gave her a wink as he reached the bottom of the ladder. He drew Connie into his arms. "How about a kiss and a prayer for God's grace on this event?"

Connie accepted his kiss with enthusiasm. They then clasped hands and prayed for God's will to be done. When Lance left, Connie suddenly felt lonely and anxious. She gazed into the trees and at the streamers fluttering in the gentle breeze. A chill suddenly overcame her. What if this didn't work? What if all this planning was for naught? She refused to allow doubt to creep in at this important moment. She wouldn't be like the ocean waves rolling in and out, going nowhere, as the Bible talked about in the book of James. She believed God would perform a miracle here in this grove by the river, if not for Gene and Bette, then for her and Lance.

Time slowly ticked by. When the hour drew near, Connie took her place behind some nearby bushes to await the gathering. Five minutes passed. Ten. Twenty. She saw Lance and his granddad moseying up the paved walkway. Panic assailed her. Claudia and Hilda were nowhere in sight. Where were they? Had something happened? She saw Lance pause with his granddad, talking about something, yet she could clearly see the worried look on his face.

"Looks like someone is having a party here," Silas Westerfield noted.

"It sure does." Lance glanced at the bushes toward Connie. When his grand-dad wasn't looking, he mouthed the words, *Where is Bette?*

Connie shrugged her shoulders and pointed to her watch, telling him they were late.

Forty-five minutes had elapsed. Lance and his granddad had already moved along with their walk. Connie felt she might faint. Her limbs began to tremble. The emotion of it all was too great. All their plans, all that seeking, everything had fizzled out before it began. She wanted to break down and cry. Instead, she shoved the strap of her purse over her shoulder and made for the trees, ready to take everything down.

Suddenly she heard voices in the distance.

"Why, it does look like a party," Claudia was saying. Connie darted behind the bushes. Her heart thumped wildly. She saw Hilda guiding Claudia over to the grove.

"We wanted to make sure you had a proper send-off," Hilda said. "So we had lunch catered. Today you will be served like a queen." Hilda pulled out a chair at the small table for Claudia to sit.

Connie wanted to cry. Hilda was doing such a splendid job with all this. Now if only Lance would return with his granddad. At last she saw them heading back down the paved path that led through the park. Lance backpedaled and disappeared. Hilda, as well, took her husband by the arm and walked off, telling Claudia they were going to find the caterer.

"Wait a minute!" Claudia exclaimed, getting to her feet. She turned and, to her shock, saw Gene approaching the outdoor dining area. "What's going on? I thought this was supposed to be a going-away party given by friends."

He looked around. "I guess all these friends had other plans."

She began to shake. "This was all a setup, wasn't it? I don't believe it."

"I do. Don't you see what's going on here, Bette? There are people who really love us. They want us to take time to be alone."

"I was deceived." She began to walk away in a huff.

"Yes, you have been deceived for a very long time. Forty years, to be exact. Maybe it's about time you tasted a bit of the truth." Gene limped over and took a seat. To his apparent surprise, Bette suddenly turned around and sat down opposite him. She kept her gaze focused on her lap.

"I don't believe they did this," she murmured. "And Hilda, of all people. Why?"

She looked up, and her jaw dropped when a waiter and an assistant appeared in the grove, carrying silver dishes full of food. Lance's granddad pulled a handkerchief from his pocket to wipe his eyes and blow his nose.

"Look at this," his voice choked out as the table was arranged. The waiter poured out goblets of sparkling cider. Slowly Gene lifted his glass. "Bette, even if our paths take us in opposite directions, I'm glad we can at least enjoy the love that others have for us together. It will be a fond memory."

Bette's hand shook as she raised her glass to her lips. She took one tiny sip, then set it down. "I don't think I can go through with this."

Gene lifted a silver cover off the platter to reveal the steaming chicken cordon bleu, wild rice, and asparagus encircled with red pimento. "You mean you can't enjoy this wonderful meal? Look at the love, not to mention the money and effort that went into this. Even if you say nothing more to me the rest of the meal, we can pretend to enjoy it and be gracious toward those who thought enough of us to do such a wonderful thing."

Lance curled his arm around Connie, watching from their place behind the bushes as Bette and Gene began to eat. Perhaps for the first time in forty years, they would actually share a pleasant conversation over a meal together. What she saw and heard filled her with expectation.

The couple continued to eat the lunch. At one point, Connie saw her neighbor lift her head and laugh. She squeezed Lance's hand. It seemed almost unbelievable to see this happening after the events they had witnessed at the antique center.

Just then Lance took her by the hand and propelled her away.

"What are you doing?" she whispered. "Don't you want to see what's happening?"

"I've seen plenty to know that they need to be alone, and I mean really alone. They've both been through a lot. Only God can make right what's happened between them."

"But—" Connie stared back at the grove of trees and the streamers waving as if to say farewell. The mere idea that she couldn't see the end results of their handiwork left her with a nagging feeling inside. Now she would have to wait for the results, and for how long, she didn't know.

"Besides, I thought maybe you would like to go on a walk with me." When she didn't say anything, he tugged on her hand. "Connie?"

"Of course I want to take a walk with you. But maybe they could use. . ."

"Our help?" He laughed. "I think we've done enough. Sometimes you have to let go and allow people to find their own course in life. If you try to do it all on your own, you can get hurt if things don't work out the way you planned."

"I know. I've been there, many times." When she did let go and allowed God to work, events happened that she couldn't begin to explain. Then she knew it came from His hand and no one else's.

The soft breeze felt wonderful on her face after all the stress of the last few hours. What felt even more wonderful was the presence of Lance at her side. They stopped at a picnic table. Nearby on a patch of sandy ground, a furious game of volleyball was in progress.

"Have you ever played?" he asked.

"I'm terrible at it."

"Let's see." He grabbed her hand and led her forward.

"Lance, what are you doing?"

He didn't answer but asked the team leaders if they could join in. Connie found herself and Lance on opposing teams. *This is all I need, another embarrassing moment in my life.* Why was he making her do this? Thankfully the ball rarely came to her. Instead, she watched Lance's athletic abilities as he dove for the ball, including several spikes that sent cheers rippling through his team. When it came time for Connie to serve, she looked at the ball with uncertainty. Lance stood near the net, a smile on his face and waving at her to serve the ball to him. She served, sending the ball sailing over the net between two players.

"Hey, good serve!" said a guy next to her.

Connie's confidence rose. She served another ball, which Lance dived to intercept. Instead, he fell flat on his face. Sand covered his fine trousers and polo shirt. Yet he looked as if he were having the time of his life. After several more serves, Connie decided to call it quits. Her wrist stung from the smack of the ball. Lance thanked the teams for allowing them to play and escorted her back to the picnic table.

"Was that fun or what?"

"Or what," she pronounced, massaging her reddened arm.

He took up her arm and kissed the tender area. "I hope you don't mind that we played. I used to love volleyball as a kid. Sometimes when the going gets rough, it's good to be a kid again."

"I'm learning more about you every day, Lance Adams. Especially the man who doesn't mind getting rough and tough in his nice clothes."

"I hope you'll want to know even more. And I want to know everything about you, too." He took her hand and held it in his.

Connie inhaled a short breath. It seemed their relationship was growing more serious by the moment. Yet the mere notion that a marriage proposal might be looming on the horizon made her shudder. Was she ready for it?

Chapter 15

Connie waited patiently for some word as to how the picnic in the park finally ended. When she called Lance for the news, he only said his grandfather told him little about the event. "We're just going to have to be patient."

Connie sighed. How she hated waiting. If the picnic didn't unite the two of them, nothing would, in her humble opinion. She took the matter to prayer, entrusting it to God as she prepared for a day of yard sales. Donna had agreed to tag along with her. That morning she had rushed out to buy the paper and, to her delight, found a place that was selling a used rocking chair. When Donna arrived, she immediately told her they were on a scouting expedition for the chair.

"I have my list, also," Donna said. "Lamps, some glasses, Avon cosmetics, red pumps—"

"Wow. Do you really think you're going to find all that?"

"Honey, with you I never know what's going to happen!"

Connie smiled and grabbed her purse. They drove down the road, slowly past her neighbor's house that now appeared dark and dismal since the sale closing had finalized. In another few weeks, a young couple would be moving in. If only she knew what had transpired between her neighbor and Lance's grandfather.

As if reading her mind, Donna asked, "Have you heard the results of your little dinner escapade at the park?"

Connie shook her head. "Nothing. The picnic went well, I thought, but Lance says his grandfather has been tight-lipped about it all. To me, that must mean bad news."

"At least everything is on track between you and Lance, right?"

Connie became silent at that point. Donna cast her a look. "Don't tell me you two had an argument."

"No, no. It's just that I think Lance is ready for the fast track, and I'm still trying to find my way through the jungle."

"I thought you were the one who said marriage was on the horizon, and you were ready to accept it with open arms."

"Donna, it didn't seem real back then. It was more like a fairy tale. Now that it might be happening, I'm scared to death."

Donna patted her arm. "You have nothing to fear. This is a great guy you've snagged. I knew it from the get-go. Besides, you're the one telling me that we should be trusting God with our lives."

"You're right. If this wasn't in God's big plan, He wouldn't let me go through with it."

Donna said little else as they continued the drive out to the country and a large home with many wares spread out on tables. At once, Connie made for the rocking chair. It was a nice piece, similar in style to the ones she had seen in Claudia's book on antiques. When she asked the price, it seemed a little steep. But Sally had said to pay whatever price, especially if the piece was in excellent condition.

Once more, Connie handed over all the money in her wallet, including some of her own cash as well as the money Sally had given her. She knew Sally would pay back the difference. Donna also found several items, among them a pair of red high heels.

"This is great," Connie exclaimed when they returned to the car, lugging the chair. They heaved it into the trunk, then tied down the back hatch with a piece of rope. "Success at last! Honestly, after the episode with the clock, I never thought I would go to another yard sale."

"Yeah, you and that clock of yours. What a tale you have to tell."

Connie had to admit it was an interesting twist in her life, bringing with it the blessing of Lance Adams. Pondering it all and the way she and Lance worked together to unite two long-lost loved ones eased her misgivings about a future commitment. It didn't matter to Lance that she worked under him at the department store with a salary that barely covered the monthly bills. What mattered to him was the love in their hearts, placed there by God Himself.

Connie arrived back at her apartment with the rocking chair, only to find a strangely familiar car parked out in front of her apartment. She gazed back at Donna thinking, *Not again!* Inside the vehicle were two passengers. One of them slowly came out of the car, dressed in a pantsuit and a necklace that glimmered in the sunlight. It was Claudia Rowe, alias Bette.

She waved at Connie, her face one huge smile. Connie stared so hard she thought her eyes would go dry.

"Is that who I think it is in the driver's seat?" Donna asked.

Sure enough, it was Silas "Gene" Westerfield, decked out in a black suit. He waved, as well, but remained behind the wheel of the car. Connie didn't know he owned a car; then she recognized the vehicle as the one that had sat for ages in Claudia's driveway.

"I hope you don't mind this intrusion," Claudia said. "I just had to see you."

"Of course. Come on in." They stepped inside the house, just as the cuckoo had finished a round of chirping. "This is my friend Donna. Donna, my neighbor Mrs. Rowe."

Donna politely shook her hand.

"Again, I hope you don't mind me stopping in," Claudia began. "Gene and I are on our way to Fredericksburg. There are some fine antique shops there, you know. And he's taking me out to dinner afterward."

Connie wanted to shout *Hallelujah!* when she heard this news. Instead, she said, "I'm so glad, Mrs. Rowe."

"I. . .well, we also wanted to thank you for caring about us so much. I honestly thought you were a strange young woman with strange ideas. Maybe even a busybody. But I'm so glad you were. I'm still in shock." A lone tear drifted down her cheek. Connie handed her the tissue box, which she took with a smile as if remembering their first visit. "I once thought my children were the only ones who cared about me. It took all of this to realize what love is really all about. You and that young man of yours had the heart to bring together two old people who might have lost something very special."

"Connie knows how to do everything up big," Donna added.

"Yes, she does, and more. Without her, I wouldn't have understood the terrible mistakes I had made. And why Gene decided to come back to me after all this time—it simply amazes me. I guess that's love, right?" She wiped her tears away with a tissue. "I must admit, one of the best things that ever happened to me was your coming to my yard sale that Saturday and buying the cuckoo clock. If I had buried it away or even thrown it out, I would have thrown away the best opportunity to experience love again."

Connie reached out and gave her a brief hug. "I'm so happy for you."

Claudia blew her nose. "Anyway, I just had to tell you this personally. Gene is waiting for me, so I need to go."

"Wait a minute, please." Connie gazed at the cuckoo clock that had accomplished yet another miracle. Slowly she took it down from its place on her wall. "You forgot something. I believe this is yours."

"Oh no. You keep it."

"Mrs. Rowe, it's not my name on the back. I can look for another one. As I recall, a handsome man once gave you this clock and with the most romantic words I've ever heard. 'As time endures, so will our love.'"

Claudia again blew her nose. "Yes, he did say that. All right, I will accept it. At least we can pay you for it."

"No, that's fine. You both have paid me more than the clock is worth and then some." Connie went to the back room to retrieve the dusty box and carefully packed up the timepiece. "So long, Mr. Cuckoo. You're going home."

Claudia bid her farewell with the box tucked under her arm. Connie peeked out between the blinds as Claudia entered the car and promptly showed the clock to Gene. He rolled down the window and, to Connie's surprise, gave her a thumbs-up signal.

"Can you believe that?" Connie said with a laugh. "Isn't it amazing?"

Donna watched the car speed away. "All of this is unbelievable," she murmured. "You think so?"

"This whole saga. I know I gave you encouragement and ideas about getting those two back together, but honestly I had no idea it would really work. And there they are, taking off like two lovebirds. It's unreal."

"Miracles can happen, Donna, especially when God is in control."

Donna fingered the lace curtain adorning the window. "Hey, Connie, would it be okay if I try out your church tomorrow?"

"That would be great, Donna! I'd love to have you come along. Did you know it's the same church Lance goes to?"

"I'm really interested in what's happened here. I'll have to admit, I wouldn't mind a miracle or two in my life. Just seeing this all play out, especially how you and Lance were determined to make things work, has got me thinking. I never went to church much. My family didn't practice religion except on holidays. If God was around, He was just a building with a steeple on top. But you live like He's real, standing right there beside you."

"It's hard to understand, Donna, but it's true. He's closer than any friend. He cares so much about each of us. He knows what's best for us, even if we don't know ourselves. Tell you what—Lance and I will pick you up; then we'll catch brunch at our newest hangout. It's this wild place that Lance introduced me to not long ago. They make a great breakfast, be it a little greasy."

"Okay." She offered a hesitant smile before picking up her yard sale purchases. "See you later."

Connie felt a rush of the warm fuzzies after what she had witnessed this day. It began with finding the rocking chair, then the miraculous encounter with Claudia Rowe, only to end with Donna interested in attending church. Now there remained but one puzzle piece left to complete the picture of blessing.

Sunday came. Donna appeared to enjoy the service immensely. Connie was glad to see her enthusiasm. She would have rejoiced more were it not for Lance's unexplained absence. She decided he must either be sick or involved in something important. She tried calling him at home but received no answer. He had never let her go more than a day or two without some method of communication, whether at work or by phone. Connie ended up taking Donna to Baby Jim's by herself, then spent the rest of the day at the apartment wondering what was going on.

The next morning, Connie anticipated seeing Lance at the store. She made up her mind to be friendly to him, even if he did leave her in the dark about his absence over the weekend. To her disappointment, he never appeared. When she moseyed on back to the office to check on him, the secretary said he was away on business. Connie thought it odd that he would go on a trip without telling her. On her lunch break, she tried numerous times to reach him on his cell phone, but his voice mail was full. There was still no response at home either.

When several more days trickled by without a word from him, Connie finally decided to give his grandfather a call. It was the only thing left to do.

"All I know is that he said he would be out of town, Miss Ortiz."

"He didn't leave a message or anything about what he's doing?"

"He did say he would be seeing the family. I'm sure he will call you when he gets back."

Connie hung up the phone, more confused than ever. It just didn't seem like Lance to take off without saying anything. Suddenly fear hit her broadside like a car smashing into a brick wall. What if his family had talked him out of associating with her? Just like Silas Westerfield, when Claudia's family turned her against him and they were forever shut out of each other's lives. Connie began biting her nails, something she hadn't done since she was a teenager. Maybe one of his sisters had run a check on her and found out how poor she was. Maybe they didn't like the idea of him associating with someone who had a Hispanic background. Now it had come down to this.

She began to pace, looking up at the empty wall space where the cuckoo clock once hung. There was nothing to fill the void, nothing but the awful image of Lance sending her a letter informing her this wasn't going to work between them, that his family had said no, or he had found a wealthy woman who was the manager of a sister store. Oh, why hadn't she been truthful about her feelings at the onset? She should have come right out and told him she loved him, that she wanted to spend the rest of her life with him no matter how much money they earned. Instead, doubt clouded her vision.

The week passed so slowly Connie didn't think she would see the end of it. When she miscalculated a refund to a customer who came storming back, asking her if she had taken math in high school, Connie thought she was about to lose it. The precious peace she had tried to hang on to was gone. Even prayers were hard to offer up anymore.

"What's the matter?" Donna finally asked. "You aren't yourself at all."

"Lance flew the coop."

"Huh? What are you talking about?"

"He's been gone a week and didn't even tell me he was leaving. He never called either. His grandfather said he had gone home. For all I know, his family talked him out of our relationship. The curse that affected Gene and Bette has happened once again."

"Honey, you'd better stop with these wild ideas of yours. You know Lance is crazy about you."

"If he was, then don't you think he would have told me what he's doing? Maybe he's gone off to see another woman."

"Connie, you know better than that. You had brothers. Did they ever tell your mother where they were going?"

"Hardly ever." Louis and Henry were very bad at alerting the family of their whereabouts, nor did they ever remember the telephone for notifying the family. Many nights Mom waited up late, wondering if they would walk through the door alive. She would scold them for not finding the phone booth to call, even after giving them money. These days she would have given them a cell phone, but that didn't always work either as Connie discovered with Lance.

"That's men for you. They tend to be a little preoccupied at times. So just be patient. You know the saying 'Absence makes the heart grow fonder'?"

For Connie, Lance's stark absence only lent itself to more strange stories and scenarios. When Saturday arrived, she decided to work some overtime, unwilling to spend the weekend at home wondering what Lance was up to. She again tried calling his place and still received no answer. She thought of trying his grandfather one more time, but he had seemed nonchalant about the whole venture as if there was nothing to worry about. *So stop worrying, Connie,* she told herself.

At church on Sunday, she finally saw Lance scurry in late to the service. Instead of going to see her, he rushed forward to greet others in the congregation. Connie bit her lip. Salty tears burned her eyes. It was just as she feared. His family disapproved of her, and now it was over between them.

Connie didn't even wait for the service to conclude but headed straight for her car, brushing away the tears as she went. She didn't intend to make a spectacle of herself in front of everyone in church. She opened the car door, preparing to leave, only to find a gift-wrapped box sitting on the driver's seat.

"What is this. . . ?" she began. Her hands trembled. She sat down in the driver's seat and began fumbling with the wrapper. Inside was a brand-new cuckoo clock, exactly like the one that once hung in Grandma's house—the instrument that once imparted so much comfort, then and now. On a whim, she turned the clock over and found a small box taped to the back. "What is this. . . ?" she said again.

Just then a familiar hand touched hers through the open door of the car. She trembled, knowing at once the presence and the scent of cologne. *Lance.*

"Let me get that for you." He moved around to the other side of the car and slid into the passenger seat.

Connie didn't know what to say. Everything became a blur. When he untaped the small box and gave it to her, the tears flowed freely down her face.

"Connie," he began, concerned by her reaction.

"I thought they talked you out of it," she moaned, opening the box to reveal a beautiful diamond ring. "I thought your family would tell you to go find someone rich."

"I did find someone rich, Connie Ortiz. Rich in mercy, rich in compassion, rich in love. I know this isn't exactly the greatest place to ask for your hand, here in your car. Maybe we can go somewhere quiet."

"This is perfect. And the answer is yes!" She slipped the ring onto her finger.

He smiled. "I hope you weren't totally put out when I didn't tell you my plans. As you can see, I was on a secret mission. Granddad said you'd called."

"I must admit, I wasn't sure what to think."

"Now you know. By the way, I did see my family. All my sisters want to plan the wedding, from the shower down to the reception. So you're covered."

"They really want me to be a part of the family?"

"Of course they do. They would like to meet you as soon as possible. After I got done sharing with them what's happened these last few weeks, there wasn't a dry eye in the house. Connie, you made a great impression. But most important of all, you made an impression on me." He leaned over to kiss her.

Instead, Connie stood the clock up, adjusted the settings, and pulled the chain all the way to the floor of the car. The bird appeared with its first greeting.

Lance jumped at the sound. He looked at Connie and laughed. "What was that all about?"

"Don't you know? Time's up!" She set down the clock and fell into his tender embrace.

Epilogue

Connie opened a side door to peek in at the eager crowd. Instantly her jitters increased. Nearly every seat in the church was taken as young and old came out in their best dress, with smiles on their faces, to witness their marriage.

"You know better than to do that," Donna reprimanded her, shutting the door firmly. "Anyway, do you want Lance to see you? The groom isn't supposed to see the bride until the ceremony."

Connie felt for the veiled hat perched on her head. She'd always wanted to wear a hat on her wedding day. Now that day had arrived. It seemed hard to believe, nearly like a dream, and all because of a cuckoo clock purchased at a yard sale. It amazed her still how God could do such wonders with the simplest things in life. "Does the hat look all right? I hope Lance likes it. I mean, it's not a regular veil. . . ."

"Better than all right. You look fantastic. Stop worrying."

Connie inhaled a sharp breath, thinking of the crowded sanctuary she had seen. Among the many guests was the entire contingent of her father's family, who had flown in from Guatemala. Even when she managed a peek through the open door, she'd seen them sitting in the front two rows, smiles etched on their faces, murmuring to each other in their native tongue. It was wonderful seeing them all together. But among all her family, an empty chair remained, one she had hoped might be filled, even though she'd heard no word. Lance and she had tried their best to locate her youngest brother, Henry, using whatever detective skills they had in their possession, to no avail. He seemed to have disappeared. How she wished he would be here, that he might be a part of the festivities and the family pictures. But it was not to be.

"Now what?" Donna asked.

"Nothing." Again she fooled with her hat.

"You're making it crooked," Donna scolded, adjusting it once more. "Stop with the bridal shakes already. It's going to begin anytime."

"I know. I was just hoping maybe Henry would sneak in or something to surprise me. I've been hoping all morning. It would be so nice to have my whole family together, especially today."

"You know that isn't going to happen. There's been no word. Your parents don't even know where he is, nor does Louis."

Connie looked at her simple bouquet of mixed flowers.

"Don't let it bother you." She felt Donna poke her in the arm. "Just settle down and have a great time. This is all about you and Lance."

Me and Lance. How could she tell Donna it was much more than that? It was also about a union of people, besides her and Lance, who otherwise might have been left in sorrow and despair. Like the cuckoo clock uniting two lonely people who even now were planning their own marriage—Lance's grandfather, Silas Westerfield, and her neighbor, Claudia Rowe. She'd seen them sitting together on the groom's side of the aisle, holding hands. Connie sighed. Despite the sadness over the absence of her youngest brother, Connie knew there was much to rejoice this day. And when the first chords of music began, she felt an even greater reason to rejoice, that she would be united in love forever with the perfect man God had chosen.

When the ceremony had concluded, Lance managed to sneak Connie away to a coat closet for a private kiss. "You look beautiful," he told her, nuzzling his nose in her neck.

"Do you like the hat?"

"Of course. I love the hat. I love the lady wearing the hat." He stepped back. "But you don't look very happy. Is something bothering you?"

"Oh, I'm happy, Lance. Really I am. I only hoped Henry might have made it. That God would have done a miracle."

He sighed. "You have to give him over to the Lord, Connie. There's nothing else you can do."

"But all your family is here. All four sisters, to be exact, plus all their families. But when they take the picture of my family, he won't be there."

"Connie, he hasn't been a part of your family for years. He made his decision. And we made ours." He took her in his arms. "We have the limo waiting, you know, to take us to the reception. So let it go, and let's have fun. Okay?"

Connie nodded. Lance escorted her to the foyer of the church where well-wishers lingered to offer their congratulations. When they settled in the limo, Connie watched the trees go by as they made their way to the park where the reception would be held. Once within its boundaries, Lance pointed out the paths they had walked when they planned the clever trap to snag his grandfather and her neighbor. They could see from their seat the place where they had arranged a special dinner for the couple beneath the shade trees and how God had fanned the flame of love kindled long ago. Connie squeezed Lance's hand. "I'm so glad we were a part of it all," she said. "It's still hard to believe we did what we did. Sometimes I look back on it and wonder how I could have been so bold."

Lance chuckled softly. "Did you know Granddad even asked me that once? How we could do what we did to see him and Mrs. Rowe reunited?"

"It's all God working in our hearts," she murmured when the limo pulled around to the site of a huge white tent erected in a field. She smiled as Lance hurried to escort her from the car. She placed her hand in his, allowing his strength to bring her to her feet, even as her other hand swept up the wedding gown around her.

Suddenly she saw him, but just for a moment. Lanky. Disheveled. A beard. But she knew it must be him. Her heart leaped. He stared at first, then began walking away, back behind the tables of food being arranged by the caterer.

She caught her breath. "Henry?"

"Connie?" Lance asked. "What's the matter?"

She couldn't respond. Instead, she gathered up her gown and hurried over, even as the bearded man tried to evade her. "Henry, please wait!"

He shook his head until she managed to find him standing behind a tree. "I—I don't want Mom and Papa to see me," he muttered.

"Henry, I can't believe it. I'm so glad to see you." She came forward, her arms open wide, even as he again began to retreat.

"Everyone is coming over here," he mumbled.

Connie turned to see Lance venturing forward, followed by a few curious family members. She hurried back to them and offered a quick smile. "I thought I saw someone I recognized from long ago," she said, ushering them into the main tent. She glanced back to see a look of relief on Henry's face. Inwardly her heart pounded. Oh, how she wanted to talk to him, to welcome him, to tell him that despite everything, even when he sent her doll careening down Grandma's laundry chute long ago—an event that now spawned a smile—she loved him.

"What was that all about?" Lance wondered.

"It's Henry, Lance! He's here, but he doesn't want anyone to see him just yet. He and my father have never gotten along well. But he came. I can't believe it. He really came."

After a quick nod, Lance stepped away, claiming a need to talk to someone. When he returned, he took Connie's hand in his. "Come with me." Lance managed to sneak her behind the tent and to several large trees where Henry stood waiting. "No one can see you here." Lance then moved off to engage the guests arriving for the reception.

"Henry, I've missed you. Are you all right?"

"I've been in drug rehab," he told her, his foot scuffing the ground. "Papa won't care. He thinks I'm a drug addict anyway. That I'm scum."

"I don't. I'm just glad you're here. Please, will you consider coming to say hello to the family and telling them what you're doing? That you're in rehab? I think it will make Mom feel better to know you're all right."

"They'll stand there and judge me. Tell me I'm no good. Especially Papa. I don't want to cause a scene."

"Henry, all of us do wrong things. No one does right. And sometimes we judge those wrongs, thinking some are worse than others. But we have no right to judge. God is greater than all of that. And He has a plan for your life. He had a plan for mine by bringing me a wonderful man. And I know He has a plan for you and wants to help you overcome all this."

"I don't really have anything to do with God," he said stiffly.

"That's okay. But He has everything to do with you. He cares. He counts every hair on your head. And I care, too." She reached out her hand. "Please. I want you to be a part of this. We're going to have pictures taken soon. Please come and join the family and don't worry about Papa. It will be the best wedding gift you could give me."

Henry thought on it for a moment, teetering on the brink of indecision, then reluctantly stepped forward. At first the family appeared shocked to see him. Then Connie's mother threw her arms around him and hugged him close. Louis offered him a handshake and a smile. Papa said little, but at least Connie was glad to see some acceptance from her family. And when it came time for the family pictures with the bride and groom, her heart rejoiced over God's restoration of the long-lost sheep, even if Henry's heart still remained far from Him.

When the lines formed for the food, Lance again whisked her aside. "Once again, you are hard at work reuniting people," he told her with a laugh. "There's no stopping you, is there?"

"Lance, if I ever stopped at anything God wants me to do, I would stop living."

"Good. Then let's keep right on going. Who shall we help next?"

Connie laughed before glancing around. "I see a few employees from the store we could go greet."

Lance laughed long and loud, while his arms swept her up in an embrace. For a moment, Connie thought she heard the cuckoo sing, but it was only the melody of a bird chirping a song in the trees above. Like the cuckoo clock hanging on the wall of her home, the song serenaded a perfect ending to a perfect dream come true.

The Wish

Chapter 1

O uch, that hurt!"

Debbie Reilly yanked her finger away to observe the trickle of blood oozing out. She climbed down the stepladder and dodged the string of Christmas lights that dangled from the doorway into the third-floor nurses' lounge.

"What happened?" inquired the registered nurse, Mrs. Whitaker. She stood by her cart of medications, pouring pills into cups to distribute during the coming noon hour.

"Must be a broken bulb up there or something." Debbie strode off to the clean utility room to find a bandage. From the hallway of the White Pines Health Care Facility where she worked as a nursing assistant, Debbie could hear the variety of voices emanating from the rooms of the residents. There were Harold White, a World War II veteran who complained about the rations he had to eat; Sylvia Hubble, who babbled about working in a dress shop; and Delores Masterson, who stroked and talked to a pretend cat nestled in her lap. A few others were calling out the names of loved ones.

Debbie fetched a bandage from a box. She began removing the wrapper when, above the noises in the hall, she heard a faint voice like that of an angel, singing a song from days gone by. Debbie smiled to herself as she neatly wrapped the bandage around her sliced finger. The singing beckoned her to the room, and Debbie peeked in to find Elvina Jenson struggling to force her chubby arm through the sleeve of a blouse.

"Let me help you with that," Debbie said to her.

A smile spread across her plump face. "Thank you so much, dear."

Debbie helped her fit one arm at a time through the sleeves, then buttoned the blouse down the front. She stepped back and watched the unseeing gray blue eyes of the woman stare straight ahead from where she sat on the edge of the hospital bed.

"Now, would you mind getting me my earrings?" Elvina asked.

Debbie opened the drawer of the nightstand to fish out the pair of gold earrings Elvina insisted on wearing every day. When she did, her leg brushed a rectangular box sitting on a stool. Debbie handed Elvina the earrings, then turned to see the gift tag still attached to the top with a piece of tape. Bits of Christmas wrapping paper clung to the sides of the leather case. *To Gram*, she read on the tag, *With love always, Nathaniel J.* "An early Christmas gift?" she inquired of Elvina whose fingers fumbled to attach the pretty gold earrings to her earlobes. "Or a late Thanksgiving gift?"

Her head turned in the direction of Debbie's voice. "What was that?"

"The box here. I hadn't noticed it before, but I see the tag on it."

Elvina's face again broke open into a broad smile. "Oh, my box. Nathaniel gave it to me last evening. He said he couldn't wait but insisted that I have it now. We laughed at the songs we played on it last night. I love it so much."

Debbie furrowed her forehead in puzzlement. "You mean it plays music?"

"Of course, dear. It's a record player."

Debbie unfastened the twin clasps and lifted the lid to find an old-fashioned turntable, arm, and needle that fit into the grooves of the record. "You don't see these around," she confessed. "I remember my family owning one when I was little. Then, one day, they became obsolete. Now we have Internet downloads. A whole new wave of music."

"Nathaniel is so kind," the older lady continued. "He told me about those fancy music boxes they have nowadays, but I wanted my record player. You see, mine was taken from the house when I came here. Most of my most precious things were sold." Debbie watched the tears well up in the woman's eyes. "But Nathaniel searched in antique shops all over the Roanoke area until he found one exactly like my old one. He wouldn't tell me what he paid for it. Can you imagine?" She shook her head. "And to think that things like that would end up in an antique store. Now, can you help me put on my lipstick?"

Debbie went once more to the drawer, sifting through the combs, bobby pins, and other assorted junk tucked inside before finding the tube of lipstick. Elvina sat patiently on the bed while Debbie traced Elvina's dry lips with color. In an afterthought, she put a dab of lipstick on each pale cheek and rubbed it in lightly to produce a blush.

Elvina chuckled. "Trying to doll me up so I can get a man?"

Debbie's cheeks heated at Elvina's question. "Why not? You're young at heart."

Elvina laughed merrily. "You're so sweet. I was hoping you would be working today. I tell Nathaniel all the time about my nurse who comes and takes care of me during the day. He's still single, you know. I tell him all the time he needs to settle down. But he has his own way of doing things." She reached out and patted Debbie's arm. "Do you have a man in your life?"

Debbie slid the cover over the tube of lipstick and tossed it back into the drawer. "No man yet." She tried to suppress the thought that stirred up a wave of emotion.

"That's too bad. How old are you, dear?"

"Twenty-eight."

"Dear me. Twenty-eight and no man. I had four babies by the time I was your age. I had six children, you know."

Debbie gazed at the picture frame decorating the bedside table. In the middle of the portrait sat Elvina in a huge chair, surrounded by her family. Two men and three women stood beside the chair, all with graying hair. A host of grandchildren and great-grandchildren formed a semicircle around them. The photographer probably had to use a hefty, wide-angle lens to capture all the smiling faces that comprised the huge family. For a moment, Debbie wondered which one in the photograph was this Nathaniel whom Elvina so highly praised.

As if Elvina could see Debbie examining the photo, she said, "Six babies, even though there are only five in the picture. One was killed in Vietnam. Albert, my oldest. He was Nathaniel's father."

Debbie focused once more on the old record player and the writing scrawled on a gift tag in the shape of a Christmas bell. *Nathaniel J.* "The *J* must stand for his middle name?" she wondered out loud.

"Nathaniel James," Elvina supplied. "He signs everything to me *Nathaniel J.* He's just like his father, with his own way of doing things. I so wish Nathaniel could have known his father, but Nathaniel wasn't even born when Albert died in a helicopter crash over Vietnam. Albert was just like his father before him, you see, joining the army and all."

Debbie listened while Elvina reminisced about her family. She wished she could stay all day and listen to her stories. The time displayed on a small alarm clock alerted her to the work she still needed to accomplish before noon, including hanging the rest of the colored lights over the doorway of the nurses' lounge. "Let me help you into your wheelchair, Elvina," she said as she slid a pair of shoes on over the cotton socks Elvina wore to bed every night. "Then I have to run and check on a few of the other residents." Elvina nodded and held up her arms. Debbie bent her knees, encircled the resident with her arms, and slowly propelled her into a wheelchair outfitted with a soft pad. She placed a flowered robe across Elvina's lap, then took up a comb and gently fluffed out her curly gray hair.

"You always do such a nice job," Elvina commented. "Now before you leave, would you mind putting on a record for me?"

Debbie turned to the box, unfastened the clasps once more, and lifted the top. Beside the box lay several records. "You want to hear the one about the doggy in the window?"

"That would be fine. It's my favorite."

Debbie slipped the record out of its jacket, placed the large disc on the turntable, and positioned the needle carefully on the record. A scratching noise came through the small speakers inside the box before the female vocalist began the opening bars of Elvina's favorite song. The tune followed Debbie out into the corridor, where several of the residents in their wheelchairs had paused in the hallway to listen. She returned to the string of lights still hanging from the doorway, examining the bulbs, one by one, for the culprit that had lacerated her finger.

"What's that racket I hear?" asked Trish. The fellow nursing assistant sat inside the lounge sipping a mug of coffee.

"Elvina's record player." Debbie yanked out the broken bulb. "Do we have any extra bulbs?"

"Look in the first drawer on the left at the nurses' station," Trish replied. "You know, I haven't heard a song like that since I visited Granny's house when I was little. 'Course that was before my parents split up. Never got to see her after that. Then she died."

Debbie pulled out the drawer to fetch a package of bulbs. "Elvina's grandson bought the record player for her. He found one like her original in an antique store."

"So that's what the mystery gift was," said Trish. Debbie couldn't help but peer inside the lounge at the aide who sat there smirking. "Her grandson came strutting in here last week while I worked an evening shift, saying he was buying his grandma a gift to remember. Wish he would get me a gift to remember. . .like a diamond ring."

"A diamond ring!" Debbie said in astonishment, mounting the stepladder to finish fastening the string of lights above the doorway.

"You've never met the hunky grandson? Wow, is all I can say. And he's so devoted to her. What guy do you know comes in almost every evening to spend time with an old lady? Guess that's why he's not married. No social life. Though he can come here anytime his little ol' heart desires, just as long as he eventually asks me out. Better yet, make it a marriage proposal. I'm not getting any younger."

Debbie fumbled with the tacks, trying to stick them into the wall above the doorway to anchor the lights, but she found Trish's words distracting.

"Normally I never pay attention to the visitors who come walking in here," Trish went on. "You can't help but notice him, though. Tall. Huge shoulders. Wavy dark hair and eyes to die for. I'll bet he's the reason everyone on the evening shift wants to be assigned to the rooms in the front hall. They fight like cats and dogs over who will take care of Elvina so they can spend time with the handsome grandson."

Debbie could just imagine the nurses on the evening shift, circling the nurse in charge like a pack of wolves and fighting over the string of rooms located in the front corridor. She never once considered asking for certain rooms just so she could interact with the visitors. For some reason, Mrs. Whitaker always assigned her room 307 where Elvina resided. It became routine. But now with all this talk of the handsome grandson, Debbie wondered if she should switch to the evening shift for a week, just to see what the hubbub was about. Then she thought better of it. Trish and the gang would no doubt vie for the treasured room. As it was, Debbie couldn't stand how Trish cared for the residents. Trish took shortcuts that irritated her to no end.

"All done," Debbie announced, stepping back to admire the colored lights glimmering from the doorway. Around the nursing station, she had strung a rope of plastic holly and berries. Inside the lounge, a Christmas tree decorated a far table that once held the huge coffeepot. Another tree of red ribbons and white lights decorated the inside of the solarium where the residents congregated for meals, entertainment, or television. Debbie always found the holidays difficult at the facility. Some of the residents would become depressed at the idea of spending the most celebrated time of the year cooped up inside a health-care facility rather than at home with relatives. A few were fortunate enough to have families willing to keep them over the holidays, but most spent their holidays here with the nursing staff. Knowing she was scheduled to work on Christmas, Debbie was determined to make the time as festive as possible. She made a mental list of the things she wanted to do—bake up a batch of Christmas cookies for those who could have sweets, coax the church youth choir into performing a selection of Christmas carols at the facility on Christmas Eve, and buy a few gifts for her favorite residents, like Elvina. For a moment, she wondered what this Nathaniel would think if she came walking in on Christmas morning with a gift for his grandma—like a few new records to play on the ancient record player. Would he smile at her and show her some interest?

Forget it, Debbie. Don't get yourself all worked up. You've managed to strike out with every guy you've ever met. Remember how the one you loved ended up marrying your roommate? So don't set yourself up for further disappointment. Debbie sighed, recalling with pain her close friendship with Brad. She always assumed one day their friendship would turn to love—until she discovered his real interest lay with her roommate, Tonya. When the fact came to light, Debbie felt both betrayed and used. Brad and Tonya were now married and living in Washington, D.C., with their two kids. She received a Christmas picture card from them every year, and every year, she would gaze at his handsome face and think of all she had lost. *Guess I'm just not cut out for love.*

Despite this, the thought of Nathaniel, whoever he might be, sent a snippet of hope rising up within her. Perhaps some day he would discover that it was she who kept his grandma looking so fine each day. Maybe then he would want to find out more about her. *Dream on. He won't even notice me among all the rest here. I'm one out of many.*

Debbie strolled over to her small steel cart to put away the linens left from the morning care, still thinking about the man called Nathaniel J. He must be a one-of-a-kind guy to forgo a social life to spend evenings with Elvina. Even going to great lengths to find her a treasured keepsake like the record player. Debbie inhaled a breath. *I would like to meet him someday, even if it goes no further than that.*

⌘

Debbie stepped out into the frigid December air after a long day at work. Inhaling the breath of wind that brushed her face, she detected the faint scent of smoke drifting from a nearby fireplace or woodstove. Her feet scuffed along the slick sidewalk, still covered by patches of ice from a recent storm. The cold wind ripped through her jacket while she gazed up into the darkening skies above. Behind her stood the brick building of the White Pines Health Care Facility, framed by a grove of pine trees, glazed with ice, which gave the facility its name. Twin wreaths decorated the front doors. White lights glimmered in pretty array on the bushes. A few cars drifted into the parking lot, bearing visitors who came to sit with their loved ones through the dinner hour. She watched them arrive one by one, wondering which one might be this Nathaniel J. Some were older people dressed in their heavy wool coats. Others toted children along with them. Debbie smiled, knowing how much the elderly residents loved seeing the faces of children. Every year, Debbie coordinated a Christmas Eve performance and a few youth groups would come to the facility to sing traditional Christmas carols, including the youth group from her own church. At that moment, she wished the group could sing Elvina's favorite song about the doggy in the window. Debbie smiled, thinking how surprised Elvina would be if the group suddenly broke out into the song from long ago. She could imagine the scene—the tears drifting slowly down Elvina's plump cheeks, her gnarled hand fumbling to find Debbie's and give a squeeze of gratitude. "You made my day," her voice would crack. And standing behind her, smiling in approval, would be her grandson, Nathaniel J.

Stop it, Debbie, she scolded herself. *Get the guy out of your head. He's probably already got a girlfriend, for all you know.*

She continued down the road, still thinking about an encounter with Elvina's grandson, when her feet flew out from underneath her. She fell hard on her backside in the road, just as a car swerved around the bend to enter the parking lot of the facility. Brakes squealed as the car came to an abrupt halt by the curb opposite her. Debbie slowly sat up, her tailbone screaming in pain.

"Are you all right?" inquired an anxious voice.

"Yeah," she sputtered, trying to get to her feet. Instead, she felt a shooting pain running down each leg. Her legs wobbled, and she collapsed onto the road with a grunt.

"Here, let me give you a hand." A tall figure, dressed in a wool overcoat,

240

offered her his gloved hand. She grasped his hand, squeezing her eyes shut to ward off the pain, and gingerly got to her feet.

"It's pretty slippery out here," said the man's voice.

"Yeah," Debbie mumbled again, hobbling along the sidewalk. "Thanks."

"Can you drive?"

"My car's in the garage. I walked today. My apartment's not that far. I can make it."

"Pretty dangerous to be walking in this kind of weather along a major highway. I'll gladly give you a lift."

Debbie stared into his dark eyes, and he peered back in concern. He didn't seem to fit the description of someone trying to take advantage of her. No doubt he was a visitor coming to see someone at the facility. "I'm fine, but thanks for the offer." Debbie continued down the road, even as her back erupted into spasms with every step she took. Once more her feet slipped on the ice. She would have fallen a second time had she not, at the last moment, grabbed hold of a young tree at the corner.

"I don't think you're going to make it without doing more harm than good," the man said, rushing to her side. He offered her his arm.

"You don't need to help me. I'm sure you've got things to do. I'm okay, really."

"You're not okay. If you're as close as you say, it probably won't take me ten minutes, tops, to drive you home. I have plenty of time. I'm meeting a fine lady, and she won't mind if I'm being a hero in disguise. She likes heroes."

So he has a girlfriend who works at the facility, Debbie thought. *Guess there's no harm in getting a lift then.* She allowed him to guide her to his car. She eased herself into the passenger seat, wincing in pain as the tender area of her back pressed against the seat.

"I take it you work at White Pines," he said, pointing at her baby blue nursing pants that peeked out from beneath the coat she wore and her white clogs in desperate need of polish.

"I just got off the day shift. Normally I get off at three, but they needed a few extra hands for a couple of hours until help arrived. It looks like I may be working late the rest of this week."

"How long have you worked at White Pines?"

"Eight years," Debbie said. She hunkered down in the seat and watched the scenery flash by. "When you get to town, turn right at the next stop sign. My apartment building is on the left."

"Do you like nursing?"

"It's okay. The holidays are tough, though. We try to do what we can to make it special for the residents."

He steered the car into an empty space in front of the building.

"Thanks a lot."

"Sure. You need help getting to the door?" He added quickly, "Of course I won't go in or anything. I just want to make sure you don't fall."

Debbie detected a gentlemanly quality about him that put to rest any remaining fears. She accepted his assistance and grasped the crook of his proffered elbow.

He paused at the door. "Better put some ice on that bump you have and take some ibuprofen." He laughed. "Hey, wait a minute. Why should I be telling you what to do? You're a nurse."

"A nursing assistant," she corrected.

"What's the difference?"

"I didn't earn a college degree. LPNs and RNs have degrees and a license to practice. I took a training course, but that's all. I don't deal with medications, procedures, that sort of thing. I basically take care of the residents' needs like bathing, dressing, feeding, etc."

He nodded his head. "I see. You do all the labor."

"I guess so, in a way. Though the RNs have to make all the tough decisions. I've thought of one day getting a full-fledged degree, but I'm not sure I could take the stress of being the boss." Her smile ignited a grin on his face. His bright teeth matched the bit of snow that frosted the bushes. "You'd better get going so you aren't late for your date."

His dark eyebrows lifted at the comment before another grin swept across his face. "My date," he repeated. "I'll have to tell her that one. She'd get a kick out of it. Take care of yourself, and no more spills. Ice can hurt." He nodded and strode to his car.

Debbie watched his departure from her doorway as he turned the car around in the parking area and sped off in the direction of White Pines. She leaned against the door frame before the shooting pain in her back reminded her of her need for rest. *So long, my wonderful benefactor,* she thought with a sigh. *Too bad you already have someone else.*

Chapter 2

"Hey, Gram."

"Nathaniel, I just knew it was you walking through the door. I can tell because you're wearing that Blue Ice cologne I gave you." Her face erupted into a broad smile. "Now you sit right here by me and tell me how your day went."

"You never change," he said with a smile, stooping to kiss her wrinkled cheek. He withdrew at that moment to find a small blotch of color on her cheeks. "Where did the blush come from? I don't remember Aunt Grace sending any blush. Just tubes of that hot red lipstick."

"It's my little nurse who takes care of me during the day, don't you know? She put some on my face. I told her I'm all set now to meet a man."

He snickered as he sat down beside her and took her hand in his. "Gram, you're something else."

"I asked her if she had a man, and she said no. Maybe you should see if she's right for you?"

Neil, as he was nicknamed by his friends and family, could only shake his head, even though Gram could not see the look on his face. She never changed but kept after him about the relationship thing as though it were a secret mission of hers. Just then a nurse from the evening shift bopped in for a moment and offered him her brightest smile. Soon after, she came strolling in again with a tray bearing cups of ice, sodas, and Gram's favorite sugar cookies, freshly baked in the facility kitchen. *Not again,* he groaned to himself. He began feeling more and more uncomfortable visiting Gram in the evening with all the nurses who came snooping around the room. Some, like this one, offered goodies. Others asked him questions about work, interests, cars, and the like. He knew they were trying to determine his eligibility. Gram always laughed at the attention and poked him in the arm, asking him when he would invite one of the young ladies out.

"Nurses aren't my type," he would tell her.

"Why not? They're caring individuals."

Neil twisted his lips. *Not this crew. They are looking to make a conquest, like I'm the Bachelor of the Year or something.*

"Nathaniel, you're upset," Gram now said. "I can tell by the way you're holding my hand. Is it the evening nurse who just came in?"

243

"She's doing the usual routine to make some kind of impression. Your cookies, my soda. I'm surprised she didn't give me a business card with her phone number on it and the nights she's available for dinner."

"Oh, you," Gram said, squeezing his hand. "None of them can help it. You're a wonderful young man. This wouldn't be happening if you found yourself the right girl to settle down with."

"She's nowhere around here, I can tell you that."

"What about Roanoke? It's a very large city with plenty of fine ladies. Maybe a coworker at that insurance place where you work? Or your church?"

How could he tell his grandmother that out of all the coworkers in the place, one was already married, one was divorced with three kids, and another was old enough to be his mother? In church, the women were either fresh out of college and just beginning to taste life or already married. No one in the middle, like him. The lonely middle man.

"The trouble with you is that you don't go out enough. You spend too many evenings here instead of going to where the young people are. I used to love attending the opera with Joe, you know. Why don't you do something like that?"

Neil nearly laughed at the suggestion but kept his lips pressed tight. Still, he could envision himself decked out in a tuxedo with a lovely lady in evening apparel on his arm. Perhaps the suggestion wouldn't be so farfetched if there were a lovely woman to escort to such a venue. He'd had a few female interests in the past, but nothing came of them. Between work and then coming here for nightly visits, as Gram said, there wasn't much time.

"Gram, I don't go out because I would miss seeing you. You're my lady friend. In fact, the nurse I helped out today thought I was going on a date."

Elvina straightened in her wheelchair. "You helped a nurse? When? Where?"

"She took a fall on the ice and landed right in the road. She refused my help at first, but I talked her into letting me drive her home."

"Do you like her? Since you come here every day, you could see her at the same time. Something like that would work."

"Gram, let it go."

"I would, except for the fact you're the son of my oldest boy. Not to mention that you're thirty-five years old. That's too old. I want you to find a wife and have children. I want another Nathaniel in the family."

He laughed. "I'd think having one around is enough for you."

"It's never enough." She sighed. "Oh, if only you'd known your father. You're so much like him. He married your mother late, too. He gave me the same excuses. There was no one he liked. He was too busy to care, anyway. So I guess I should expect his son to do the same."

Neil said little. There wasn't much to say. Whenever anyone talked about his father, he listened politely.

"And the little nurse who takes care of me during the day is twenty-eight years old. Can you imagine? Twenty-eight and never been married. Tsk, tsk."

"People are waiting longer to get married these days, Gram. They don't do it fresh out of high school like in the old days. They have careers, and they want to make sure that the one they're marrying is the right one. I prefer the idea of going slow. Maybe we wouldn't have so many divorces nowadays if people chose their mates better."

"If you go any slower, I won't live to attend your wedding, let alone enjoy any great-grandchildren. I want the son of my Albert to be happy."

He had heard how close his father and Gram were until his father ended up in the service and then died in Vietnam. For years after, Gram had struggled with depression, only cheering up whenever his mother brought him and his siblings over for a visit. Now as an adult, Neil's visits with his grandmother continued as they had back then. He felt a special bond with Gram because of it all. Over the years, she had shared all she could remember about his father, to the point that Neil felt he knew him, even if he'd never met him. And it probably cheered Gram to know that, though he was the product of a son who lived no more, something of his father, Albert, still lived on. It would have been great, of course, to have a dad. Someone to take him to baseball games. Someone to lean on when the going got rough. Even someone to talk to about these women issues. But he let it go as he did with most things. God had His reasons, even if Neil didn't understand them all.

After dinner, Neil bade Gram farewell and headed for the elevator. Passing by the nursing station, he ignored the stares from every corner and the faces peeking out from the lounge. Heat flooded his cheeks. If only he could come here for a visit without thinking he was a chunk of meat on display. As it was, he never considered himself the type with that kind of appeal. In the mirror, he saw a normal guy with brown hair and eyes to match. There were no dimples, no flashy smile, nothing that should attract this amount of attention. Maybe there were no other guys his age visiting the residents. And for certain, the ratio of single men to women in this small town left much to be desired.

For now, he decided to dismiss the thought of women and think about Gram and what he would like to give her for Christmas. He had an idea brewing and wondered if he could make it work. What if he could arrange to have her taken out of this facility to spend Christmas with his mother and siblings? Christmas at home, surrounded by her loved ones, would be the ultimate present, in his opinion—a wish come true for Gram, and one she would treasure always. He would take her to his home if he could, but a high-rise apartment in downtown Roanoke was hardly the place for a wheelchair-bound woman. His mother had plenty of room, if he could convince her. He would make it as easy as possible.

Arrange for everything and hire a nurse to help.

He strode out into the cold night for the drive home to Roanoke. All around were the signs of the blossoming holiday season—twinkle lights glimmering from homes, shop windows bursting with unusual gift ideas, bell ringers for charity organizations stationed in front of the shopping centers, and even the faint hum of a distant carol in the air. He thought about presents and the great idea of bringing Gram home for the holidays. He could just imagine her face on the big day when he rolled her into the family home to greet her loved ones. He had to make it happen somehow.

Suddenly the injured nurse on the road came to the forefront of his thoughts. He could chat with her about the idea and what equipment he might need. Maybe he could even hire her. She seemed to care about the residents. She had experience, working there at White Pines for eight years. Maybe she would do it if the price was right. The thought buzzed in his head as he drove along, making a mental note to arrive at the same time tomorrow in the hopes of catching the nurse on her way home.

Another busy workday at the White Pines facility had come and gone when Debbie emerged from the building, bleary-eyed from the lack of sleep over her bruised tailbone and worn-out from having to float to another floor because of a nursing shortage. She still shuddered over the day's work—contending with several belligerent residents who, as they put it, "did not like her style of nursing." She missed the peace of her own unit and the residents she had come to know and love. Now she looked forward to a relaxing bath, then curling up in front of the fireplace with a good book—if she could get a fire going in the small fireplace inside her apartment. Camping and fire building were not her forte. In Girl Scouts, she specialized in selling those great cookies. That and earning the first aid badge. She loved bandaging and caring for the sick.

Debbie took the walk slow this time, careful to avoid the glistening ice that gave her the colorful mark decorating her backside. She was so intent on staring at the pavement she did not hear a car pull up beside her until a voice startled her.

"Hello? Anybody home?"

Debbie whirled around to find a shadowy face peering at her from the car window. Shuddering, she ignored the car and continued on down the sidewalk. The car followed slowly behind. She began feeling hot in her jacket. Her nerves stood on edge, thinking of muggers who sometimes stalked young nurses walking home from work. If only she had her car back. She would be safe and sound, driving away at breakneck speed. *How long does it take for a garage to get the right parts anyway?*

"Is something the matter?" the voice persisted.

A car door slammed, followed by footsteps. Debbie searched for a place to run when she found herself face-to-face with a familiar figure dressed in a black overcoat.

"I didn't mean to scare you. I'm the guy who helped you out yesterday, remember?"

"Oh, it's you." She sighed in relief. "I'm not used to having strange men following me."

"Is your back doing better?"

Debbie shrugged. "I'll survive. It was hard today, trying to work with it. I never knew a bruised tailbone could hurt so much."

"Maybe you should take off a day or two and let it heal up."

"Call in sick this time of year? You must be joking. As it is, everyone seems to be taking off early, leaving us very short-staffed. In fact, I had to work on another floor today, which was no fun. Different residents and different nursing personnel with their own philosophies and ways of doing things." She bent her head, studying the patches of ice decorating the sidewalk. "Then I had several residents who were not very friendly. One even swung his fist at me."

The man's eyes widened in alarm. He took a step closer. "Swung his fist at you? You're kidding."

"Don't worry. He missed. A good thing, too, or I'd have a bruise on my face to match the one on my tailbone."

"Look, it must still be hard walking, especially after a day like today. I can drive you home again. It's no trouble."

"What are you, the White Pines taxicab service?"

"When someone is injured and has had a rough day, I am. Better yet, how about we get ourselves some hot chocolate at the coffee shop in Daleville? I hear when life gives you lemons, drink chocolate."

She laughed. "You mean, when life gives you lemons, make lemonade."

"Hot chocolate in the winter. Lemonade in the summer."

Debbie snuggled her hands into the pockets of her jacket, feeling the warmth radiating through her at this friendly invite. Her first gift of chocolate, be it hot chocolate, presented by a good-looking man. Now that was a treat she could hardly turn down. "Sure, why not? I guess I deserve it."

He smiled and led the way back to his car. "By the way, I suppose we should introduce ourselves. I'm Neil."

"I'm Debbie."

He performed a U-turn and drove off in the direction of Daleville.

"So where do you work?" Debbie wondered. "Around here somewhere?"

"I live and work in Roanoke. I man a desk job at an insurance firm. Definitely not the fast lane."

"So you pick the pockets of the injured," she said with a laugh. "No wonder you were curious about my accident."

"I would be if your car was insured through my company and involved in an accident. I work in the auto division."

"Hey, maybe you can help me out. I've had my car in the garage now for five days. It seems they've lost the parts. Either that or they have the parts and don't know what to do with them. They were supposed to have my car fixed in a day or two. Something about replacing a few noisy valves. Now it's turning into a weeklong ordeal."

"Sounds fishy to me. If you want, I can stop by the garage and check it out for you."

Debbie sighed. A man of chocolate and a rescuer of one in the throes of being ripped off. She was more impressed by the minute. "That would be great. Thanks. It's Hank's Auto Service. I wonder if Hank knows what's going on. Anyway, I'd hate to think the garage is taking advantage of me just because I'm a woman. You never know." She gazed at the storefronts and homes, decked out in holiday greenery and lights. "Nary a Nativity scene to be found," she murmured.

"What was that?"

"Oh, I was just looking at all the worldly portrayals of the Christmas season. You know, elves, Santa, animals, stockings. But hardly any Nativity scenes and certainly none in the town squares. Too bad." She paused then, uncertain how he would take her opinions or the fact that she was a Christian.

"We live in strange times. No one has a need for God and especially no reminders of Him. Every major holiday is replaced by some symbol, like Easter bunnies for the Resurrection. And even the public schools call it winter break and not Christmas break so one doesn't have to say the word *Christ*. It's crazy."

Debbie couldn't help but be delighted by his words, despite the seriousness of them. Neil thought the same way she did. This picture was getting rosier by the minute.

Sitting at the coffee shop a short time later, with a mug of hot chocolate topped off by a swirl of whipped cream, Debbie thought she had died and gone to heaven. She felt more relaxed than if she had submerged herself in that bathtub full of bubbles. Neil's dark eyes perusing her from across the table added to the pleasure. If not for the thought in the back of her mind about the date he had with a worker at White Pines yesterday, she might actually wonder if God was performing a wondrous miracle in her midst.

They talked about their days in school, their jobs, and what was on their wish list for Christmas. Debbie talked of owning a luxury SUV and laughed.

Neil shifted in his seat after draining his mug of chocolate and folded his hands on the table. "Debbie, there is another reason behind this little get-together."

Here it comes. He left the other nurse he's seeing at White Pines and wants to go out with me. She tried to hold her eagerness at bay, along with a twinge of anxiety. What if he did ask her out on a real date? What would she do? What would she wear? First things first. "Yes?"

"Since it's Christmas and we're talking about gifts, I have an extra special gift I'd like to give someone close to me. You see, I have a grandmother in White Pines who would love the best present of all—Christmas at home, surrounded by her family."

"So you visit your grandmother?"

"I go see her most evenings. That's where I was going when I saw you out there in the middle of the road."

Wow. So the date I thought he had with another woman in the facility was really a visit with his grandmother. What a guy. Kind, considerate, thoughtful of those in need. And looking pretty good right now. "That's sweet of you to think of her. Half the residents would love to go home to be with their families, but it just doesn't happen."

"I'm hoping I can make it happen for Gram. For as long as I can remember, she and I have always been close. Unusually so, I think, due to my father's death."

"I'm sorry to hear that."

"Don't be. I never knew him. My mother was carrying me at the time, so I never laid eyes on him. Anyway, I want to bring Gram home to be with the family over the holidays. I have no space for her at my old bachelor pad in a high-rise. I need to convince Mom to go along with the idea, and I think hiring a nurse to take care of her might be just the ticket. I think Mom would agree to the plan, knowing I've already set up round-the-clock care. I would pay you well and—"

Debbie straightened in her seat, wincing at the spasm in her back. "You want to hire me? That's nice of you, Neil, but you see—"

"If money is the problem, I will definitely make it worth your while. I know you would rather be home with your family, so it's a big sacrifice."

"Yes, but I—"

"Believe me, Gram is the greatest person to take care of. You wouldn't have to do much, honestly. How does five hundred a day sound? Is that too low? I don't know how much private-duty nurses get. Maybe I need to scope it out a bit more so I'm giving fair wages, especially over the holidays. We're talking three twenty-four-hour days most likely, depending on what Gram needs."

Debbie nearly choked on the amount. Fifteen hundred smackaroos. That was more pay than she earned in several weeks of work. *If only*— She sighed. "Neil, I would love to do it, but I'm already working Christmas."

His cheeks pinked. He stirred in his seat, clearly flustered. "What?"

"I said, I'm working Christmas. . .at White Pines. It's my turn this year."

"You work Christmas?" His cheery countenance instantly changed to one of disappointment.

"We are scheduled to work every other Christmas. I was off last year, so it's my turn. And believe me, there's no way I can get that time off, either. It's a dead issue as far as work goes."

Neil tapped on the side of the mug. "I see." He drained the mug, then checked his watch. "Sorry, I need to get going. I have a few things to do before I see my grandmother."

Debbie winced. All the joy of the meeting quickly evaporated. Now that the air had cleared, she could see at once that he wasn't interested in her personally. He was after one thing, a nurse to take care of his grandmother. She should have known he would only take her to a coffee shop with some other motive in mind, rather than trying to get to know her. It had been this way all her life with guys, like Brad who she thought was looking her way but instead had his eye on her roommate.

Debbie swallowed down her indignation and managed to thank him for the hot chocolate. They strode out to the car in an uncomfortable silence. When he arrived at her apartment, he asked if he could check on her car.

"Don't worry—I can take care of it. Thanks anyway." Before he could respond, she gave him a brisk thank-you and darted into her apartment, shutting the door behind her. *Serves me right, getting my hopes up that a man might finally be looking my way.* He was looking for service, though a good kind of service, she had to admit. If only she didn't wrestle so much with expectations that went flying out the window at the least provocation. If only she could rely more on the plan God had for her life and not some preconceived notion. *Lord, please let me know what that plan is,* she prayed.

250

Chapter 3

Neil strode into the White Pines facility that evening without the usual exuberance that marked his step. Gram would know something was up as soon as he gave her a welcome kiss on the cheek. Despite being blind, she could read his every mood—when he had a bad day at the office or when something else ailed him. Before heading to her room, he stopped in the hall to collect his composure. He couldn't tell her the real reason for his disappointment this night: that he had failed in hiring the nurse he thought perfect for his plan to bring her home. Not only that, but he knew they had left the coffee shop on shaky ground, which didn't make him feel any better. Guess he had not been a gentleman with the lady. He had managed to get her angry after a mere sixty-minute encounter.

He glanced at the nurses walking back and forth, some greeting him with a smile. Perhaps he would need to swallow his indignation at being chased by this colorful flock in their printed smocks and find a smiling face willing to help him with Gram. Maybe something could be gained from all the attention.

He noticed a rather tall nurse brush by him, rolling her cart of linen supplies in the direction of his grandmother's room. She turned and gave a smile before flinging back her dark blond hair.

"Hi, Neil. How's it going?"

He stopped dead in his tracks, startled that she knew his name. Had they met before?

"I'm Trish, and I've got your grandma for the evening." She pulled out her notepad with scribbles on it. "Usually I work days, but I'm pulling a little overtime tonight. Is there anything she would like this evening?"

"Actually, yes. There's something I need."

The nurse straightened, her eyes wide, as if ready to give him anything he wanted. Any other time and he would have cast the interest into the dust. Not this time. He planned to make full use of it. "I was wondering. Are you by chance off this Christmas?"

"Why, yes, I am."

"You've probably already made plans though, right?"

"Nothing that can't be changed, of course. What's up?"

"I'm looking to hire a nurse for a few days to take care of Gram at my mother's house. It will be sort of her big Christmas gift, you might say. Would you be interested? I'll pay five hundred a day for three days."

Trish's eyes lit up. "Wow! Sure, I'd love to take care of your grandma. I pretty much know her routine, you see, since I take care of her a lot."

Neil sighed in relief, thankful he had solved his dilemma. But he couldn't settle a nagging sensation of doubt rising up within. Was that God nudging his heart? The truth be known, he wanted Debbie to be Gram's nurse. There was something about her that intrigued him. He could tell she loved the residents and wanted to care for them in the best way possible. But he couldn't have her. She was already taken—besides the fact that she was mad at him. He brushed away the feeling and offered a small smile. "Great, thanks. We'll talk over the specifics at a later date."

"Let me give you my name and cell number," she said, hurriedly writing down the information on a slip of paper before tearing it off and handing it to him. "If you want, maybe we can grab a bite to eat sometime, and you can fill me in on all the details."

"Sure," he said, stuffing the note inside the pocket of his overcoat before heading into Gram's room.

She sat in her wheelchair, humming a tune along with her favorite record. Immediately she paused, lifted her head, and smiled. "Hello, Nathaniel."

"Hi, Gram." He gave her the usual welcome kiss.

A frown settled on her face. "Oh dear, what happened? The boss give you trouble? Was it the traffic? Is it snowing out? Someone told me there may be another snowstorm soon."

"No, just gray skies out." He pulled up a chair and plunked himself down. "I have a lot on my mind."

Gram turned in her wheelchair and sniffed the air. "You went out somewhere. . .to dinner maybe? Did you eat out with a young lady? Oh, I hope so. It must get very boring eating with an old lady like me every day. You need to get out more."

Neil turned red and shifted in his seat. He never considered that his coat would carry the scent of the coffee shop. With Gram's loss of sight, her senses of smell and hearing were quite keen. "I did go to the coffee shop," he admitted.

"Who with?"

"The nurse I helped on the road yesterday."

Gram beamed. "Wonderful! I'm so glad, Nathaniel. Did it go well?"

"Uh, not really. I mean she's nice and everything, but she's. . .uh, she's not the right one for me."

"Oh, honestly. You take a girl out once and think she's not right for you? Don't be so picky. Take her out again. For my sake."

"Gram. . . ," Neil began. A choking sensation filled his throat. "Please don't pressure me like this."

Immediately she shrank down in her wheelchair and became quiet.

Neil exhaled a loud sigh. "I'm sorry I said that. If it means so much to you, I'll take her out again. As it is, we really didn't talk about anything. . .that is, anything personal and all. It was more like a business conversation."

"Oh, give it a chance. Talk about things she likes. Be that considerate man I know and love. I'm sure she's pretty, too."

Neil considered Debbie's characteristics—her cheeks tinted pink by the wind, her blue eyes shining in the fading sunlight, the way she smiled over her cup of hot chocolate with the steam caressing her face. "I guess so. I didn't look at her in that way."

"You take her out again and then introduce me to her. I'll know if she's the right one for you."

"Gram, you're something else." He chuckled and leaned over to plant another kiss on her cheek.

"I'm more than something. I'm the one who's going to make sure you aren't alone in life." She paused then. He thought he saw tears gathering in her eyes. "To be left alone is the worst thing in life. Don't ever let it happen to you, you hear me?"

Her face at that moment remained branded within him—that hollowed look of loneliness. He was glad he had decided to arrange for her to be home for the holidays. Her words confirmed the plan—and perhaps other ideas that now began to well up in his thoughts.

ⁿ

Debbie was glad to leave work on time at the end of the regular day shift. She headed straight for home, thankful she didn't run the risk of seeing Neil outside the facility. The scene at the coffee shop still rubbed her nerves raw. Why did she have a problem with this anyway? Was she that desperate to be noticed by a man, like all the other nurses? Wouldn't it be better to yield such desires to God, who was quite capable of handling all the issues of her life?

Despite the emotional pain of her falling-out with Neil, at least her back seemed to be on the mend. Using a handheld mirror, Debbie could make out the bright blue and purple pattern left by the pavement. *I look like a genuine stained glass ornament,* she observed with a chuckle. The comment made her think of her Christmas decorations in storage in the basement of the small apartment building. With the few snow flurries floating around outside the window of her apartment, Debbie decided that Christmas decorating would help her forget her troubles and shift her moodiness to the joy of the upcoming holiday.

Dragging up the two boxes from storage, she rested for a bit to calm the aching in her back. Inside one box were ornaments, a music box, and a treasured Nativity set made of porcelain that immediately took a prominent position on the lamp table. The other box held an assortment of lights in one tangled ball of wire and bulbs thrown into a plastic bag. Debbie put on a CD of her favorite Christmas carols and set to work untangling the mess. *I should have done this the right way and put these strands back in their proper packaging,* she thought. But the mere idea of trying to press two hundred lights into the plastic prongs of the light boxes made her shudder. *So now I pay the price.*

Hoping not to push her frustration button, which she didn't need to do right now, she delved into a gusty rendition of a Christmas carol that drifted out of the stereo speakers. "O come, let us adore Him!" she sang. "O come, let us adore Him. . ."

"O come, let us adore Him. . .Christ the Lord," a deep voice echoed in reply.

Debbie set down the light strand. A chill swept through her. She hurried to the front door and peeked through the security hole to find Neil standing there, covered in a dusting of snow. She opened the door to the living snowman who waved his leather glove at her. "What are you doing here?"

"I've been standing here for ten minutes, listening to the carols. I figured the best way to make my entrance known was to sing along."

"I have a doorbell."

Neil shrugged. "I rang it a couple of times, but it's hard for door chimes to compete with Christmas carols. They sound like they're part of the music."

Debbie stepped aside, allowing him in. He seemed different today—joyful, interested, witty. He took off his coat and hung it over a chair to dry. "You're in the Christmas spirit, I see," he said, noting the tangled web of lights on the carpet.

"This is a royal mess, actually. Do you want to thaw out over a cup of tea? I have different flavors, like peach."

"Peach tea would be great, thanks."

Debbie entered the kitchen, fumbling to put a mug of water in the microwave. She could not recall the last time a man had graced her humble abode, except for the days of Tonya and Brad. And that was a time she'd rather forget. She dipped a teabag into the mug decorated with a bear in a nursing uniform before presenting it to Neil. He chuckled when he saw the design. "Sorry about the mug. My family thinks it's cute to give me mugs with nursing stuff on it. I get a new one every year for Christmas. I have eight of them. So you're kind of stuck with it."

"Do you plan to continue working at White Pines?"

"I guess so. There's nothing else I can do right now. I have a few college credits to my name, but no other degree." She plopped down in a chair and put her feet up on a stool. "I suppose I could go on and get a real nursing degree if I had the money and the time."

"Being a nursing assistant probably doesn't pay much, though."

She shrugged before scanning the small, one-bedroom garden apartment. "It's enough to pay the bills. Of course I can't buy new things. I get hand-me-downs from the family. Or I check out the Salvation Army store for bargains out of the bin."

"Old relics never die," he said with a nod. "Look what you get nowadays—plastic mailboxes or even blow-up furniture. There are hardly any of the old wood drawers around anymore, or stuffed armchairs that never wear out. If you can believe it, I have several old pieces inside my place."

"Really?"

"Got them at an antique store. Oh sure, my sister, Sandy, rants that I need to go contemporary. Black-and-white, I guess. But I like older stuff. It lasts much longer, even over brand-new. All one has to do nowadays is poke a pin through one of those blow-up sofas and watch it sail out the window."

Debbie suppressed a laugh. All the ideas she had conceived from their earlier meeting at the coffee shop likewise had flown out the window. She enjoyed hearing how he preferred old furniture. He certainly wasn't a stuffy, stick-your-nose-in-the-air type of person used to a lavish lifestyle. In fact, he seemed relaxed, easygoing, even tempered. *A great catch. Maybe.* She breathed out a sigh, determined not to go that way, to keep her expectations in check. One step at a time.

Neil picked up several strands of lights knotted together. Slowly, with an overwhelming patience that amazed her, he began the tedious task of untangling the lights. "I should get a few boards for you to wrap the strands around when the season is over," he remarked. "Then you won't have to deal with this again."

Debbie turned to her own set of tangled lights, hoping he didn't see the flush creeping into her face. He was being too kind. Surely there must be some other motive for this impromptu visit. "So why did you come tonight, Neil? Like I said at the coffee shop, I can't help out with your grandmother at Christmas. Switching with others is out. And if I don't show up, I'll likely be canned."

"I know. You told me." He paused, surveying the knot of lights. "This is more complicated than some of those jigsaw puzzles I used to do with Gram when I was a kid. Boy, was she a whiz at putting them together. Put me to shame." He gave a tug. "Anyway, there is a reason I came barging in here like this."

Here it comes.

"I didn't like how we left each other at the coffee shop yesterday."

Debbie stared in amazement.

"I could tell you were kind of put off by what happened. And I don't blame you." He set down the clump of lights to take a swig of the peach tea.

"Well, you didn't pull any punches. You came right out and told me the reason for splurging on the hot chocolate. I guess chocolate and hiring nurses do go together." Debbie frowned at her rising irritation. "Sorry. I guess I was put off. I was hoping it would be more of a friendly kind of thing, you know. Not that I don't understand what you were trying to do. I mean, having your grandma come home for the holidays is very noble. I'm glad you want to do it. Really."

"I'll admit that was my main goal. But looking back on it all, I realize I didn't go about it the right way. I guess, at the moment, with the idea fresh in my mind, I wanted to make it work. I think it would make a great gift for Gram, something money can't buy—the idea of Christmas with the family, singing carols, watching an old Christmas movie, even roasting a chestnut or two." He looked at her with the most beautiful coffee-colored eyes she had seen in a good, long while. And she liked the small tuft of dark hair that fell over his forehead. "We all have our traditions, I guess."

"We have traditions. In my family, we always started Christmas Eve night by going to our favorite barbecue place. Then Dad insisted on taking us on a grand tour of the lighting displays. This one place had fantastic illumination with every sculpted light and plastic figurine known to mankind. They must start decorating as soon as summer is over. Dad used to do some big decorating when we were kids. You know, stringing up those lights with the megasize bulbs. He even made a model of a church once." Debbie caught herself when she realized how easily she had launched into her childhood with such eagerness. She'd never shared memories like this. With the girls at work or church, it was things like clothes or activities. This was new, different, even exciting. And especially with Neil here, soaking up every word.

"I'd like to see a big display like that sometime," he said. "And barbecue is one of my favorite foods. I would travel down to North Carolina just to get the real stuff." He returned to the lights and managed to untangle a long strand that spanned the length of the room.

Debbie pulled over the chair, ready to climb up and tack them around the windows. Neil stood below, feeding her lights as they continued to talk about Christmas memories. In an instant, everything else faded but the twinkle of lights and a handsome man helping her decorate her apartment. Could this really be happening? Well, why not? Why couldn't she relish the thought of a man helping her decorate and enjoy every bit of it? Why did she need to bask in past disappointment? The days of Brad and her roommate, Tonya, were long gone. They had their own lives. And she had hers, which was becoming even more interesting as time slipped by. Time to let go of the past and embrace the future.

They stood together, observing the lights for a moment longer, before Neil went for his coat.

"Thanks for helping me with the decorations," Debbie said.

"Hope you aren't mad anymore about the coffee shop scene."

The flush in her face returned, hotter than ever. "I'm not mad. Not really. I just have to work out a few things, which don't have anything to do with you. Besides, I think what you're doing for your grandmother is great. I'm sure she will be thrilled by it all."

He nodded, a small smile breaking out across his face. "Maybe we can do the hot chocolate thing again sometime. Start over. Get back on track."

Debbie nodded, unable to speak. When he said good night, Debbie felt another rush of warmth invade—and not from the millions of lights now warming her home or the tea inside her tummy. It was the warmth of a good night to a sweet and considerate man. Good night and sweet dreams. And she knew who would dominate her dreams tonight.

Chapter 4

O h, Debbie, dear! Your boyfriend is calling you."
Debbie paused in midstride, carrying a tall stack of linens to make up the beds inside a room. How she wished she could just think about the meeting with Neil in her apartment a few nights ago. Instead, the craziness of work consumed her. Nearly all the residents seemed overdemanding, asking her for this or that. There were numerous accidents to clean up. Several refused to eat, forcing her to alert the head nurse, Mrs. Whitaker.

Trish looked into the room, a sardonic smile plastered on her face. Debbie knew she couldn't possibly mean Neil. No one knew about him, not that he was her boyfriend, by any means. Maybe soon he would enter that arena, if all went as planned. It did irk her some that she hadn't heard from him since the evening he helped her untangle the Christmas lights. She hoped they weren't at another impasse. She thought the evening had gone pretty well. And he had left it open-ended, with another coffee or chocolate meeting to come in the near future.

Suddenly Debbie heard a loud voice echoing down the hallway. "Shore up that line! Get to the top of the ridge on the double. I know the Germans are coming. We'll get murdered standing here. Move on out!"

Trish leaned against the door frame. "Mrs. Whitaker asked if you could calm dear Harold down. I guess you have a knack for that kind of thing. He probably thinks you remind him of his girlfriend from the 1940s or something."

Debbie gritted her teeth and plunked the stack of linens on a bed. How she disliked Trish's demeaning ways. She could certainly think up a good retort, were it not for Christian virtue that made her bridle her tongue. She prayed for patience as she brushed by Trish to hear the racket that grew louder as she approached. When she peeked inside Harold's room, she found the poor man sliding halfway out of his wheelchair. His hair stood up like a wild man, his face unshaven. She exhaled loudly. Harold was Trish's patient, no doubt. He bore all the telltale signs.

Debbie came around behind and hoisted him up so he sat properly in his chair. "What's the matter, Harold?"

He looked back at her with a wild look in his eyes. "What are you doing? Don't you know there's a war going on? Duck down 'fore the enemy sees you."

Debbie calmly walked over to the nightstand and took a comb out of the drawer. "Harold, we've had these talks before. World War II has been over for sixty years."

"What? That's impossible. I'd be an old man if the Great War ended sixty years ago."

Debbie bit her lip to keep from laughing. He did have a sense of humor, despite his memory lapses.

"In fact, if the war's been over sixty years, I'd be in my eighties at least, and I'm only twenty-four."

He was absolutely right. Debbie marveled at the way Harold could make rationalizations like these, even if he did say other irrational things. But to his mind, everything made perfect sense and she was the one off her rocker. Maybe a little reality check might set things straight and clear his thoughts. She wheeled him into the bathroom and to the mirror hanging low on the wall. "See, Harold? You're not in your twenties anymore. You're a man of wisdom."

He said nothing but stared. She heard a sniffle and looked down to find tears glistening on his cheeks. "Get me out of here," he ordered. Debbie hurriedly wheeled him back into the room. He continued to sit there, staring, the tears drifting down.

Her lower lip trembled. Regret instantly filled her. For all she knew, Harold found comfort in his youthful identity, and in an instant, she had shattered it. "I'm so sorry, Harold. I thought it would be good for you to see that you aren't a young man anymore."

He only turned away from her to stare at the wall. Debbie twisted her face in dismay. What did it hurt if Harold wanted to believe he was still young? If it made him happy and made him feel as if he still had a life to live, even in his advanced years, then why not? Instead, she had ripped it all away from him.

Debbie shook her head and retreated to the hall to find Trish standing just outside the door, a wide grin painted on her face. "Bravo! What a show. Did you really think crazy old Harold would want to see himself in the mirror?"

Debbie began to stew. "I don't know. I thought it was worth trying to get him to see reality."

"Honey, none of these people here think they're old. They all think they're swinging singles from way back when hoopskirts were in fashion."

"You're a little off. They didn't wear hoopskirts in the 1940s. Anyway, maybe you could clean Harold up a little more. And he could use a shave."

"So now you're the high-and-mighty nurse who knows everything? Where is your advanced degree that says you can order me around? Huh?"

Debbie blew out a sigh and hurried off to the room where the linens still sat on the unmade bed. She shouldn't have opened her mouth about Trish's untidy habits. Now the whole floor would know what she said and be on her case about it. Debbie shook her head. She needed to talk to Mrs. Whitaker about Trish anyway. The woman shouldn't even be working here, considering the way she treated the residents. Not that Debbie had seen Trish do anything horrendous like the stories she had heard about abuse in these places. But the way Trish kept her charges looking so untidy or offered snide remarks, in Debbie's eyes, was akin to maltreatment. Even so, after being here eight years, Debbie knew well what could happen if she did make waves. Trish had plenty of friends on staff who could make Debbie's life miserable. And others before her had been chased away for littler things.

Making the bed in rapid fashion, Debbie walked down the corridor and paused by Harold's door. He was sitting better in his wheelchair. His clothes were neat, but he still looked listless. His eyes stared blankly from his unshaven face. Debbie glanced up the hall and, seeing no sign of Trish, ventured back inside. "Let's get a shave, Harold. Spiff you up a little for all the girls."

"Huh? What for? I'm just an old geezer. Everyone tells me I'm old, that I look old, that I am old."

"I'm sorry about what happened, Harold. Please, can I give you a shave?" She held up the electric razor.

He said nothing as she approached. Only when she turned on the razor did he flinch. His extremities began to quake. Fear was clearly spelled out in his eyes that grew all the more wild. "We're gonna have to get off these boats," he said to her. "But I see the bullets. The enemy's already firing at us. But we gotta head for the beach anyway. There's no turning back."

"Where are we headed, Harold?"

"To Omaha, of course. We're supposed to take Omaha Beach. Me and Sam, we're going together. We trained together. Got on the same landing craft together. We're both real scared, too. He's my best friend, you know."

Debbie recalled the movies she had seen about that awful day at Normandy on the shores of France. She remembered thumbing through her father's multitude of coffee-table books about World War II. But here sat a man who had witnessed, firsthand, a time period that lived in infamy. Why hadn't she even considered it before trying to make him see the reality of living in the present day?

"Sam got sick to his stomach," Harold went on. "Seasickness, I guess. He used his helmet as a bucket until I told him to just lean over the side of the boat. Then we heard the bullets. He was tugging on my jacket. I said there weren't nothing to fear, that the enemy couldn't hit the broadside of a barn."

"It must have been real scary," she said, running the electric shaver around his chin. He lifted his head higher so she could shave his neck.

"When the boys started dying, it was. They died right in front of me. One by one." Suddenly his shoulders began to heave. The tears bubbled over. "They died. Sam died. Everyone in my company died, except me. I was on my own. I didn't know anyone on the beach. I was all alone with bullets all around."

Debbie stood there, mesmerized by the story. Just then his grisly hand took hers. His skin was dry, the veins crisscrossing the top of his hand like the streets on a road map. "Don't ever be alone, young lady. Being alone with the enemy closing in is the worst thing in life."

Debbie managed to pat his hand before putting back the razor. Just as quickly, Harold lapsed into a quiet pensiveness, staring straight ahead. She looked at him, thinking of all the scenes that replayed over and over in his mind like a rerun with no end. She felt sorry for him.

Debbie ventured to the nurses' station to check the assignment sheet and found Trish loitering there along with two cohorts, Meg and Natasha. When they saw her, they gathered together like a flock of hens and began their clucking. Debbie refused to embrace the old fear left over from the high school days of students talking behind her back, though she was certain the nurses were doing just that.

"So old Harold has you wrapped around his finger, eh?" Trish said with a huge smile painted on her face. The other two nurses giggled.

"Why don't you leave him alone? He doesn't have long to live in this world anyway. No one here does. They have to spend the rest of their existence here, so we should make it as nice as possible for them. We're the only real family they have."

"They're not my family," Natasha announced in disgust, staring at her set of purple polished fingernails. "I'm only in this place until I find a better job."

"The problem with Debbie is that she thinks these people are her pets," Trish added.

"Actually, Trish, it's you who treats them like dogs," she muttered and headed back down the hall.

Trish followed. "Excuse me? What did you say?"

Debbie felt the heat rise in her neck even as she tried to look the other way.

"If you have something to say, say it to my face."

Debbie whirled. "Okay. Leave Harold alone. And don't call him names. If anything, he should be treated like a hero. A lot of men like Harold bled and died so you could stand there and say the things you do."

Trish hooted. "Honey, no one died for me, 'specially little old Harold who doesn't even know what planet he's on."

Jesus died for you, Debbie thought, but this was hardly the time or atmosphere to delve into her heartfelt beliefs. "People need to look more at history. See what soldiers have accomplished and the freedoms they have won for us. Our country would be a much different place without their sacrifices."

"Huh? What are you talking about?"

Debbie could see this conversation was going nowhere fast. She excused herself to check on several patients, with Trish glaring at her as she hurried down the hall. Ducking inside a linen alcove, she steadied herself. Maybe Neil was right. Maybe it was time to look for another job, not only to bring in more money but also to escape people like Trish. . . .

. . .that is, until she heard a voice shouting at some unseen German enemy invading White Pines. Down the hall she went, with a strength greater than herself. If no one else on earth needed her, Harold did and maybe Elvina, too. And that was enough to keep her feet entrenched in this place, at least for now.

Despite trying to turn things around and salvage the day at White Pines, Debbie left work feeling depressed about where she was going in life. She wondered if her faith was at all evident to the staff and patients. For certain, the staff disliked her. If it weren't for the residents like Elvina and Harold and the relationships she'd fostered with them, she might be tempted to move away from this area altogether. What was keeping her here anyway? None of her family lived here. They made their home in northern Virginia where her father still negotiated the nightmare of Interstate 66 at rush hour, trucking it into Washington, D.C., every day. For herself, Debbie couldn't stand the thought of working in some metropolitan city that extended far beyond the borders of the District of Columbia. She made a big break after two years of community college, venturing as far south as possible, back to country living with less stress—or so she thought. She took a six-month nursing assistant course at a community college, then went looking for a job. Settling here in the foothills of the Blue Ridge in the tiny hamlet of Fincastle, she found something about the area that she enjoyed. Maybe the hilly surroundings with the grand scope of the Blue Ridge spanning the distant horizon. Fincastle also had quaint homes, some dating back generations, and held its own unique niche in history as the hometown of Julia Hancock, the wife of William Clark of the famous Lewis and Clark expedition. It was a nice area. But was it enough to keep her here, especially with what she had to endure at work and beyond?

Okay, quit throwing yourself a glorified pity party. She entered her car, thankful to have her set of wheels back—finally. The very next day after untangling the Christmas lights and sharing peach tea with Neil at her apartment, Hank's Auto Service called to say the car was ready. And the price was far cheaper than what she had originally been quoted. *Did Neil have a hand in me getting my car back, I wonder?* The mere thought made her feel better.

Driving to the store in Daleville to pick up a few groceries, Debbie made the decision to look on the bright side of things. God had placed her at White

Pines for a reason. She felt good about being around the residents and caring for their needs, both physically and emotionally. Maybe the attacks from people like Trish were confirmations that she was doing the right thing, even if she felt beaten down by them at times.

Debbie hadn't been cruising the store aisle more than fifteen minutes when she heard a familiar male voice whistling an old-time Christmas carol. Neil stood in the aisle with his own shopping basket in hand that held a can of shortbread cookies, a package of mints, and a bag of lozenges. She couldn't help but laugh, first at the idea of running into him in the same aisle of a huge grocery store, and second at the items he had chosen.

"Hi, Neil. Great start to the dinner you have planned," she teased.

He spun around. "Debbie, hi! So you like my choices, do you?"

"It's certainly unique."

He acknowledged his basket. "I plan to start off the evening fare with an appetizer of mints. Nothing like a sugar high to get you off on the right footing. Then a main course of shortbread cookies. And for dessert, assorted throat lozenges to cool the palate."

Debbie laughed long and loud, a freeing kind of laugh where the frustrations of life took flight in a hurry. "Mine isn't much better," she acknowledged, looking down at the contents of her basket—chocolate-covered ice cream bars, hot cocoa mix, and a stick of deodorant.

"I see chocolate. Is someone having another bad day?"

His observation sent tears springing to her eyes.

His voice softened. "Is your back still hurting you? I think you'd better have a doctor take a look at it. My sister once hurt her back and never got it checked. It bothers her even still. Sometimes she's in bed for a few days. She can't lift anything over twenty pounds."

"No, it's not that." Debbie rested the basket on a display of canned fruit. "What can I say? Life these days is definitely making me want to mix up a batch of lemonade. In fact, I'd better go get some."

"Put your stuff back," he ordered. "Time for that second round of hot chocolate I promised you."

She gazed at him. A smirk played on his lips, offset by the seriousness in his eyes.

"Guess I should. The ice cream bars aren't going to make it home anyway. But you can still buy your exotic dinner for that special someone."

He laughed. "Meet you in the front of the store."

Twenty minutes later, they were sitting at the same table they had occupied the week before, with two cups of chocolate before them. When Neil got to the punch line of a joke he'd heard at work, Debbie laughed and blew on the steam before taking a sip. She had to admit this encounter was much better than the first. Especially since Neil appeared sensitive to her woes and expressed a desire to help. She delved into the shortened version of the day's struggles, including Harold's battle with Normandy versus the twenty-first century and the callous mistake she'd made in showing him his reflection in the bathroom mirror.

"There's nothing wrong with trying to point an elderly gentleman to reality," he said.

"But you should have seen the reactions of my fellow coworkers. They thought it was some joke, like it's a scream to poke fun at an older man."

He rolled his eyes. "I can tell you for a fact that most of them don't even know what planet they're on. They don't want to be working there, and it shows. And for sure, they don't care about the residents the way you do."

"How do you know I care?"

He leaned over the table. "Is that a trick question? I can hear it in your voice. You're concerned you might have upset this Harold fellow by showing him his image in the mirror. And then your interest in his past. Seems to me, these days, no one wants to know about another's past, present, or future."

She took another sip. "Okay. So what about your past, present, and future?"

He hesitated at first. "Well, let's just say my past is better left right where it is. My present, I will have to wait for Christmas to see. Probably socks and underwear. And only God really knows the future, if we are patient enough to wait and find out."

Again a funny smirk spread across his face, this time accompanied by a twinkle in his eyes. So this Neil did have a bit of humor about him. But Debbie sensed there were other things left unspoken, as well. She had to admit, his comment about the past stirred up her curiosity to know more. But she wouldn't pry. She would wait.

"And you?" he asked.

"I grew up in northern Virginia in the fast lane. Or rather the HOV lane. My present would be a cruise to Alaska. And my future is like yours. Whatever God wants." She bowed her head then, feeling the warmth in her cheeks, even as he stared at her. She could sense a bond already forming. It amazed her. And here she thought she wasn't cut out for love. Maybe God was trying to show her otherwise. "Anyway, I'll get through this time somehow. He's been faithful to help me every day."

"That's right. And you are meant right now to work at White Pines, even if it gets a little tough. Just keep doing what you're supposed to do and don't worry about everyone else. We're told to take care of our neighbor. 'Love one another,' as the Bible says. And I hate to say it, but that includes those who treat us like junk sometimes, such as your coworkers, for example."

"Easier said than done," she mumbled, thinking of Trish.

"It's happened to me. I had a coworker of the higher-ups give me extra caseloads because he didn't like me, or so I thought. I sat there and wondered if maybe he had a falling-out with someone at home. A bad family life. Disappointment. If you can put the person in a different light, it helps."

"You need to come to work with me and be my conscience. Like Jiminy Cricket in *Pinocchio*. You can even wear a top hat and a red umbrella to go along with your black coat."

Neil laughed. "Debbie, I think you already have things figured out. Just hang tough. Take each day, one at a time. It's all any of us can do, you know."

As long as her days were filled with him, washed down with cups of hot chocolate, she had no doubt they would be good days. She left the shop feeling renewed. Sure, life's troubles were still there in one form or another, but at least they seemed smaller. Even insignificant. And that was a welcome change.

Chapter 5

Debbie awoke the next morning feeling better than she had in ages. Something about her encounter with Neil put everything in a new light. She decided to employ some of his wisdom to her situation and see what transpired. She would think of Trish, Natasha, and all the rest as women wrapped up in a perpetual fog of unhappiness, unable to see anything clearly. She would consider them as Jesus would—lost people who needed love not confrontation. Though it would be difficult to assert such love when following behind Trish, picking up after her, and tending to the care she'd left undone, Debbie would do her best.

With her new attitude in place, Debbie found the day proceeding smoothly. The fact that Trish also had the day off didn't hurt matters. Mrs. Whitaker did not assign Debbie to Elvina's wing but to the other wing that included Harold's room. He perked up when he saw her, smiling a toothless grin for the first time that she could recall. Debbie took her time pampering him a little, giving him a thorough shave, scouring around for some aftershave lotion to smooth on his face, and dressing him in a new sport shirt.

"Did you ever get married, Harold?"

"No. Never had a girl. Sam did, but I didn't. He talked about her all the time. His Liv, he called her."

"Liv? Was that short for Olivia?"

"Don't know. When he went off to fight, Sam left her and the boy behind. He told me all about them, how he was gonna marry her and be a real father to that little boy. He told me. . .told me to. . ." Harold stopped then, as if a switch had been turned off. A strange look distorted his rough features.

"Harold?"

He began to tremble and then looked off in the distance. "Hey, you there! What are you doing out of line? Get back in line right now, or the major's gonna have it in for you."

Debbie sighed. Once more he had lapsed into that strange battle state of sixty-some-odd years ago. When she tried to coax him back again, he refused. For a man who sometimes did not delve in reality, Harold had a knack for stubbornness. Sometimes she sensed pride holding him in that time period. Or, perhaps Harold found comfort in a wartime frame of mind, as if the present day proved more painful than D-day. Why he would think that, she had no idea.

"Debbie, I need a favor." Mrs. Whitaker stood in the doorway with the medication cart. She was of the "old school" of nursing, clad in her pure white dress with the nursing button of her alma mater prominently displayed, white hose, and white nursing shoes. Debbie was thankful the nursing assistants could wear colorful tops and white clogs. Her favorite smock this time of year was the one with holly and berries sprinkled across the fabric. And in January, Debbie liked to wear one covered in flowers to remind her of the coming spring.

"Can you work overtime tonight? I had two call in sick for the evening shift, and we're running short. If you can work until seven, that would be great."

Debbie quickly agreed. *More time on my mission field,* she decided. She would love to have Neil tagging along with her, telling her what to do, being her encouragement, lifting her head up when it sometimes sank to her chest in dejection. Then she realized Neil was merely a messenger. God was the source of her encouragement—her head lifter.

The rest of the day went smoothly with these thoughts singing in her head. Even when most of the day shift went home and Debbie remained behind, she felt light on her feet as if she had barely worked an eight-hour shift already. When Debbie got a break, she decided to pay Elvina a visit. Debbie came in whistling, hoping to put on a record for her and hear her sing. Elvina sat in her wheelchair by her bedside, staring toward the door with her hands folded on her lap as if waiting for something. "Hi, Elvina, it's Debbie."

"Oh, it's my little nurse. How are you, dear? I haven't seen you in such a long time. Are you working this evening?"

Elvina, with her eyes blinded to everything around her, had never literally *seen* Debbie, but Debbie knew what she meant. "Yes, for a few hours. For some reason, I've been assigned the other hall the last week or so. Do you want me to put on a record for you?"

"No, thank you. I'm waiting for Nathaniel to come. He's late today. I already hear the dinner carts coming down the hallway."

Debbie looked at her watch. "It's 5:30."

"Tsk, tsk. He always comes at 5:00. Must be there was a lot of traffic."

"I'm sure he will be here." Suddenly it dawned on her that she would get the opportunity to see this infamous grandson of Elvina's, the one who had given her the record player, the one everyone on staff raved about. She wondered why she had always missed seeing the man when working overtime. Oh well. Tonight, the mystery of Elvina's Nathaniel would be solved. Debbie chuckled to herself until she glanced at Elvina's nightstand. Sitting on top was a tin of shortbread cookies that looked vaguely familiar.

"What are you up to?" Elvina asked.

Leave it to Elvina to sense something was up. She had eyes in the back of her head. "Oh, nothing. Just wondering if you've eaten any of the cookies yet?"

"Are you hungry? Help yourself. I was going to ask the nurses if they would like to have them. To be honest, why Nathaniel thinks I should have cookies, I don't know. Yes, I do have a sweet tooth, but I'm afraid you sweet things will hurt your backs trying to get me out of bed if I keep eating cookies and candy."

Debbie wondered if it would be too presumptuous to open Elvina's drawer and check for throat lozenges. Just then she heard the nurses' station paging her. She hurried off, not giving it another thought until she returned half an hour later. Debbie went to check on Elvina and see if her grandson had made it in. She peeked in and saw a man with a rugged build sitting by Elvina's wheelchair. His back was to her, but she plainly saw the shocks of dark hair. He and Elvina were laughing. Debbie sucked in her breath. She didn't want to give the appearance of being overzealous as so many of the staff had been known to do. She decided simply to stride in, in a businesslike fashion. Maybe she could take the two dinner trays while stealing a quick glance.

Lifting her head high, Debbie marched in. "Let me get those trays out of your way," she declared, swiping up the trays.

"Oh, Nathaniel, this is the sweet nurse I was telling you about," Elvina said.

Nathaniel turned. They stared at each other.

"Neil?"

"Debbie?"

She burst out laughing, in keeping with the season of unpredictable joy. The surprise tickled her all the way to her toes inside her white clogs, as did the delightful smile erupting on Neil's face. "My day is complete."

"Mine, too."

❧

Neil couldn't believe that the nurse his grandmother adored turned out to be Debbie, though he wasn't totally surprised. Debbie had a fondness for the residents that was unmistakable. He could tell right away the two of them shared a special bond, which he hoped to share with Debbie, as well. When Gram launched into how Debbie made her feel beautiful with makeup and combing her hair, Neil cast a smile in Debbie's direction. He was getting more impressed by the minute.

"Debbie cares, Gram. She's a great person."

She sat up straighter in her chair. "You know her, Nathaniel?"

A blush filled Debbie's face, making her appear all the more attractive—though he thought her attractive anyway, with the way her soft brown hair lay on her shoulders. Recalling her hunched over that hot chocolate, the steam in her face, he couldn't help but stare. The holly and berries printed on her nursing smock, coupled with her cheerful countenance, brightened his day—especially a cold and dreary December one like today.

"This is simply wonderful," Gram cooed. "Nathaniel has been telling me all about a nurse who had fallen in the road. Was it you, Debbie? You're still here, aren't you?"

"I'm right here, Elvina. Yes, I did take a fall about a week or two ago. If it weren't for your grandson, I might have been turned into a human waffle under the wheels of a delivery truck."

Gram picked up Neil's hand and gave a squeeze. A tear or two trickled out of her eyes. "This is so sweet, I can't help but cry," she confessed. "How I prayed you would find a nice lady to settle down with. I just know you two are perfect for each other."

Neil glanced at Debbie who was using a fork from one of the trays to trace an imaginary line across the bedside table. He could tell that she was trying to decide how to take all this. The truth be known, Neil had been thinking quite a bit about Debbie. He had that trip back and forth from Roanoke, with plenty of time for contemplating and planning. Of course, one could hardly plan out a future relationship. That fell in God's department. Neil didn't want to make a mess of things. But he did like the feeling he got whenever he was around Debbie. And presto, here she was—caring for Gram, no less!

Debbie picked up the trays. "I guess I'd better get these into the cart before the cafeteria guys roll it away."

"Let me get the other tray," Neil offered. Gram looked on, grinning from ear to ear, as if she had planned this all out and everything was proceeding on cue. The whole notion made him suddenly bashful. The words became tangled in his throat as he walked a few paces behind Debbie down the hallway. At the large metal cart, they each slid in their respective trays.

"So you come here every evening to eat with Elvina, I mean, your grandmother?" Debbie asked.

"Most evenings."

"Small world."

"Small facility." He nodded toward the hallway that branched off into another part of the building. "Who would've thought you would be working on this floor."

"Actually I'm only here another hour or so. I usually work days, but they needed an extra hand until seven."

"I'll probably be leaving around then. I'd offer you a ride, but I take it you have your car back, right?"

Debbie nodded. He wondered then if they should do something after her shift was over. What does one do on a Wednesday evening? He'd already had his dinner. He didn't know if she'd eaten or not. Maybe get a pizza? That sounded like teenybopper stuff. They had done the coffee shop scene, even run into each other at the grocery store. He wasn't about to invite himself over to her apartment again. Downtown Fincastle offered little in the way of entertainment, and meeting at the shopping plaza at Daleville seemed lame. Roanoke held many possibilities but was too far out of the way for a midweek outing. He considered it for a time until he saw Debbie staring inquisitively.

"Something wrong?"

"No. Just thinking."

"Well, I have to check on the other residents. Have a good visit."

He sighed, wishing he had come up with something, but let the idea slide for the time being. Instead, he returned to his grandmother to find her sitting there quietly, looking distant, as if in deep thought. "You okay, Gram?"

"Oh, of course. Just thinking about you two gets me thinking about my sweetheart when I was young."

Neil grimaced. He was never good at talking to her about Grandpa Joe, who had passed away two years ago. Gram seemed to take it well when she learned her husband had died in his sleep. But comments like this always threw him for a loop, wondering what to say or how to react.

"My long-lost love." She straightened then, her gray blue eyes growing deeper in color to a near navy blue. "You never saw what he looked like. A pity."

The remark puzzled him. "Sure I have. Plenty of times."

"No, you haven't. I don't think your mother has a single picture of him anywhere. No one does that I know of. Your father was too small to have pictures. He was only three when his dad left. I don't think he gave him a picture, but he should have."

What is she talking about? This was getting more confusing by the minute. Of course there were pictures of Grandpa Joe. He began to panic, wondering if Gram was having some kind of memory lapse. Maybe some disease lay lurking there for a long time, like that dreaded Alzheimer's disease, and now it had surfaced. "Gram, I've seen many pictures of Grandpa. Mom has them sitting there on the mantel."

She shook her head. "If only I knew how to say these things right, but I don't. I do wish you knew him, Nathaniel. You remind me of him. The way you greet people. The way you treat a lady—like helping my little nurse when she fell. He was chivalrous. He would help anyone."

"Gram, I know it was hard to lose Grandpa, but he's in heaven. He was a fine Christian man."

"I don't know where he is," she said hollowly. "I don't know if he's alive or dead. I wish I did. If there were one wish I could have, it would be to see him one last time. If only he could tell me why he wrote just one letter and why I never heard from him again. If only I could tell him about your father—what a fine young man he turned out to be, and then the fine children he had, like you. He would be so proud."

Neil stared, his hands sinking deeper into his pockets. None of this was making any sense. He whirled and walked out into the hallway, scanning the nurses' station. Everyone was gone, probably involved in evening care to ready the residents for the night. He needed to talk to someone, a doctor maybe, someone who could tell him if his grandmother was suffering a mental defect. Debbie would know. She knew Gram like the back of her hand. At least he hoped she did. He walked down the hall, peeking in each room until he found her.

"Hi, Neil." She paused. "Is something wrong?"

He waited until she came out into the hallway. "It's Gram. Something's not right. She keeps talking about Grandpa like she hasn't seen him in thirty years. He just died a couple of years ago. And now she's asking to see him again."

Debbie sighed. "I'm sorry, Neil. Sometimes a mind can wander in the evening. It's just temporary. She'll be better in the morning."

"I've never heard her say these things before. She says there are no pictures of him either and that I've never even seen what he looks like. Debbie, I have a picture of Grandpa Joe sitting on my bureau at home. I knew him very well."

"I don't know what to say, Neil. If you want, I can try and talk to her."

"No. It might make her more confused and upset. I just wish I knew what to do." Neil strode away, staring at the floor tiles. It had finally happened. His dear grandmother had gone senile, and when he least expected it. Looking at his watch, he decided to call it an evening before anything else absurd came forth. Heading back to her room, he paused in the doorway to study her. She appeared sweet and innocent, so lucid really, talking about a long-lost love, her sweetheart, as if he were a real person. Maybe he was, in her mind.

When Neil walked into the room, her head turned. "I thought you had left without saying good-bye. That's not like you."

"Gram, I'm worried."

"About what?" She said it as if he were the one going senile.

"What you said about Grandpa Joe. It doesn't make any sense."

"I wasn't talking about Joe. Dear Joe. I know he's in heaven, bless his heart. I just wondered what happened to your other grandfather."

My other grandfather? "What? You mean my mom's dad?"

She waved at him. "No, no, no. Your father's father. Your real grandfather. Oh, never mind. It's getting late. Can you send for Debbie? I need to get ready for bed. And you need to go home before it gets too late." She turned her wrinkled cheek toward him, waiting for him to bestow the nightly ritual of a kiss on her cheek. He obliged, only to have her pinch his own in an affectionate way.

"Don't worry about things. I'm fine."

"I'll try not to," Neil managed to say.

Leaving White Pines that night, he felt like he was walking in a daze. *My dad had another father who wasn't Grandpa Joe?* If so, he knew nothing about him. Could it be something that had been hidden away all these years, only to come forth now? He kicked up a stone. And why now, when other things were on his mind. He didn't need this disruption in his life. He was considering things that he had never considered before: being together with Debbie, believing life might finally—at age thirty-five—be coming together for him. Why did this have to come out now?

Chapter 6

Neil drove home in a cloud of confusion and questioning. Not even the flashing Christmas lights in the windows or the outlandish blow-up snowmen and Santas in the front lawns made him turn his head. Instead, he only stared at the road ahead. *What other man is Gram talking about?* He hoped the cold night air, blowing on him through the car vent, would wake him up to reality. Maybe this was just a temporary lapse in Gram's thinking and everything would be back to normal when he saw her next. He gripped the steering wheel as he drove onto Interstate 81, heading for Roanoke. Maybe he should call the floor tomorrow and let Gram know he was under the weather and wouldn't be in. That would give them both time to clear their heads and set things straight. He needed it. Right now his felt like a fog machine had been turned on inside. He couldn't even see.

Maybe I should talk to Debbie or the head nurse and find out if they've switched her medication. Once, they had given Gram a new sleeping pill so she could rest. That night, she became completely delirious, climbing out of bed and trying to walk around the room. She nearly fell. Maybe they had given her a new pill, and now the side effects were showing up as a delusion of some man contrived in her mind, some sweetheart, someone she even insisted was his true grandfather, of all things.

His cell phone played a tune, interrupting his thoughts. He struggled for it, buried under gloves and some papers from work. Looking at the number, he saw it was White Pines. *This is it.* They were going to tell him that his grandmother had indeed taken a turn for the worse, that her mind and emotions were completely off the wall, that everything he knew and loved about her was gone.

"Neil, it's Debbie."

He tensed. "Don't tell me there's something else wrong with Gram."

"Nothing's wrong. I'm just concerned about you."

"How did you get this number?"

"Off Elvina's—I mean, your grandmother's—chart."

"It's good you called, actually. I need you to find out for me if they have her on some kind of new medication. Something that may be giving her hallucinations."

"I can ask the charge nurse, but I don't think she's on anything new. Neil, I wish that you would tell me what's going on."

He gripped the tiny phone until his hand went numb. "It's just that she's talking about things that make no sense. Like her mind has snapped or something."

A pause came over the line. "Neil, I've been with her the last twenty minutes. In fact, I'm even staying until nine to make sure she's okay. She seems completely lucid to me when I'm with her. But I can tell she's worried about you. She thinks she upset you."

An understatement, to say the least. She might as well have thrown a bucket of ice water on me. "I just don't know what to think with the way she is carrying on about my grandfather."

"It's that time of year," Debbie's soothing voice came over the phone. "People tend to think more about loved ones. They get to reminiscing."

"You don't seem the least bit concerned."

"No. And neither should you. Just pray about it. I'm sure when you see her tomorrow everything will be better."

"I'm not coming in tomorrow. I think I'll lay low and wait for this to pass." He paused before adding, "Actually, when she found out about you and me, that's what brought this on—all this talk about some sweetheart. So I think we also need to cool it for a while."

A pause came over the line. "Exactly what is it I'm supposed to cool?"

He could hear her vexation on the rise but thought little of it. "Just tell Gram that we aren't interested in each other, okay? Tell her we just happened to bump into each other, that kind of thing. We hardly know each other anyway, so it doesn't matter."

He heard a gasp followed by, "Sure. Whatever you want."

Then silence.

Great, Neil thought. *She hung up. Well, what am I supposed to do? The reason Gram got off on this whole sweetheart idea was because she thought Debbie and I were going out. All I want to do is push Gram back into the reality of her husband and my grandfather named Joe, the only grandfather I've ever known.*

Neil felt no better when he arrived in Roanoke. Everything looked so cheerful with white lights decorating the office buildings. Some houses were decked out in so many lights that the air traffic in the skies above would have no problem zeroing in on Roanoke. But his mood right now didn't match the gleaming decorations. Nor was he in the mood to head for his lonely apartment, even if the guy in the condo next door would likely call him up, looking to play a computer game.

Instead, he drove to the suburbs of Roanoke. Soon he was passing places where he learned to ride a bike with training wheels, sold oranges and magazines to neighbors for school fund-raising projects, played street hockey with the neighborhood kids. At the end of the cul-de-sac stood the family home, a modest one-level ranch over a basement. And here, he stopped.

"Neil!" his mother exclaimed when she answered the door. "I wasn't expecting you."

"I should have called first, instead of just showing up on your doorstep."

She gave him a kiss. "I'm always glad to have you drop by. No one seems to do it anymore. Everyone's too busy."

The television blasted from the family room. Neil figured the chatter of the tube probably kept her company. Thankfully this wasn't her night to be with her friends at the quilting club, the Red Hat Club, or any number of her other clubs that kept her occupied. When he thought about it, he realized he should probably come by more often for a visit. "Have you heard from Sandy or Dick?" Neil asked.

A smile broke out across her face. "Yes. They're planning to be here for Christmas. Isn't that wonderful? I'll have all my kids together. I'll bake all your favorite cookies. You can start a fire in the fireplace. I haven't used the thing since the last time you all were here; was it Thanksgiving a few years back? We'll have a wonderful time."

"Great to hear, Mom. Anyway, there are a few things I need to talk about concerning Christmas."

She led the way to the living room, where they sat down. All at once, his eyes fell on twin portraits of his paternal grandmother and grandfather. Gram and Grandpa Joe. There they were, as plain as day. Maybe he should ask Mom if he could borrow the pictures to give Gram a reality check.

"You look like something's on your mind," she observed. "Have you had dinner? I can make you up something quick."

"I ate with Gram."

"Oh yes, of course. How is she doing? I need to go see her soon."

"Look, I went to see her tonight, and she was saying some pretty strange things."

She straightened in her chair, a look of distress distorting her features. "Oh dear. Don't tell me she's going downhill. I've heard people say that the holidays are hard on older people. I understand because the holidays are hard on me, too."

"Mom, this may sound strange, but tonight Gram was talking about another man. Some sweetheart of hers from long ago. She said no one probably has ever seen him, that there were no pictures. And she denied that this was Grandpa Joe. Do you have any idea what she's talking about?"

Her eyes widened. She shifted in her seat and looked off in the direction of the miniature Christmas tree sitting on a table. "Neil, you know older people. I'm sure it was some old boyfriend from long ago." She added in a high-pitched voice, "Though I don't know why on earth she would mention him. She had a wonderful marriage with your grandfather."

"Which grandfather?"

She turned pale. "What are you talking about? Grandpa Joe, of course." She pointed to the picture.

"That's not what Gram said. She called this man my other grandfather. She said Dad had a different father. And he wasn't Grandpa Joe."

Her jaw tightened. "Neil, honestly. Your grandmother is over eighty. She's already lost her sight and her mobility. Who knows what's happening to her mind? I'm sure she just came up with this because she's feeling lonely. I know what it's like to be lonely, even though your father would have wanted me to re-marry. But I couldn't do it, even though I came close. He was my one and only."

"So there isn't anything to what she says? This is purely old age and nothing else?"

She began to fidget before standing and walking into the kitchen. "Do you want something to drink?"

"Sure, thanks."

He ventured to the doorway, observing her pour soda out of a two-liter bottle. He was never good at picking up on emotional responses, but clearly his mother seemed troubled by something. Maybe his grandmother wasn't so crazy after all. Maybe there was something slowly being brought to light. When Neil took the glass of soda from his mother, she refused to make eye contact. He drank it down, wishing he could muster some time to scout around the house for clues. But what clue was he supposed to find? He didn't even know where to begin. And Mom wasn't being helpful at all.

He thought of broaching the other subject, his once glorious idea of inviting Gram to spend Christmas with them. That had to take a backseat right now. One stress point at a time. He had to get this ironed out first.

The rest of the evening was consumed by the mundane. What his brother and sister were doing. His nieces, his sister Sandy's kids, and what Mom planned to buy them for Christmas. Dick's new job. He wondered if his siblings were privy to this mystery surrounding an alternate grandfather, if they had heard of such a thing or knew of a skeleton hanging in the family closet.

He picked up his coat, telling his mother he had to go.

"Neil, please forget about what Elvina said," she said, staring in concern. "You're making yourself upset over nothing. Let it go."

"I wish I could, Mom. But I think there may be more here than meets the eye." He made for the door.

She nearly ran to him, putting her hand on his arm. Her lower lip quivered, and tears welled in her eyes. "Neil, I'm begging you. Let it go. Whatever it is, it's not worth rehashing."

He carried the memory of his mother's troubled face into the cold winter's night. Something was afoot. Something strange. A secret kept under wraps for years—until now. How could he possibly let this go? This had to do with his flesh and blood, after all. His lineage. His heritage. He had a right to know the truth.

As soon as he got into the car, Neil picked up his cell phone. He wasted no time contacting his sister to tell her what was happening.

She only laughed. "Neil, Gram's an old lady. Let her have some fun with her memories or whatever."

He grimaced. How typical of Sandy to make light of something this serious. She always said older people made her feel uncomfortable. She couldn't understand why he would want to spend evenings with their grandmother when he could be out on the town, living it up. For all he knew, she had never put one foot in White Pines. "I hardly would call this fun. It's serious. You and I may have some grandfather other than Grandpa Joe. Our father's father could be a stranger we never knew existed."

"Even if we did, he's long gone by now. What's the big deal? So what if Gram had a lover before Grandpa Joe and they shacked up together. That's the way life is these days. Guess back in her day, too."

He winced at these words. To Sandy, this all seemed as natural as baseball games and apple pie, even if she should be concerned about the consequences of immorality as the mother of two daughters. "If she did, do you realize that makes our father illegitimate?"

"Really, Neil. That's disgusting. You shouldn't be saying such things, especially since you never knew Dad. I was three when he died, and I remember him in his uniform and everything. He died fighting for his country. The least you can do is honor his memory. He doesn't deserve to be slapped with a label, especially over something that isn't his fault."

"I'm not doing anything of the sort. I am honoring his memory by finding out the truth for the sake of our family."

"Sometimes the truth is better left unsaid. I don't want you spoiling Christmas by bringing this up. We're all going to be together, and we're going to have a good time. So please, for all our sakes, let it go."

That was the proverbial saying of the night. *Let it go*. And just how was he supposed to do that? Life had been turned upside down in an instant. And now he was facing it head on.

⸼

Neil slept little that night, spending hours on his computer, scouring the Internet, and trying to find out more information about the family genealogy. He ran into brick walls on every turn. Without details and specifics, such as the phantom grandfather's name, he had little hope of discovering the truth.

During his time away from White Pines in his pursuit of the truth, he called the nursing unit to check on Gram. He had the nurses tell her he was under the weather, an understatement, to say the least. He never felt worse. All the respect he held for Gram, all the love he had for her, was now being put to the test. What if she did have a child out of wedlock, who happened to be his father? People do make mistakes. But Gram's swooning over his dad's father, when the man's memory should have been put away long ago, made Neil angry. If anything, such sin should be a closed book, not thrust wide open for all eyes to see.

When three days had passed, Neil realized he would have to venture back to White Pines and face the situation head-on. He didn't relish the encounter. The joy of spending that special time with Gram was lost on the heels of all this. It would be difficult concealing his feelings about it, too. Gram would sense something was up. She was far from senile but, rather, was as sharp as a tack. She'd know—which maybe was for the better. Maybe he could put this to rest, once and for all.

Arriving at White Pines, Neil decided to get his act together before he ventured up to Gram's room. He headed for the cafeteria and a cup of coffee, hoping he could come up with a way to salvage his relationship with Gram while finding out information at the same time. Hunkered down at the table, he was nursing his dilemma over a cup of hot brew laced with cream and sugar when he heard a friendly hello. He looked up to see Debbie standing over him, holding her own cup of coffee. He never thought the vision of a sweet and friendly face would stir him as much as her face did at that moment.

"Everything all right?"

He shrugged and took a swallow of coffee.

"I wanted to call, but you made it pretty clear that I should avoid you. So I did."

"That was a big mistake on my part."

She raised an eyebrow.

"I thought the two of us got my grandmother on some kind of strange track that made no sense. Now, after talking to my family, I think there may be something to her story."

"About your grandfather?"

"How he may not be the man I thought. My dad's father is not Grandpa Joe but a man I know nothing about."

Debbie sat down, her mouth a perfect O.

He nodded. "Mom acted pretty strange when I asked about it. My sister laughed it off, like the idea of Gram shacking up and having a child out of wedlock is no big deal. But it is to me. If I find out it's true, that we're all illegitimate, do you realize what kind of a stigma that is to live with?"

"Neil, if your grandmother did something in her past, it's like every other sin in our lives. God can erase it, as far as the east is from the west. He can make something good come out of it. And I think He already has. Look at you."

Neil wanted to accept the compliment she offered. Instead, he found himself sagging under the weight of it. To him, this sin left a stain that could not be erased. It would always be a part of him, this bloodline that was not Grandpa Joe's but some stranger's. "I have to find out from Gram who this man is, but I don't know how to go about asking. My family told me to forget about it. But I can't."

"Neil, if it will help, I'll gladly ask Elvina about it. I can talk pretty openly with the residents. I'll try to discover what's going on so you won't be caught in the middle."

"That might be better. The truth is, I don't feel comfortable asking Gram about her past. I feel like a busybody. But, maybe, if you were to do a little probing. . ."

"Sure. As it is, Elvina's been pretty depressed since you stopped visiting. She won't eat her dinner. So you need to get up there on the double and assume your post." Debbie shot him a grin before looking at her watch. "Dinner is being served as we speak."

"So she isn't eating, huh?" He drained his coffee. "I can't have that happening. I'd better make tracks. And, Debbie. . .thanks a lot. You're a godsend."

Her smile warmed his heart and set him at ease. Despite the situation he now found himself in, he thanked God for leading Debbie across his path.

Chapter 7

Debbie mulled over everything as she drove to work the following morning. How does one handle a delicate matter like this, one so fragile that the situation could break apart if she wasn't careful? She didn't have the slightest idea. This was a tough walk, like trying to walk on pavement made of glass. Not only must she consider Elvina's feelings but Neil's, too. She liked the man a great deal and spent a good amount of time thinking about what had happened and the stress he must be enduring. She wasn't immune to stress herself, by any means, and couldn't help feeling sorry for his situation. Now he was depending on her to be a clever gumshoe in his time of need. She sighed, a bit fearful, and hoped she wouldn't let Neil down. Maybe if she succeeded, they would also succeed in their relationship, which appeared about ready to blossom. Maybe if they could handle this crisis successfully, they truly would be inseparable.

Debbie drove down the main road of Fincastle and spied a small antique store with windows decked out in holiday trim. A thought came to her. Parking in front of the establishment, she wandered inside. To her delight, she stumbled upon a box of old records, some from an era that Elvina was certain to enjoy on her old-fashioned record player. She went ahead and purchased the entire box. Maybe it would pave the way to a closer kinship with Elvina and perhaps an open door to her past.

Arriving at work, Debbie groaned when she saw Trish there. It had been peaceful the last few days on the floor with Trish taking some time off. Even Harold was calmer and not shouting down the menacing Germans like he usually did. It was as if the residents were more relaxed without Trish around.

"What is that?" Trish inquired, pointing to the phonograph records in Debbie's possession. "You never give up, do you? You still want to be the belle of the floor."

"I care about the residents."

"Ha. You mean you want them singing your praises so it makes the rest of us look bad." She glanced over at Natasha who nodded.

"Trish, I don't know why you're so concerned about what I'm doing. It would be nice if we all just worried about our own lives."

Mrs. Whitaker ducked into the nurses' lounge, telling them it was time to get their assignments. When she saw Debbie's armful of record albums, she asked about them.

"They're for Elvina," Debbie said proudly.

"What a wonderful idea. Maybe it will lift her mood a little. Since her grandson stopped visiting regularly, she hasn't been acting quite right. I think this is a great idea."

Debbie could nearly see the fire and brimstone spurting out of Trish's nostrils. As she went about her day, she sensed Trish glaring at her and whispering to the other nurses. Then things began to happen. Debbie's linen cart mysteriously disappeared. All the call lights for her patients came on at once. When she answered them, only to find nothing amiss, they were turned on again. She began to fume. If things weren't difficult enough, now she had to deal with coworkers acting like grade school kids.

When Trish and company left for lunch, Debbie used the time to present her gift to Elvina. She found the older woman sitting in her chair positioned in front of the window, though Debbie knew she couldn't see the pretty view of the evergreen trees. Love welled up within her at the sight of the woman, especially with the knowledge that this was Neil's beloved grandmother. "Hi, Elvina."

She turned her head and smiled. "Debbie, how are you?"

"I'm doing well."

"Why don't I have you today? I have that one who always sounds like she has a cold."

"I wish I had control over the assignments, Elvina, but it's the head nurse who makes them out." Debbie took a seat beside her. "I have something for you." Gently she placed a record on Elvina's lap.

"What is this?" She sniffed it. "Smells old. A record?"

"Yes. I found several of them in an antique store, and I thought you might like to hear some new tunes. There's one that has a song about a woodpecker, of all things."

Elvina began to glow. "How wonderful. I would love to hear it. I could use some laughter right about now."

Debbie obliged by starting up the player and putting on an album. Soon the room filled with the crazy tune. In no time, they were singing away with the lyrics and mimicking the song's funny woodpecker noises.

They both broke out in laughter at the song's conclusion. "Could your husband sing?" Debbie asked.

"Joe? Dear me, no. He couldn't carry a tune in a bucket, poor thing. He once told me how he tried out for the choir. The choirmaster thought he should do other things. He was very good at building. He made me a wonderful cabinet to store all my fine china. I certainly hope my daughter is taking good care of it."

Debbie began to fidget, wondering how she should broach the subject of the other man Elvina had talked to Neil about. "I think the oldies are still goodies."

"Oh, they certainly are. Now my Samuel, he had a wonderful singing voice. He would make me swoon with his voice. I told him he should go to Hollywood and star in a musical."

Debbie caught her breath. It seemed almost too good to be true. Elvina was actually talking about *him*! "I don't think I've heard about Samuel. Was he one of your sons?"

Elvina laughed long and loud. "Oh, you are a funny thing. Certainly not, though I often thought of naming one of my sons after him. I don't think Joe would have approved. He knew how close Samuel and I once were. I think Joe was afraid the man would show up on my doorstep one day, ready to whisk me away or something."

Even as Elvina spoke, Debbie began to rationalize all this out. Elvina must have once had two boyfriends competing for her love. Maybe they had tried to woo her in different ways, one with flowers and song, and the other with trips to the store for an ice cream float. Debbie had to admit she wouldn't mind two men fighting over her. There was a certain romantic lure to it all. Two men, each one interested, each one thinking she was special, each one wanting to share their life and love forever. Then she chastised herself. What was wrong with one special man wooing her with hot chocolate and a great smile? Neil was more than enough, in her opinion, and she hoped the feeling was mutual.

"I don't know what happened to him." Her voice softened. "For all I know, Samuel died on the battlefield."

Battlefield? Now Debbie was all ears.

"Maybe he never came back. Or if he came back, he never tried to contact me. Maybe even now he's wondering what happened to his Albert. But I did what he wanted. I took care of his little boy while he was gone. I treated him as if he were my own."

"Hello! Excuse me! If this isn't much of a bother, your people are ringing their call lights, Debbie. And Harriet is nearly on the floor."

Debbie whirled to see Trish standing in the doorway, her arms folded. She stood up and followed Trish to the solarium to find one of the residents, the elderly Harriet Watson, leaning a bit sideways out of her chair. "Anyone could have helped her," Debbie grumbled, helping the woman sit upright with pillows at her sides to support her.

"We have enough to do without looking after your residents while you sing some dumb woodpecker song and hold Elvina's hand," Trish said in a huff.

Debbie burned with anger. Everything took flight, even the bit of joy over the way Elvina was beginning to open up about her past. Debbie soon began snapping at the residents. When one accidentally tipped over his tray of food, spilling it on the floor and leaving colorful patterns on her smock, she scolded him.

"Debbie, may I see you for a minute?"

Mrs. Whitaker spoke from the doorway of her office. Heat flooded Debbie's face at the thought of the head nurse witnessing her outbursts.

"Is everything all right?" asked Mrs. Whitaker. "I've never seen you lose your temper with the residents."

"I'm fine."

"Sometimes it can get very stressful around the holidays. The residents get more demanding."

"The personnel aren't much better."

Mrs. Whitaker raised her eyebrow.

"I'll be frank, Mrs. Whitaker. Trish and I do not get along at all."

"It's not like I haven't noticed. But we must do what we can in order to give the residents the best care possible. They are our priority."

"Trish doesn't think so. More than once, I've had to clean up after her. She doesn't brush their teeth. She never combs their hair. And she gets the praise of everyone on the floor just because she has the biggest mouth."

Mrs. Whitaker stood silent and still, studying her. Debbie knew she had blown it big-time. She'd let her irritation get the best of her. Though she wanted Mrs. Whitaker to know about Trish's work habits, she never expected it to come out this way. But maybe it was just as well. The truth had finally been let out of the bag instead of being hidden away for far too long.

"I will follow Trish and see what's happening. But I suggest, Debbie, that you concentrate on what you're doing. I can say that, after what I observed today, you are no different than Trish. Raising your voice with the residents is not proper care either."

"I know. I shouldn't have done it. I wasn't mad at them but at other things. And I took it out on them, which I shouldn't have."

"Debbie, I know we all experience frustrations here. I have my moments, too. But we have to be doubly careful to keep ourselves under control at all times." She nodded before returning to the computer screen to complete the day's charting.

Debbie shuffled out of the office, only to see Trish standing at the nurses' station, a funny grin painted on her face. If only she had an ally on this floor, someone who would vouch for her and what she had witnessed concerning Trish. But there was no one. No one cared. She was on her own. Talk about being on the battlefield of the enemy, alone, just like Harold warned. She was living it.

The work shift had ended by the time Debbie ventured back to see Elvina. She made certain that Trish and her cohorts had left before she returned to the room. Elvina was listening to one of the records she had brought. "I'm back, Elvina."

"I was thinking of you and wondered where you went."

"I had to take care of some residents." She shrugged. "It's just like one of the other residents said—I'm here on a battlefield without a friend in the world."

"Now, now." Elvina reached out her hand, which Debbie took. The older lady squeezed it. "You're my friend."

"Thanks, Elvina."

"In fact, I do believe you're my best friend. I don't have friends here. I don't talk to anyone except the girl at the beauty parlor. And, of course, Nathaniel."

"Why don't you go play bingo or do some crafts?"

"I like the minister at the Sunday services. But I think people see me and decide they can't talk to me because I'm blind and can't see them. Or maybe I make them uncomfortable, and they think they will say the wrong words."

"It must be hard."

"I was thankful to see what I could before the glaucoma took away my sight. I saw my dear husband and my children."

"And you saw Samuel, too."

"Samuel! I told you about Samuel? My goodness, I haven't told anyone about Samuel. I saw him before he left to go to war. World War II, you know. And he told me. . ." She paused.

All at once, Debbie saw her gray blue eyes fill with tears. Elvina's hand fell away to rest in her lap, which was covered by a knitted lap robe.

"He asked me to take care of his little boy. He had a boy, you know. The little boy's mother died in childbirth. That's what Samuel told me. And he asked me to look after his Albert while he was gone to war. And I did, Debbie, even when Samuel didn't come home. Little Albert became part of our family when I married Joe. He grew up and married Terrie. And they had three children: Richard, Sandra, and Nathaniel J. But Albert died so young, the poor thing. He died in Vietnam."

Debbie stared in disbelief. Despite the sadness of it all, the truth rang loud and clear. Neil indeed had another grandfather, a man he never knew, a man who went off to war and left his father in Elvina's care. "And you have no idea what happened to Samuel?"

She shook her head. "I heard from him once. I used to have the letter. I don't know whatever happened to it. I should have put it in a frame. It's gone now, as are most of my things. But I can remember it clearly, as if he had written it yesterday. He told me how rainy and cold it was in England. He said they would soon go and free France. He said there wasn't anything better than fighting to free others. He told me to give Albert a hug and tell him his father loved him."

Tears trickled down her plump cheeks. Debbie leaned over and plucked two tissues out of the box, one for Elvina and one for herself.

"I read the letter to Albert. He was only three. He took it in his hands and held it to his heart. What a sweet sight. It was the closest he ever came to his father since he left for war, the handwriting on that paper. I would show the letter to him every so often, telling him his father wrote it after he went off to war. When he was about ten, he asked about the war. I told him as best I could. But I didn't want to share how I used to feel about Samuel, since I was married to Joe, you know. Those things shouldn't come out. I loved my Joe." She blew her nose. "And yes, I loved Samuel, too. But it was different. A different kind of love. In a different time and place. And that time is gone. But I wish it would come back. I wish I could know where he is. I wish I could see him one last time, show him his grandchildren. He would be so proud. But it's a Christmas gift well beyond anyone's ability to give."

Debbie left White Pines, her thoughts fairly spinning over this emotional revelation. It seemed too unbelievable to be real, yet it was. And she was in on it all, along with Neil. *Neil.* She would have to tell Neil the truth. What would he think? How would he react? Would the news push them away or bring them closer? She didn't know as she hugged her arms around her to ward off the chilly December night. She would have to tell him and let God handle the rest.

Chapter 8

Neil felt like Watson meeting Sherlock, only Debbie didn't appear for this meeting dressed in a full-length trench coat. Instead, she sat opposite him in the coffee shop in a fuzzy blue sweater. A shaggy scarf dangled around her neck, and she wore gold hoop earrings. She looked radiant. When she called earlier to invite him for coffee, he nearly fell over. A woman hadn't invited him to do anything in ages. He took the coffee-and-bagel invite as the next best thing to dinner at a five-star restaurant. Of course this was hardly some special date. From the seriousness of her expression as she sipped her cappuccino, this was strictly business. But he hoped more might come out of the conversation in the end.

"You were right, Neil," she began.

I was right? That was news to him. So far, it seemed he hadn't been right about anything. After the fiasco at his mother's, the phone call to his sister, and a fruitless Internet search to try and hunt down clues to his past, he only saw doors slamming in every direction.

"You have a different grandfather on your dad's side."

The coffee caught in his throat. He coughed, quickly covering his mouth with a napkin before he made a fool out of himself by splattering coffee down the front of his sweater.

"Are you all right? I can hit you on the back or something, but if you're coughing, that usually means you're okay."

"I'm okay," he said in a raspy voice. "I should have swallowed first before you broke the news. How did you find out?"

"Elvina told me. Took awhile, but she finally did. His name was Samuel."

"Samuel what?"

Debbie's full red lips turned pouty. For some reason, she looked absolutely kissable at that moment, and he couldn't figure out why. She had just dropped a bombshell of some unknown grandfather. Kissing should be the furthest activity from his mind. Maybe he should simply ditch all this soap opera stuff—the strange grandfather, his family's weird reactions, Gram's longing to see some old flame—and enjoy this budding relationship. That would be nice. Maybe soon. First he had to get this resolved.

"She never mentioned his last name. All I know is, he went off to war."

"Which war? We've had plenty."

"The Civil War."

A twinkle in her eye now accompanied her upturned lips. If not for the table separating them at this moment and the seriousness of this discussion, he might be forced to act on his impulses and skip to the kissing part. "Very funny. We've had several wars in the twentieth century. World War I and II. Korean War, Vietnam. Desert Storm. Afghanistan. Iraq. Of course I'm pretty sure it wasn't any of the later ones."

"World War II. He left his boy behind, Elvina said, asking that she take care of him while he was away. The little boy's mother had died giving birth, it seems. How sad. And the boy's name was Albert."

Again his throat tickled, but at least he wasn't in the midst of swallowing coffee. He coughed. "That was my dad's name. Albert Jenson."

"He must've had a different last name, though, before he was adopted into the Jenson family. Maybe you can ask your mom what it was."

He shuddered at the thought of another confrontation with his mother. "I don't think I can. She wasn't too keen about me prying into this matter in the first place. All she and Sandy told me to do was let it go. But I think I have the right to know who my true grandparents are. There's nothing wrong about wanting to know one's heritage."

"Or knowing, for instance, if you're predisposed to hereditary traits," Debbie added. "I mean, when you fill out physicals, you have to give a family history of illnesses, such as heart disease, cancer, or some other diseases in the family."

He began turning his cup. A bit of coffee spotted the table, probably from the first coughing episode, and now it made a perfect brown ring. "Did Gram say what happened to Samuel?"

"No, and that's where the real mystery comes in. She said she never received word about his circumstances. Once he shipped out overseas, she got one letter from him, and that was all. I think it's strange that a man who left behind a son he obviously loved would suddenly disappear. My thinking is, he probably went missing in action."

"Maybe. Then why would Gram want to see him again?"

"I suppose she wants to know what happened—to close that chapter in her life. She has little else to think about in her wheelchair all day, you know. You get to thinking about the past. And obviously she has been thinking about Samuel."

Neil sighed. He wished there were more to go on. Like a last name for the man. What unit he was with. He might have been able to do some further research on the Internet. It might take another trip home, maybe when his mother was preoccupied with her quilting bee. He had a key to the house. He could

287

go over there and do some hunting to avoid further family turmoil over this. Though he wished his mother would just come out and tell him what she knew and save him the trouble of digging for answers. Obviously the idea of some other man in the family line raised questions some would rather leave unasked. But it was important to him. His bloodline was not of the true Jenson. He was not a true relation to Gram—or to any of those relatives on his dad's side he saw at holidays or at reunions. He had no true grandmother, paternal aunts, uncles, or even cousins, as far as he knew.

He sucked in his breath. Is this how his father once felt? Did he, too, wonder who his real parents were? If he had any other siblings? Or did he just accept Gram, Grandpa Joe, and those who loved him, casting away the mystery concerning the identity of his real parents. If only Neil could ask him. If only he knew his own dad, too. Now he had two lost loved ones, his grandfather and his dad, who didn't know that he, Neil, lived and breathed, that he carried on their characteristics, that he was alive and doing pretty good for himself, all things considered.

"Neil?" Debbie asked, staring at him with a questioningly look in her deep blue eyes. Against the fuzzy blue sweater, those eyes looked even more intense. "Are you okay?"

"Oh sure."

"I'm not so sure. You look like one of the Lost Boys in Never-Never Land. You haven't said anything."

"Maybe I am a lost boy. I don't know who I am, at least half of me, that is. I don't know my grandparents on my dad's side. I don't know my relatives. Not even my father. I feel like a half-baked orphan. I never would have believed it until just a few days ago. Then some deep, dark secret pops out when you least expect it. Now I have to deal with it. To be honest, I don't know if I want to."

"It has to be hard. But you realize there are people who love you even if you don't have a direct bloodline to them. Like Elvina. Despite everything, you're her grandson, through and through. And that's what counts—the love you've had for each other all your lives. You need to look at it that way, Neil."

He chuckled. "We're sure good for each other, Debbie, telling each other how to have a positive outlook. I would almost venture to say we were made for each other."

He saw her inhale swiftly. A red tide flooded her cheeks. She stared down at her cappuccino. Nothing came out for several moments. The seconds of solitude were agonizing. "What I meant is, we seem to have the right words to say to each other when the going gets rough," he added hastily.

"I guess we do."

The conversation became stilted after that. A short time later, they were saying good-bye and going their separate ways. Neil sighed in disappointment. He shouldn't have brought the conversation to such a personal level. He didn't need to thrust all his problems on her, even if he did feel an unmistakable attraction for her. Though he did agree with his assessment that they were made for each other. They helped each other when life dealt out one trial after another. They stood together, supporting one another. And God showed He cared, through an attractive woman named Debbie.

Neil spent the rest of the day idle, paying little attention to the insurance claims mounting on his desk at work. Instead, he gazed at the table and a miniature twinkling Christmas tree that one of the secretaries had placed there. He considered his past, present, and future, even though he had made light of it when Debbie first asked him. The past had now reared its head; even when he wanted to leave it alone, God had seen fit to resurrect it. Maybe he needed to deal with it—not only the other grandfather issue, but the idea of not having a dad and losing out on that part of his life. Until now, he hadn't realized that, perhaps, there were things he needed to resolve in his heart, a deep aching, a hole that a dad never did fill. Sure, Mom had brought his uncles around for the influence of men in his life. But as he'd recently learned, they weren't even his true relatives on his dad's side. They weren't truly his family. And it made him feel strange.

Later that evening, Neil headed to his mom's house. It sat dark and silent but for the white lights left burning on a few outside bushes. Using the key to open the kitchen door, he ventured inside. Immediately he inhaled the delicious aroma of dinner earlier that night. *Meat loaf.* Raiding the refrigerator to make a meat loaf sandwich, he then headed to the basement and Mom's place for storing everything under the sun. He was looking for a clue, something that would link him to this strange man who went off to fight at Normandy. Some name that could help him with an Internet search. Something tangible he could hold on to and not let go.

An hour later, he was still rummaging through boxes of old snapshots. There were a few of his father as a youth. He recognized Gram in many of them. Scribbled on the back, in his grandmother's stately handwriting, were the words: Al, 1950, ten years old. Al, 1952. Then he found one labeled Al, 1948. He was getting closer. His heart began to thump in anticipation.

Suddenly a door banged upstairs. *Oh no!* Was it time for his mother to be home already?

"Who's here?" her voice called out. "Sandy?"

Neil froze. He stuffed the pictures back in the box as footsteps sounded on the stairs. "Just me, Mom."

"Neil?" His mother appeared as he sat guiltily on the floor, surrounded by photo boxes. "What on earth are you doing?"

"Gram confessed to a friend of mine, Mom. Grandpa Joe is not my true grandfather. His name was Samuel."

Her hand flew to her forehead. "I have a terrible headache, Neil. That's why I came home early. I can't take this right now."

"I'm sorry you don't feel good, Mom. But please, I just need a little information. Like Dad's real name before the Jenson family adopted him. That's all I need. Then I'll be out of your hair. Promise."

"Why do you insist on doing this, Neil?"

He stared, surprised she would ask him. "So I can find out about my true grandfather. Mom, this is important. It's like any adopted child who wants to know about their real parents. What if this man had some kind of family gene we don't know about? Like genes for cancer, heart disease, or a blood condition. Sandy and Dick should know, too. I can research the Internet for the family tree."

"Well, what harm is there? All right. His last name was Truett. T-R-U-E-T-T." She collapsed in a chair. "Your father told me about the man from what Elvina relayed to him as a youngster—that his father's name was Samuel Truett and that he went off to war. He fought in the Battle of Normandy. He wrote Al and Elvina once and then was never heard from again."

"Does anyone know what happened to him?"

"No one knows. Elvina always hung on to the hope that he was alive, maybe living somewhere in France. If that were the case, then why didn't he check on Al? We always believed he died in the war. But no one knows for certain. There was no record. I think he was even listed as missing in action, but I'm not sure."

"I know there was a lot of confusion at the Battle of Normandy, with GIs being in the wrong place and with the wrong units. He must've gotten lost in it all."

"Really, Neil, it was so long ago. I don't know why Elvina is bringing this up and dragging you into the middle of it. It just isn't right." She stood up and headed for the stairs. "I need some hot tea. But after tonight, I don't want to hear anything more about it."

Neil looked at the box of pictures at his feet. He felt bad, putting this kind of stress on his mom. Maybe he should let things go and let the past stay the past. But he couldn't shake the vision of Gram wanting to know what happened. And this was Dad's father. He had a desire to know. A right, even. And he hoped Mom would understand.

⸎

Neil wasn't certain what to say or do when he came to see Gram a few evenings later. He had called the facility to leave a message that he would not be in for several days. He spent that time hunkered down at his computer, doing every kind of a viable search for Samuel Truett. There were Web sites devoted to veterans of the Normandy invasions. He managed to find Samuel's unit and where they fought, but little else. There was not even conclusive evidence as to where he might have ended up, whether dead on the beach or somewhere in France. It was a bit of consolation, at least, to see the name of his actual grandfather there on the computer screen. He wished he knew what the man looked like. Looking in the mirror earlier that day as he readied himself for work, he wondered if he possessed any of the characteristics on his dad's side. Maybe the nose? The color of eyes? That persistent small tuft of hair that drooped down over his forehead?

He was glad to share all this with Debbie over the phone that evening. He told her what he'd learned, about Samuel's full name and his place in history on D-day. As usual, she was her own confident self, claiming that God was about ready to blow wide open the doors on his past. He hoped so.

As he arrived at White Pines that evening, he prayed that Gram would be in the mood to talk about things. It all depended on her frame of mind.

In the parking lot, he saw a tall nurse with blond hair unlocking the door to her car. She looked up then. A smile easily formed with teeth that gleamed like pearls. "Hi, Neil."

I'm not in the mood for this. And I have a nurse I like very much, thank you. Try the next guy.

"I'm Trish, remember? You hired me to take care of your grandma over Christmas."

The comment stopped him in his tracks. With everything else going on, he had forgotten his idea to bring Gram home, and the plan for this Trish to care for her.

"Hey, listen. I have a few minutes. Wanna grab some coffee, and we can talk about her care?"

His fingers began to curl inside the pockets of his coat. "Actually I haven't yet arranged for it all. I'll have to let you know when things are settled." He wanted to ask if there was any way she might switch with Debbie and allow her to come, but before he could form his thoughts into words, Trish stepped forward.

"Hey, I was talking to Natasha, and she was telling me about this great movie that just came out. Some kind of funny Christmas comedy. A bunch of us nurses on the floor were thinking of going. Wanna come along with us?"

The invitation momentarily stunned him. "Is this some kind of floor event?"

"Yeah, we nurses like to get together sometimes and go to the movies. Kind of a tradition every year to see the season's latest Christmas flick. But since there aren't many guys working here, except in the cafeteria or in maintenance, we'd love to have you come along to give us some atmosphere. I mean, you're a regular on the floor. You practically live there, kind of." She giggled.

He chuckled in response. If this was a floor event, no doubt Debbie was also going. That idea appealed to him, considering how his life had been topsy-turvy recently. A few laughs with Debbie and her nursing buddies might be just the thing he needed. "Okay."

Trish's face lit up as if she had been plugged like a strand of Christmas lights into a socket. "Great!" Trish exclaimed. "We're going tomorrow night at seven. The Regal Theater in Roanoke. You can visit your grandma and then join us. It's going to be great."

He shuffled off, glad for some kind of outing with Debbie besides the coffee shop, even if it were with the other nurses on the floor. They had done little else but immerse themselves in this grandfather mystery. Maybe in the theater, he could sneak her away from the crowd to a seat on the opposite side. There they could indulge in a bucket of popcorn and conversation. For once, he had something to look forward to besides thinking about his family situation. And that made things easier to handle, at least for now.

Chapter 9

Hey, Debbie, Neil here. Hope you're doing well. Looking forward to seeing you tonight. Should be a lot of fun. I'm planning to pick you up around six. See you then."

Huh? What is he talking about? Debbie heard the cryptic message loud and clear on the answering machine but couldn't quite believe it. She racked her brain, trying to remember if she had agreed to do something with Neil tonight. Had they made plans during the coffee outing a few days ago and she'd forgotten about it? Looking at the calendar, there was nothing written in. But they must've set up something for him to say what he did on the answering machine. As it was, ever since the encounter at the coffee shop, she found herself in a daze. Despite the conversation about Neil's grandfather, it wasn't like other past encounters. Something had changed in Neil. . .an interest that had not been there before, as if their casual friendship had taken a personal turn. Of course Debbie would like nothing better, but it still made her feel jittery, like a girl on her first date. Was she ready for this new turn onto some unknown path with a man she had only recently begun to understand?

She decided to go along with whatever the preplanned engagement was, in the hopes that something might clue her in. Maybe this was Neil's way of leading her by the hand down that new path in their relationship. Staring at her wardrobe, she wondered what to wear for a mystery date, finally settling on a jean skirt and a Christmas sweater. That should work for almost anything.

When the doorbell rang, Debbie opened her door to find a cheerful and expectant Neil. *This must be a great time we set up,* she thought with a sigh. *If only I knew what.*

"Do you have any idea what movie you were going to see?" he asked as they stepped out into the blustery evening air. "I know where the theater is in Roanoke, but I haven't been by there in a while to see what's playing."

"Uh. . ." *Did I agree to see a movie?* "I'm not sure, Neil."

"So Trish didn't tell you, huh? I guess it doesn't matter."

Trish? What does she have to do with this? "No, she didn't. We don't talk much."

"Hmm. I know it's some kind of comedy. I think it has something to do with Christmas."

Debbie was growing more uncomfortable by the minute and more depressed at the thought of Neil and Trish conversing. Obviously Trish had invited him to see a movie. Then why was he dragging her along? To be a chaperone? To dump her somewhere when the timing was right and run off to be with Trish? *Really, Debbie, get a life. This guy is no Brad. He's a gentleman.* Besides, they had been getting along famously. He had shown an obvious interest at the coffee shop. Then why was Trish suddenly mixed up in all of this?

"You're awfully quiet," he observed.

How do I tell him nicely that I have no idea *what is going on?* "Neil, I have no idea what is going on." The statement popped out of her mouth like an exploding cork.

"What do you mean?"

"I mean, tonight. You leave me a message on the answering machine, but I don't recall us setting up any kind of special outing to a theater."

"You know—the annual movie gig you gals go to every Christmas. Trish told me all about it—how you nurses get together to see the latest Christmas movie playing. She decided since I was a regular on the floor, I could tag along."

I don't believe it. That woman is too much. "Neil, I'm sorry to say this, but I know nothing about our floor's staff attending a movie tonight. That's not to say they aren't going. Trish gets the other nurses together to do things, even has them over to her place. They go out to the mall in Roanoke and other places—a regular groupie thing. But I've never been invited to those events. I don't fit into their mold, I guess, which is probably for the best."

He looked as if he didn't believe her. "I assumed you were a part of this, being a floor thing. That's the main reason I said yes, thinking you'd be there."

At least that part proved gratifying and even endearing. "Look, I'll be honest with you. Trish and I don't get along at all. She really dislikes me, and I must say, the feeling is mutual, despite the fact I've tried not to make enemies."

He turned off at the nearest exit and came to a stop in the parking lot of a gas station. "I had no idea. Wow, I'm sorry. I shouldn't have assumed all this. It was pretty dumb."

"It's okay. You can just take me home and go on to see the movie, whatever it is."

"So you still don't want to go? We can get our own seats. It'll be fun. We deserve it."

"I'm sorry, but sitting in the same theater with Trish would be the worst kind of agony. I know that sounds mean. I wish I could say that things were okay between us, but they aren't." Then it all came tumbling out—how Trish was considered the belle of White Pines, even though her work ethics left much to be desired. The way she treated the residents. How everyone loved Trish but left others like Debbie hanging out to dry. How Debbie wished she had the right words to say. Why people didn't notice her efforts but applauded Trish instead. "I just wish I could tell the head nurse, Mrs. Whitaker, about it all."

Neil sat there, still and silent, as if Debbie had delivered a major blow to his life. "I wish I had known about this earlier," he said glumly. "Now what am I supposed to do?"

"Sorry. I didn't mean to burst a bubble or something."

"I hired this Trish gal to take care of Gram for the holidays."

"You what?" Debbie nearly jumped in her seat. "Neil, you can't have her do that."

"No, I can't, not after what you've been telling me about the way she treats the residents. No wonder Gram always seems depressed whenever Trish takes care of her. I thought it was because of the holiday season or the memories of this other grandfather. How could I have been so stupid?"

Debbie saw the anger fill him. His fingers tightened around the steering wheel.

"I don't like being taken for a ride."

"Neil, you didn't know. You were trying to give your grandmother a nice Christmas. There's still time to find someone else."

He didn't seem to hear her. She sucked in her breath, watching the rigid lines forming on his face. "Hey, it's no big deal."

"I don't like someone pulling the wool over my eyes, and that's all I've been enduring these last few weeks. A wool coat thrown over my head. Maybe a whole coatrack. Between this whole grandfather scenario and some whacked-out dame pulling a few fast ones, I don't know what's going on. But I plan to set the record straight, once and for all."

Tires spit gravel as the car took off, making a fast U-turn and heading back toward Fincastle. Debbie had no idea what to say so she kept quiet until Neil drove into the lot of her apartment building. Debbie offered to brew him a cup of the peach tea he liked, hoping it might calm him down enough to think rationally. But the lines of irritation were clearly written on his face like lines drawn in the sand.

Moments later, she handed him the freshly brewed tea in the bear nursing mug. "Neil, all I ask is that you don't do something you and I will both regret. Especially me. I still work at that place, you know. You stir up the hornet's nest, and guess who will get stung."

"I understand, Debbie, but some things in life need to be said. And it's high time someone told it like it is and didn't beat around the bush. The fact is, this woman needs to respect and treat human beings with dignity and not like playthings for her amusement. And you said so yourself that you wanted people to know about it."

Debbie flushed. She could just imagine the reaction if he strode in there with his emotional guns fully loaded. *But he doesn't understand Trish, nor does he have any inkling where this all might lead. And it won't be Trish's head that rolls.* There were all sorts of scriptures that told how to treat one's enemy—such as turning the other cheek when someone strikes you, or heaping coals of fire on another's head by not reciprocating evil for evil but rather answering evil with good. She mentioned them. "So just tell her that the plans have changed, that you don't want her working for you. Please don't go to Mrs. Whitaker about it. Let it go at that."

He slapped his hand across his forehead. "Good grief, there it is again—'Let it go.' The saying of the century." He laughed long and loud on a sarcastic note. "That's all I've been hearing. I should get a T-shirt made up with those words on the front: LET IT GO. Let your grandfather go, Neil. Let everything go and allow the chips to fall where they may. Let people lie to you. Let the past sneak up on you. Forget that you have another grandfather or that some women will do anything to sucker you in." He threw the tea down his throat. "Guess what? I won't let it go. Not when there's a manipulative woman out there trying to take advantage of the elderly and others. These things need to be straightened out. If we let people do whatever they want, how is justice served?"

"If you must be the judge, at least be tactful. Don't storm in there and nail her to the wall. It will only backfire. There are ways to be wise as a serpent but gentle as a dove."

But the way Neil was looking at the moment, being tactful and acting like some dove were the furthest thoughts from his mind. And no amount of warm peach tea was going to stem the tide either. She sighed. There was nothing she could do. She was witnessing Neil's raw side. Better it came out now, she supposed. She wanted to find out more about him, didn't she? And now she was, even though she wondered where it might lead in the end.

శ

Something definitely had changed when Debbie walked onto the floor a few days later. It began with her floating to another unit instead of staying on her normal floor. She disliked being away from the residents she had come to cherish. And her reassignment wasn't just for one day. Every day, she showed up to work on her own unit, and every day, Mrs. Whitaker sent her elsewhere. In the corner of the nursing lounge, she could see Trish sitting there with a wry smile, chattering with her friends. Debbie couldn't help but wonder what was going on. She didn't want to think Neil had anything to do with this. What had he said about the whole scenario that led to this change? Had he arranged to have her moved from the floor to keep her and Trish apart?

Debbie tried to involve herself in her work, but she felt like she was walking on a sheet of ice, slipping and sliding, ready for another bruising. All the joy she had found in her work had vanished. At the noon hour, she went back to the floor and asked to see Mrs. Whitaker. The head nurse seemed preoccupied when she arrived, shuffling papers, looking at her watch, appearing as if she would rather be anywhere else than in a meeting with her. Or was it simply Debbie's imagination?

"I don't understand why I've been assigned to float, Mrs. Whitaker," Debbie started, taking a seat in the office. "I haven't been on this unit all week."

She sighed. "Debbie, it's my duty to send extra nurses on staff to where the need is the greatest."

"But no one else is floating. Just me."

Her face became rigid. "I have it in confidence that several people have witnessed some rather shocking things from you recently with regard to the residents and staff here on this floor. And I've even had some complaints from the residents."

She sat there, stunned. "What? But I haven't done anything."

"There have been complaints of you being short with the residents. I've seen it myself. You've let your assigned residents fall out of their wheelchairs. Trish even said she had to help because you weren't there. We can't have residents falling on the floor, breaking bones."

Debbie fumed, remembering but a single such incident, when she had been singing a song with Elvina and Trish informed her of a resident sliding out of her chair. But Trish had placed far more residents in harm's way in one week's time than Debbie had in her eight years of working here. "Trish isn't telling the truth. . . ."

"It isn't just Trish, but just about everyone on the unit who is complaining. I'm sorry, Debbie, but I think it's best if you float for now until I have you transferred to another floor. I know how you told me that you and Trish don't get along. So I think it's for the best if the two of you work on different units."

Trish and her gang are at it again, and this time at full throttle. Anger welled within her. Debbie felt her cheeks heat to a high intensity. "Trish should be the one transferred instead of me. I've done nothing wrong."

"Debbie, I've made up my mind. Trish has been here longer than you anyway. So we will look to having you transferred as soon as there's an opening. If you will excuse me, I have some paperwork to do."

Debbie felt as though she were living out her worst nightmare. The fog of life grew even thicker as she stumbled out of the office. How could this be happening? She knew why it happened. Neil must have made everyone irate, and now Trish had gathered the troops to have her permanently removed from the floor. Debbie had enemies worse than the Germans who plagued Harold's waking state, and her enemies worked right here with her. They had succeeded in taking her away from the residents she loved with all her heart.

Debbie went into the bathroom, locked the door, and sat down on the floor. Great heaves rose up in her throat. The injustice, the pain, was overwhelming. Is this what it felt like to be condemned without cause? To be punished for doing nothing but caring for others? *Is this what it's like, Jesus? I can't stand it. It hurts. I hurt.* She began to choke, almost as if she needed to vomit up the injustice. Slowly standing up, she gazed at her reflection in the mirror. Her eyes were red. Her brown hair hung in disarray. She looked as defeated as she felt.

Debbie could hardly wait for the shift to be over. Before she left, she decided to go and see Harold. She felt a kinship with him now that a real-life enemy had come to do battle. Harold would understand, somehow. When she arrived, he didn't look much better than she felt. He sat in his chair, leaning over to one side, his chin sunk into his hand, his bloodshot eyes staring blankly. Likely he was seeing images of the war again. Little did he know there was a fierce war going on right now. A spiritual war. A war of good and evil.

"Hi, Harold."

His head lifted. "It's you! Where have you been? I've been looking for you everywhere."

"I've been battling an enemy," she said glumly.

He gripped the armrests of his wheelchair as if the words brought him to life. "You've seen the enemy? Report your findings to the major. We need an accurate report of their movements."

For some reason, his words imparted comfort. He didn't know what had happened to her, but his propensity for war and battle seemed appropriate for the occasion. "There are enemies right here on this floor, you know."

"I know that. I've seen them. They pretend to wear white, but they are wolves in sheep's clothing."

She stared in wonder and amazement at the scriptural quote that proved quite apropos to her situation. For a man supposedly not in tune with reality, Harold knew his Bible. And he knew what was happening all around him. "You are so right, Harold."

"I know them. Spies, they are. They work for the enemy. You have to be careful of them because they are here among our troops. Walk carefully. Keep alert."

"Yes, they're sneaking around, telling lies. And the lies seem to be working. They are having too much influence on the higher-ups." *Way too much,* she thought glumly.

He took her hand and gripped it. "It may seem that way, but, my dear girl, you should never give up. Don't think for a minute that they've won."

"That's all easier said than done. If only I knew what to do."

"Just keep quiet for now. Lay low. Wait. And when the moment comes, you can expose them for who they are."

She had to smile until the reality of her situation sobered her. "I won't have the time to expose their deeds. I'm being transferred."

"You're being transferred?"

"The boss thought it was for the best. I won't be a part of this unit anymore."

Harold shook his head. "You can't do that. Not now. It's the enemy playing tricks. You have to watch them. They are crafty. But don't you go. Tell the major you need to be here. Tell him you need to finish your mission. If you go, others are gonna die. You have to accomplish your mission."

She stared in wonder at the frail man sitting there in his wheelchair. Harold spoke more like a messenger from God than Debbie could have imagined. If only she could believe it and not think of him as lost in another time and place. "Thanks, Harold."

He smiled and sat back as if his own mission were accomplished. But to Debbie, it looked like her mission had folded under the attack of the enemy. The mere thought depressed her greatly.

Heading for the car that afternoon, she decided this spelled the end. She would give her resignation at the end of the pay cycle and be done with all this misery.

Chapter 10

Once inside the safety of her apartment, Debbie chose not to turn on the lights. Instead, she put on the night-light above the stove and sat in the tiny living room in the dark. The dismal surroundings mirrored her soul at the moment, shadowed by a dark thundercloud. Angry tears smarted her eyes. She hoped she could disappear from this area and never be heard from again. Dad knew northern Virginia like the back of his hand. She would go back to her roots and look for a job there. Start fresh. Her parents would be happy to have her home. They would provide all the help she needed in finding a job and another place to live. She could search out old friends from high school, people she'd abandoned to come here. She missed good friends. It would be a safe refuge and a great escape. She would leave the whole mess behind her—Trish and her gang, Mrs. Whitaker's accusations, everything, and start over. Just so long as none of it followed after her.

Debbie went into the kitchen, turned on a light, and began taking down dishes to start the packing process. The nursing mugs promptly went into the garbage. Time to move on with her life. Leave here and never look back. Pretend White Pines, Elvina, Harold, and, yes, Neil never happened. She paused.

Neil.

She picked out the mug from the garbage she had used to serve him tea. Staring at it, her eyes welled with tears before she put the mug back in the trash can. She had no choice. This was the best way.

At that moment, the doorbell rang. Debbie contemplated ignoring it. Instead, she crept over to the door and peeked through the security hole.

Oh no! It's him.

"Debbie? You in there?"

Yes, and I'm perfectly miserable. You wanted to take revenge, and I end up the casualty, just like I thought I would. Wounded and about ready to run.

"Debbie, I saw your car parked in front of your place, so I know you're in there."

She chewed on her lip. "What do you want?"

"I heard what happened. Gram told me. She heard you were being transferred. Let me in, okay?"

"Just leave me alone."

"Debbie, please. I'm here to say I'm sorry."

She leaned closer to the door, intrigued by the concern radiating in his voice.

"This is my fault entirely. Please let me in."

In an instant, she opened the door. He stood dressed in his thick wool coat, staring at her, his eyes hollow. "You lose electricity or something?"

Debbie turned on a light in the living room. "I like it dark. Fits my mood."

Slowly he shed his coat and sat down on the sofa. "I know what's been happening to you, and I blame myself entirely. Gram told me you haven't been on the unit all week. She said you were working on other floors. A nurse told her."

"Big deal."

"I know you cautioned me to use tact when confronting Trish. I'll admit I didn't, and I have a feeling this is revenge."

"I don't know what was said, but somehow those people are painting me out to be the villain—telling the head nurse the things that Trish has done wrong and blaming them on me. None of it is true either. I don't know what to do." She slumped down, resting her chin in her hand.

"Then I'll make sure that woman is locked up with the key thrown away." Neil stood up and began to pace.

"Neil, it's that kind of attitude that got me into this mess in the first place."

He whirled around.

"I asked you to please use tact. I don't know what you said, but it really backfired. Now everyone hates me."

He sighed. "I guess displaying tact was the furthest thing from my mind. I really laid into Trish. I told her flat out that she isn't going to work with my grandmother or anyone else until she gets her act together. And I warned her to leave you alone. Obviously my threats didn't accomplish what I intended."

"No, they didn't."

"You warned me. I guess I let my anger get the best of me."

"Trish hired her cronies to back up her story about me being a wretched aide. And the head nurse, Mrs. Whitaker, is buying it all. She's going to fork over my transfer even before the ink on the paper is dry. But I don't plan on giving her—or anyone there—the satisfaction of watching me being run off the floor."

Neil stiffened. His hand reached out to her. "Debbie, I'm really sorry this happened. I'll talk to the head nurse myself and straighten this out."

"No, thanks." She stood up. "As far as I'm concerned, this is my signal to move back to my hometown. I'm giving my resignation in a week and leaving this place." She returned to the kitchen to take pots out of the cupboard. "Even if things do get straightened out, there'll still be tension on the unit. I think it's best for all our sakes if I make tracks and leave. It's almost the end of the month. I can get out of my rental agreement easier then, too."

"What? Are you crazy?"

"Everyone else thinks I am. I can make a break. Dad has been asking me to move back to northern Virginia anyway. There are plenty of jobs around there. Maybe I can even finish my education and become an RN."

His face turned pasty white as he looked at the dishes mounting on the table. "Debbie, please don't do this."

"It's better this way. For everyone."

He stared in disbelief. "So, because of my stupidity, you're going to jump ship?" He snapped his fingers. "I never pegged you for a quitter, even if things got a little rough. This can be fixed, you know. I will do whatever it takes."

Her anger escalated within. "I'm not quitting. I'm moving on to bigger and better things. You try working in a place like that. Nurses ganging up on you. Residents who don't care what you do for them. Never getting any thanks but a slap in the face, and for something you didn't even do. Then you went and told everyone off when I pleaded with you not to. You took matters into your own hands, as though my opinion didn't count. And now I end up being the one who gets burned."

His cheeks turned from white to crimson red. "So you've made up your mind, and nothing I can say is going to change it."

"That's about right."

He went to the living room and gathered up his coat. "Look, I know I blew it. I'm willing to fix this. But if all you want to do is bolt, then it makes no sense for me to do anything, does it?"

He stood for a few lingering moments, no doubt hoping she would change her mind. When she didn't answer, he turned and left. As soon as the door shut behind him, Debbie looked back at the dishes. She went to the trash can and again took out the nursing mug in which she had served Neil the tea. Fingering the bear dressed in a nursing uniform, she promptly broke into tears.

What can I do, God? I made this mess, and now Debbie is moving away because of it. Help me figure this out.

The dilemma plagued him all night. Another sleepless night. Another night of contemplation, and this time it did not concern his grandfather. He was about to see the one woman who stirred him like no other leave the area, never to be heard from again. The woman with whom he was falling head over heels in love was now a casualty. To lose Debbie would be like losing a part of himself. They were alike in so many ways. They thought alike. They both loved God. But, if Debbie had already made up her mind to leave, there was little he could do. He could try to remedy the situation at her workplace, yes. Pray, yes. But the decision to stay or go was hers alone. He only wished she would consider him in the equation. Maybe she had no deep feelings for him. Maybe he was just a buddy, a brother, a temporary friend until the going got rough. There was no meaningful relationship to keep her here, and that's why she felt she could leave.

Neil decided he must try to fix this, even if Debbie was determined to leave. He had not followed her advice. He had approached Trish with his anger evident, telling her he wouldn't hire her if she were the last nurse available, ordering her to show some respect for the residents instead of treating them as objects for her amusement. Debbie had asked him to be tactful, but tactful he was not. Debbie's bit of wisdom might have saved him a lot of heartache and the confrontation he must now endure. But he would do what he must to keep Debbie from leaving.

Arriving at White Pines that evening, he felt like a soldier ready to encounter a hail of bullets. Maybe this was a feeling akin to what his grandfather felt on his approach to the beaches of Normandy. Of course, that was totally different—a life-threatening scenario—but Neil's anxiety remained, nonetheless.

At that moment, he saw a nurse locking the doors to her car. He recognized the blond hair, square nose, and thin frame. Exiting his own vehicle, he sank his hands deep into the pockets of his wool coat and approached her. "Trish?"

She whirled. "Huh? What's the matter? What did I do?" She then chuckled. "Oh, it's you. You need to do something about that coat. I thought you were some kind of detective."

"Actually I am. Bet you didn't know that when we first met, did you?" He offered his hand. "Detective Neil Jenson."

At first, she looked stunned. Then a smile crept across her face. "You're no detective. You work with insurance or something."

"I changed occupations for this meeting. This is detective work of the likes you've never seen. Speaking of which, I've heard how my girlfriend is about to get the boot off the floor. All this seems to be coming on the heels of the discussion you and I had the other day."

She began fidgeting with her purse strap.

"I just can't figure out why you would stoop to spreading lies about her and to the head nurse. Are you jealous for some reason?"

Her head jerked around, eyes blazing. "Ha. I am *not* jealous of Debbie, believe me."

"Well, something must not be right to go to these lengths. Unless, of course, you want to tell everyone the truth, which would help in the long run."

"I have," she said, lifting her head high.

Neil felt his irritation rising. "Good. So I can say for a fact that Debbie isn't getting a transfer, nor will she face any further character assassinations. If things get turned around with your head nurse, I won't make more waves about this whole, sad scenario. If not, then I'd be careful if I were you. Two can play at this game."

"Oh, really? And what can you possibly do to me?" she asked, the uncertainty clearly evident in her voice.

"Just clear things up and keep them clear, Trish. I mean it. Or it's gonna get ugly. I can promise you that."

They stared at each other for a moment before she whirled about and hurried off.

Neil blew out a sigh. *So much for tact.* But, at this point, love was on the line. And he meant what he said. If she got his boiler going any hotter, he was liable to create a firestorm of trouble that would smoke her right out of this place.

He sighed. *One down.* Now he needed to confront the head nurse. Before going up to the third floor, he grabbed a cup of coffee in the cafeteria to ponder the situation. Even with his human frailty, Neil believed God was looking out for him somehow. But as he nursed his cup of coffee, with the steam caressing his face, he wondered if he was only digging a deeper pit for himself and Debbie. There were other ways to deal with such problems—like praying and letting God handle the vindication. He took a swallow of coffee. But he had to do something. How else could he keep Debbie from running? He had to show her he cared. He had to tell her, somehow, that moving away was not the answer, that the real answer for her life could be found only by seeking God's will for her life and, yes, with a guy named Neil by her side. And the best way to do that was to get this Mrs. Whitaker to reconsider, to keep her where she loved the residents like Gram, to make her stay somehow, someway.

"No, I don't think so. Thanks anyway."

Neil cringed as he steered his car onto the highway. His fingers gripped his cell phone. This is what he feared—Debbie giving him the brush-off when he suggested they meet for dinner. The plan was simple enough in his mind—whisk her away to a restaurant and share what was on his heart. But so far, she was not cooperating one iota. How could he display tact in such a situation? He certainly couldn't order her to go out with him. That would send her packing in no time flat.

"So it's final then," he said. "You're moving away?"

"I am looking for another job, if that's what you mean. I made some calls home, and Dad is looking into some possibilities for me. I'm just laying all my options out on the table."

"Good. And I would like to be one of those options. The least you can do is let me take you out to dinner so we can discuss it."

A pause came over the line. "Neil, this just isn't going to work out between us. You know it."

"Look, it's not what you think. That is, I'm not the option. It's what I have to say that is." *Am I making sense?* "There are some things I've discovered that you need to hear. If you aren't willing to look at the big picture, Debbie, then I would say you've grown a bit close-minded."

He could almost feel the coldness seep over the phone line and the, *"I am not!"* ringing loud and clear, though she said nothing. He heard a click and thought she had hung up.

"Okay, I'll go. I won't be labeled close-minded, even if everyone has labeled me a host of other things. You can give your little spiel. It's only fair, I suppose."

He exhaled rapidly. "Good. I'll pick you up at six." He clicked off his cell phone and shoved it into a small compartment above a used coffee cup. At least he'd convinced her to hear him out. He didn't know what good it would do, but he could try. And if it didn't work out, then God must have other plans for the two of them, though he hated to think what those plans might be.

Debbie wore a different sweater when he arrived to pick her up. A cherry-colored one this time, which poked out from above the jacket she wore. Her face did not bear that soft touch either but appeared stony, with glazed blue eyes to match.

"So where are we going?" she asked. "To the old hangout?"

"No. Somewhere different. My mother always liked this place."

He drove for a time. Debbie stared out the window at the Christmas decorations until her teeth began to chatter. "Do you mind turning on the heat? It's cold in here."

"Of course. Sorry about that. I can think clearer when it's cold."

"No wonder you have to wear a heavy wool overcoat. And black leather gloves. Bet you can see your breath in here." She blew into the air. "Well, now that the heat is on, I don't see it."

Her attitude had definitely changed. It was colder, harsher, like the weather that turned frigid with the arctic blast that roared through just yesterday. How does one warm up a woman chilled by her circumstances?

In another fifteen minutes, he pulled up to a famous country restaurant. "I love this place," Debbie announced.

You hit the bull's eye. Way to go, Neil. He smiled. "Good. Mom always liked to look around the country store inside before they called our name off the waiting list to go into the restaurant."

"Not a very private place to put one's options out on the table," she mused.

"Daleville isn't the best place for a cozy atmosphere. I could take you to Roanoke if you want. Plenty of places there."

"No, this is fine." She immediately left the car and headed into the store. In no time, she immersed herself in the assortment of products for sale. Neil gave the waitress his name and then joined her as she perused handblown glass ornaments, old-fashioned toys, glassware, candles, and everything else women loved to coo over. Just to see Debbie relaxed and enjoying her time of browsing made all this worth his while and more.

Suddenly the waitress called out, "Mr. and Mrs. Jenson, your table is ready." Debbie whirled, gaping at him.

"I didn't tell her to say that," he said swiftly, feeling the hot flush crawl into his face.

"I sincerely hope that is *not* the option you plan to fork out onto the table."

She laughed loudly as if it were some great joke. They followed the waitress to the rear of the room and, to Neil's relief, a small table tucked away in the corner. So far God was smiling on this little plan of his, minus the Mister-and-Missus routine. Though he did find the idea of being a married couple appealing, in a strange sort of way. He could picture himself spending his life with Debbie. If only she felt the same way. But that was not on his agenda, at least not yet. First things first. He had to make certain she stayed put.

"Get the hash brown casserole," Debbie urged. "You'll love it. By the way, isn't this menu great? It's like being sent back in time, with the old-fashioned parchment paper and writing. And, of course, the good home cooking."

After they gave their orders, Debbie picked up the pegboard puzzle at their table and began playing with it. "I can never leave less than four of these pegs in here," she murmured. "Guess I'm not that smart."

"I think you're very smart." *And beautiful, caring, the perfect match for me. . .if it's God's will for us.*

"Most folks around here wouldn't agree with your assessment of my abilities. In fact, they think I belong somewhere else. Though, at least they haven't yet transferred me off the floor. In fact, Mrs. Whitaker took me off the float list. I wanted to ask her why, but I didn't." She jumped the pegs over each other and tossed them into a small pile.

Neil hid his reaction behind a menu, thanking God silently for small victories.

"Okay, you're hiding something, Neil Jenson."

He glanced over the top of the menu. "Who, me?"

"Yes, you. I can tell. You had something to do with my transfer back to the floor, didn't you? There's no way I could suddenly be back in everyone's good graces without a little help."

"Look, Debbie, I think Mrs. Whitaker realizes the mistake she made. She knows what a positive impact you have on the residents, how well that World War II vet you talk about responds to you. Even Gram went and asked her where you were and why you weren't around, that you were deeply needed and sorely missed. Yep, my grandmother, the crusader. Trish and her crew had convinced Mrs. Whitaker that you were the one causing the problems on the floor, but I think she's beginning to see who the true ringleader is. And I must admit, I think she's a tad bit embarrassed by it all."

"I've worked with her long enough. I can't believe she would take Trish's word over mine."

"Trish has a way about her that is very convincing. I mean, she threw me for a loop about the movie bit. She can be quite the conniver."

"Trish would bite off a hand if it suited her. She doesn't care about anyone, especially the residents. I doubt she'd help a soul unless it was to her advantage, or unless it was a man dressed in a black overcoat and wearing black gloves. She's almost forty, you know, and she wants so badly to be married. I'm just glad you saw through it." Debbie removed a few more pegs. "Hey, I got down to three pegs. I'm getting better at this."

"I'm really sorry work is so tough. But you have to think that God must want something important accomplished in that place, maybe even among those who dislike you. And you can bet when the going gets rough that you must be doing something right. So I hope you'll hang in there and not give up."

The food arrived. Neil prayed for the meal and immediately tackled his hash brown casserole. Debbie only sat there, staring at the food in front of her—the chicken potpie with a side dish of hash brown casserole. She made no move to pick up her fork.

Neil immediately tensed. "What's the matter? Are you sick?"

"No." She paused. "Overwhelmed, I guess. I don't know anyone who would stick his neck out for me the way you have. No one I know would go and confront people for my sake. Or buy me dinner in one of my favorite restaurants. And certainly no guy, for that matter. I mean, I've eaten with people before. The girls from church. Things like that. I guess I'm not sure what to say or do at this point."

Neil acknowledged her plate. "C'mon. Enjoy your option then. It's sitting right on the table like you said it would be."

Her forehead wrinkled in confusion. "My option?"

"I'm forking out my option. This is it—dinner out with me. You eat this, and you're stuck here for good. You know it. Skip it and leave, and I guess this really is good-bye."

She stared before a slight smile teased the corners of her lips. "I'm too hungry, and this is simply too good to walk away from." She picked up her fork. "I never thought a way to a woman's heart would be by way of a sweet country restaurant and a man dressed in a black overcoat. But I guess this time it is."

Neil laughed heartily. He never had a more pleasant meal and was sorry to see it end so quickly. But they both had jobs to go to the next morning, and he needed to return to Roanoke. On the drive back to her place, they talked some more. Debbie even broached the topic of his grandfather, Samuel, and asked how things were going in that department.

"I'm at a little bit of a roadblock as far as that's concerned," he admitted. "Maybe it's better that I stop where I am. I should leave the past alone. 'Let it go' like everyone's been telling me to do and concentrate on getting Gram home for a few days over the holidays." Arriving at the apartment building, he wasn't sure if he wanted to let everything go. He had refused to let Debbie go, and through dinner and conversation, she had changed her mind about leaving. But what else could he do? Besides, there were more important things, after all. His life. Debbie's life. And where life was taking them at the moment. And he was glad that they both finally seemed to be heading in the right direction.

"Thanks for dinner. It was great."

"Debbie, I hope you know I care about you. A lot."

She sat still for a moment, pulling the zipper to her jacket up and down. "I know. That's why I couldn't eat my dinner at first. It hit me right then that you really do care what happens to me. It's not just some passing whim. I've gone through that, you know. I thought it was real once, but the guy wanted someone else. My roommate."

"This is *not* some passing fancy. Believe me, it's very real. In fact, I'll even show you how real it can get." He leaned over to kiss her. At first she seemed tense by the encounter. He felt her lips tremble against his. Then she fumbled for the door, and before he knew it, she disappeared into the night.

Startled, Neil flopped back in his seat. Had he made a mistake? Did he move too fast? He only meant it as a kiss of joy, an answer to prayer, and all the proof required to show that they were right for each other.

If only she felt the same way.

Chapter 11

Debbie giggled at a singsong rhyme of love trickling through her head, even as she prepared to tackle another day at White Pines. She found it hard to believe all her desires could be realized so quickly and so completely. Never did she think Neil would end the evening the way he had. Reflecting on their past encounters, she could see how much he cared. He wasn't a Brad by any means. He was Neil, his own man, and a wonderful man at that. And no, she wasn't about to leave. Not now, not ever. She could already hear wedding bells pealing, at least in her heart. Maybe one Saturday, she would venture to Roanoke and shop around for a dress. She'd ask her younger sister Kris and some friends from church to be bridesmaids. She would plan out the flowers, the caterer, everything.

She sighed. Forget dreaming about a wedding and then life with Neil in some glorious two-story, four-bedroom home in Roanoke and her with a full-fledged nursing degree, four kids, and a minivan to cart them around in. Time to get back on track, at least for the present. She still had all her Christmas shopping to do and cards to write up. Not to mention her work at White Pines.

Today she was assigned to Harold. He sat in his wheelchair in the usual combat mode, talking about Hitler's Germans and what the troops needed to do to secure victory. "So how are those spies you've been seeing?" he asked Debbie while she combed his hair. "Did you turn them in?"

He remembered their last conversation. "Well, they didn't quite confess, but at least the lies have stopped and the head command has kept me on the unit."

"Yeah, but things can start up again at any moment. Keep alert. And make sure to wear your helmet and keep your gun at the ready, just in case."

Wise words. The Bible talked about keeping one's armament ready when facing the enemies of life. The helmet of salvation, the breastplate of righteousness. The sword of the Spirit or the Word of God, among the other accoutrements.

"They're slick, the enemy," Harold continued. "And they're dug in good up there. They had all that time, you know, to dig in and wait for us to come. It could have been worse. They all thought we would land in Calais, commanded by General Patton." He chuckled. "But we fooled them good. Yep, we sure did, when General Eisenhower moved us to the landing at Normandy."

Normandy. The name triggered something within her, something she had kept buried since the falling-out on the unit and, most recently, Neil's kiss. She recalled the conversation about Neil's true grandfather going off to battle across the ocean. "I know someone who was at Normandy," she said to Harold.

Immediately he perked up. "Was he in my unit? I can't find my buddies anywhere. And Sam, I told you about Sam."

Sam! She began to think. Neil's grandfather was called Samuel. "Did your friend go by Sam or Samuel?"

"Sam, of course. No good man would go by Samuel, 'lessen he was some good ol' boy from back home." Harold laughed and then turned somber. "Poor Sam."

"Tell me about him, Harold."

"He was a great man. A good friend. He had a girl back home. Liv, he called her. And he had a boy, too. Cared about him a lot, he did. Talked about him all the time."

"A boy? How old?"

"Don't recall. Young boy, I think. A few years old. Sam loved that boy. Sent him some letters, I think."

Debbie put the comb away and sat down in a chair. She pulled Harold's wheelchair around to face her. "Harold, what else do you know about Sam? Did you have more than one soldier named Sam serving in your unit?"

"Only one Sam in my unit. But there were heaps more in the division, of course."

"The man I'm thinking about, his name was Samuel Truett. I'm sure you've never heard of him."

A smile spread across the elderly man's face. "Sure I have. That's his name. Sam Truett."

Shock waves rippled through her. She steadied herself. Maybe he was only repeating what she had said. "Did Sam Truett and you go to war, Harold? Was he your friend?"

"Sure. He was my best friend. And he..." Harold paused. "Someone get up to the beachhead! Someone's gotta do it. And I can't. I can't face it anymore."

He had lapsed back into his battle state. Somehow the questions had triggered a memory too painful to consider. Harold was again mumbling battle scenarios of Normandy. Yet, the confession coming out of his mouth couldn't help but intrigue Debbie. She didn't know if he was confessing the truth or not, but with this information, Neil might be able to find out on the Internet if the men did, indeed, serve together in the same unit.

Debbie could hardly keep her mind on her work after that. It didn't even bother her that nurses were whispering behind her back, that Trish was dishing out strange looks all day, or even that Mrs. Whitaker looked at her in an odd sort of way during the course of the shift. She could only think of Neil arriving tonight and the news she couldn't wait to share.

On her coffee break, Debbie couldn't wait any longer. Neil had to know what she might have stumbled upon. She sneaked off to a phone booth, placed a call to his cell, and left a message on voice mail, ending with, "I'll wait around for you to come in. I'll be in the cafeteria at four, and I can fill you in on the details then."

All day she waited for his call and his voice exclaiming her news that Harold may have very well known Samuel Truett. The phone stayed strangely silent. She tried not to read anything into it. Certainly the news should have sent him racing to return the call. Maybe he was on a case overload at the insurance company. Or his cell phone wasn't charged up. Or he never checked messages until the end of the day. For whatever reason, the day shift ended with no word from him.

Finally someone notified her she had an outside call. Debbie nearly tripped over a linen cart to answer it at the nurses' station.

"Hey there," Neil said cheerfully. "I got your message. What's up?"

She opened her mouth, ready to spill out everything she had learned concerning Harold. But first, she had to find out something important. "Did your grandma ever have a nickname?"

He laughed. "You mean you called to ask me that? C'mon, Debbie. Why did you really call?"

"No, I'm serious. Did she?"

"Okay, I'll play along, just so long as you're the prize. Grandpa Joe used to call her Liv. Of course we wondered why he would call Gram a name like that. I mean, people 'live,' don't they? Why did he have to call her Liv unless he was glad she was living?" He laughed at his wit.

Debbie could barely catch her breath she was so excited. Harold was telling the truth. He would not know such information unless Samuel Truett once shared it with him. They were all related. It was too unbelievable to be real.

"Do you have a nickname?" he went on, oblivious to the seriousness of this.

She wanted to keep the conversation on topic but decided to wait and reveal her reason for the question when he arrived at White Pines. "Sure. You can call me Sneaky."

"Sneaky. I like that. Why are you sneaking around?"

"Come to White Pines as soon as you can, and I'll tell you."

"Wow, now that's an offer I can't refuse. Be there quick as a flash."

She replaced the receiver, only to find several of the staff giving her inquisitive looks. Didn't anyone believe in privacy anymore? Well, it didn't matter. She knew now she had stumbled upon something extraordinary. *A miracle.* And she couldn't wait to see the look on Neil's face when all was revealed. It would be priceless. If only she had a camera to record all this for posterity's sake. For his children. Maybe *their* children. She tried to steady her breathing and began to pace. She would go see Elvina, but she feared her anxiety would be detected. She would wait for Neil instead.

She checked her watch. He didn't say where he was. For all she knew, he was still hiking it down from Roanoke and she had another forty minutes to wait with the rush hour traffic. Maybe she should just sit in the lounge and read one of the many magazines.

"You seem awfully anxious," the unit secretary noted.

Debbie gave a small smile, realizing she was attracting attention, and strode off to the elevator. She pushed the button. She would wait for him in the lobby. And then she would take him right to where he needed to go.

The doors parted, and suddenly he was there, black overcoat and all, coming toward her. The next moment, she was on the floor, having tripped over her own feet. He looked as startled as she was.

"Wow, what a greeting." Neil offered her his hand.

Debbie winced as the old back wound flared up once again.

"Not your back," he groaned.

"Same place."

"I'm sorry." He shook his head, but his eyes told a different story, one of tenderness, compassion, and—dare she think it?—love. He gently massaged her upper back in a circular motion. "Let's get some ice on it right away."

"I haven't got time, Neil. This can't wait. I'm dying as it is."

His concern was quickly replaced with confusion. "Huh?"

"There's someplace I have to take you."

"Can't I first say hello to my favorite lady? I promised her I'd be here, and I'm already a little late." He walked off toward Elvina's room, leaving Debbie standing in the hallway. She tried to maintain her composure, but inwardly she felt like a Mexican jumping bean. She began to pace again, even as her back still smarted from the contact with the floor.

"Gram, I think there's something important Debbie needs to tell me," she heard Neil say. "I'll be right back."

Debbie had all she could do to keep from dragging him down the hall. "Neil, I've discovered something really big."

"So have I," he said, pulling her to a stop. His finger traced her cheek and then her lips.

"No, please be serious. This is about your grandfather. Your other grandfather."

His finger dropped. The tender expression melted away. "I told you I've given up on all that. It's time to move on. 'Let it go,' as everyone's been saying."

Debbie took him by the hand. "No, you can't let this go, believe me. I want you to meet someone."

"I'm not really in the mood for other visitations right now, except with you and Gram."

"You will be, don't worry." As they walked, the words rushed out. "Remember me telling you about Harold? The World War II vet who fought at the Battle of Normandy? Well, he was talking about his best friend in the army. And guess what his name was? Sam! You know, Sam. . .short for Samuel."

"So what? There are plenty of Sams in this world, Debbie."

"I'm telling you, there's a connection." She could see the look of confusion distorting his face as he followed her into the room.

"Hi, Harold," Debbie greeted. "I brought a friend of mine. He's a soldier at heart."

Harold gripped Neil's hand and shook it heartily. "Glad to meet you. We need some strong, young men to join our forces. We have so little. Omaha took everyone away."

Neil cast a sheepish look in Debbie's direction, uncertain how to respond.

"Yes, and guess what, Harold?" Debbie interjected. "Neil here says he knows Sam, too."

"Really? Wasn't he a great man?"

"I—I know a Samuel Truett," Neil began.

"Sure, Sam Truett. From Wheeling, West Virginia. Were you also in the same unit?"

Neil stared in disbelief. Debbie nudged him. "I, uh, I heard he had a son."

"Sure did. He loved that little boy. Little Albert. He was sure sad to have to leave him." Harold straightened up in his chair. "You know, I saw that little fella before we left. It was raining real hard. Good weather for ducks. I saw them together that day, when they said good-bye."

Neil grabbed for the man's hand, his eyes large. "You saw my dad? And my grandfather? I don't believe it. This is unbelievable. What did they look like? What did they say?"

Harold shrank down in his wheelchair. His bloodshot eyes filled with fear and confusion. "I—I don't know what you're talking about."

Uh-oh, Debbie thought. "Harold, what Neil meant to say is that he knows Sam and Al, also. They were close, too, like family relations, you see."

Harold relaxed when he heard this. "Sam was like a brother to me. He was a tall man. Bushy dark brown hair, almost looked black, though they made him cut it short. And his boy looked exactly like him."

Debbie glanced at Neil's hair. Wavy hair. Dark brown, nearly black. Excitement bubbled up within her. She wondered if Neil was feeling the same thing, but by the look on his face, he appeared far from it. In fact, he looked ghostly white, as if in a state of shock.

Harold continued chattering about the army and then the Battle of Normandy. All at once, Neil whirled and stumbled out of the room.

"Neil?" She hurried out after him. "What's wrong?"

He glared at her. "How could you put me through that? That man doesn't know my grandfather or my dad. He doesn't even know what year it is. He still thinks he's at Normandy."

"Neil, you're wrong. He knows more than you think. You need to go back and talk to him some more."

"He isn't right in the head, Debbie. I think it's cruel to have planted these things in his mind, only to have him spit them back at me. What do you think this is? A game?"

Debbie stared, horrified. "I never planted anything in his mind. What he's saying is genuine. Besides, I can prove it. He was telling me all about Sam's girl whom he called Liv. The girl he left behind. You were the one who told me your grandmother's nickname was Liv. Harold couldn't have known that fact unless he heard your grandfather, Samuel Truett, say it."

Neil stared into Harold's room where they could hear the man listing off the supplies left after the initial engagement. "This is too unbelievable to be real."

"I know. It's a miracle happening right in this very place. Here is a living link to your grandfather and your past. Please, Neil, go back and talk to Harold. If you don't, you'll regret it the rest of your life."

He considered it for a moment. Slowly he made his way back into the room. Harold had just finished checking the list of first aid supplies on hand and detailing how the medic had been killed. He stopped when he saw Neil. "You're supposed to be on guard duty, young man. What did you say your name was?"

"Neil. Neil Jenson."

"Good-sounding name. I'm Harold White."

"Yes, and you know Sam Truett. Is he. . .is he here? I, uh, I need to talk to him."

The man's lips began to quiver. Tears filled his eyes. "You didn't hear the news then."

"We, uh, we never got a statement from the War Department, if that's what you mean."

"Fools. They should have told you. You should know. He died right next to me. Right there on the beach. Took a slug in the belly. And he said. . ." He stopped. "Uh-oh. Keep to your feet, men."

Debbie could see the pain of the past driving Harold back into a state of war. She came to his side. "Please, Harold, please tell us what happened to Sam. It will help Neil accept what happened if you tell us. He never got the telegram. Neither did Liv. They need to know."

"Liv doesn't know either? Sam talked about her with his dying breath. Told me to tell her that he loved her."

"She wants to see him. It's her Christmas wish."

Harold's head dropped to his chest.

Debbie heard a noise she hadn't anticipated. Weeping.

"Sh–she won't see him no more. He's gone. And she—she will have to take care of Sam's little boy. I'm sorry, Sam. I know I promised you, and I'm sorry." He lifted his face, damp with tears, and looked at Neil. "I'm sorry, young man. I told Sam I would take care of Liv and the boy. On his dying breath, I promised. But I didn't. I didn't do what I said I would do. When the war was over, I came home and did nothing. I didn't even check to see how Albert was doing." Great heaves shook his frail form. "I'm sorry, Sam."

Neil ventured forward and took the feeble man in his arms. Unresolved grief filled them both. Debbie looked on, the tears bubbling in her own eyes, as Neil embraced the closest link to both the grandfather and the father he never knew.

Chapter 12

I f that wasn't a bomb falling out of the skies, I don't know what is."

Debbie couldn't help but agree with Neil's assessment of the encounter with Harold White. They decided on a drive to look at Christmas lights for a change of pace but were really using the occasion to mull over everything. Though shocking, she recognized the news provided answers Neil desperately needed. And she was glad for it. Neil had a living testimony of one who witnessed his roots.

"I'm amazed that Harold actually knew him," Neil went on. "That they were best friends, of all things. That he saw my grandfather die there on the beach. What do you wager the odds are of such an occurrence?"

"A million to one at least. Which is why this has to be God's doing."

He began tapping on the steering wheel. "I can see why God tells us not to worry about tomorrow, that it will take care of itself. He orchestrates the future. I could never have brought all this together. Think of all the minute details that had to come forth to make this reunion work. For instance, if you hadn't taken that tumble in the road, none of this would've happened."

Debbie chuckled, even as her hand went to her battered tailbone. "I guess this is one time I can say a bruise on the backside was worth it."

Suddenly she saw one of his large hands sneak over and take hold of hers; then he gave a gentle squeeze.

"And I'm happy, too, that you decided not to move away. I would've never discovered the truth. You've made such a difference in my life, Debbie. I can't begin to say."

"Please don't put me on a pedestal. Remember, Mrs. Whitaker thought I was the worst thing to come storming onto the floor."

"She didn't know what a good nurse she had. And that's what I told her, plain and simple. That she should be proud to have you there, caring about the residents more than all of her staff combined. That you gave your life to them every day. And she owed you big-time."

"Boy, I'll bet that went over like a lead balloon. Neil's good-hearted tact." She giggled.

He laughed in response. "Hey, she listened. And she stopped sending you off to other floors. I know Gram is very glad to have you back." He gave her hand another gentle squeeze. "So am I. I was miserable when we were apart. I couldn't sleep or eat." He paused.

The symptoms sounded familiar to her. No appetite. Loss of sleep. Could it be the symptoms of that sickness called love? She sucked in her breath, at a loss for words.

"And now I need you more than ever."

She looked at his hand, still curled around hers, and wondered what he meant. As a companion? His one and only? She sucked in her breath, suddenly nervous. Were all her fantastic dreams about to come to pass? If so, was she ready to handle them?

"Somehow we're going to have to break the news to Gram about Harold and this Sam Truett fellow. Well, I guess he isn't just some fellow down the street. He was my grandfather. But she needs to know the truth. It's been her wish to find out what happened to him. I know it will hardly be a great Christmas gift, but maybe she can find some peace, after all is said and done."

Debbie blew out a sigh. He hadn't said what she thought he would say, but then again, maybe it was for the better. She didn't think she was yet ready for dreams to come true anyway. "So how do you plan on springing the news?"

"I'm not sure. I was hoping you'd be able to give me some ideas. If I just came out and said it, she might not believe me. Then we'd be in real trouble."

Debbie had little time for contemplation as they slowed to a stop behind a row of cars lined up along the road. Up ahead, she saw colored lights and oversized glimmering snowflakes hovering in midair. She lowered the window and strained to see. "Neil, you won't believe this, but there's a house down the road here that has every kind of light display imaginable."

"Must be something big. The traffic has come to a dead halt."

They inched their way forward until they came to a large sign welcoming all visitors, and an arrow pointed to where cars could park in a farmer's field. Debbie nodded to Neil's inquiry as to whether or not they should investigate. He turned into the field and parked. "This is great," she squealed. "You'll get to share in a family tradition. The house is decorated up like the one I described to you when I was a kid."

"I'll gladly look at any tradition that has to do with you. Let's go see what this is all about."

Debbie stared in amazement at the displays—at least six different lighted Nativity scenes, snowflakes positioned high up in the trees, dancing bears, tin soldiers, a huge train, and so many more it nearly took her breath away. They walked through lighted tunnels, past Mary and Joseph looking upon the newborn Babe. They strolled along a pebbled path to a tiny house that held at least a hundred animated Santas, carolers, angels, and music boxes, all playing carols with glee.

"A genuine Christmastown, USA," Neil commented. "I'd love to see their electric bill."

"These people do love Christmas," she agreed. Walking by the main house, Debbie gazed upon the dozens of lighted roses on the ground like a winter's garden. "Beautiful."

"Seeing this, I can't help thinking about Gram," Neil said. "She would get a kick out of it all. She loves light displays. I want her to have a nice Christmas, but I don't know if I can pull it off. And now we're going to have to break the news to her about my grandfather."

"It will work out fine, don't worry," she said, drawing closer to his coat, which felt better than any security blanket. "Look over there."

Her sights fell on a large tent where inside a band played lively tunes. They looked at each other and walked over to find people sitting in folding chairs, clapping away to gospel tunes praising God. At a large table, an older woman offered hot chocolate and Christmas cookies.

"You have quite a setup here," Neil remarked.

"We do it every year. We like to bless the community."

"It must take you all year to put up the lights and take them down again."

She laughed. "We start in early fall. And usually it takes until the end of January to tear it all down. We have several sheds in the back where we store it all. But we love doing it." She nodded toward the band. "This way, people will also stop by the tent here and learn something about God."

"Interesting," Neil said, taking a seat beside Debbie to hear the band. "They set up all these lights to draw people in, and then arrange to have a band play gospel songs and talk about the real reason for the season. What a great way to minister to the people."

"I'd love to do something like this one day," Debbie mused. "But I would do my place up entirely in white lights. I'd serve cinnamon stars. And mulled cider."

Neil snickered. "You'll have to marry a guy who likes to do that kind of stuff."

Debbie looked down at the steaming hot cocoa she held in her hands. How she hoped Neil, sitting there in his black wool coat, might be that kind of guy.

"I'm lucky if I can even screw in a lightbulb," he added.

For some reason, the comment saddened her. Maybe she had been living in a cloud these days since they shared a kiss, convinced that God had brought the right man into her life. Or was she only caught up in some emotional whim and not seriously thinking and praying about this? Of course Neil had many special characteristics that appealed to her. The way God brought them together through his grandmother had been a miracle, as well. "You were good at untangling that strand of lights in my apartment," she remarked.

He laughed. "Yes, I did do a pretty good job. Maybe there's hope for me in the decorating department, after all."

Debbie hoped so, too, as a rousing rendition of "Amazing Grace" filled the tent. The music followed them out into the wintry night. Again Debbie felt Neil's thickly gloved hand slip around hers. They walked toward the car and gazed upon the many lighted forms of forest animals tucked back in the woods.

"There really has been amazing grace in my life," Neil said, staring at the animated deer that nodded their heads as if in agreement to what he said. "All grace. Grace to figure out this thing with my grandparents. Grace for my desk job. Grace to get through the latest fiasco at White Pines with the nurses. Grace on my family. Grace to know more about you, Debbie, and make sure I don't ignore any of your instructions ever again. And grace to remember that tact is the key." He chuckled.

She sighed. *God, how can this man not be for me? He must be. He knows You so well. Look what we've been through. Even when I wanted to leave, he remained steadfast, firm, unrelenting. I will even teach him how to string up white lights, if only You would finish this work in us.*

When she opened her eyes, he was gazing at her intently. She thought perhaps he might kiss her, but the moment passed. Neil coaxed her toward the car. She sighed. It was better for them to travel the road of love one step at a time, to wait on God's leading and not act out of impulsiveness.

Once inside the car, Neil sat in his seat as if frozen, staring out the window.

"What are you thinking about?" she asked.

"The work I have to do. Like telling Gram the news, which I hope doesn't shock her to death."

"Neil, we'll sleep on it tonight and see if we have any ideas on how to tell her. I know when we do come up with an idea, it will be perfect."

"Debbie, you're something else."

A kiss of gratitude followed in the most perfect moment possible. As far as she was concerned, her Christmas wish had already come, wrapped in a big black wool overcoat, and with a future waiting to be had. There was no better fulfillment to a season of giving and joy.

✦

"Please?"

The elderly woman shook her head and looked away.

"But, Gram, you need to talk to him."

She shook her head again. "I'm not speaking about private things to some man I don't even know. Really, Nathaniel. How can you even suggest such a thing?" She drew up her lap robe as if to guard herself.

Neil felt his frustration level rising. He glanced back at Debbie who nodded her head, her eyes wide, as if encouraging him to stand firm. "Gram, this is the only way. Believe me. I talked to him. He knows everything. Even your nickname. How would he know that unless he knew Sam? Your Sam? Sam Truett."

"Nathaniel, you don't live here. I hear things all the time. The poor people calling out for loved ones. One lady asking for her cat. They have lost their minds, many of them. And I'm not about to trust something this personal, this dear to me, to some crazy old man." Her voice heightened. "Anyway, I don't want to get to know any more men. I had two men, and they both left me alone to live in this place. So please don't force me to meet some crazy man."

Neil retreated into the hall. He felt sick to his stomach, even as Debbie laid her soothing hand on his shoulder. "What am I going to do? She won't talk to Harold. I guess we are similar in a way, even if we aren't blood relations. I didn't want to talk to the man either, at first. But it was the best thing I ever did."

"We can't force her, Neil. Maybe she's afraid to face the truth. It's scary confronting the past. Let it go."

He began to chuckle scornfully. " 'Let it go.' Honestly, if I hear that statement again, I think I'll go crazy." He'd no sooner spoken than regret seized him. "I'm sorry," he said to Debbie. "But this is something I've just got to see through." He turned on his heels and started to walk down the hall. When Debbie asked where he was going, he told her he was going to think. He spoke the truth, but he also wanted to see that man again. Harold. The man who knew his grandfather. The one who knew his father. The only living, breathing link left to his past.

He brushed by the nurses, many of whom only gave him a passing glance. He was glad for small miracles. Word had spread about him and Debbie being an "item," and it made him happy. Now, if he could just resolve this situation, it would be a merry Christmas all the way around.

He arrived at the open doorway of Harold's room to find Trish standing inside, scolding Harold as she tried to make him sit properly in his wheelchair.

"Who do you think you are, talking to him like that?" Neil snarled.

Trish whirled around, her face white.

"You don't deserve to work here. It's an honor to work with people like him. You treat them like they're dirt on the floor."

She said nothing but only stared. Even Harold stared, his eyes wide.

"You know, if you can't do a job right, you shouldn't be doing it. These people deserve better. You should be giving them all the respect they can get. Now please leave."

Trish said nothing but hurried out of the room. Harold shook his head in wonder. "I would promote you if I had the authority, young man."

Neil pulled up a chair and sat down beside him. "Do you remember me, Harold?" He saw the tears of recognition.

"W–Why did you come back?"

"I need a favor. A big one."

"I. . .uh. . ." Harold stared off into the distance. "Hey, I see them. Here they come!"

Neil gently took the man's face in his hands, turning it so their eyes met. "Harold, it's time to face reality. The war's long over, and now I need your help."

"I can't help you."

"Yes, you can. You knew my grandfather, Sam Truett. You knew my dad, Albert, when he was a little boy. You can help me in more ways than you know. You already saved me from an enemy of confusion and all the unanswered questions. Now you can save a woman who has been living with questions all her life. You can fulfill her one wish at this moment."

"But. . .I don't know any women."

"Liv. You can help Liv."

His wrinkled hand gripped Neil's. "Liv! You mean, she's here?"

"Yes, she lives here. Down the next hall. A miracle of God, really. She's Sam's Liv, the one he talked about on the battlefield, the woman who took care of Sam's little boy. And I'm that little boy's son."

Harold began to tremble. "It can't be. You can't be."

"Harold, I am. And right now I need you to go talk to Liv. I need you to tell her what happened to Sam that day on the beach. Let her heart rest in peace."

He shook his head. "I can't do that."

"Look, I know what you said. How you made Sam a promise when he lay there dying. You think you didn't live up to it. But now is the time. You can fulfill the promise to Sam by meeting Liv and telling her the truth. Don't you think Sam would want her to know what happened to him?"

"But he wanted me to take care of them. And I didn't. I did nothing. I came home and tried to forget."

"Harold, you have to let that go." Neil nearly laughed at his use of the expression—*let it go*. But maybe there was more to the saying than met the eye. "Now you can do something, something really big, to put Liv's heart at rest. She told me the best Christmas present she could have was to know what happened to Sam. And you're the one who can make it happen."

Harold sat there, seemingly frozen in place in his wheelchair. At least he was no longer murmuring words of war, seeing the enemy, talking of bullets and death. For the first time, he was not immersing himself in the past but facing it.

"All right."

"What?" Neil could hardly believe what he heard.

"I'll talk to Liv and tell her that I knew Sam and what happened to him. Where is she?"

Neil brushed his hand across his face, unsure if this was real. "Wow, Harold. Okay." His thoughts became muddled. "Look, I'll try to set up a meeting place, okay? You two should have privacy. I'll get back to you."

Harold shook his hand. "You grew up to be a nice young man," he said. "Sam would be proud. In fact, you look like him."

Neil couldn't hold the tears that teased his eyes. He was his father's child and his grandfather's grandson. A part of both men lived on. He felt proud then, proud to be a product of men like that. He only prayed the life he lived would preserve their honor.

Chapter 13

H ow do you think it went?" Debbie wondered.

Neil tried hard not to let his nervousness show, even as his skin crawled with prickles of anxiety and curiosity. He picked up a travel mug of coffee. He didn't even want to wager a guess. As it was, he'd convinced Gram to go to the meeting on a slightly false pretense, telling her that a friend from long ago had come to see her. Now he wondered if he'd made yet another awful mistake. Maybe he should have come right out and told her. But if he had, he was certain she would have refused the encounter. This was the only way.

"You aren't saying anything."

He took another gulp of the stale coffee before tucking the mug into the car's cup holder. "I don't know. I guess I'm trying not to think about it too much. I just hope and pray I haven't made the worst mistake of my life by having the two of them meet. If this ends up killing Gram, I'll never forgive myself."

Immediately Debbie put her hand on his, steadying his nervous tremors. "Neil, please don't say that. We need to believe that everything is going to work out right. We didn't come this far to let it all go downhill. God knows your heart, that you want good to come from a situation that has been going on now for over sixty years."

"No matter how this ends, I plan to visit Harold as much as I can. The man is my relative, even if he is not a blood relation. He's my only living link, besides Gram, to my grandfather and my father. He deserves all the attention I can give him, and so much more, really."

"I'm sure he'll love having you for an adopted grandson. I think it will do wonders for him. And it will do wonders for your grandmother, too."

Neil tried hard not to fidget while he glanced out the car window. He had wanted to go back and be with Gram after the meeting was all said and done, but he was glad he hadn't. Better to give Gram time after something of this magnitude. He only hoped their close relationship as grandmother and grandson still remained intact.

"Hello?" Debbie whispered in his ear. "You okay?"

"Yeah. I guess we gave the best medicine we could. Now we have to wait for the healing."

She nodded before planting a light kiss on his cheek. "I agree. Maybe you can rest easier tonight, knowing all this is finally out in the open."

"I hope so." That would be a nice change to a Christmas season that had begun in ways he never could have imagined. He glanced over at Debbie. Her eyes were wide, cheeks all aglow, a vision of beauty during a difficult and unpredictable time. He was glad to have her by his side, and he hoped she'd stay forever.

"So let's change the subject and concentrate on our job for today. Did you bring your Christmas shopping list?" Debbie reached inside her pocket and pulled out a sheet of paper filled with scribbles.

Neil shrugged.

"You don't have one? Then how are you supposed to remember who to buy for and what?"

Lists. They were as foreign to him as picking up a dust rag and cleaning the apartment. He usually relied on his brain to do the remembering, but these days, his mind felt more like a colander, with ideas dripping into oblivion. "I'll see what you buy, and maybe it will give me some hints."

When Debbie suggested a shopping trip to Roanoke to while away the hours on this Saturday afternoon, Neil thought it a good idea. He felt the need for an escape, and Debbie was a good distraction—until he found himself thinking again about Christmas and all the great ideas he had still not put into motion. He hadn't talked to his mother about inviting Gram home for the holidays, nor had he looked into another private-duty nurse to replace Trish. With the weight of the grandfather issue, it had taken a backseat.

"Don't worry about the list," Debbie went on. "We'll make one right now. You tell me who you need to buy for, and maybe I can make a suggestion." She took out a scrap of paper and a pen from her purse.

"Gram," he began. "I still need a private-duty nurse."

"You mean you haven't gotten one yet? Neil, you can't leave important things like that to the last minute. As it is, it's probably too late."

"So there's no chance of you doing it? What if you called in sick? Or said that a loved one needed special care over the holidays?"

The look she gave communicated her answer, though he hoped a miracle might still be in the works. When she launched into getting docked a week's pay for not showing up on Christmas, along with the horror of telling a lie to boot, he immediately retreated. Maybe with all the turmoil brewing this year, he should just forget about inviting Gram to Mom's house. But the more he considered dropping the idea, the less peace he felt. It seemed perfect having her there with all his siblings together, especially after the Harold incident. His aunts and uncles would stop by for hors d'oeuvres on Christmas Eve. It would be like a reunion. Gram would have a ball, holding newborn great-nieces and great-nephews, seeing her great-grandchildren, laughing, and reminiscing about the old days. He wanted to make it work, but so far, nothing was falling into place the way he'd intended.

He put his thoughts aside then and made small talk about gift ideas for others in the family. When they arrived, the mall in Roanoke was fairly bursting at the seams with shoppers. Once inside, they paused at several stores to do some window-shopping. Fuzzy sweaters like the kind Debbie wore graced the mannequins. Neil wondered if she would like another one for her wardrobe. Did she own a black one? He liked black. Or was a sweater too personal? Maybe he should stick to old-fashioned notepaper in a flowered box. Or a large potted poinsettia. A bouquet of red roses better illustrated his heart. A diamond ring would be the ultimate gift, if he thought she would say yes. She had to say yes. They had been through so much. She had seen the inner struggles of his heart and the goings-on with his family. She had become a crucial part of his life. They were being knit together as one.

A poke in his arm drew him back to the reality of the shopping experience. Debbie had stopped at some bath boutique. Flowery scents assaulted his senses. Looking across the way, he saw a computer store. That was more his style. He was curious to know what new games would be out for the coming New Year. Maybe he could find something for his brother, Dick.

"I think you can find some nice stuff in here for your mother and sister." She poked him again. "And stop thinking about buying yourself a computer game," she said with a teasing tilt.

"I can't get anything past you, can I?" He smirked and followed her inside. There wasn't a guy in the place, only women perusing the multitude of soaps and lotions in every color of the rainbow. The warring scents assaulted his nostrils.

Debbie opened a bottle of pink stuff and placed it under his nose. "Isn't this nice?"

"Smells like a lollipop. What is it?"

"It's called Raspberry Dream. You really don't seem into this."

"Tell you what. . ." He took out his wallet and pulled out a few bills. "Why don't you buy my mom and Sandy something for me? I'm no good at this kind of stuff. To me, everything smells the same."

"You aren't leaving me for that computer store across the way, are you?"

"No. I was hoping to check my voice mail for any messages. Here," he said, handing the cash to Debbie, "you can spend up to fifty bucks on each."

"Wow! Okay." Debbie looked as though he had given her the key to the bank. She grabbed a shopping basket and began performing the sniff test on various products.

Neil moseyed outside the store, took out his cell phone, and hit the auto-dial button to access his messages.

"Neil, this is Mom. I just got a call from the charge nurse at White Pines. Elvina isn't doing very well. She won't take her pills for the nurse. Maybe you can go over there and see what's happening. I'll try to see her tonight."

His hand tightened around the phone. *What? How can that be?* It didn't sound like Gram at all.

He listened to the next message.

"Neil? This is Trish from the White Pines Health Care Facility. I'm calling about your grandma. We've been having a hard time getting her to take anything. She won't eat or even take her medications. Everyone here is very concerned. If she doesn't take her pills soon, she may be transferred to the hospital. Please give the floor a call back. You can ask for Mrs. Whitaker."

Even Trish was calling? A chill fell over him, despite the warmth of the mall and the fact that he was perspiring heavily inside his wool sweater. A message from the head nurse, Mrs. Whitaker, followed, echoing her concern over Gram's condition.

Neil hurried back inside the store to find Debbie carrying two gift baskets full of bath products. "Hey, Neil, how about gift baskets? Don't they look nice?" Her cheerful face deteriorated into one of concern. "What's the matter?"

"Tell you in a minute. Go ahead and get them. We have to go." He waited until she paid and handed him the change. "Gram is refusing to take everything. Food, pills." He swept his hand across his face.

"Neil, I'm so sorry!"

He took the bags. "This is it, Debbie. She's going to die. Grandpa Joe's gone. My dad's gone. Now this whole Sam and Harold story. I guess she thinks she has nothing left to live for. She's given up."

"Neil, we have to pray that won't happen," she said as they hurried toward the escalator. "God isn't going to let anything or anyone take her until it's time. You have to believe that."

"Maybe this is the time." He bumped the shopping bags into the door in his haste to leave. Outside, the parking lot was filled to capacity with last-minute shoppers. "This is a nightmare. How am I going to get out of here?"

"Neil, it will be okay."

Debbie appeared so calm, cool, and collected. Maybe if it were her flesh-and-blood relative in dire straits, she would act differently. She, too, would be angry at the shoppers and traffic, realizing she was still an hour away from a loved one ready to sink into eternity without even saying good-bye.

"I should have never set up that meeting between her and Harold," he said gruffly, trying to pull out of the parking spot. Debbie warned him about an on-coming car. "I see it. This is nuts. We're never going to get there in time. She'll die, and it's my fault."

"No, it isn't your fault, Neil Jenson. So stop it right now."

The tone of her voice made him stare at her in surprise. He managed to steer the car out of the parking lot and to the main road heading for the interstate. "I don't know, but it's obvious things aren't resolved. And now she's doing this, like she's decided to take revenge or something."

"So they told you she isn't eating?"

Neil nodded. "Yeah, and not taking her pills. Her refusal to take her blood pressure medication has me worried. She could have a stroke if her blood pressure isn't in check. She's already had a mild one, you know. A few years back." He then muttered about the crazy drivers. "This is nuts." He abruptly rolled down his window. "Hey, how would you like me to cut you off?" he shouted at a driver in the passing lane.

Debbie sank down in her seat and stared out the window.

Neil frowned. He knew he was acting like a wild man, controlled by anxiety and confusion, guilt and blame. He didn't know what to say or how to react. His emotions were doing all the talking. But maybe Debbie needed to witness the raw side of him—see that he wasn't all dapper and kind, helping his elderly grandmother, being a hero. He had his share of faults and problems, too. He was a regular flesh-and-blood guy, not some stained glass saint.

He began to grind his teeth as negative thoughts drove away peace, joy, and faith to some black void of nothingness. Debbie reached over and inserted a CD. Christmas carols filled the car. He tried to listen to them, but all he could envision was Gram, pale as a ghost, her hand lying across her chest, her breathing ragged as she spoke her final words.

I'm dying, Nathaniel. Now that everyone I love is gone, I might as well see them in heaven. Kiss the family for me. Tell them there's nothing more they can do for me.

"Neil, watch out. You're driving on the shoulder."

Neil quickly brought the car back onto the highway. Gram had sometimes refused to eat, but never had he known her not to take her blood pressure medication or any of the other colorful pills she took each day and night. She was trying to make herself die.

"I won't have her committing suicide," he growled out loud.

"Neil?"

"She's trying to kill herself. Keeping herself from medication. As a Christian woman, she should know that's wrong."

Debbie scraped tiny images with her fingernail into the frost forming on the window. Two hearts intertwined. A star. A candle. A mural of Debbie's mind began materializing on the window. "Neil, she's acting out on her feelings. A cry for help, you might say. This is a tough time of year for the residents. We just need to take it one step at a time and not go in there looking to condemn her.

Something is making her do this. If we can find out the reason, we might be able to deal with it." Now she set to work on a small stable, no doubt the beginnings of the Nativity.

In no time, they were on the road headed for White Pines. Neil wasn't sure what to say or do when he arrived. He knew Debbie was right, that he needed to keep his opinions in check. He couldn't march right in there and force-feed Gram the pills, though he might be tempted to do so if necessary.

He ran into the facility with Debbie trying in vain to keep up. He didn't even notice until he entered the elevator and pushed the button that he'd left her behind. His thoughts were on one person and one person alone. When he exited, the head nurse was standing there next to the medication cart. From the look on her face, the news was not good.

"Mr. Jenson, I'm sure you're here about your grandmother."

"Is she dying?"

"I wouldn't say that. But if she keeps going the way she is, it's not looking good. I was going to put in calls to your other relatives. Since you're the one who sees her so much and your name is listed first on the chart, I wanted to wait until you came in. But I will be obliged to share the information with her power of attorney, a Mr. Kevin Jenson."

"He's her oldest living son. So what brought this on?"

"I was hoping you could tell me. She seemed perfectly fine a few days ago, and suddenly this happened. Not that I want to pry into personal matters, but I hope everything is all right. I know disagreements can happen from time to time."

"Actually there was a wake-up call of sorts." He described in abbreviated detail the scenario surrounding his real grandfather, Gram's first beau, and how Harold knew him from the war.

"Isn't that amazing? I would think Elvina would be happy to hear such news. To know that there's a resident right on this floor who was so close to your family."

"I guess it did the opposite. Now she feels there's nothing left to live for."

Mrs. Whitaker nodded in sympathy. "I'm so sorry. You realize if she doesn't take her pills we may have to transfer her to the hospital. As it is, her blood pressure is beginning to spike. And she needs fluids."

The mere mention of all this made him sick inside. "I'll get her to take her pills," he said with a huff. He came to the doorway where Gram lay in bed, her eyes closed, looking like a pale doll. It didn't seem possible that she had been reduced to a feeble state in such a short period of time.

When he came to her bedside and spoke, her eyelids fluttered open. Her gray blue eyes stared straight ahead. "I know why you're here, Nathaniel, but it's my decision. You've made your decision. I've made mine."

"It isn't your decision, Gram. Not when it comes to life and death. That's God's decision."

Her cheek muscles tightened. "Nathaniel, I won't debate this with you."

"Gram, you've just had the greatest encounter with a man who knew Sam and was with him when he died. Harold's the last living person Sam talked to. The one who heard Sam's last words, and they were all about you. Isn't that worth something?"

"You might have at least told me who it was I was meeting and not some fancy story about an old friend from long ago. You lied to me, Nathaniel."

He hadn't lied. Harold was a friend from the past, a very good friend of Sam's. "I knew you wouldn't have met him if I told you everything. You have to admit it's a miracle, Gram. That a man living on the very same floor as you knew Samuel Truett."

"Harold is a very nice man. And I appreciate what he had to say, even if I think he made it up."

"He isn't making it up. He even knew your nickname because Samuel told him. So, Gram, there's no reason to do this to yourself. None at all."

"I've made my decision. I want to be home with my dear Joe."

"This isn't your decision to make. Life-and-death decisions are in the hands of the Lord. He's the One who decides. You do this, and you're playing God."

She closed her eyes. "Please leave. I want to rest."

"You can't do this. Think about your family." *And me,* he added silently.

"I have thought of my family. And who really cares anyway? None of them come to see me, except for you. I have been more of a burden than anything. You know it, and so do I. There really isn't anything more to say."

Neil stood there speechless. What was he supposed to do? He couldn't make the family come see her. But he had visited her. Didn't that matter to her? Didn't all that count? He wanted to shout, to make her see reason, to tell her how selfish this all was. He thought about putting on a record to calm the situation, but right now he needed something more powerful. Something that would speak louder than mere human words could say. He picked up her Bible. "Can I read you a few verses, Gram?"

She shrugged. At least she didn't order him to leave and never come back. He clung to any signs of hope at this crucial time. Flipping through the scriptures, he prayed for a word to minister to her heart. He cleared his throat. "I've always liked these verses, Gram, in Proverbs, chapter three, especially when I'm trying to figure out things in my life.

" 'Trust in the Lord with all your heart and lean not on your own understanding; in all your ways acknowledge him, and he will make your paths straight.

Do not be wise in your own eyes; fear the Lord and shun evil. This will bring health to your body and nourishment to your bones.'"

He looked up to see Gram's eyelids beginning to close from fatigue. With a sigh, he shut the Bible, placed it on her bedside table, and whispered good-bye. He had done all he could. The rest was up to God. Exiting the room, he nearly stumbled into Trish. She appeared to be lingering in the hallway. She said nothing but pretended to arrange her linen cart. He glanced back to see Trish enter another room across the hall. Neil wondered if she had been eavesdropping. What did it matter? Gram wanted to die. He might as well leave here and never come back, for what good he seemed to do. Nothing was working out, no matter what he did.

Neil never felt so burdened. He strode down the hall, and suddenly he was in front of Harold's room. He peeked inside. Harold had wheeled his chair into the bathroom and was combing his hair. To Neil's amazement, the veteran was singing a song. He stared in disbelief. How could the man look so alive when only a week ago he seemed confused and out of his mind? And now Gram was the one acting confused. *It's like they switched places*. The sight of the man, renewed in spirit, cheered Neil immensely. Finally some good fruit to be had after weeks of bad.

"Harold?" he said softly, stepping inside.

Harold wheeled his chair around. "Neil. I'm glad to see you. Come in."

It felt good to be acknowledged in such a friendly manner. He sat down slowly in a chair.

"You don't look too good," Harold observed. "What's wrong?"

"It's Gram. Liv, that is."

"What's the matter? Is she sick?"

"She won't take her medicine. Her blood pressure is rising. She's decided it's her time to die."

He twisted his face. "Is it because of me?" He said it matter-of-factly but with innocence and vulnerability. Tears welled up in his stark gray eyes. "It is because of me, isn't it? Because I didn't take care of her and Albert. She won't forgive me. That's why she's doing this."

"No, Harold. It's a bunch of different things. She's decided to feel sorry for herself and doesn't care about the consequences. Maybe you could talk to her again."

Harold shook his head. "I don't see what good that will do. As it is, I'm responsible. She was fine until. . .until. . ." He began to mumble something under his breath.

"No. She's lonely, and I don't think she knows what she's truly lonely for. I can't fulfill her needs, even though I come to visit. No one can. Only God can fulfill them, whether here in White Pines or in her own house. But it's hard convincing her of that. Gram's lived through a lot of loss. Maybe it's finally caught up with her. I know you've been through a lot, too. That's why I think you can reach her when no one else can."

"But I wouldn't know what to say or what to do. I talked to her once already. It didn't seem to do much good."

"Sometimes the best thing you can do is nothing at all. Maybe you can just sit there for starters. Let her know someone else cares in this world besides me. Let her see God through you."

Harold turned back to the bathroom mirror, staring at his reflection. "I suppose I could sit there for a little while anyway."

Neil breathed a sigh of relief. He helped wheel Harold down the hallway, past the curious onlookers who had gathered at the nurses' station. Trish stared at them as if this were some kind of evolving soap opera. Neil brought Harold to the doorway of Gram's room.

Harold said nothing, only stared at the woman lying in bed with her eyes closed. Neil saw his dry, cracked lips begin to move. Harold was praying! The sight of it moved Neil as well as convicted him. *'Pray without ceasing.' Harold is right. Pray when the going gets rough. Pray and don't stop. God, please make this work out all right. You saved me. You helped my family by revealing a secret from so long ago. You helped me by bringing Debbie into my life and blessing our developing relationship. Please save my grandma.*

Chapter 14

I don't know why you're here."

"You know why I'm here. Your grandson even said so. He says you aren't eating or taking your medicine. You have to eat."

"It doesn't matter. No one cares. Once they leave you in this place, that's the end. Sometimes people come to visit. But really, we are just a burden to everyone."

Silence weighed the air.

Debbie's skin began to crawl. Harold and Elvina were in the room talking, but she couldn't help overhearing. Neil's heart would break if he knew what they were talking about. Thankfully he was gone. She had heard, of course, how Neil talked to Harold yesterday, convincing him to meet with Elvina. Harold had come, but she refused to see him. Now today, by some miracle, she had agreed to a visit. "One last time," as she put it, "before I leave this world. There's nothing worth living for anyway."

But there is, despite the situation, Debbie thought. God was an ever-present help in times of need. He remained in control, even at White Pines. He cared. His love knew no bounds, whether in a house or here in a facility. And it was God to whom people needed to look to for comfort and consolation. If only she knew how to convey these things so despair didn't rule the night. She had had to learn it well herself when she thought despair would overcome her. She was a living example. No one was immune, whether they lived on the outside looking in or the inside looking out. And through it all, she discovered He was sufficient for everything, in every situation.

"That may be," Harold continued to Elvina, "but it still doesn't give you the right to hurt yourself and others, like Neil for example. He's done a lot for you. He's given up his life for you. And what have you done?"

"Why! I never."

"In the army, it was considered the worst kind of cowardice to harm yourself just so you could get out of the war. And that's what you're doing here, Liv."

"This isn't some kind of battlefield, Harold."

"Maybe you don't think so, but it sure can be. The same evil I fought long ago is still around. Sin don't go away. It's still the same. There's no difference in God's eyes. Sin is still sin, whether it's Hitler killing God's people or you wanting to kill yourself. And the problem is, you'll end up hurting a lot of other people if you do. Nothing is worth that, no matter where you end up living out your life. And here there are nice people, kind people helping you and loving you, like Neil and Debbie and even that head nurse there. So don't be so selfish. Think about other people besides yourself for a change."

Debbie could hardly believe this was the same Harold who spoke such words. It was like he had awakened from some kind of coma after all this time and now was speaking righteous words full of life-changing power.

Just then she felt a breeze and turned to see Trish rolling her linen cart along. "Playing matchmaker?" she asked with a teasing lilt to her voice.

Debbie picked up a pillowcase from her linen cart, pretending to fold it. "Hardly. But it's nice to see the change in Harold."

Trish paused to observe the two residents having a conversation with one another. "Wonder of wonders. And Harold doesn't think Elvina is some enemy soldier either."

"That's because he knows her. Indirectly, that is. Harold knew a man who was close to Elvina before the war. His name was Sam. Harold and Sam fought side by side in Normandy. Harold was there when Sam got shot and took his last breath. Elvina never knew what happened to Sam—that is, until now, sixty years later." Debbie drew in a breath.

Trish stared, her mouth forming a circle. "So you mean Elvina had another husband named Sam?"

"Sam was like her boyfriend, I guess you could say, before she got married. He was a widower with a small son when they met. I think his wife died in childbirth. Anyway he wanted Elvina to take care of his little boy while he was away in the army. He never came home. Elvina adopted the boy and made him a part of the family even after she married her husband, Joe. That adopted boy turned out to be Neil's father. That's why Neil calls her his grandmother to this day, even though there is no blood relation."

Trish stood transfixed. "This is too weird."

"Yes. It's a miracle."

She hesitated. "I know what it's like to be adopted."

The words came out so matter-of-factly that Debbie was taken aback. "What?"

"I'm adopted. I always wanted to know who my real parents were. My mom told me some young thing gave me away when she was a teenager. I was a teenage birth. It always kind of got to me, though, thinking about being adopted, wondering if my real parents thought about me or how I turned out."

Debbie could hardly believe the words flowing out of Trish. It made her feel badly that she'd thought so little of her. She could have been more patient with Trish and more of a friend. Maybe it would have helped them both in the long run. "Wow, I'm sorry to hear that."

"Don't be. You have nothing to feel sorry for."

"I know how Neil felt when he heard his paternal grandparents weren't his blood relatives, that his father was adopted into the family. It was hard. I don't know the feeling myself."

"I just wish my stepdad wasn't so drunk all the time when I was growing up. Good thing my folks split when they did. And I know my adopted mom cared about me, until she died of breast cancer last year." Trish took hold of the cart and rolled it away. Debbie stared after her, dumbfounded over the confession. What was the proverbial saying—*Don't judge a book by its cover*? And here she had judged Trish big-time without asking God for wisdom and understanding.

Just then she heard a sound she didn't think she would ever hear again. Laughter coming out of Elvina's room. It jolted her like an electrical current passing through an outlet. Elvina and Harold were sharing stories of a bygone era and laughing away. It played like music to her ears. She couldn't help but shed a tear before a smile came forth to match the merriment. She couldn't wait to tell Neil. He needed a good laugh right now, almost as much as they did.

❧

He stared, his brown eyes fixed. She could've waved her hand over them, and he wouldn't have blinked. "They laughed?"

"Yes, Neil. They laughed. Ho, ho, ho."

He swiped his hand through his hair. "And then you saw her take the pills Mrs. Whitaker gave her?"

"With a big glass of juice. And she looked different. Peaceful. Calm."

"Wow. I can't believe it. I was hoping of course. Praying up a storm that there might be a change. I'm glad, Debbie. Really glad." He took her hands in his. "How shall we celebrate? Dinner out?"

"Actually I need your help. Dinner's at my place. Stir-fry."

He smiled. "Sounds good. After all this, I could eat up a storm. Hope you make enough."

She smiled a bit coyly. "Oh, there will be plenty."

❧

Neil handed Debbie several peeled carrots and watched her slice them up. "That's an interesting tale, I must say. But it doesn't excuse past behavior, like how she treated both you and Gram."

Debbie dumped sliced carrots into a bowl. She had just finished telling Neil about Trish, expecting him to react the way she had upon hearing of Trish's past. He didn't. She sighed. Neil hadn't done anything she expected the past few weeks she had known him. She tried to keep her nerves in check, all the while wrestling with the idea of truly knowing the man standing beside her. "This isn't just a tale, Neil. It's a moving story. And it makes me understand Trish a bit better."

"There is no way one can understand a woman like that. I mean, I had a tough life growing up in a single-parent home. But I don't persecute insurance claimants just because I had no father."

"So what should I do? Treat her like an outcast for her many sins?"

Neil opened his mouth to spout out a retort, then clamped his lips shut. Finally he said, "You should do whatever God tells you."

"Good. Because I invited Trish to join us for dinner."

"You did what?" His gaze swept the counter. "No wonder you're cooking up enough to feed an army. And here I thought this was all for me."

"I hope that isn't a problem. Jesus ate with the outcasts, as I'm sure you know. And since you two have something in common, growing up in different family situations, I thought it would be good."

Just then she felt the sweep of his hand on hers. "Debbie, I don't care to eat with Trish."

"Huh?" The statement both startled and puzzled her.

"Hello?" He tapped her gently on the head. "We've had encounters in the past, none of which were overly pleasant. Before that, she and all the rest of her crew were like vultures after a kill. I don't care to give out any more mixed signals, especially since my signal is set."

"What do you mean, your signal is set? Set to what?"

He pried the knife carefully from her fingers and laid it on the counter. His touch sent a tremor through her. "I'll give you one guess." He drew near, pulling her into his embrace.

She wiggled out of his arms. "I know you may think your light is green, Nathaniel J., but mine is yellow and rapidly turning red." She grabbed a red Christmas hand towel and held it in front of her. "And if you don't watch it, the police will give you a little ol' ticket for running a red light." He withdrew, a grin still on his face, even as she picked up the knife again to tackle the veggies. "I wouldn't worry about Trish getting the wrong signal," she added. "She decided to also invite a friend. Her new boyfriend, I think. I told her you would be here and that you love computers. This guy does, too, it seems. So you two can chat."

His cheeks turned rosy. "Now you tell me. Thanks a lot, missy."

"You didn't ask." She felt like giggling the way his face contorted into a picture of discomfort. She continued to chop and dice, even as she sensed his gaze on her. The chemistry was so strong between them. She felt like a chemistry student, ready to watch her experiment in love boil over. Yes, this man was having a profound effect on her and growing by leaps and bounds as each day passed.

The feelings abruptly subsided when the doorbell rang. Neil went to answer it.

Voices soon filled the living room. A sense of peace flowed through Debbie. God was good, even if things didn't look quite right in her eyes. He was in control.

Trish came to dinner bearing some new records for Neil's grandmother. "I thought maybe Elvina would like hearing some of these. They are left over from my stepmom. Guess I inherited them."

Debbie thought Neil would keel over right there. He gave a sheepish thank-you, avoiding eye contact. Debbie thanked God for the change she'd seen in Trish and for bringing her here.

"I see the guys are already talking about the latest computer games," Trish noted, moseying on into the tiny kitchen where Debbie was working. She helped herself to a carrot.

"Boys must have their toys. I took Neil shopping for his family the other day at the mall, and I could tell he only wanted to check out the computer store across the way from the bath boutique."

Trish laughed. "It's so typical, isn't it? Stu only wants to talk computers, too. I didn't even have a computer until he hooked me up. Now I love chatting with friends." She stood still, watching, even as Debbie sensed her own nervousness. "You know, I wonder why you and I never got along."

The comment took Debbie by surprise. "I'm not sure. I guess because we both do things differently."

"Well, you might as well know—I'm quitting White Pines after the New Year. I'm going to work in the same computer store as Stu, handling the cash register. I'm just not cut out to work at the facility anymore."

"You've been there a long time."

"Too long. It's time to move on. But I think you need to go on with nursing, Debbie. Go to college and get your degree. Become an RN like Mrs. Whitaker."

"Huh?" Debbie's knees turned to gelatin.

"Sure. You have what it takes. I mean, we all see it. Maybe that's why we've had problems. You're a natural at taking care of these people. Some of us, well, it's just a job. But to you, this is your life. You pour everything into these people's lives. You live for them really."

Debbie never imagined anyone observing her in such fine detail, except when she made a blunder. Now Neil's words of long ago came back—how her mission field was right where God had placed her, inside the White Pines Health Care Facility. She prayed she might make a difference. Come to find out, her life had been speaking loud and clear, more than mere words could say. "I do like it," she admitted. "I don't know, though, if I have the money and the stamina to become a full-fledged nurse. I see what Mrs. Whitaker has to do."

"My sister—actually my stepsister—is a nurse. She works in the ER and loves it. I wouldn't be caught dead handling gunshot wounds and all that. But you should really think about it."

"Maybe I will. Thanks." For the first time, Debbie could see going to the mall with Trish, or maybe a movie, as remarkable as that seemed a mere week ago. How rapidly things could change—and when she least expected it!

Dinner was a rousing success. While they ate dessert, Trish laid down her fork. "Hey, I want to make an announcement."

"You're engaged," Debbie said with a sigh. She tried to avoid Neil's eye as he turned to look at her.

"No way," Stu said loudly.

Trish laughed. "That will take some convincing. Actually, Neil, I know that you were looking to hire a nurse to take care of Elvina over the holidays. Have you filled the post yet?"

"No," he answered, a bit cautiously.

"I told Trish she must have New Year's Eve off," Stu added. "I've got it set for us to go to Times Square to watch the ball drop."

"So since Neil needs a nurse for Christmas, do you want to switch with me, Debbie? I'll work Christmas if you'll work New Year's Eve. And that leaves you free to take care of Elvina if you want to."

Debbie could hardly believe it. And from the look on Neil's face, neither could he.

"I don't know what to say, Trish."

"Merry Christmas." She handed over her plate. "And another helping of that carrot cake, please. It's simply divine."

When the evening wrapped up and Trish and Stu said good night, Neil came to help Debbie with the dishes. She could only sing the praises of God for doing a great work. "Neil, I must admit, you were right again."

He nearly dropped the red dish towel. "I don't think I can handle all this praise, Debbie. It's giving me a swelled head. What did I do this time?"

"When you talked about our unique mission work, giving our jobs to God and letting Him use us... Trish said some really wild things tonight. Not only, of course, about switching holidays and all. But she commented on my work with the residents and thinks I should become an RN like Mrs. Whitaker. She says I have what it takes."

"I agree wholeheartedly. In fact, if you need a loan for school, I'd be happy to help out."

"What? But I haven't even decided if I'm going to be one or not."

"I think it's a great idea. And who would have thought your old nemesis would confirm it?"

No one. No one but God, that is. He had a knack for coming up with surprises in the most unexpected fashion. But becoming a nurse might mean jumping from the frying pan into the fire. Or it might mean the satisfaction of a dream fulfilled, to have a degree and a good job, like everyone else in her family. To feel a sense of accomplishment while doing something near and dear to her heart—caring for the injured, the aged, those in need. "Think I'll be any good at it?"

"Is that a trick question?"

"It might be. I'm asking you if you think this is something I should do, or is everyone just trying to be nice."

"I doubt Trish would say it just to be nice. She has nothing to lose or gain at this point. Maybe she's seen the light for the first time. I didn't tell you this, but when I was reading the Bible to Gram that day she refused to take her pills, I saw Trish standing outside in the hall. I wondered then if she had heard the words. Somehow I think this has really affected her."

Debbie couldn't help but agree.

"And as for me," Neil said, "I've been trying to be nice for a very long time and wondering if I'd been failing at it miserably. Especially when you wanted to leave this area and never return. It made me wonder if we were on the right track or not."

She didn't blame him for thinking that. He had been nice. In every word and deed, a true friend. And maybe more. Working side by side, doing dishes, and chatting, she felt completely at home with him. They seemed right for each other. She had seen the light, and maybe now her very own Christmas wish stood poised to become a reality.

Chapter 15

This has been so wonderful; I don't know what to say."

Debbie watched from afar as Elvina sat with her grandchildren and great-grandchildren in Neil's mother's home, surrounded by gifts and love. The last two days had gone so well she could hardly believe it. Elvina was a different person—strong, determined, even able to take a few steps from her bed to the wheelchair. She acted younger. At times, she even seemed to see: She expounded on things that were happening all around her, such as when one of the great-nieces snitched a Christmas cookie from the plate. It had made a world of difference in her life to be here with her loved ones. And Debbie had to admit, it made a difference in hers, too, just to be here with Neil's family. At times, she caught members of his family looking at her strangely. Maybe he had mentioned their relationship to them in passing conversation. Or maybe they knew something she didn't.

She chuckled in hindsight, recalling the day Neil asked her to come and help during Christmas. Though she expected to hear about it after Trish's offer to exchange holidays, he hadn't mentioned anything until one day when he came knocking on her apartment door. He told her in an excited voice how everything was arranged. "We're set to have Gram come to my mom's house for Christmas. I tiptoed in with the issue to Mom, and she agreed, as long as I took care of all the details. I've arranged for the bed and the necessary supplies. I lack only one tiny detail."

"And what would that be, pray tell?"

He winked. "I need a certain nurse willing to help me out. The one who kissed me the other week at Christmastown, USA, would do nicely."

He opened his arms to pull her into his embrace, and they kissed again, right after she said, "I will." She half expected an engagement to follow on the heels of all this, but then again, Neil remained too absorbed with preparations for his grandmother's Christmas visit for something that drastic. And rightly so. Though she did dream of the big night when he would whisk her away for a candlelight dinner and ask for her hand on bended knee. Maybe New Year's—the perfect time for a new beginning.

Debbie glanced at her watch. After the gift exchange, Neil left to run an errand. Why he felt the need to escape somewhere on Christmas morning, she couldn't imagine. No stores were open, as far as she knew. Ninety minutes had already passed. What could be keeping him?

She turned her attention to the Jenson family—Neil's mother giving Elvina a cup of juice; his sister, Sandy, talking to Elvina about her job; the two great-granddaughters looking over some new jewelry; and Neil's brother, Dick, immersing himself in the computer game Neil had given him. Both Neil's mother and Sandy loved their bath products in the baskets.

"Did you pick this out?" Neil's mother had asked him after unwrapping her gift.

Sandy laughed outright. "Oh, Mom, really. Can you imagine a guy buying bath products? Obviously he conned Debbie into doing it for him. You can see the woman's touch. You did it, didn't you, Debbie?"

Debbie remembered the loving glance Neil had given her, even as her fingers traveled over the pure black sweater he had wrapped up for her in bright Christmas paper. He laughed at the new black hat she had given him to match his black overcoat and black gloves. "Now I am definitely the man who wears black," he said with a chuckle.

"And it looks like you're getting Debbie to follow suit," Sandy added, pointing to the black sweater.

It didn't matter to Debbie. She loved the sweater, and yes, she had fallen in love with the man, too. They were made for each other, as he once said. Now she was getting edgy for his return. Without him here, she felt like an intruder among his family, even though she was hired to care for Elvina.

"Where could Neil be?" his mother asked.

"You know him," Sandy said. "He has something up his sleeve. Remember when he once came for Christmas with that puppy, Mom? I thought you would die when he said it was for you."

"Yes, and I gave the dog to a lonely member in my church who needed the companionship much more than I did. I only hope Neil gets back in time to help carve the roast. He's the only one who knows how to work my electric knife."

At last, Debbie heard the rumble of an engine and a car door slam.

"Debbie, can you give me a hand with this gift?" Neil called out. "It's very fragile."

Debbie offered a meek smile to the inquisitive looks displayed by the family before darting out the door. To her surprise, Harold sat in the front seat of Neil's car, grinning from ear to ear. "This is the best day of my life," he told them as they helped him into a portable wheelchair. "The best day. Look at that sun. Look at the blue sky."

"So this is your secret errand," Debbie murmured to Neil with a smile. "What will your family think?"

"He's just here for the afternoon. And besides, I'm not doing it for them. I'm doing it for Gram. This is her Christmas wish come true, in a way."

Debbie looked at him in confusion until it dawned on her—Elvina's wish that she learn what happened to her beloved Samuel. Harold was the link to it all. When they brought Harold into the house, Neil's family was on their feet in an instant.

"Why, Neil!" his mother exclaimed.

"What on earth are you doing?" Sandy added.

"I'm bringing Gram her special Christmas present, so don't say anything else," he announced, slowly wheeling Harold over to Elvina, who stared expectantly. "It's a present she specifically asked for." Then to his grandmother, he said, "Hold out your hand, Gram."

"Oh, dear. I hope you didn't get me anything too expensive or large, Nathaniel," she said. Neil took Harold's hand and placed it in his grandmother's. She grew rigid. "I—I don't understand." Her fingers traced the pathway of Harold's jagged veins and long, bony fingers.

"Merry Christmas, Liv."

Her hand fell away. "It can't be. Whatever are you doing here, Harold?"

He looked to Neil for help.

"Merry Christmas, Gram," Neil said with a laugh.

She turned white. "I don't understand. How is Harold my Christmas gift?"

Neil knelt beside her and took her other hand in his. "Gram, remember how you said you had one big Christmas wish, to know what happened to the man who means a great deal to you and to our family? The one who gave me a great dad, even if I never knew him? That's why Harold is here. He knew our real grandfather. He knew our dad. And he was the last one to speak to Sam before he left this world. He's the answer to your Christmas wish—in an indirect way, that is."

No one said anything for several agonizing moments. Debbie looked at each family member. Some wore expressions of disbelief. Neil's mother's eyes harbored tears. Debbie could barely draw a breath, wondering what would happen next. Would this special gift be accepted? Would the wounds from long ago find healing? Would the family open their hearts and accept Harold?

Finally Elvina turned to Neil. "Well, Nathaniel, are you going to put on a Christmas carol or two? I brought my record player and albums with me, you know."

Neil grinned. In no time, the bars of a favorite Christmas carol, "Joy to the World," filled the room. When they finished, the family pressed in around them, asking Harold about his friendship with their Sam and how he and Elvina had come to meet. Debbie never saw Harold so filled with warmth and love. What a far cry from just a few weeks ago, when he was but a sad and lonely man.

What a beautiful day, too. Now Debbie was witnessing a freedom in Harold's spirit, and in Elvina's, as well. They no longer held expressions of confusion, weariness, or dismay, but life and even love. When Harold's hand reached for Elvina's, taking it up in his own, Debbie's heart flip-flopped at the sight.

"I do have one other request to play," Neil announced. He took up another record, one of the older versions Debbie had purchased at the antique store a few weeks back. "This is Harold's gift to Gram." All at once, Harold's rich bass voice filled the room as he sang a love song from days gone by. Everyone chuckled in glee. Elvina sat there, mesmerized by the man who sang to her so lovingly.

Suddenly Harold brought forth a small box out of his shirt pocket. Before Elvina could say anything, he took out a ring and slipped it carefully on her ring finger. "Liv, will you marry me?"

"Harold. . . ," she began, her fingers touching the ring. "Oh, Harold!"

Debbie sucked in her breath in astonishment. Shock resounded throughout the family circle. Sandy sat unmoving, her eyes glued to the scene. Neil's mother stared with the same confused expression. "Don't you think you're moving a little fast with all this?" she wondered. "I mean, didn't you both just meet at White Pines a short time ago?"

Harold squirmed in his chair. Debbie sucked in her breath, wondering if she should say anything. She saw Neil slowly shake his head at her. This was Elvina and Harold's to handle. She could only watch and pray for God's will to come forth.

"I know it seems very fast," Harold began.

"Oh really, Terrie," Elvina remarked. "Look at us." A tear began sliding down her cheek. Her finger gently stroked the ring she held. She then lifted her face. A smile broke out. "I think two lonely people like us still have a few years left for happiness. Don't you?"

No one could say anything after that. When Debbie's gaze fell on Neil, he wasn't looking at the elderly gentleman proposing to his stately grandmother or responding to the questioning glances of his mother. He was staring straight at her.

While the family marveled at the Christmas Day engagement in their midst, Debbie went to fetch Elvina's medication for the afternoon. Her hand shook as she fumbled with the pills. She could hardly believe what had happened. One gift on top of the other. And she was here to see it all, thanks to Trish. *It's a fact. The Lord does work in mysterious ways.*

All at once, she heard footsteps behind her. She turned to find him leaning against the door frame, his arms folded. *Neil. Dear, sweet, thoughtful Neil.* She really did love him. What would be their future? More mysteries to solve? More places to explore? More hot chocolate to drink? Or maybe each other to have and to hold one day when the time was right?

"Great moment, huh?" he said.

"Wow, I should say. One for every history book and fairy tale there is. Weren't they cute? Who would have thought?"

"No one. At least not me—until Harold told me what he had in mind."

"So you knew Harold would propose?"

"He talked to me about it a few days ago. He said that Liv had done something miraculous in him. He couldn't stop thinking about her. He asked me what it was that made him feel that way. I said, 'Love, my man!' He wondered if they dared marry, if that could happen with their residence in White Pines. I said, 'Why not?' So he asked me to find an antique ring, something old but meaningful. We set this all up for today."

"Neil, you're something else. You really do like making wishes come true, don't you?"

"Only God can make it a reality. Sometimes what we wish for isn't always the best thing for us. But He can make it all come out right in the end. He is faithful."

She listened, deep in thought, wondering about her secret desire, if it was a part of God's great plan or simply wishful thinking. But she knew better than to second-guess at this point. She had witnessed a wonderful miracle—and on Christmas morn, when the greatest miracle of all had come forth. On top of it all, she could delight in the love of a man God had brought into her life when she needed him most. "Yes," she agreed, allowing his arms to impart an embrace of warmth and of love. Their lips met. "He is very faithful, to the end."

Epilogue

The tiny White Pines chapel never looked more beautiful to Debbie. Red roses stood in a vase on the altar. Bows decorated the pews. And the time was perfect, too, for celebrating love, as Elvina and Harold exchanged their wedding vows that afternoon. *Valentine's Day. The day of love.* She exhaled a sigh, even as her gaze drifted over to Neil, standing beside Harold as his best man. How handsome he appeared in a dark suit and tie with a red-rose corsage pinned to the lapel. She steadied the bouquet of roses she held in her hands. The heavenly scent filled her. It was a blessed event come true, and one she hoped to experience in her own life. But for now she and Neil had made an agreement to take it slow. Take the time to know each other more. To seek God in everything. And allow their relationship to grow. Yet she couldn't help but think of her own wedding in the process. *I will definitely have roses,* she decided. *The red roses of love. And a dove white wedding dress with a long veil that reaches to the floor.*

When Harold and Elvina's wedding kiss came, followed by applause, tears filled Debbie's eyes. The newlyweds looked radiant as they moved up the aisle in their respective wheelchairs to the rear of the chapel where they would receive congratulations from family and friends. Debbie followed to take her place in the receiving line, when she felt the warmth of Neil's hand sliding into the crook of her elbow.

"You made it through the ceremony and didn't faint," he whispered. "See? I knew you would do fine."

Debbie smiled, recalling her nervous jitters just before the ceremony was about to commence. But peace ruled the day and her heart, and for this, she could only thank God. They came to stand with Elvina and Harold, greeting Elvina's children and grandchildren, along with a few staff members from White Pines. When Debbie caught sight of Trish and her intended, Stu, among the guests, she felt her legs tremble.

Trish showed Debbie her hand and the sparkling diamond. "It's official. See?"

"Congratulations. You both didn't waste much time."

Trish laughed. "Hey, we plan to open our own computer store in the next few months. So I told him if he wants me to be a partner, then he'd better make it official with a proposal. And I didn't mean a business contract either."

Debbie laughed along with Trish until a lump of emotion filled her throat.

She cast a sideways glance at Neil. *What about us, God? What is Your will for us? Will I have a diamond ring, too, one day? I don't mean to be impatient. I guess I just need to be content, grateful for Neil and for what You have done in our lives.*

When the receiving line had come to an end and the gathering wandered toward the solarium for a small reception, Debbie stepped away for a breath of fresh air. She pushed back her damp hair and sighed, only to find Neil coming toward her.

"Well, you did it," she said, loosening his tie.

"Thanks, I was getting hot. So what did I do?"

"Made a wish come true. Or you were instrumental in bringing about a wish, I guess I should say. Maybe even more than a wish."

"Debbie, it took two. In more ways than one."

"I didn't do that much."

He raised an eyebrow. "Well, I could stand here and make a list of your many accomplishments, as well. But that would both make us pretty late for the reception and Gram a bit miffed. But before we go, I do want to let you in on a little secret."

"Yes?"

"I had a wish, too, like Gram. I could sing the Jiminy Cricket song of wishing on a star, but I can't sing worth anything. Besides, I took my wish to the One who knows what's best for me."

Debbie thought she might melt like a snowflake on the warm ground when she heard these words. If only she could tell him her desire, too—that she would love to spend a lifetime with him. *If only.* "So what might your wish be?"

When she saw the velvet box in his hand, she gasped. Their wishes were one and the same! "Me?"

"You. My one and only. Marry me?"

"Yes!" she cried with tears in her eyes. There was a special guy just for her in this whole wide world, and God knew it most of all.

Thank You, God. Wishes do come true.

A Letter to Our Readers

Dear Readers:

In order that we might better contribute to your reading enjoyment, we would appreciate your taking a few minutes to respond to the following questions. When completed, please return to the following: Fiction Editor, Barbour Publishing, Inc., P.O. Box 719, Uhrichsville, OH 44683.

1. Did you enjoy reading *Virginia Weddings* by Lauralee Bliss?
   ❑ Very much—I would like to see more books like this.
   ❑ Moderately—I would have enjoyed it more if _____ .
   _____

   _____

2. What influenced your decision to purchase this book?
   (Check those that apply.)
   ❑ Cover   ❑ Back cover copy   ❑ Title   ❑ Price
   ❑ Friends   ❑ Publicity   ❑ Other

3. Which story was your favorite?
   ❑ *Ageless Love*   ❑ *The Wish*
   ❑ *Time Will Tell*

4. Please check your age range:
   ❑ Under 18   ❑ 18–24   ❑ 25–34
   ❑ 35–45   ❑ 46–55   ❑ Over 55

5. How many hours per week do you read? _____

Name _____

Occupation _____

Address _____

City_____ State_____ Zip_____

E-mail_____

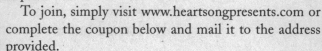